Picture yours  **hostile territor** **of instant dea** **every shadow.** You are a spy bound on a mission that a sane man would have refused. An impossible assignment, but you have all the time you need as long as it isn't over 24 hours.

Now you are hunted through the snow like an animal, but an animal of great strength and many special skills. You have been trained in a hard and bitter school. But so have your enemies.

All around you are the Security Police. As you lie hidden in a snowbank, a handkerchief stuffed in your mouth to prevent your chattering teeth from betraying you, you hear them calling to each other, over the belling of leashed hounds.

You decide without wonder or self-recrimination that you probably have a minute left to live.

Fawcett Books
by Alistair MacLean:

H.M.S. ULYSSES 14083-0 $1.95
THE GUNS OF NAVARONE 14171-3 $1.95
SOUTH BY JAVA HEAD 14023-7 $1.95
THE SECRET WAYS 14010-5 $1.95
NIGHT WITHOUT END 14129-2 $1.95
FEAR IS THE KEY 14011-3 $1.95
THE BLACK SHRIKE 13903-4 $1.75
THE GOLDEN RENDEZVOUS 23624-2 $1.95
THE SATAN BUG 14009-1 $1.75
ICE STATION ZEBRA 23234-4 $1.75
WHEN EIGHT BELLS TOLL 23893-8 $1.95
WHERE EAGLES DARE 23623-4 $1.75
FORCE 10 FROM NAVARONE 23934-9 $2.25
PUPPET ON A CHAIN 23318-8 $1.75
CARAVAN TO VACCARES 23361-8 $1.75
BEAR ISLAND 23560-2 $1.95
THE WAY TO DUSTY DEATH 23571-8 $1.95
BREAKHEART PASS 22731-6 $1.75
CIRCUS 22875-4 $1.95
THE GOLDEN GATE 23177-1 $1.95
SEAWITCH 23597-1 $2.25

UNABLE TO FIND FAWCETT PAPERBACKS AT
YOUR LOCAL BOOKSTORE OR NEWSSTAND?

If you are unable to locate a book published by Fawcett, or, if you wish to see a
list of all available Fawcett Crest, Gold Medal and Popular Library titles, write
for our FREE Order Form. Just send us your name and address and 35¢ to help
defray postage and handling costs. Mail to:

FAWCETT BOOKS GROUP
P.O. Box C730
524 Myrtle Ave.
Pratt Station, Brooklyn, N.Y. 11205

(Orders for less than 5 books must include 75¢ for the first book and 25¢ for
each additional book to cover postage and handling.)

Alistair MacLean

THE
SECRET
WAYS

FAWCETT GOLD MEDAL • NEW YORK

THE SECRET WAYS

All characters in this book are fictional,
and any resemblance to persons living or
dead is purely coincidental.

Copyright © 1959 by Gilach A. G.

Published by Fawcett Gold Medal Books,
a unit of CBS Publications,
the Consumer Publishing Division of CBS Inc.,
by special arrangement with Doubleday & Co., Inc.

All rights reserved, including the right to
reproduce this book or portions thereof.

ISBN: 0-449-14010-5

Printed in the United States of America.

30   29   28   27   26   25   24   23   22   21

1

THE wind blew steadily out of the north and the night air was bitterly chill. Nothing moved across the snow. Under the high cold stars the frozen plain, empty, desolate, stretched endlessly away on every side until it vanished into the blurred distance of an empty horizon. Over everything lay the silence of death.

But the emptiness, Reynolds knew, was illusion. So were the desolation and the silence. Only the snow was real, the snow and that bone-deep, sub-zero cold that shrouded him from head to toe in a blanket of ice and continuously shook his entire body in violent, uncontrollable spasms of shivering, like a man suffering from ague. Perhaps that feeling of drowsiness that was beginning to creep over him was only an illusion also, but he was aware that it, too, was no illusion; it was real and he knew only too well the meaning it carried with it. Resolutely, desperately almost, he crushed down all thought of the cold, the snow and sleep, and concentrated on the problem of survival.

Slowly, painstakingly, careful to make not the slightest unnecessary sound or movement, he slid one frozen hand under the lapels of his trench coat, fumbled his handkerchief out of his breast pocket, rolled it into a crushed ball, and stuffed it into his mouth: betrayal of his position could come only by sight or sound, and the folds of the handkerchief would break up the heavy condensation of his breath in the frosty air and muffle the chattering of his teeth. Then he twisted round cautiously in the deep, snow-filled ditch by the roadside into which he had fallen, reached out an exploratory hand—now curiously mottled blue and white by the cold—for the trilby that had been knocked from his head when he had tumbled off the overhanging branch of the tree above him, found it, and inched it slowly towards him. As thoroughly as his numbed, now almost useless fingers would permit, he covered crown and brim with a thick layer of snow, crammed the trilby deep over the giveaway black hatch of his head, and lifted head and shoulders in almost grotesque slow motion until first the hatbrim and then his eyes cleared the level of the ditch.

In spite of its violent shivering, his whole body was as taut as a bowstring as he waited, in tense, sickening expectation, for the shout that betokened discovery, or the shot or the numbing crash that carried oblivion with it as a bullet found the exposed target of his head. But there was no sound, no shot, and his awareness only heightened with the passing of every moment. His first quick scanning of the circuit of the horizon was now complete, and there could be no doubt about it: there was no one there, at least close at hand, either to see or to be seen.

Moving just as carefully, just as slowly, but with a long-drawn-out easing of his pent-up breath, Reynolds straightened until he was kneeling upright in the ditch. He was cold and shivering still, but was no longer aware of it, and the sleepiness had vanished as if it had been a dream. Once again his gaze travelled in a full circle around the horizon, but slowly, probingly, this time, the keen brown eyes missing nothing, and once more the answer was the same. There was nobody to be seen. There was nothing to be seen, nothing at all but the icy twinkle of the stars in the dark velvet of the sky, the level white plain, a few small isolated groves of trees, and the curving ribbon of road beside him, its surface hard-packed by the snow treads of heavy trucks.

Reynolds lowered himself back down into the deep trench which the impact of his falling body had carved out in the drifted snow in the ditch. He had to have time. He had to have time to recover his breath, to ease his still gasping lungs' demands for air and more air: a scant ten minutes had passed since the truck in which he had stolen a lift had been stopped by the police block, and the brief, fierce scuffle, clubbed automatic in hand, with the two unsuspecting policemen who had investigated the rear of the truck, the sprint round the providential bend in the road, and then the mile-long, grinding run till he had reached the grove of trees beside which he now lay had brought him to the point of exhausted collapse. He had to have time to figure out why the police had given up the pursuit so easily—they must have known that he would be bound to keep to the road: leaving the road for the deep virgin snow on either side of it would not only have slowed him to a trudging walk but also, but virtue of the fresh tracks so easily visible on that starlit night, would have instantly given him away. And, above all, he had to have time to think, to plan out what he must do next.

It was typical of Michael Reynolds that he spent no time in self-recrimination or in wondering what might have happened had he chosen some other course of action. He had been trained in a hard and bitter school, where such idle luxuries as self-blame for what was irrevocably past and done with, useless post-mortems, crying over spilt milk, and all negative speculations and emotions which might possibly contribute to a lessening of over-all efficiency were rigidly proscribed. He spent perhaps five seconds considering the past twelve hours, then dismissed the matter completely from his mind. He would have done the same thing over again. He had had every reason to believe his informant in Vienna that air travel to Budapest was temporarily out—airport security precautions during the fortnight of the forthcoming International Scientific Conference were reported to be the most stringent ever. The same applied to all the main railway stations, and all long-distance passenger trains were reported to be heavily patrolled by Security Police. That left only the road: first an illegal crossing of the frontier—no great feat if one had expert help, and Reynolds had had the best there was—and then a stolen ride on some eastward-bound truck. A roadblock, the same Viennese informant had warned him, would almost certainly be in operation on the outskirts of Budapest, and Reynolds had been prepared for this: what he hadn't been prepared for, and what none of his informants had known of, was the block east of Komarom, some forty miles outside the capital. Just one of those things—it could have happened to anyone and it just so chanced that it had happened to him. Reynolds gave the mental equivalent of a philosophic shrug, and the past ceased to exist for him.

It was equally typical of him—more precisely, perhaps, it was typical of the rigorous mental conditioning he had undergone in his long training—that his thoughts about the future were rigidly canalised, channeled along one all-exclusive, particular line of thought, towards the achievement of one specific objective. Again, the emotional colorings which would normally accompany the thought of the potentialities of a successful mission or the tragic consequences of failure had no part in his racing mind as he lay there in the freezing snow, thinking, calculating, planning, assessing chances with a cold and remote detachment.

"The job, the job, always the job on hand," the colonel had repeated once, twice, a thousand times. "Success or failure in what you do may be desperately important to others, but it must never matter a damn to you. For you, Reynolds, consequences do not exist and must never be allowed to exist, and for two reasons: thinking about them upsets your balance and impairs your judgment—and every second you give up to thinking along these negative lines is always a second that should and must be used to working out how you're going to achieve the job on hand."

The job on hand. Always the job on hand. In spite of himself, Reynolds grimaced as he lay there waiting for his breathing to return to normal. There never had been more than one chance in a hundred, and now the odds had lengthened astronomically. But the job was still there; Jennings and all his priceless knowledge must be reached and brought out, and that was all that mattered. But if he, Reynolds, failed in this, then he had failed and that was all there was to it. He might even fail tonight, on his first day of the assignment after eighteen months of the most rigorous and ruthless specialist training aimed at the accomplishment of this task alone, but that made no difference whatsoever.

Reynolds was superbly fit—he had to be, all the colonel's specialist handful of men had to be—and his breathing was again as near normal as made no difference. As for the police mounting the roadblock—there must be half a dozen of them, he had caught a glimpse of several others emerging from the hut just as he had rounded the bend—he would have to take a chance on them: there was nothing else he could do. Possibly they had only been stopping and searching eastbound trucks for contraband and had no interest in panic-stricken passengers who fled away into the night—although it seemed likely enough that the two policemen he had left groaning in the snow might take a rather more personal interest in him. As for the immediate future, he couldn't lie there indefinitely to freeze in the snow or risk discovery by the sharp-eyed drivers of passing cars or trucks.

He would have to make for Budapest on foot—for the first part of the journey, at least. Three or four miles' heavy trudging through the fields and then regain the road—that, at least, he would need to take him well clear of the roadblock before he dared try a lift. The road to the east curved left before the block, and it would be easier for him to go to the left also, to short-circuit the bend of the road across the base of the triangle. But to the left—the north, that was—lay the Danube at no great distance, and he baulked from finding himself trapped in a narrow strip of land between river and road. There was nothing for it but to strike off to the south and round the apex of the triangle at a discreet distance—and on a clear night like that, a discreet distance meant a very considerable distance indeed. The detour would take hours to complete.

Teeth again chattering violently—he had removed the handkerchief to draw in the great, gasping breaths of air his lungs had demanded—chilled to the bone and with his hands and feet useless and empty of all feeling, Reynolds pushed himself shakily to his feet and began to brush the frozen snow off his clothes, glancing down the road in the direction of the police roadblock. A second later he was once more flat on his face in the snow-filled ditch, his heart thumping heavily in his chest, his right hand struggling desperately to free his gun from the pocket in his coat where he had stuck it after his fight with the police.

He could understand now why the police had taken their time in looking for him—they could afford to. What he could not understand was his own folly in supposing that discovery could result only from some betraying movement or incautious sound made by himself. He had forgotten that there was such a thing as a sense of smell—he had forgotten all about the dogs. And there had been no mistaking the identity of the leading dog as it nosed eagerly along the road, not even in the semi-darkness: a bloodhound was unmistakable where there was any light at all.

With the sudden shout from one of the approaching men and the excited jabber of voices, he was on his feet again, reaching the grove of trees behind him in three short steps: it had been too much to hope that he hadn't been spotted against that vast backcloth of white. He himself, in turn, had seen in that last quick glimpse that there were four men, each with a dog on leash: the other three dogs weren't bloodhounds, he was sure of that.

He drew in behind the bole of the tree whose branches had lately given him such brief and treacherous refuge, freed the gun from his pocket, and looked down at it. A specially made, beautifully machined version of a Belgian 6.35 automatic, it was a precise and deadly little gun, and with it he could hit a target smaller than a man's hand, at twenty paces, ten times out of ten. Tonight, he knew, he would have difficulty even in hitting a man at half that distance, so unresponsive to the mind's demands had his numbed and shaking hands become. Then some instinct made him lift the gun up before his eyes, and his mouth tightened: even in the faint starlight he could see that the barrel of the gun was blocked with frozen slush and snow.

He took off his hat, held it by the brim and about shoulder height, jutting out from one side of the tree, waited a couple of seconds, then stooped as low as he could and risked a quick glance round the others. Fifty paces away now, if that, the four men were walking along in line abreast, the dogs still straining on their leashes. Reynolds straightened, dug out a Biro pen from his inside pocket, and quickly but without haste began to free the barrel of the automatic of the frozen slush. But his numbed hands betrayed him, and when the Biro slipped from his fumbling fingers and disappeared point downwards in the deep snow, he knew it was useless to search for it, too late for anything more.

He could hear the brittle-soft crunch of steel-shod boots on the hard-packed snow of the road. Thirty paces, perhaps even less. He slid a white, pinched forefinger through the trigger guard, placed the inside of his wrist against the hard rough bark of the tree, ready to slide it round the trunk—he would have to press hard against the bole to keep his shaking hand even reasonably steady—and with his left hand fumbled at his belt to release the knife with its spring-loaded blade. The gun was for the men, the knife for the dogs, the chances about even, for the policemen were advancing towards him shoulder to shoulder across the width of the road, rifles dangling loose in the crooks of their arms, unskilled amateurs who did not know what either war or death was. Or, rather, the chances would have been about even but for the gun in his hand: the first shot might clear the blocked barrel, it might equally well blow his hand off. On balance, then, the chances were heavily against him, but then, on a mission such as this, the chances would always be against him: the job on hand was still on hand, and its accomplishment justified all risks short of the suicidal.

The knife spring clicked loudly and released the blade, a five-inch sliver of double-edged blued steel that gleamed evilly in the starlight as Reynolds edged round the bole of the tree and lined up his automatic on the nearest of the advancing policemen. His trigger finger tightened, held, slackened, and a moment later he was back behind the tree trunk. Another and fresh tremor had seized his hand, and his mouth had gone suddenly dry: for the first time he had recognized the other three dogs for what they were.

Untrained country policemen, however armed, he could deal with; bloodhounds, too, he could handle, and with a fair chance of success; but only a madman would try conclusions with three trained Doberman pinschers, the most vicious and terrible fighting dogs in the world. Fast as a wolf, powerful as an Alsatian, and a ruthless killer utterly without fear, a Doberman could be stopped only by death. Reynolds didn't even hesitate. The chance he had been about to take was no longer a chance but a certain way to suicide. The job on hand was still all that mattered. Alive, though a prisoner, there was always hope: with his throat torn out by a Doberman pinscher, neither Jennings nor all the old man's secrets would ever come home again.

Reynolds placed the point of his knife against a tree, pushed the spring-loaded blade home into its leather scabbard, placed it on the crown of his head, and crammed his trilby on top of it. Then he tossed his automatic at the feet of the startled policemen and stepped out into the road and the starlight, both hands held high above his head.

Twenty minutes later they arrived at the police-block hut. Both the arrest and the long cold walk back had been completely uneventful. Reynolds had expected, at the least, a rough handling, at the most a severe beating up from rifle butts and steel-shod boots. But they had been perfunctory, almost polite in their behaviour, and had shown no ill will or animosity of any kind, not even the man with his jaw blue and red and already badly swelling from the earlier impact of Reynolds' clubbed automatic. Beyond a token search of his clothing for further arms, they had molested him in no way at all, had neither asked any questions nor demanded to see and inspect his papers.

11

The restraint, the punctiliousness made Reynolds feel uneasy: this was not what one expected in a police state.

The truck in which he had stolen a lift was still there, its driver vehemently arguing and gesticulating with both hands as he sought to convince two policemen of his innocence—almost certainly, Reynolds guessed, he was suspected of having some knowledge of Reynolds' presence in the back of the truck. Reynolds stopped, made to speak and if possible clear the driver, but had no chance: two of the policemen, all brisk officiousness now that they were once more in the presence of headquarters and immediate authority, caught his arms and hustled him in through the doors of the hut.

The hut was small, square, and ill made, the chinks in its walls closed up with wadded wet newspaper, and sparsely furnished: a portable wood stove with its chimney sticking through the roof, a telephone, two chairs, and a battered little desk. Behind the desk sat the officer in charge, a small fat man, middle-aged, red-faced, and insignificant. He would have liked his porcine little eyes to have a cold, penetrating stare, but it didn't quite come off; his air of spurious authority he wore like a threadbare cloak. A nonentity, Reynolds judged, possibly even, in given circumstances—such as the present—a dangerous little nonentity, but ready for all that to collapse like a pricked balloon at the first contact with real authority. A little bluster could do no harm.

Reynolds broke away from the hands of the men holding him, reached the desk in two paces, and smashed down his fist so heavily that the telephone on the rickety little desk jumped and gave a tiny, chimelike ring. "Are you the officer in charge here?" he demanded harshly.

The man behind the desk blinked in alarm, hurriedly sat back in his chair, and had just begun to raise his hands in instinctive self-defence when he recovered himself and checked the movement. But he knew his men had seen it, and the red neck and cheeks turned an even darker hue.

"Of course I'm in charge!" His voice started off as a high squeak, dropped an octave as he came on balance again. "What do you think?"

"Then what the devil do you mean by this outrage?" Reynolds cut him short in midsentence, drew his pass and identification papers from his wallet, and flung them on the table. "Go on, examine these! Check the photograph and thumbprints, and be quick about it. I'm late already, and I haven't all night to argue with you. Go on! Hurry up!"

If he had failed to be impressed by the display of confidence and righteous indignation, the little man behind the desk would have been less than human—and he was very human indeed. Slowly, reluctantly, he drew the papers toward him and picked them up.

"Johann Buhl," he read out. "Born, Linz 1923, now resident of Vienna, businessman, import-export dealer, machine parts."

"And here by the express invitation of your Economic Ministry," Reynolds added softly. The letter he now threw on the table was written on the Ministry's official notepaper, the envelope date-stamped Budapest four days previously. Negligently Reynolds reached out a leg, hooked a chair towards him, sat, and lit a cigarette—cigarettes, case, lighter, all made in Austria: the easy self-confidence could not be other than genuine. "I wonder what your superiors in Budapest will think of this night's work?" he murmured. "It will hardly increase your chances of promotion, I should think."

"Zeal, even misplaced zeal, is not a punishable offence in our country." The officer's voice was controlled enough, but the pudgy white hands trembled slightly as he returned the letter to its envelope and pushed the papers back to Reynolds. He clasped his hands on the desk before him, stared at them, then looked up at Reynolds, his forehead creased. "Why did you run away?"

"Oh, my God!" Reynolds shook his head in despair: the obvious question had been a long time coming, and he'd had plenty of time to prepare. "What would you do if a couple of thugs, waving their guns around, set on you in the darkness? Lie down and let them butcher you?"

"They were police officers. You could——"

"Certainly they're police officers," Reynolds interrupted acidly. "I can see that now—but it was as black as night inside the back of the truck." He was stretched out at his ease now, calm and relaxed, his mind racing. He had to end this interview quickly. The little man behind the desk was, after all, a lieutenant in the police or its equivalent. He couldn't possibly be as stupid as he looked; he might stumble across an awkward question at any moment. Quickly he decided that his best hope lay in audacity: the hostility was gone from Reynolds' manner, and his voice was friendly as he went on.

"Look, let's forget about this. I don't think it's your fault. You were just doing your duty—unfortunate though the consequences of your zeal might be for you. Let's make a deal: you provide me with transport to Budapest, and I'll forget it all. No reason why this should ever reach the ears of your superiors."

"Thank you. You are very kind." The police officer's reception of the proposal was less enthusiastic than Reynolds had expected; one might even have imagined a hint of dryness in the tone. "Tell me, Buhl, why were you in that truck? Hardly a normal method of transport for businessmen as important as yourself. And you didn't even let the driver know."

"He would probably have refused me—he had a notice forbidding unauthorized passengers." Far back in Reynolds' mind a tiny little warning bell was ringing. "My appointment is urgent."

"But why——"

"The truck?" Reynolds smiled ruefully. "Your roads are treacherous. A skid on ice, a deep ditch, and there you were—my Borgward with a broken front axle."

"You came by car? But for businessmen in a hurry——"

"I know, I know!" Reynolds let a little testiness, a little impatience, creep into his voice. "They come by plane. But I have 250 kilos of machine samples in the boot and back of my car: you can't lug a damned great weight like that aboard a plane." Angrily now he stubbed out hs cigarette. "This questioning is ridiculous. I've established my bona fides and I'm in a great hurry. What about that transport?"

"Two more little questions, and then you shall go," the officer promised. He was leaning back comfortably in his chair now, fingers steepled across his chest, and Reynolds felt his uneasiness deepen. "You came direct from Vienna? The main road?"

"Of course! How else would I come?"

"This morning?"

"Don't be silly." Vienna was less than 120 miles from where they were. "This afternoon."

"Four o'clock? Five o'clock?"

"Later. Ten past six exactly. I remember looking at my watch as I passed through your customs post."

"You could swear to that?"

"If necessary, yes."

The police officer's nod, the quick shifting of his eyes took Reynolds by surprise, and before he could move three pairs of hands had pinioned his from behind, dragged him to his feet, twisted his arms in front of him, and snapped on a pair of shiny steel handcuffs.

"What the devil does this mean?" In spite of the shock, the cold fury in Reynolds' tone could hardly have been bettered.

"It just means that a successful liar can never afford to be unsure of his facts." The policeman tried to speak equably, but the triumph in voice and eyes was unmistakable. "I have news for you, Buhl—if that is your name, which I don't for a moment believe. The Austrian frontier has been closed to all traffic for twenty-four hours—a normal security check, I believe—as from three o'clock this afternoon. Ten past six by your watch indeed!" Grinning openly now, he stretched out a hand for the telephone. "You'll get your transport to Budapest all right, you insolent impostor—in the back of a guarded police car. We haven't had a Western spy on our hands for a long time now: I'm sure they'll be delighted to send transport for you, just especially for you, all the way from Budapest."

He broke off suddenly, frowned, jiggled the receiver up and down, listened again, muttered something under his breath, and replaced the receiver with an angry gesture.

"Out of order again! That damned thing is always out of order." He was unable to conceal his disappointment; to have made the important announcement personally would have been one of the highlights of his life. He beckoned the nearest of the men.

"Where is the nearest telephone?"

"In the village. Three kilometers."

"Go there as fast as you can." He scribbled furiously on a sheet of paper. "Here is the number and the message. Don't forget to say it comes from me. Hurry, now."

The man folded the message, stuffed it into his pocket, buttoned his coat to the neck, and left. Through the momentarily opened door Reynolds could see that, even in the short time that had elapsed since his capture, clouds had moved across the stars and slow, heavy snowflakes were beginning to swirl across the silhouetted oblong of darkening sky. He shivered involuntarily, then looked back at the police officer.

"I'm afraid that you'll pay heavily for this," he said quietly. "You're making a very grave mistake."

"Persistence is an admirable thing in itself, but the wise man knows when to stop trying." The little fat man was enjoying himself. "The only mistake I made was ever to believe a word you said." He glanced at his watch. "An hour and a half, perhaps two, on these snowy roads, before your—ah—transport arrives. We can fill in that time very profitably. Information, if you please. We'll start off with your name—your real one this time, if you don't mind."

"You've already had it. You've seen my papers." Unasked, Reynolds resumed his seat, unobtrusively testing his handcuffs: strong, close-fitting over the wrist, and no hope there. Even so, even with bound hands, he could have disposed of the little man—the spring-knife was still under his trilby—but it was hopeless to think of it, not with three armed policemen behind him. "That information, those papers, are accurate and true. I can't tell lies just to oblige you."

"No one is asking you to tell lies, just to, shall we say, refresh your memory? Alas, it probably needs some jogging." He pushed back from the desk, levered himself heavily to his feet—he was even shorter and fatter standing upright than he had seemed sitting down—and walked round his desk. "Your name, if you please?"

"I told you——" Reynolds broke off with a grunt of pain as a heavily ringed hand caught him twice across the face, backhanded and forehanded. He shook his head to clear it, lifted his bound arms, and wiped some blood from the corner of his mouth with the back of his hand. His face was expressionless.

"Second thoughts are always wiser thoughts," the little man beamed. "I think I detect the beginning of wisdom. Come now, let us have no more of this disagreeable foolishness."

Reynolds called him an unprintable name. The heavily jowled face darkened with blood almost as if at the touch of a switch; he stepped forward, ringed hand clubbing down viciously, then collapsed backwards across his desk,

16

gasping and retching with agony, propelled by the scythe-like sweep of Reynolds' upward swinging leg. For seconds the police officer remained where he had fallen, moaning and fighting for breath, half lying, half kneeling across his desk, while his own men still stood motionless, the suddenness, the unbelievable shock of it holding them in thrall. It was just at this moment that the door crashed open and a gust of icy air swept into the hut.

Reynolds twisted round in his chair. The man who had flung open the door stood framed in the opening, his intensely cold blue eyes—a very pale blue indeed—taking in every detail of the scene. A lean, broad-shouldered man so tall that the uncovered thick brown hair almost touched the lintel of the doorway, he was dressed in a military, high-collared trench coat, belted and epauletted, vaguely greenish under a dusting of snow, so long-skirted that it hid the tops of his high, gleaming jackboots. The face matched the eyes: the busy eyebrows, the flaring nostrils above the clipped moustache, the thin chiselled mouth—all lent to the hard, handsome face that indefinable air of cold authority of one long accustomed to immediate and unquestioning obedience.

Two seconds were enough to complete his survey—two seconds would always be enough for this man, Reynolds guessed: no astonished looks, no "What's going on here?" or "What the devil does all this mean?" He strode into the room, unhooked one of his thumbs from the leather belt that secured his revolver, butt forward, to his left waist, bent down, and hauled the police officer to his feet, indifferent to his white face, his whooping gasps of pain as he fought for breath.

"Idiot!" The voice was in keeping with the appearance, cold, dispassionate, all but devoid of inflection. "Next time you—ah—interrogate a man, stand clear of his feet." He nodded curtly in Reynolds' direction. "Who is this man? What were you asking him and why?"

The police officer glared malevolently at Reynolds, sucked some air down into his tortured lungs, and whispered huskily through a strangled throat.

"His name is Johann Buhl, a Viennese businessman—but I don't believe it. He's a spy, a filthy Fascist spy," he spat out viciously. "A filthy Fascist spy!"

"Naturally." The tall man smiled coldly. "All spies are

filthy Fascists. But I don't want opinions, I want facts. First, how did you find out his name?"

"He said so, and he had papers. Forgeries, of course."

"Give them to me."

The police officer gestured towards the table. He could stand almost upright now. "There they are."

"Give them to me." The request, in tone, inflection, in every way, was a carbon copy of the first. The policeman reached out hastily, wincing with the pain of the sudden movement, and handed him the papers.

"Excellent. Yes, excellent." The newcomer riffled expertly through the pages. "Might even be genuine—but they're not. He's our man all right."

Reynolds had to make a conscious effort to relax his clenching fists. This man was infinitely dangerous, more dangerous than a division of stupid bunglers like the little policeman. Even trying to fool this man would be a waste of time.

"Your man? Your man?" The policeman was groping completely out of his depth. "What do you mean?"

"I ask the questions, little man. You say he is a spy. Why?"

"He says he crossed the frontier this evening." The little man was learning lessons in brevity. "The frontier was closed."

"It was indeed." The stranger leaned against the wall, selected a Russian cigarette from a thin gold case—no brass or chromium for the top boys, Reynolds thought bleakly—lit a cigarette, and looked thoughtfully at Reynolds. It was the policeman who finally broke the silence. Twenty or thirty seconds had given him time to recover his thoughts and a shred of his courage.

"Why should I take orders from you?" he blustered. "I've never seen you in my life before. I am in charge here. Who the devil are you?"

Perhaps ten seconds—ten seconds spent minutely examining Reynolds' clothes and face—elapsed before the newcomer turned lazily away and looked down at the little policeman. The eyes were glacial, dispassionate, but the expression of the face showed no change: the policeman seemed to shrink curiously inside his clothes and he pressed back hard against the edge of the desk.

"I have my rare moments of generosity. We will forget for the present what you said and how you said it." He nodded towards Reynolds, and his tone hardened almost imperceptibly. "This man is bleeding from the mouth. He tried, perhaps, to resist arrest?"

"He wouldn't answer my questions and——"

"Who gave you authority either to question or injure prisoners?" The tone of the voice cut like a whip. "You stupid bungling idiot, you might have done irreparable harm! Overstep your authority once again, and I personally will see to it that you have a rest from your exacting duties. The seaside, perhaps—Constanta, for a start?"

The policeman tried to lick his dry lips, and his eyes were sick with fear. Constanta, the area of the Danube-Black Sea Canal slave-labour camps, was notorious throughout central Europe: many had gone there, but no one ever returned.

"I—I only thought——"

"Leave thinking to those capable of such difficult feats." He jerked a thumb at Reynolds. "Have this man taken out to my car. He has been searched, of course?"

"But of course!" The policeman was almost trembling in his eagerness. "Thoroughly, I assure you."

"That statement coming from such as you makes a further search imperative," the tall man said dryly. He looked at Reynolds, one heavy eyebrow lifting slightly. "Must we be reduced to this mutual indignity—my having to search you personally, I mean?"

"There's a knife under my hat."

"Thank you." The tall man lifted the hat, removed the knife, courteously replaced the hat, pressed the release catch, thoughtfully inspected the blade, closed the knife, slid it into his coat pocket, and looked at the white-faced policeman.

"There is no conceivable reason why you should not rise to the topmost heights of your profession." He glanced at his watch—as unmistakably gold as the cigarette case. "Come, I must be on my way. I see you have the telephone here. Get me the Andrassy Ut, and be quick about it!"

The Andrassy Ut! Even though he had been becoming surer of the identity of the man with the passing of every moment, confirmation of his suspicions still came to Reynolds with a sense of shock and he could feel his face tightening in spite of himself under the speculative gaze of the tall stranger. Headquarters of the dreaded AVO, the

Hungarian Secret Police, currently reckoned the most ruthless and implacably efficient behind the Iron Curtain, the Andrassy Ut was the one place on earth he wanted at all costs to avoid.

"Ah! I see the name is not new to you." The stranger smiled. "That bodes no good for you, Mr. Buhl, or for your bona fides: the Andrassy Ut is hardly a name on every Western businessman's lips." He turned to the policeman. "Well, what are you stuttering about now?"

"The—the telephone." The voice was high and squeaking again and faltering badly: he was afraid now to the point of terror. "It's out of action."

"Inevitably. Matchless efficiency on every hand. May the gods help our unfortunate country." He produced a wallet from his pocket, opened it briefly for inspection. "Sufficiently good authority for the removal of your prisoner?"

"Of course, Colonel, of course." The words tripped over one another. "Whatever you say, Colonel."

"Good." The wallet snapped shut, and the stranger turned to Reynolds and bowed with ironic courtesy.

"Colonel Szendrô, headquarters, Hungarian Political Police. I am at your service, Mr. Buhl, and my car at your disposal. We leave for Budapest immediately. My colleagues and I have been expecting you for some weeks now and are most anxious to discuss certain matters with you."

2

IT was pitch-dark outside now, but light streaming from the open door and uncovered window of the hut gave them enough visibility to see by. Colonel Szendrô's car was parked on the other side of the road—a black left-hand-drive Mercedes saloon already covered with a deep layer of snow, all except the front part of the bonnet, where the engine heat melted the snow as it fell. There was a minute's delay while the colonel told them to release the truck driver and search the inside of the truck for any personal luggage Buhl might have been forced to abandon there—they found his overnight bag almost immediately—and then Szendrô opened the front right-hand door of the car and gestured Reynolds to his seat.

Reynolds would have sworn that no one man driving a car could have held him captive for fifty miles, only to find out how wrong he was even before the car started. While a soldier with a rifle covered Reynolds from the left-hand side, Szendrô stooped inside the other door, opened the glove compartment in front of Reynolds, fetched out two lengths of thin chain, and left the glove box open.

"A somewhat unusual car, my dear Buhl," the colonel said apologetically. "But you understand. From time to time I feel that I must give certain of my passengers a feeling of—ah—security." Rapidly he unlocked one of the handcuffs, passed the end link of one of the chains through it, locked it, passed the chain through a ring or eyebolt in the back of the glove box, and secured it to the other handcuff. Then he looped the second chain round Reynolds' legs, just above the knees, and, closing the door and leaning in through the opened window, secured it with a small padlock to the armrest. He stood back to survey his work.

"Satisfactory, I think. You should be perfectly comfortable and have ample freedom of movement—but not enough, I assure you, to reach me. At the same time you will find it difficult to throw yourself out of the door, which you would find far from easy to push open anyway: you will observe that the pull-out handle is missing from your door." The tone was light, even bantering, but Reynolds knew better than to be deceived. "Also, kindly refrain from damaging yourself by surreptitiously testing the strength of the chains and their anchors: the chains have a breaking load of just over a ton, the armrest is specially reinforced, and that ring in the glove box bolted through onto the chassis—— Well, what on earth do you want now?"

"I forgot to tell you, Colonel." The policeman's voice was quick, nervous. "I sent a message to our Budapest office asking to send a car for this man."

"You did?" Szendrô's voice was sharp. "When?"

"Ten, perhaps fifteen minutes ago."

"Fool! You should have told me immediately. However, it's too late now. No harm done, possibly some good. If they are as thick in the head as you are, a circumstance of which it is admittedly difficult to conceive, a long drive

21

in the cold night air should clear their minds admirably."

Colonel Szendrô banged the door shut, switched on the rear light above the windshield so that he should have no difficulty in seeing his prisoner, and drove off for Budapest. The Mercedes was equipped with snow tires on all four wheels, and in spite of the hard-packed snow on the road Szendrô made good time. He drove with the casual, easy precision of an expert, his cold blue eyes forever shifting to his right, very frequently and at varying intervals.

Reynolds sat very still, staring right ahead. He had already, in spite of the colonel's admonitions, tested the chains: the colonel hadn't exaggerated. Now he was forcing his mind to think coldly, clearly, and as constructively as possible. His position was almost hopeless—it would be completely so when they reached Budapest. Miracles happened, but only a certain kind of miracle: no one ever escaped from the AVO headquarters, from the torture chambers in Stalin Street. Once there, he was lost; if he was ever to escape it would have to be from this car, inside the next hour.

There was no window-winding handle on the door—the colonel had thoughtfully removed all such temptations; even if the window had been open he couldn't have reached the handle on the outside. His hands couldn't reach the wheel: he had already measured the arc of radius of the chain and his straining fingers would have been at least two inches away. He could move his legs to a certain extent, but couldn't raise them high enough to kick in the windscreen, shatter the toughened glass throughout its length, and perhaps cause a crash at fairly high speed. He could have placed his feet against the dashboard, and he knew of some cars where he could have heaved the front seat backwards off the rails. But everything in this car spelt solidity, and if he tried and failed, as he almost certainly would, all he'd probably get for his pains would be a tap on the head that would keep him quiet till they got to the Andrassy Ut. All the time he deliberately compelled himself to keep his mind off what was going to happen to him when he got there: that way lay only weakness and ultimate destruction.

His pockets—had he anything in his pockets he could use? Anything solid enough to throw at Szendrô's head, shock him for a length of time necessary to lose control and crash the car? Reynolds was aware that he himself might be hurt as seriously as the colonel, even though he had the advantage of preparation, but a fifty-fifty chance was better than the one in a million he had without it. He knew exactly where Szendrô had put the key to the handcuffs.

But a rapid mental inventory dismissed that hope: he had nothing heavier in his pocket than a handful of forints. His shoes, then—could he remove a shoe and get Szendrô in the face with it before the colonel knew what he was doing? But that came only a second ahead of the realisation of its futility; with his wrists handcuffed, the only way he could reach his shoes in any way unobtrusively was between his legs—and his knees were lashed tightly together. . . . Another idea, desperate but with a chance of success, had just occurred to him when the colonel spoke for the first time in the fifteen minutes since they had left the police block.

"You are a dangerous man, Mr. Buhl," he remarked conversationally. "You think too much—Cassius—you know your Shakespeare, of course."

Reynolds said nothing. Every word this man said was a potential trap.

"The most dangerous man I've ever had in this car, I should say, and a few desperate characters have sat from time to time where you're sitting now," Szendrô went on ruminatively. "You know where you're going, and you don't appear to care. But you must, of course."

Again Reynolds kept silent. The plan might work—the chance of success was enough to justify the risk.

"The silence is uncompanionable, to say the least," Colonel Szendrô observed. He lit a cigarette, sent the match spinning through the ventilation window. Reynolds stiffened slightly—the very opening he wanted. Szendrô went on: "You are quite comfortable, I trust?"

"Quite," Reynolds' conversational tone matched Szendrô's own. "But I'd appreciate a cigarette too, if you don't mind."

"By all means." Szendrô was hospitality itself. "One must cater for one's guests—you'll find half a dozen lying loose inside the glove compartment. A cheap and undistinguished brand, I fear, but I've always found that people in your—ah—position do not tend to be overcritical about these things. A cigarette—any cigarette—is a great help in times of stress."

"Thank you." Reynolds nodded at the projection on top of the dashboard at his own side. "Cigar lighter, is it not?"

"It is. Use it by all means."

Reynolds stretched forward with his handcuffed wrists, pressed it down for a few seconds then lifted it out, its spiral tip glowing red in the faint light from above. Then, just as it cleared the facia, his hands fumbled and he dropped it on the floor. He reached down to get it, but the chain brought his hands up with a sharp jerk inches from the floor. He swore softly to himself.

Szendrô laughed, and Reynolds, straightening, looked at him. There was no malice in the colonel's face, just a mixture of amusement and admiration, the admiration predominating.

"Very, very clever, Mr. Buhl. I said you were a dangerous man, and now I'm surer than ever." He drew deeply on his cigarette. "We are now presented with a choice of three possible lines of action, are we not? None of them, I may say, has any marked appeal for me."

"I don't know what you are talking about."

"Magnificent again!" Szendrô was smiling broadly. "The puzzlement in your voice couldn't be improved upon. Three courses are open, I say. First, I could courteously bend over and down to retrieve it, whereupon you would do your best to crush in the back of my head with your handcuffs. You would certainly knock me senseless—and you observed very keenly, without in any way appearing to do so, exactly where I put the key to these handcuffs." Reynolds looked at him uncomprehendingly, but already he could taste defeat in his mouth.

"Secondly, I could toss you a box of matches. You would strike one, ignite the heads of all the other matches in the box, throw it in my face, crash the car, and who knows what might happen then? Or you could just hope that I'd give you a light, either from the lighter or cigarette: then the finger judo lock, a couple of broken fingers, a transfer to a wrist lock, and then the key at your leisure. Mr. Buhl, you will bear watching."

"You're talking nonsense," Reynolds said roughly.

"Perhaps, perhaps. I have a suspicious mind, but I survive." He tossed something on to the lap of Reynolds' coat. "Herewith one single match. You can light it on the metal hinge of the glove box."

Reynolds sat and smoked in silence. He couldn't give up, he wouldn't give up, although he knew in his heart that the man at the wheel knew all the answers—and the answers to many questions which he, Reynolds, probably didn't know ever existed. Half a dozen separate plans occurred to him, each one more fantastic and with less chance of success than the previous one, and he was just coming to the end of his second cigarette—he had lit it off the butt end of the first—when the colonel changed down into the third gear, peered at the near side of the road, braked suddenly, and swung off into a small lane. Half a minute later, on a stretch of the lane parallel to and barely twenty yards from the highway, but almost entirely screened from it by thick, snow-covered bushes, Szendrô stopped the car and switched off the ignition. Then he turned off the head and side lights, wound his window right down in spite of the bitter cold, and turned to face Reynolds. The roof light above the windshield still burned in the darkness.

Here it comes, Reynolds thought bleakly. Thirty miles yet to Budapest, but Szendrô just can't bear to wait any longer. Reynolds had no illusions, no hope. He had had access to secret files concerning the activities of the Hungarian Political Police in the year that had elapsed since the bloody October rising of 1956, and they had made ghastly reading: it was difficult to think of the AVO—the AVH, as they were more lately known—as people belonging to the human race. Wherever they went they carried with them terror and destruction, a living death and death itself, the slow death of the aged in deportee camps and the young in the slave-labour camps, the quick death of the summary executions, and the ghastly, insane, screaming deaths of those who succumbed to the most abominable tortures ever conceived of the evil that lay buried deep in the hearts of the satanic perverts who find their way into the political police of dictatorships the world over. And no secret police in modern times excelled or even matched Hungary's AVO in the nameless barbarities, the inhuman cruelties and all-pervading terror with which they held hopeless people in fear-ridden thrall; they had learnt much from Hitler's Gestapo during the Second World War, and had that knowledge refined by their current nominal masters, the NKVD of Russia. But now the pupils had outdistanced their mentors, and they had developed flesh-crawling refinements and more terribly effective methods of terrorisation such as the others had not dreamed of.

But Colonel Szendrô was still at the talking stage. He turned round in his seat, lifted Reynolds' bag from the back, set it on his lap, and tried to open it. It was locked.

"The key," Szendrô said. "And don't tell me there isn't one or that it's lost. Both you and I, I suspect, Mr. Buhl, are long past that kindergarten stage."

They were indeed, Reynolds thought grimly. "Inside ticket pocket of my jacket."

"Get it. And your papers at the same time."

"I can't get at these."

"Allow me." Reynolds winced as Szendrô's pistol barrel pushed hard against lips and teeth, felt the colonel slip the papers from his breast pocket with a professional ease that would have done credit to a skilled pickpocket. And then Szendrô was back on his own side of the car, the bag open: almost, it seemed, without pausing to think, he had slit open the canvas lining and extracted a slim fold of papers and was now comparing them with those he had taken from Reynolds' pockets.

"Well, well, well, Mr. Buhl. Interesting, most interesting. Chameleonlike, you change your identity in a moment of time. Name, birthplace, occupation, even your nationality, all altered in an instant. A remarkable transformation." He studied the two sets of documents, one in either hand. "Which, if any, are we to believe?"

"The Austrian papers are fakes," Reynolds growled. For the first time he stopped speaking in German and switched to fluent idiomatic Hungarian. "I had word that my mother, who has lived in Vienna for many years, was dying. I had to have them."

"Ah, of course. And your mother?"

"No more." Reynolds crossed himself. "You can find her obituary in Tuesday's paper. Maria Rakosi."

"I'm at the stage now where I would be astonished if I didn't." Szendrô spoke also in Hungarian, but his accent was not that of Budapest, Reynolds was sure of that—he had spent too many agonising months learning every last Budapest inflection and idiom from an ex-professor of central European languages of Budapest University.

Szendrô was speaking again. "A tragic interlude, I am sure. I bare my head in silent sympathy—metaphorically, you understand. So you claim your real name is Lajos Rakosi? A very well-known name indeed."

"And a common one. And genuine. You'll find my name, date of birth, address, date of marriage all in the records. Also my——"

"Spare me." Szendrô held up a protesting hand. "I don't doubt it. I don't doubt you could show the very school desk on which your initials are carved and produce the once-little girl whose books you once carried home from school. None of which would impress me in the slightest. What does impress me is the extraordinary thoroughness and care of not only yourself but the superiors who have so magnificently trained you for whatever purpose they have in mind. I do not think I have ever met anything quite like it."

"You talk in riddles, Colonel Szendrô. I'm just an ordinary Budapest citizen. I can prove it. All right, I did have fake Austrian papers. But my mother was dying, and I was prepared to risk indiscretion. But I've committed no crime against our country. Surely you can see that. If I wished, I could have gone over to the West. But I did not so wish. My country is my country, and Budapest is my home. So I came back."

"A slight correction," Szendrô murmured. "You're not *coming* back to Budapest—you're going, and probably for the first time in your life." He was looking Reynolds straight in the eyes when his expression changed. "Behind you!"

Reynolds twisted round, a split second before he realised Szendrô had shouted in English—and there had been nothing in Szendrô's eyes or tone to betray his meaning. Reynolds turned back slowly, an expression almost of boredom on his face.

"A schoolboyish trick. I speak English"—he was using English now—"why should I deny it? My dear Colonel, if you belonged to Budapest, which you don't, you would know that there are at least fifty thousand of us who speak English. Why should so common an accomplishment be regarded with suspicion?"

"By all the gods!" Szendrô slapped his hand on his thigh. "It's magnificent, it's really magnificent. My professional jealousy is aroused. To have a Britisher or an

27

American—British, I think, the American intonation is almost impossible to conceal—talk Hungarian with a Budapest accent as perfectly as you do is no small feat. But to have an Englishman talk English with a Budapest accent—that is superb!"

"For heaven's sake, there's nothing superb about it," Reynolds almost shouted in exasperation. "I *am* Hungarian."

"I fear not." Szendrô shook his head. "Your masters taught you, and taught you magnificently—you, Mr. Buhl, are worth a fortune to any espionage system in the world. But one thing they didn't teach you, one thing they couldn't teach you—because they don't know what it is—is the mentality of the people. I think we may speak openly, as two intelligent men, and dispense with the fancy patriotic phrases employed for the benefit of the—ah—proletariat. It is, in brief, the mentality of the vanquished, of the fear-ridden, the cowed shoulder that never knows when the long hand of death is going to reach out and touch it." Reynolds was looking at him in astonishment—this man must be tremendously sure of himself—but Szendrô ignored him. "I have seen too many of our countrymen, Mr. Buhl, going, as you are, to excruciating torture and death. Most of them are just paralysed, some are plainly terror-stricken and weeping, and a handful are consumed by fury. You could not possibly fit in any of these categories—you should, but, as I say, there are things your masters cannot know. You are cold and without emotion, planning, calculating all the time, supremely confident of your own ability to extract the maximum advantage from the slightest opportunity that arises, and never tired of watching for that opportunity to come. Had you been a lesser man, Mr. Buhl, self-betrayal would not have come so easily. . . ."

He broke off suddenly, reached and switched off the roof light just as Reynolds' ears caught the hum of an approaching car engine, wound up his window, deftly removed a cigarette from Reynolds' hand, and crushed it beneath his shoe. He said nothing and made no move until the approaching car, a barely perceptible blur behind the sweep of its blazing headlights, its tires silent on the snow-packed road, had passed by and vanished to the west. As soon as it was lost to sight and sound Szendrô had reversed out on the highway again and was on his way, pushing the big car almost to the limit of safety along the treacherous road and through the gently falling snow.

Over an hour and a half elapsed before they reached Budapest—a long, slow journey that could normally have been done in half the time. But the snow, a curtain of great feathery flakes that swirled whitely, suddenly, into the flat-topped beams of the headlights, had become steadily heavier and slowed them up, at times almost to walking pace as the labouring wipers, pushing the clogging snow into corrugated ridges on the middle and at the sides of the windshield, swept through narrower and narrower arcs until finally they had stopped altogether; a dozen times, at least, Szendrô had had to stop to clear the mass of snow off the screen.

And then, a few miles short of the city limits, Szendrô had left the highway again and plunged into a mass of narrow, twisting roads; on many stretches where the snow lay smooth and deep and treacherously masking the border between road and ditch, theirs was obviously the first car that had passed since the snow had begun to fall, but despite the cars and concentrated attention Szendrô gave the roads, his flickering eyes found Reynolds every few seconds: the man's unflagging vigilance was almost inhuman.

Why the colonel had left the main road Reynolds couldn't guess, any more than he could guess why he had stopped and drawn off the road earlier. That he wanted, in the earlier instance, to avoid the big police car racing west to Komarom and now to bypass the police block on the city limits of which Reynolds had been warned at Vienna was obvious enough, but the reason for these actions was a different thing altogether. Reynolds wasted no time on the problem: he had problem enough of his own. He had perhaps ten minutes left.

They were passing now through the winding, villa-lined streets and steeply cobbled residential avenues of Buda, the western half of the city, and dropping down to the Danube. The snow was easing again, and, twisting round in his seat, Reynolds could just vaguely see the rock-bound promontory of the Gellert Hill, its grey, sharp granite jutting through the wind-blown snow, the bast bulk of the St. Gellert Hotel, and, as they approached the Ferenc Josef Bridge, the St. Gellert Mount where some old-time bishop who had incurred the wrath of his fellow man had been shoved into a spiked barrel and heaved into the Danube. Bungling amateurs in those days, Reynolds thought grimly, the old bishop couldn't have lasted a couple of minutes; down in the Andrassy Ut things would doubtless be much better arranged.

Already they were across the Danube and turning left into the Corso, the one-time fashionable embankment of open-air cafés on the Pest side of the river. But it was bleak and desolate now, as deserted as were nearly all the streets, and it seemed dated, anachronistic, a nostalgic and pathetic survival from an earlier and happier age. It was difficult, it was impossible to conjure up the ghosts of those who had promenaded there only two decades ago, carefree and gay and knowing that another tomorrow would never come, that all the other tomorrows could only be the same as today. It was impossible to visualise, however dimly, the Budapest of yesterday, the loveliest and happiest of cities, all that Vienna never was, the city to which so many Westerners, of so many nations, came to visit briefly, for a day, for two days, and never went home again. But all that was gone, even the memory was almost gone.

Reynolds had never been in the city before, but he knew it as few of the citizens of Budapest would ever know it. Over beyond the west bank of the Danube, the Royal Palace, the Gothic-Moorish Fisher's Bastion, and the Coronation church were half-imagined blurs in the snow-filled darkness, but he knew where they were and what they were as if he had lived in the city all his life. And now, on their right, was the magnificent Parliament of the Magyars, the Parliament and its tragic, blood-stained square where a thousand Hungarians had been massacred in the October rising, mown down by tanks and the murderous fire of the heavy AVO machine guns mounted on the roof of the Parliament itself.

Everything was real, every building, every street was exactly where it should be, precisely where he had been told it would be, but Reynolds could not shake off the growing feeling of unreality, of illusion, as if he were spectator of a play and all this was happening to someone else. A normally unimaginative man, ruthlessly trained to be abnormally so, to subject all emotion and feeling to the demands of reason and the intellect, he was aware of the strangeness in his mind and at a loss to account for it. Perhaps it was the certain foreknowledge of defeat, the knowledge that old Jennings would never come home again. Or it could have been the cold or tiredness or hopelessness or the ghostly veil of drifting snow that hung over everything, but he knew it was none of these things, it was something else again.

And now they had left the embankment and were turning into the long, broad tree-lined boulevard of the Andrassy Ut itself: the Andrassy Ut, that street of well-loved memories leading past the Royal Opera House to the zoo, the Fun Fair, and the city park, had been an inseparable part of a thousand days and nights of pleasure and enjoyment of freedom and escape to tens of thousands of citizens in days gone by, and no place on earth had lain nearer to the hearts of the Hungarians: and now all that was gone, it could never be the same again, no matter what befell, not even if peace and independence and freedom were to come again. For now the Andrassy Ut meant only repression and terror, the hammering on the door in the middle of the night and the brown lorries that came to take you away, the prison camps and deportation, the torture chambers and the benison of death: Andrassy Ut meant only the headquarters of the AVO.

And still the feeling of remoteness, of detached unreality remained with Michael Reynolds. He knew where he was, he knew his time had run out, he was beginning to know what Szendrô had meant by the mentality of a people who had lived too long with terror and the ever-present specter of death, and he knew, too, that no one who ever made a journey such as he was making now could feel exactly the same again. Indifferently, almost, with a kind of detached academic interest, he wondered how long he would last in the torture chambers, what latest diabolical variations of destroying a man lay in wait for him.

And then the Mercedes was slowing down, its heavy tires crunching through the frozen slush of the street, and Reynolds, in spite of himself, in spite of the unemotional stoicism of years and the shell of protective indifference in which he had armoured himself, felt fear touch him for the first time, a fear that touched his mouth and left it parched and dry; his heart, and left it pounding heavily, painfully in his chest and his stomach as if something heavy and solid and sharp lay there, constricting it upon itself: but no trace of any of this touched the expression on his face. He knew Colonel Szendrô was watching him closely; he knew that if he were what he claimed to be, an innocent citizen of Budapest, he should be afraid and fear should show in his face, but he could not bring himself to it—not because he was unable to do so, but because he knew of the reciprocal relationship between facial expressions and the mind. To show fear did not necessarily mean that one was afraid, but to show fear when one *was* afraid and fighting desperately not to be afraid would be fatal. . . . It was as if Colonel Szendrô had been reading his mind.

"I have no suspicion left, Mr. Buhl, only certainties. You know where you are, of course?"

"Naturally." Reynold's voice was steady. "I've walked along here a thousand times."

"You've never walked here in your life, but I doubt whether even the city surveyor could draw as accurate a map of Budapest as you could," Szendrô said equably. He stopped the car. "Recognise any place?"

"Your H.Q." Reynolds nodded at a building fifty yards away on the other side of the street.

"Exactly. Mr. Buhl, this is where you should faint, go into hysterics, or just sit there moaning with terror. All the others do. But you don't. Perhaps you are completely devoid of fear—an enviable if not admirable characteristic, but one which, I assure you, no longer exists in this country; or perhaps—an enviable *and* admirable characteristic—you *are* afraid, but ruthless training has eliminated all its outward manifestations. In either case, my friend, you are condemned. You don't belong. Perhaps not, as our police friend said, a filthy Fascist spy, but assuredly a spy." He glanced at his watch, then stared at Reynolds with a peculiar intentness. "Just after midnight— the time we operate best. And for you, the best treatment and the best quarters—a little soundproof room deep below the street of Budapest: only three AVO officers in all Hungary know of its existence."

He stared at Reynolds for several seconds longer, then started the car. Instead of stopping at the AVO building, he swung the car sharp left off the Andrassy Ut, drove a hundred yards down an unlighted street, and stopped again long enough to tie a silk handkerchief securely over

Reynolds' eyes. Then minutes later, after much turning and twisting which completely lost Reynolds all sense of place and direction as he knew it was designed to do, the car bumped heavily once or twice, dropped steeply down a long ramp, and drew up inside an enclosed space— Reynolds could hear the deep exhaust note of the car beating back off the walls. And then, as the motor died, he heard heavy iron doors clanging about behind them.

Seconds later the door on Reynolds' side of the car opened and a pair of hands busied themselves with freeing him of the restraining chains and then resecuring the handcuffs. Then the same hands were urging him out of the car and removing the blindfold.

Reynolds screwed up his eyes and blinked. They were in a big, windowless garage with heavy doors already locked behind them, and the brightness of the overhead light reflecting off whitewashed walls and ceiling was momentarily dazzling after the darkness of the blindfold and the night. At the other end of the garage, close to him, was another door, half open, leading into a brightly lit whitewashed corridor: whitewash, he reflected grimly, appeared to be an inseparable concomitant of all modern torture chambers.

Between Reynolds and the door, still holding him by the arm, was the man who had removed the chains. Reynolds looked at him for a long moment. With this man available, the AVO had no need to rely on instruments of torture—those enormous hands could just tear prisoners apart, slowly, piece by piece. About Reynolds' own height, the man looked squat, almost deformed in comparison, and the shoulders above that great barrel of chest were the widest Reynolds had ever seen: he must have weighed at least 250 pounds. The face was broken-nosed and ugly but curiously innocent of any trace of depravity or bestiality, just pleasantly ugly. Reynolds wasn't deceived. In his line of business, faces meant nothing: the most ruthless man he had ever known, a German espionage agent who had lost count of the number of men he had killed, had the face of a choirboy.

Colonel Szendrô slammed the car door and walked round to where Reynolds was standing. He looked at the other man and nodded at Reynolds.

"A guest, Sandor. A little canary who is going to sing

us a song before the night is through. Has the Chief gone to bed?"

"He is waiting for you in the office." The man's voice was what one would have expected, a low, deep rumble in the throat.

"Excellent. I'll be back in a few minutes. Watch our friend here, watch him closely. I suspect he's very dangerous."

"I'll watch him," Sandor promised comfortably. He waited till Szendrô, with Reynolds' bag and papers in his hand, had gone, then propped himself lazily against a whitewashed wall, massive arms folded across his chest. Hardly had he done so when he pushed himself off the wall and took a step towards Reynolds. "You do not look well."

"I'm all right." Reynolds' voice was husky, his breathing quick and shallow, and he was swaying slightly on his feet. He lifted his shackled hands over his right shoulder and massaged the back of his neck, wincing. "It's my head, the back of my head."

Sandor took another step forward, then moved swiftly as he saw Reynolds' eyes turning up till only the whites showed, beginning to topple forward, his body twisting slightly to the left as he fell. He could injure himself badly, even kill himself if his unprotected head struck the concrete floor, and Sandor had to reach forward quickly, arms outstretched to cushion the fall.

Reynolds hit Sandor harder than he had ever hit anyone in his life. Thrusting forward off the ball of his foot and pivoting his body with whiplash speed from left to right, he brought his manacled hands scything down in a violent, vicious, chopping blow that carried with it every last ounce of power of his sinewy arms and shoulders. The flat edges of his two hands, pressed hard together, caught Sandor across the exposed neck, just below the line of jawbone and ear. It was like striking the trunk of a tree, and Reynolds gasped with the pain: it felt as if both his little fingers were broken.

It was a judo blow, a killing judo blow, and it would have killed many men: all others it would have paralysed, left unconscious for hours—all others, that is, that Reynolds had ever known. Sandor just grunted, momentarily shook his head to clear it, and kept on coming, turning sideways to neutralise any attempt Reynolds might make to use feet or knees, pressing him back remorselessly against the side of the Mercedes.

Reynolds was powerless. He couldn't have resisted even had he been of a mind to, and his utter astonishment that any man could not only survive such a blow but virtually ignore it left no room for any thought of resistance. Sandor leaned against him with all his great weight, crushing him against the car, reached down with both hands, caught Reynolds by the forearms, and squeezed. There was no animosity, no expression at all in the giant's eyes as they stared unblinkingly into Reynolds' from a distance of three or four inches. He just stood there and squeezed.

Reynolds clenched teeth and lips together till his jaws ached, forcing back the scream of agony. It seemed as if his forearms had been caught in two giant, inexorably tightening vises. He could feel the blood draining from his face, the cold sweat starting on his forehead, and the bones and sinews of his arms felt as if they were being mangled and crushed beyond recovery. The blood was pounding in his head, the garage walls were becoming dim and swimming before his eyes, when Sandor released his grip and stepped back, gently massaging the left side of his neck.

"Next time I squeeze it will be a little higher up," he said mildly. "Just where you hit me. Please stop this foolishness. Both of us have been hurt, and for nothing."

Five minutes passed, five minutes during which the sharp agony in Reynolds' arms faded to a dull, pounding ache, five minutes in which Sandor's unblinking eyes never strayed from him. Then the door opened wide, and a young man—he was hardly more than a boy—stood there looking at Reynolds. He was thin and sallow, with an unruly mop of black hair and quick, nervous darting eyes, almost as dark as his hair. He jerked a thumb over his shoulders.

"The Chief wants to see him, Sandor. Bring him along, will you?"

Sandor escorted Reynolds along the narrow corridor, down a shallow flight of stairs at the end into another corridor, then pushed him through the first several doors that lined both sides of the second passageway. Reynolds stumbled, recovered, then looked around him.

It was a large room, wood-panelled, the worn linoleum on the floor relieved only by a stretch of threadbare carpet in front of the desk at the far end of the room. The room was brightly lit, with a lamp of moderate power in the ceiling and a powerful wall light on a flexible extension arm behind the desk; at the moment the latter was pointing downward on to the surface of the desk, harshly highlighting the jumble of clothes and other articles that had recently been so neatly folded in Reynolds' bag. Beside the clothes were the torn remnants of the bag itself: the lining was in tatters, the zip had been torn off, the leather handle had been slit open, and even the four studs in the base of the bag had been torn out by the pair of pliers lying beside them. Reynolds silently acknowledged the handiwork of an expert.

Colonel Szendrô was standing beside the table, leaning over towards the man seated behind it. The face of the latter was hidden in deep shadow, but both hands, holding some of Reynolds' papers, were exposed to the pitiless glare of the lamp. They were terrible hands; Reynolds had never seen anything remotely like them, had never imagined that any human being's hands could be so scarred, crushed, and savagely mutilated and still serve as hands. Both thumbs were crushed and flattened and twisted, fingertips and nails were blurred into a shapeless mass, the little finger and half of the fourth finger of the left hand were missing, and the backs of both hands were covered with ugly scars surrounding bluish-purple weals in the middle, between the tendons of the middle and fourth fingers. Reynolds stared at these weals, fascinated, and shivered involuntarily; he had seen these marks once before, on a dead man: the marks of crucifixion. Had these been his hands, Reynolds thought in revulsion, he would have had them amputated. He wondered what manner of man could bear to live with these hands, not only live with them but have them uncovered. He was suddenly possessed of an almost obsessive desire to see the face of the man behind these hands, but Sandor had halted several paces from the desk, and the blackness of the shadow by the lamp defeated him.

The hands moved, gesturing with Reynolds' papers, and the man at the desk spoke. The voice was quiet, controlled, almost friendly. "These papers are interesting enough in their own way—masterpieces of the forger's

art. You will be good enough to tell us your real name."
He broke off and looked at Sandor, who was still tenderly
massaging his neck. "What is wrong, Sandor?"

"He hit me," Sandor explained apologetically. "He
knows how to hit and where to hit—and he hits hard."

"A dangerous man," Szendrô said. "I warned you, you
know."

"Yes, but he's a cunning devil," Sandor complained.
"He pretended to faint."

"A major achievement to hurt you, an act of desperation to hit you at all," the man behind the desk said
drily. "But you mustn't complain, Sandor. He who expects
that death comes with the next breath but one is not given
to counting the cost. . . . Well, Mr. Buhl, your name,
please."

"I've already told Colonel Szendrô," Reynolds replied.
"Rakosi, Lajos Rakosi. I could invent a dozen names, all
different, in the hope of saving myself unnecessary suffering, but I couldn't prove my right to any of them. I *can*
prove my right to my own name, Rakosi."

"You are a brave man, Mr. Buhl." The seated man
shook his head. "But in this house you will find courage a
useless prop: lean on it and it will only crumble to dust
under your weight. The truth alone will serve. Your
name, please?"

Reynolds paused before replying. He was fascinated
and puzzled and hardly afraid any more. The hands fascinated him, he could scarcely take his eyes off them, and
he could see now some tattooing on the inside of the
man's wrist—at that distance it looked like a figure 2, but
he couldn't be certain. He was puzzled because there were
too many off-beat angles to all that was happening to him,
too much that didn't fit in with his conception of the AVO
and all that he had been told about them. There was a
curious restraint, almost a cold courtesy in their attitude to
him, but he was aware that the cat could just be playing
with the mouse; perhaps they were just subtly sapping his
determination to resist, conditioning him to be least
prepared for the impact of the blow when it came. And
why his fear was lessening he would have found it impossible to say; it must have arisen from some subtle prompt-
ings of his subconscious mind, for he was at a conscious
loss to account for it.

"We are waiting, Mr. Buhl." Reynolds couldn't detect

the slightest trace of an edge through the studied patience of the voice.

"I can only tell you the truth. I've already done that."

"Very well. Take your clothes off—all of them."

"No!" Reynolds glanced swiftly round, but Sandor stood between him and the door. He looked back, and Colonel Szendrô had his pistol out. "I'll be damned if I do it!"

"Don't be silly." Szendrô's voice was weary. "I have a gun in my hand and Sandor will do it by force, if necessary. Sandor has a spectacular if untidy method of undressing people—he rips coats and shirts in half down the back. You'll find it far easier to do the job yourself."

Reynolds did it himself. Inside a minute all his clothes were crumpled heaps about his feet, and he was standing there shivering, his forearms angry masses of red and blue weals where Sandor's viselike fingers had dug into his flesh.

"Bring the clothes over here, Sandor," the man at the desk ordered. He looked at Reynolds. "There's a blanket on the bench behind you."

Reynolds looked at him in sudden wonder. That it was his clothes they wanted—looking for giveaway tags, probably—instead of himself was surprising enough; that the courtesy—and, on that cold night, the kindness—of a covering blanket should be offered was astonishing. And then he caught his breath and utterly forgot about both of those things, because the man behind the desk had risen and walked round with a peculiarly stiff-legged gait to examine the clothes.

Reynolds was a trained judge, very highly trained, of faces and expressions and character. He made mistakes and made them often, but he never made major mistakes, and he knew that it was impossible that he was making a major one now. The face was fully in the light now, and it was a face that made these terrible hands a blasphemous contradiction, an act of impiety in themselves. A lined, tired face, a middle-aged face that belied the thick, snow-white hair above, a face deeply, splendidly etched by experience, by a sorrowing and suffering such as Reynolds could not even begin to imagine, it held more goodness, more wisdom and tolerance and understanding than Reynolds had ever seen in the face of any man before. It was the face of a man who had seen everything, known everything, and experienced everything and still had the heart of a child.

Reynolds sank slowly down on to the bench, mechanically wrapping the faded blanket around him. Desperately, almost, forcing himself to think with detachment and clarity, he tried to reduce to order the kaleidoscopic whirling of confused and contradictory thoughts that raced through his mind. But he had got no further than the first insoluble problem, the presence of a man like that in a diabolical organisation like the AVO, when he received his fourth and final shock and, almost immediately afterwards, the answer to all his problems.

The door beside Reynolds swung open towards him, and a girl walked into the room. The AVO, Reynolds knew, not only had its complement of females, but ranked among them skilled exponents of the most fiendish tortures imaginable; but not even by the wildest leap of the imagination could Reynolds include her in that category. A little below middle height, with one hand tightly clasping the wrap about her slender waist, she had a face that was young and fresh and innocent, untouched by any depravity. The yellow hair, the color of ripening corn, was awry about her shoulders, and with the knuckles of one hand she was still rubbing the sleep from eyes of a deep cornflower blue. When she spoke, her voice was still a little blurred from sleep, but soft and musical, if perhaps touched with a little asperity.

"Why are you all still up and talking? It's one o'clock in the morning—it's after one, and I'd like to get some sleep." Suddenly her eyes caught sight of the pile of clothing on the table, and she swung round to catch sight of Reynolds sitting on the bench and clad only in the cold blanket. Her eyes widened, and she took an involuntary step backwards, clutching her wrap even more tightly around her. "Who—who on earth is this, Jansci?"

3

"JANSCI!" Michael Reynolds was on his feet without any volition on his own part. For the first time since he had fallen into Hungarian hands the studied calmness, the mask of emotional indifference vanished and his eyes were alight with excitement and a hope that he had thought had vanished for ever. He took two quick steps towards the girl, grabbing at his blanket as it slipped and almost fell to the floor. "Did you say 'Jansci'?" he demanded.

"What's wrong? What do you want?" The girl had retreated as Reynolds had advanced, then stopped as she bumped into the reassuring bulk of Sandor and clutched his arm. The apprehension in her face faded, and she looked at Reynolds thoughtfully and nodded. "Yes, I said that. Jansci."

"Jansci." Reynolds repeated the word slowly, incredulously, like a man savouring each syllable to the full, wanting desperately to believe in the truth of something but unable to bring himself to that belief. He walked across the room, the hope and the conflicting doubt still mirrored in his eyes, and stopped before the man with the scarred hands.

"Your name is Jansci?" Reynolds spoke slowly, the unbelief, the inability to believe, still registering in his eyes.

"I am called Jansci." The older man nodded, his eyes speculative and quiet.

"One-four-one-four-one-eight-two." Reynolds looked unblinkingly at the other, searching for the faintest trace of response, of admission. "Is that it?"

"Is that what, Mr. Buhl?"

"If you are Jansci, the number is one-four-one-four-one-eight-two," Reynolds repeated. Gently, meeting no resistance, he reached out for the scarred left hand, pushed the cuff back from the wrist, and stared down at the violet tattoo: 1414182—the number was as clear, as unblemished as if it had been made only that day.

Reynolds sat down on the edge of the desk, caught sight of a pack of cigarettes, and shook one loose. Szendrô struck and held a match for him, and Reynolds nodded gratefully; he doubted whether he could have done it for himself, his hands were trembling uncontrollably. The fizzling of the lighting match seemed strangely loud in the sudden silence of the room. Jansci it was who finally broke the silence.

"You seem to know something about me?" he prompted gently.

"I know a lot more." The tremor was dying out of Reynolds' hands and he was coming back on balance again, outwardly, at least. He looked round the room, at Szendrô, Sandor, the girl, and the youth with the quick nervous eyes, all with expressions of bewilderment or anticipation on their faces. "These are your friends? You can trust them absolutely—they all know who you are? Who you really are, I mean?"

"They do. You may speak freely."

"Jansci is a pseudonym for Illyurin." Reynolds might have been repeating something by rote, something he knew by heart, as indeed he did. "Major General Alexis Illyurin. Born Kalinovka, Ukraine, October 18th, 1904. Married June 18th, 1931. Wife's name Catherine, daughter's name Julia." Reynolds glanced at the girl. "This must be Julia, she seems about the right age. Colonel Mackintosh says he'd like to have his boots back: I don't know what he means."

"Just an old joke." Jansci walked round the desk to his seat and leant back, smiling. "Well, well, my old friend Peter Mackintosh still lives. Indestructible, he always was indestructible. You must work for him, of course, Mr.—ah——"

"Reynolds. Michael Reynolds. I work for him."

"Describe him." The subtle change in tone could hardly be called a hardening, but it was unmistakable. "Face, physique, clothes, history, family—everything."

Reynolds did so. He talked for five minutes without stopping, then Jansci held up his hand.

"Enough. You must know him, must work for him and be the person you claim to be. But he took a risk, a great risk. It is not like my old friend."

"I might be caught and made to talk, and you, too, would be lost?"

"You are very quick, young man."

"Colonel Mackintosh took no chance," Reynolds said quietly. "Your name and number—that was all I knew. Where you lived, what you looked like—I had no idea. He didn't even tell me about the scars on your hands: these would have given me instant identification."

"And how, then, did you hope to contact me?"

"I had the address of a café." Reynolds named it. "The haunt, Colonel Mackintosh said, of disaffected elements. I was to be there every night, same seat, same time, till I was picked up."

"No identification?" Szendrô's query lay more in the lift of an eyebrow than the inflection of the voice.

"Naturally. My tie."

Colonel Szendrô looked at the vivid magenta of the tie lying on the table, winced, nodded, and looked away without speaking. Reynolds felt the first faint stirrings of anger.

"Why ask if you already know?" The edged voice betrayed the irritation in his mind.

"No offence." Jansci answered for Szendrô. "Endless suspicion, Mr. Reynolds, is our sole guarantee of survival. We suspect everyone. Everyone who lives, everyone who moves—we suspect them every minute of every hour. But, as you see, we survive. We had been asked to contact you in that café—Imre has practically lived there for the past three days—but the request had come from an anonymous source in Vienna. There was no mention of Colonel Mackintosh—he is an old fox, that one. . . . And when you had been met in the café?"

"I was told that I would be led to you—or to one of two others: Hridas and the White Mouse."

"This has been a happy short cut," Jansci murmured. "But I am afraid you would have found neither Hridas nor the White Mouse."

"They are no longer in Budapest?"

"The White Mouse is in Siberia. We shall never see him again. Hridas died three weeks ago, not two kilometers from here, in the torture chambers of the AVO. They were careless for a moment, and he snatched a gun. He put it in his mouth. He was glad to die."

"How—but how do you know these things?"

"Colonel Szendrô—the man you know as Colonel Szendrô—was there. He saw him die. It was Szendrô's gun he took."

Reynolds carefully crushed his cigarette stub in an ash tray. He looked up at Jansci, across to Szendrô, and back at Jansci again: his face was empty of all expression.

"Szendrô has been a member of the AVO eighteen months," Jansci said quietly. "One of their most efficient and respected officers, and when things mysteriously go wrong and wanted men escape at the last moment, there is no one more terrible in his anger than Szendrô, no one

42

who drives his men so cruelly till they literally collapse with exhaustion. The speeches he makes to newly indoctrinated recruits and cadets to the AVO have already been compiled in book form. He is known as The Scourge. His chief, Furmint, is at a loss to understand Szendrô's pathological hatred for his own countrymen but declares he is the only indispensable member of the Political Police in Budapest. . . . A hundred, two hundred Hungarians alive today, still here or in the West, owe their lives to Colonel Szendrô."

Reynolds stared at Szendrô, examining every line of that face as if he were seeing it for the first time, wondering what manner of man might pass his life in such incredibly difficult and dangerous circumstances, never knowing whether he was being watched or suspected or betrayed, never knowing whether or not the next shoulder for the tap of the executioner might be his own, and all at once, without at all knowing why, Reynolds knew that this was indeed such a man as Jansci claimed. All other considerations apart, he had to be or he, Reynolds, might even then have been screaming on the torture racks deep down below the basement of Stalin Street. . . .

"It must indeed be as you say, General Illyurin," Reynolds murmured. "He runs incredible risks."

"Jansci, if you please. Always Jansci. Major General Illyurin is dead."

"I'm sorry . . . And tonight, how about tonight?"

"Your—ah—arrest by our friend here?"

"Yes."

"It is simple. He has access to all but a few secret master files. Also he is privy to all proposed plans and operations in Budapest and western Hungary. He knew of the roadblock, the closing of the frontier . . . And he knew you were on the way."

"But surely—surely they weren't after me? How could——"

"Don't flatter yourself, my dear Reynolds." Szendrô carefully fitted another brown and black Russian cigarette into his holder—Reynolds was to discover that he chain-smoked a hundred of these every day—and struck a match. "The arm of coincidence is not all that long. They weren't looking for you; they weren't looking for anyone. They were stopping only trucks, searching for large quantities of ferro-wolfram that are being smuggled into the country."

"I should have thought they would have been damned glad to get all the ferro-wolfram they could lay their hands on," Reynolds murmured.

"And so they are, my dear boy, and so they are. However, there are proper channels to be gone through, certain customs to be observed. Not to put too fine a point on it, several of our top party officials and highly respected members of the government were being deprived of their usual cut. An intolerable state of affairs."

"Unthinkable," Reynolds agreed. "Action was imperative."

"Exactly!" Szendrô grinned, the first time Reynolds had seen him smile, and the sudden flash of white, even teeth and the crinkling of the eyes quite transformed the cold aloofness of the man. "Unfortunately, on such occasions as these some fish other than the ones we are trawling for get caught in the net."

"Such as myself?"

"Such as yourself. So I have made it my practice to be in the vicinity of certain police blocks at such times: a fruitless vigil, I fear, on all but very few occasions: you are only the fifth person I've taken away from the police inside a year. Unfortunately, you will also be the last. On the previous occasions I warned the country bumpkins who man these posts that they were to forget that I or the prisoner I had taken from them ever existed. Tonight, as you know, their headquarters had been informed and the word will be out to all block posts to beware of a man posing as an AVO officer."

Reynolds stared at him.

"But good God, man, they saw you! Five of them, at least. Your description will be in Budapest before——"

"Pah!" Szendrô flicked off some ash with a careless forefinger. "Much good it will do the fools! Besides, I'm no imposter—I *am* an AVO officer. Did *you* doubt it?"

"I did not," Reynolds said feelingly. Szendrô hitched an immaculately trousered leg and sat on the desk, smiling.

"There you are, then. Incidentally, Mr. Reynolds, my apologies for my rather intimidating conduct on the way here tonight. As far as Budapest, I was concerned only with finding out whether you really were a foreign agent and the man we were looking for or whether I should throw you out at a street corner and tell you to lose yourself. But by the time I had reached the middle of the town another and most disquieting possibility had struck me."

"When you stopped in the Andrassy Ut?" Reynolds nodded. "You looked at me in a rather peculiar fashion, to say the least."

"I know. The thought had just occurred that you might have been an AVO member deliberately planted on me and therefore had no cause to fear a visit to the Andrassy Ut: I confess I should have thought of it earlier. However, when I said I was going to take you to a secret cellar, you would have known at once what I suspected, known I could not now afford to let you live and screamed your head off. But you said nothing, so I knew you were at least no plant . . . Jansci, could I be excused for a few minutes? You know why."

"Certainly, but be quick. Mr. Reynolds hasn't come all the way from England just to lean over the Margit Bridge and drop pebbles into the Danube. He has much to tell us."

"It is for your ear alone," Reynolds said. "Colonel Mackintosh said so."

"Colonel Szendrô is my right hand, Mr. Reynolds."

"Very well. But only the two of you."

Szendrô bowed and walked out of the room. Jansci turned to his daughter.

"A bottle of wine, Julia. We have some Villanyi Furmint left?"

"I'll go and see." She turned to leave, but Jansci called her. "One moment, my dear. Mr. Reynolds, when did you eat last?"

"Ten o'clock this morning."

"So. You must be starving. Julia?"

"I'll see what I can get, Jansci."

"Thank you—but first the wine. Imre"—he addressed the youngster who was pacing restlessly up and down—"the roof. A walk around. See if everything is clear. Sandor, the car number plates. Burn them, and fix new ones."

"Burn them?" Reynolds asked as the man left the room. "How is that possible?"

"We have a large supply of number plates." Jansci

45

smiled. "All of three-ply wood. They burn magnificently ... Ah, you found some Villanyi?"

"The last bottle." Her hair was combed now, and she was smiling, appraisal and frank curiosity in her blue eyes as she looked at Reynolds. "You can wait twenty minutes, Mr. Reynolds?"

"If I have to." He smiled. "It will be difficult."

"I'll be as quick as I can," she promised.

As the door closed behind her Jansci broke open the seal of the bottle and poured the cool white wine into a couple of glasses.

"Your health, Mr. Reynolds. And to success."

"Thank you." Reynolds drank slowly, deeply, gratefully of the wine—he could not recall when his throat and mouth had been so parched before—and nodded at the one ornament in that rather bleak and forbidding room, a silver-framed photograph on Jansci's desk. "An extraordinarily fine likeness of your daughter. You have skilled photographers in Hungary."

"I took it myself." Jansci smiled. "It does her justice, you think? Come, your honest opinion: I am always interested in the extent and depth of a man's percipience."

Reynolds glanced at him in faint surprise, then sipped his wine and studied the picture in silence, studied the fair, waving hair, the broad smooth brow above the long-lashed eyes, the rather high Slavonic cheekbones curving down to a wide, laughing mouth, the rounded chin above the slender column of the throat. A remarkable face, he thought, a face full of character, of eagerness and gaiety and a splendid zest for living. A face to remember ...

"Well, Mr. Reynolds?" Jansci prompted him gently.

"It does her justice," Reynolds admitted. He hesitated, fearing presumption, looked at Jansci, knew instinctively how hopeless it would be to try to deceive the wisdom in these tired eyes, then went on: "You might almost say it does her more than justice."

"Yes?"

"Yes, the bone structure, the shape of all the features, even the smile is exactly the same. But this picture has something more—something more of wisdom, of maturity. In two years perhaps, in three, then it will be your daughter, really your daughter: here, somehow, you have caught a foreshadowing of these things. I don't know how it is done."

"It's quite simple. That photograph is not of Julia, but of my wife."

"Your wife! Good lord, what a quite extraordinary resemblance." Reynolds broke off, hurriedly searched his past sentences for any unfortunate gaffes, decided he had made none. "She is here just now?"

"No, not here." Jansci put his glass down and turned it round and round between his fingers. "I'm afraid we do not know where she is."

"I'm sorry." It was all Reynolds could think of to say.

"Do not misunderstand me," Jansci said gently. "We know what happened to her, I'm afraid. The brown lorries—you know what I mean?"

"The Secret Police."

"Yes." Jansci nodded heavily. "The same lorries that took away a million in Poland, the same in Rumania, and half a million in Bulgaria, all to slavery and death. The same lorries that wiped out the middle classes of the Baltic States, that have taken a hundred thousand Hungarians, they came also for Catherine. What is one person among so many millions who have suffered and died?"

"That was in the summer of '51?" It was all Reynolds could think to say: it was then, he knew, that the mass deportations from Budapest had taken place.

"We were not living here then, it was just two and a half years ago, less than a month after we had come. Julia, thank God, was staying with friends in the country. I was away that night, I had left about midnight, and when she went to make herself coffee after I had gone, the gas had been turned off and she did not know what that meant. So they took her away."

"The gas? I'm afraid——"

"You don't understand? A chink in your armour the AVO would soon have pried open, Mr. Reynolds. Everybody else in Budapest understands. It is the practice of the AVO to turn off the gas supply to a block of houses or flats before serving deportation notices there: a pillow on the bottom shelf of a gas oven is comfortable enough, and there is no pain. They stopped the sale of poisons in all chemists', they even tried to ban the sale of razor blades. They found it difficult, however, to prevent people from jumping from top-story flats . . ."

"She had no warning?"

47

"No warning. A blue slip of paper thrust in her hand, a small suitcase, the brown lorry, and then the locked cattle trucks of the railway."

"But she may yet be alive. You have heard nothing?"

"Nothing, nothing at all. We can only hope she lives. But so many died in these cattle trucks, stifling or freezing to death, and the work in the fields, the factories, or mines is brutal, killing, even for one fit and well: she had just been discharged from hospital after a serious operation. Chest surgery—she had tuberculosis: her convalescence had not even begun."

Reynolds swore softly. How often one read, one heard about this sort of thing; how easily, how casually, almost callously, one dismissed it—and how different when one was confronted with reality.

"You have looked for her—for your wife?" Reynolds asked harshly. He hadn't meant to speak that way, it was just the way the words came out.

"I have looked for her. I cannot find her."

Reynolds felt the stirring of anger. Jansci seemed to take it all so easily, he was too calm, too unaffected.

"The AVO must know where she is," Reynolds persisted. "They have lists, files. Colonel Szendrô——"

"He has no access to top-secret files," Jansci interrupted. He smiled. "And his rank is only equivalent to that of major. The promotion was self-awarded and for tonight only. So was the name ... I think I hear him coming now."

But it was the youngster with the dark hair who entered —or partially entered. He poked his head round the door, reported that everything was clear, and vanished. But even in that brief moment Reynolds had had time to notice the pronounced nervous tick on the left cheek, just below the daring black eyes. Jansci must have seen the expression on Reynolds' face, and when he spoke his voice was apologetic.

"Poor Imre! He was not always like this, Mr. Reynolds, not always so restless, so disturbed."

"Restless! I shouldn't say it, but because my safety and plans are involved, too, I must: he's a neurotic of the first order." Reynolds looked hard at Jansci, but Jansci was his usual mild and gentle self. "A man like that in a setup like this! To say he's a potential danger is the understatement of the month."

"I know, don't think I don't know." Jansci sighed. "You should have seen him just over two years ago, Mr. Reynolds, fighting the Russian tanks on Castle Hill, just north of Gellert. He hadn't a nerve in his entire body. When it came to spreading liquid soap at the corners—and the steep, dangerous slopes of the Hill saw to the rest as far as the tanks were concerned—or prizing up loose cobbles, filling the holes with petrol and touching it off as a tank passed across, Imre had no equal. But he became too rash, and one night one of the big T-54 tanks, slipping backwards down a hill with all the crew dead inside, pinned him, kneeling on all fours, against the wall of a house. He was there for thirty-six hours before anyone noticed him—and twice during that time the tank had been hit by high-explosive rockets from Russian fighter planes—they didn't want their own tanks used against them."

"Thirty-six hours!" Reynolds stared at Jansci. "And he lived?"

"He hadn't a mark on him, he still hasn't. It was Sandor who got him out—that was how they met for the first time. He got a crowbar and broke down the wall of the house from the inside—I saw him do it, and he was flinging two-hundred-pound blocks of masonry around as if they were pebbles. We took him in a nearby house, left him, and when we returned the house was a huge pile of rubble: some resistance fighters had taken up position there and a Mongolian tank commander had pulverised the bottom story until the whole house fell down. But we got him out again, still without a scratch. He was very ill for a long time—for months—but he's much better now."

"Sandor and yourself both fought in the rising?"

"Sandor did. He was foreman electrician in the Dunapentele steelworks, and he put his knowledge to good use. To see him handling high-tension wires with nothing but a couple of wooden bars held in his bare hands would make your blood freeze, Mr. Reynolds."

"Against the tanks?"

"Electrocution." Jansci nodded. "The crews of three tanks. And I've been told he destroyed even more down in Csepel. He killed an infantryman, stole his flame thrower, sprayed through the driver's visor, then dropped a Molotov cocktail—just bottles of ordinary petrol with bits of burning cotton stuffed into the necks—through the hatch

49

when they opened it to get some air. Then he would shut the hatch, and when Sandor shuts a hatch and sits on it, the hatch stays shut."

"I can imagine," Reynolds said drily. Unconsciously, almost, he rubbed his still aching arms, then a sudden thought occurred to him. "Sandor took part, you said. And yourself?"

"Nothing." Jansci spread his scarred, misshapen hands palm upwards, and now Reynolds could see that the crucifixion marks indeed went right through. "I took no part in it. I tried all I could to stop it."

Reynolds looked at him in silence, trying to read the expression of the faded grey eyes enmeshed in those spider webs of wrinkles. Finally he said, "I'm afraid I don't believe you."

"I'm afraid you must."

Silence fell on the room, a long, cold silence: Reynolds could hear the far-off tinkle of dishes in a distant kitchen as the girl prepared the meal. Finally he looked directly at Jansci.

"You let the others fight, fight for you?" He made no attempt to conceal his disappointment, the near hostility in his tone. "But why? Why did you not help, not do *something?*"

"Why? I'll tell you why." Jansci smiled faintly and reached up and touched his white hair. "I am not as old as the snow on my head would have you think, my boy, but I am still far too old for the suicidal, the futile act of the grand but empty gesture. I leave that for the children of this world, the reckless and the unthinking, the romanticists who do not stop to count the cost; I leave it to the righteous indignation that cannot see beyond the justice of its cause, to the splendid anger that is blinded by its own shining splendour. I leave it to the poets and the dreamers, to those who look back to the glorious gallantry, the imperishable chivalry of a bygone world, to those whose vision carries them forward to the golden age that lies beyond tomorrow. But I can only see today." He shrugged. "The charge of the Light Brigade—my father's father fought in that—you remember the charge of the Light Brigade and the famous commentary on that charge? 'It's magnificent, but it's not war.' So it was with our October Revolution."

"Fine words," Reynolds said coldly. "These are fine

words. I'm sure a Hungarian boy with a Russian bayonet in his stomach would have taken great comfort from them."

"I am also too old to take offence," Jansci said sadly. "I am also too old to believe in violence, except as a last resort, the final fling of desperation when every hope is gone, and even then it is only a resort to hopelessness: besides, Mr. Reynolds, besides the uselessness of violence, of killing, what right have I to take the life of any man? We are all our Father's children, and I cannot but think that fratricide must be repugnant to our God."

"You talk like a pacifist," Reynolds said roughly. "Like a pacifist before he lies down and lets the jackboot tramp him into the mud, him and his wife and his children."

"Not quite, Mr. Reynolds, not quite," Jansci said softly. "I am not what I would like to be, not all. The man who lays a finger on my Julia dies even as he does it."

For a moment Reynolds caught a glimpse, a glimpse that might almost have been imagination, of the fire smouldering in the depths of those faded eyes, remembered all that Colonel Mackintosh had told of this fantastic man before him and felt more confused than ever.

"But you said—you told me that——"

"I was only telling you why I didn't take part in the rising." Jansci was his gentle self again. "I don't believe in violence if any other way will serve. Again, the time could not have been more badly chosen. And I do not hate the Russians, I even like them. Do not forget, Mr. Reynolds, that I am a Russian myself. A Ukrainian, but still a Russian, despite what many of my countrymen would say."

"You like the Russians. Even the Russian is your brother?" Mask it as he tried with politeness, Reynolds could not quite conceal the incredulity in his question. "After what they have done to you and your family?"

"A monster, and I stand condemned. Love for our enemies should be confined to where it belongs—between the covers of the Bible—and only the insane would have the courage, or the arrogance or the stupidity, to open the pages and turn the principles into practice. Madmen, only madmen would do it—but without these madmen our Armageddon will surely come." Jansci's tone changed. "I like the Russian people, Mr. Reynolds. They're likeable, cheerful, and gay when you get to know them, and there are no friendlier people on earth. But they are young, they are very young, like children. And, like children, they are full of whims; they're arbitrary and primitive and a little cruel, as are all little children, forgetful and not greatly moved by suffering. But for all their youth, do not forget that they have a great love of poetry, of music and dancing and singing and folk tales, of ballet and the opera that would make the average Westerner, in comparison, seem culturally dead."

"They're also brutal and barbarous, and human life doesn't matter a damn to them," Reynolds interjected.

"Who can deny it? But do not forget, so also was the Western world when it was politically as young as the peoples of Russia are now. They're backward, primitive, and easily swayed. They hate and fear the West because they're told to hate and fear the West. But your democracies, too, can act the same way."

"For heaven's sake!" Reynolds crushed out his cigarette in a gesture of irritation. "Are you trying to say——"

"Don't be so naïve, young man, and listen to me." Jansci's smile robbed his words of any offence. "All I'm trying to say is that unreasoning, emotionally conditioned attitudes are as possible in the West as in the East. Look, for instance, at your country's attitude to Russia in the past twenty years. At the beginning of the last war Russia's popularity-ran high. Then came the Moscow-Berlin pact, and you were actually ready, remember, to send an army of fifty thousand to fight the Russians in Finland. Then came Hitler's assault in the East, your national press full of paeans of praise for 'Good old Joe,' and all the world loved a muzjik. Now the wheel has come full circle again, and the holocaust only awaits the one rash or panic-stricken move. Who knows, in five years' time all will be smiles again. You are weathercocks, just as the Russians are weathercocks, but I blame neither people: it is not the weathercock that turns, it is the wind that turns the weathercock."

"Our governments?"

"Your governments." Jansci nodded. "And of course the national press that always conditions the thinking of a people. But primarily the governments."

"We in the West have had governments, often very bad governments," Reynolds said slowly. "They stumble, they miscalculate, they make foolish decisions, they even have their quota of opportunists, careerists, and plain down-right power-seekers. But all these things are only because they are human. They mean well, they try hard for the good, and not even a child fears them." He looked speculatively at the older man. "You yourself said recently that the Russian leaders have sent literally millions in the past few years to imprisonment and slavery and death. If, as you say, the peoples are the same, why are the governments so utterly different? Communism is the only answer."

Jansci shook his head. "Communism is gone, and gone forever. Today it remains only as a myth, an empty lip-service catchword in the name of which the cynical, ruthless realists of the Kremlin find sufficient excuse and justification for whatever barbarities their policies demand. A few of the old guard still in power may cherish the dream of world Communism, but just a few: only a global war could now achieve their aim, and these same hardheaded realists in the Kremlin can see no point or sense or future in pursuing a policy that carries with it the seed of their own destruction. They are essentially businessmen, Mr. Reynolds, and letting off a time bomb under your own factory is no way to run a business."

"Their barbarities, their enslavements, and their massacres don't stem from world conquest?" The fractional lift of Reynolds' eyebrows was its own sceptical comment. "You tell me that?"

"I do."

"Then from what in the world——"

"From fear, Mr. Reynolds," Jansci interrupted. "From an almost terror-stricken fear that has no parallel among governments of modern times.

"They are afraid because the ground lost in leadership is almost irrecoverable: Malenkov's concessions of 1953, Khrushchev's famous de-Stalinisation speech of 1956 and his forced decentralisation of all industry were contrary to all the cherished ideas of Communist infallibility and centralised control, but they had to be done, in the interest of efficiency and production, and the people have smelled Freedom. And they are afraid because their Secret Police has slipped and slipped badly: Beria is dead, the NKVD in Russia are not nearly so feared as the AVO in this country, so the belief in the power of authority, of the inevitability of punishment, has slipped also.

"These fears are of their own people. But these fears are nothing compared to their fears of the outside world. Just before he died, Stalin said, 'What will happen without me! You are blind, as young kittens are blind, and Russia will be destroyed because you do not know how to recognise her enemies.' Even Stalin couldn't have known how true his words would prove to be. They cannot recognise enemies, and they can only be safe, only feel safe, if all the peoples of the outside world are regarded as enemies. Especially the West. They fear the West and, from their own point of view, they fear with every reason.

"They are afraid of a Western world that, they think, is unfriendly and hostile and just waiting its chance. How terrified would you be, Mr. Reynolds, if you were ringed, as Russia is ringed, with nuclear bomb bases in England and Europe and North Africa and the Middle East and Japan? How much more terrified would you be if, every time world tensions increase, fleets of foreign bombers appear mysteriously on the far edge of your long-distance radar screens, if you know, beyond any reasonable doubt, that whenever such tensions arise there are, at any given moment of the day or night, anywhere between five hundred and one thousand bombers of the American Strategic Air Command, each with its hydrogen bomb, cruising high in the stratosphere, just waiting the signal to converge on Russia and destroy it. You have to have an awful lot of missiles, Mr. Reynolds, and an almost supernatural confidence in them to forget those thousand hydrogen bombers already airborne—and it only requires five per cent of them to get through, as they inevitably would. Or how would you in Britain feel if Russia were pouring arms into southern Ireland, or the Americans if a Russian aircraft carrier fleet armed with hydrogen bombs cruised indefinitely in the Gulf of Mexico? Try to imagine all that, Mr. Reynolds, and you can perhaps begin to imagine—only begin, for the imagination can be only a shadow of the reality—how the Russians feel.

"Nor does their fear stop there. They are afraid of people who try to interpret everything in the limited light of their own particular culture, who believe that all people, the world over, are basically the same. A common assumption, and a stupid and dangerous one. The cleavage between Western and Slavonic minds and ways of thinking, the differences between their culture patterns are immense and, alas, unrealised.

"Finally, but perhaps above all, they are afraid of the penetration of Western ideas into their own country. And that is why the satellite countries are so invaluable to them as a *cordon sanitaire,* an insulation against dangerous capitalist influences. And that's why revolt in one of their satellites, as in this country two years last October, brings out all that is worst in the Russian leaders. They reacted with such incredible violence because they saw in this Budapest rising the culmination, the fulfilment at one and the same time of their three nightmare fears—that their entire satellite empire might go up in smoke and the *cordon sanitaire* vanish for ever, that even a degree of success could have touched off a similar revolt in Russia and, most terrible of all, that a large-scale conflagration from the Baltic to the Black Sea would have given the Americans all the excuse or reason they ever needed to give the green light to the Strategic Air Command and the carriers of the Sixth Fleet. I know, you know, that idea's fantastic, but we are not dealing with facts, only with what the Russian leaders believe to be facts."

Jansci drained his glass and looked quizzically at Reynolds. "You begin to see now, I hope, why I was neither advocate of nor participant in the October rising. You begin to see, perhaps, why the revolt just had to be crushed, and the bigger and more serious the revolt, the more terrible would have to be the repression, to preserve the cordon, to discourage other satellites or any of their own people who might be having similar ideas. You begin to see the hopelessness—the foredoomed hopelessness—of it, the disastrously ill-judged futility of it all. The only effect it had was to strengthen Russia's position among the other satellites, kill and maim countless thousands of Hungarians, destroy and damage over twenty thousand houses, bring inflation, a serious shortage of food, and an almost mortal blow to the country's economy. It should never have happened. Only, as I say, the anger of despair is always blind: noble anger can be a magnificent thing, but annihilation has its—ah—drawbacks."

Reynolds said nothing: for the moment he could think of nothing to say. A long silence fell on the room, long but not cold any more: the only sound was the scuffling of Reynolds' shoes as he tied his laces—he had been dressing as Jansci talked. Finally Jansci rose, switched out the light, drew back the curtain of the solitary window, peered out, then switched on the light again. It meant nothing, Reynolds could see; it was purely an automatic gesture, the routine precaution of a man who had lived as long as he had by never neglecting the slightest precaution. Reynolds replaced his papers in his wallet and the gun in its shoulder holster.

A tap came on the door, and Julia came in. Her face was flushed from the warmth of a stove, and she carried a tray holding a bowl of soup, a steaming plate of diced meat and diced vegetables, and a bottle of wine. She laid this on the desk.

"Here you are, Mr. Reynolds. Two of our national dishes—Gulyás soup and tokány. I'm afraid there may be too much paprika in the soup and garlic in the tokány for your taste, but that's how we like it." She smiled apologetically. "Leftovers—all I could produce in a hurry at this time of night."

"Smells wonderful," Reynolds assured her. "I'm only sorry to be such a bother to you in the middle of the night."

"I'm used to it," she said drily. "Usually there's half a dozen to be fed, generally about four o'clock in the morning. Father's guests keep irregular hours."

"They do indeed." Jansci smiled. "Now off to bed with you, my dear, it's very late."

"I'd like to stay a little, Jansci."

"I don't doubt it." Jansci's faded grey eyes twinkled. "Compared to our average guest, Mr. Reynolds is positively handsome. With a wash, brush-up, and shave he might be almost presentable."

"You know that's not fair, Father." She stood her ground well, Reynolds thought, but the color had deepened in her cheeks. "You shouldn't say that."

"It's not fair, and I shouldn't," Jansci said. He looked at Reynolds. "Julia's dream world lies west of the Austrian frontier, and she'd listen for hours to anyone talking about it. But there are some things she must not know, things that it would be dangerous for her even to guess about. Off you go, my dear."

"Very well." She rose obediently, if reluctantly, kissed Jansci on the cheek, smiled at Reynolds, and left. Reynolds looked over at Jansci as the older man reached for the second bottle of wine and broke open the seal.

"Aren't you worried to death about her all the time?"

"God knows it," Jansci said simply. "This is no life for her, or for any girl, and if I get caught she goes too, almost for a certainty."

"Can't you get her away?"

"You want to try it! I could get her across the frontier tomorrow without the slightest difficulty or danger—you know that this is my speciality—but she won't go. An obedient, respectful daughter, as you have seen—but only up to a self-drawn line. After that she is as stubborn as a mule. She knows the risks, but she stays. She says she'll never leave till we find her mother and they go together. But even then——"

He broke off suddenly as the door opened and a stranger walked in. Reynolds, twisting round and out of his seat like a cat, had his automatic out and lined up on the man before he had taken a step into the room, the snick of the safety catch plain above the scraping of the chair legs on the linoleum. He stared at the man unwinkingly, taking in every detail of the face, the smooth, dark hair brushed straight back, the lean eagle face with the thin pinched nostrils and high forehead of a type he knew well—the unmistakable Polish aristocrat. Then he started as Jansci reached out gently and pressed down the barrel of the automatic.

"Szendrô was right about you," he murmured thoughtfully. "Dangerous, very dangerous—you move like a snake when it strikes. But this man is a friend, a good friend. Mr. Reynolds, meet the Count."

Reynolds put the gun away, crossed the room, and extended his hand. "Delighted," he murmured. "Count who?"

"Just the Count," the newcomer said, and Reynolds stared at him again. The voice was unmistakable. "Colonel Szendrô!"

"No other," the Count admitted, and with these words his voice had changed as subtly, but as completely, as his appearance. "I say modestly, but with truth, I have few equals in the matter of disguise and mimicry. What you now see before you, Mr. Reynolds, is me—more or less. Then a scar here, a scar there, and that is how the AVO

57

see me. You will understand, perhaps, why I was not unduly worried about being recognised tonight?"

Reynolds nodded slowly. "I do indeed. And—and you live here—with Jansci? Isn't that rather dangerous?"

"I live in the second best hotel in all Budapest," the Count assured him. "As befits a man of my rank, naturally. But as a bachelor, I must, of course, have my—ah—diversions, shall we say. My occasional absences call for no comment . . . Sorry to have been so long, Jansci. Damned moustache stuck."

"Not at all," Jansci assured him. "Mr. Reynolds and I have had the most interesting discussion."

"About the Russians, inevitably?"

"Inevitably."

"And Mr. Reynolds was all for conversion by annihilation?"

"More or less." Jansci smiled. "It's not so long since you felt the same way yourself."

"Age comes to us all." The Count crossed to a wall cabinet, drew out a dark bottle, poured himself a half tumblerful of liquid, and looked at Reynolds. "*Barack*—apricot brandy, you would call it. Deadly. Avoid it like the plague. Homemade." As Reynolds watched in astonishment, he drank the contents without stopping, then refilled the glass. "You have not yet come to the business of the day?"

"I'm coming to it now." Reynolds pushed back his plate, drank some more wine. "You gentlemen have heard, perhaps, of Dr. Harold Jennings?"

Jansci's eyes narrowed. "We have indeed. Who hasn't?"

"Exactly. Then you know what he's like—an elderly dodderer well over seventy, shortsighted, amiable, a typically absentminded professor, in every respect but one. He has a brain like an electronic computer and is the world's greatest expert and authority on the higher mathematics of ballistics and ballistic missiles."

"Which was why he was induced to defect to the Russians," the Count murmured.

"He didn't," Reynolds said flatly. "The world thinks he did, but the world is wrong."

"You are sure of this?" Jansci was leaning far forward in his seat.

"Certain. Listen. At the time of the defection of other

British scientists, old Jennings spoke out strongly, if unwisely, in their defence. He bitterly condemned what he called outworn nationalisms and said that any man had the right to act according to the dictates of his mind, conscience, and ideals. Almost immediately, as we expected, he was contacted by the Russians. He rebuffed them, told them to get the hell back to Moscow, and said he fancied their brand of nationalism a damn sight less than his own: he had only been talking generally, he said."

"How can you be sure of this?"

"We are sure—we had a tape recording of the entire conversation—we had the whole house wired. But we never made public the recording, and after he had gone over to the Russians it would have been too late—nobody would have believed us."

"Obviously," Jansci murmured. "And then, also obviously, you called off the watchdogs?"

"We did," Reynolds admitted. "It would have made no difference anyway—we were watching the wrong party. Less than two months after the old boy's interview with the Russian agents, Mrs. Jennings and her sixteen-year-old schoolboy son, Brian—the professor married late in life— went to Switzerland for a holiday. Jennings was to have gone with them but was held up by some important business at the last minute, so he let them go on alone, intending to rejoin them in two or three days in their Zurich hotel. He found his wife and son gone."

"Abducted, of course," Jansci said slowly. "And the Swiss-Austrian frontier is no barrier to determined men: but more likely, perhaps, by boat, at night."

"That's what we thought." Reynolds nodded. "Lake Constance. Anyway, what's certain is that Jennings was contacted within minutes of arriving at the hotel, told what had happened, and left in no doubt as to what lay in store for his wife and son if he didn't immediately follow them behind the Iron Curtain. Jennings may be an old dodderer, but he's not an old fool: he knew these people weren't kidding, so he went at once."

"And now, of course, you want him back?"

"We want him back. That's why I'm here."

Jansci smiled faintly. "It will be interesting to learn just how you propose to rescue him, Mr. Reynolds, and of course his wife and son, for without them you achieve nothing. Three people, Mr. Reynolds, an old man, a woman, and a boy, a thousand miles to Moscow, and the snow lies deep upon the steppes."

"Not three people, Jansci: just one—the professor. And I don't have to go to Moscow for him. He's not two miles from where we're sitting now, right here in Budapest."

Jansci made no effort to conceal his astonishment.

"Here? You're sure of that, Mr. Reynolds?"

"Colonel Mackintosh was."

"Then Jennings must be here, he must be." Jansci twisted in his seat and looked at the Count. "Had you heard of this?"

"Not a word. Nobody in our office knows of it, I'll swear to that."

"All the world will know next week." Reynolds' voice was quiet but positive. "When the International Scientific Conference opens here on Monday, the first paper will be read by Professor Jennings. He is being groomed as the star of the show. It will be the Communists' biggest propaganda triumph in years."

"I see, I see." Jansci drummed his fingers thoughtfully on the table, then looked up sharply. "Professor Jennings, you said you only wanted the professor?"

Reynolds nodded.

"Only the professor!" Jansci stared at him. "God above, man, aren't you aware what will happen to his wife and son? I assure you, Mr. Reynolds, if you expect our assistance——"

"Mrs. Jennings is already in London." Reynolds held up his hand to forestall the questions. "She fell seriously ill about ten weeks ago, and Jennings insisted that she go to the London Clinic for treatment, and he forced the Communists to accede to his demands—you can't coerce, torture, or brainwash a man of the professor's calibre without destroying his capacity for work, and he flatly refused to carry on working till they had granted his demands."

"He must be quite a man." The Count shook his head in admiration.

"He's a holy terror when something gets his back up," Reynolds smiled. "But it wasn't all that much of an achievement. The Russians had everything to gain—the continued services of the greatest ballistic expert alive today—and nothing to lose. They held the two trump cards—Jennings and his son—in Russia and knew that

Mrs. Jennings would return, and they insisted that everything be done in the utmost secrecy. Not half a dozen people in Britain know that Mrs. Jennings is in Britain, not even the surgeon who carried out the two major operations on her."

"She recovered?"

"It was touch and go, but she recovered and she's recuperating very well."

"The old man will be pleased," Jansci murmured. "His wife returns to Russia soon?"

"His wife will never return to Russia again," Reynolds said bluntly. "And Jennings has no reason to be pleased. He thinks his wife is critically ill and that what little hope there is is going fast. He thinks that, because that is what we have told him."

"What! What's that?" Jansci was on his feet now, the faded grey eyes cold and hard as stone. "God in heaven, Reynolds, what kind of inhuman conduct is that? You actually told the old man his wife was dying?"

"Our people at home need him, and need him desperately: our scientists have been held up, completely blocked, on their latest project for ten weeks now, and they're convinced that Jennings is the only man who can give them the break-through they must have."

"So they would use this despicable trick——"

"It's life or death, Jansci," Reynolds interrupted flatly. "It may literally be life or death for millions. Jennings must be moved, and we will use every lever we can to that end."

"You think this is ethical, Reynolds? You think anything can justify——"

"Whether I think these things or not doesn't matter a damn," Reynolds said indifferently. "The pros and cons are not for me to decide. The only thing that concerns me is that I've been given a job to do: if it is possible in any way at all, I'll get that job done."

"A ruthless and dangerous man," the Count murmured. "I told you. A killer, but he happens to be on the side of the law."

"Yes." Reynolds was unmoved. "And there's another point. Like many other brilliant men, Jennings is rather naïve and shortsighted when it comes to matters outside his own speciality. Mrs. Jennings tells us that the Russians have assured her husband that the project he is working

61

on will be used for exclusively peaceful purposes. Jennings believes this. He's a pacifist at heart, and so——"

"All the best scientists are pacifists at heart." Jansci was sitting down now, but his eyes were still hostile. "All the best men everywhere are pacifists at heart."

"I'm not arguing. All I'm saying is that Jennings is now at the stage where he would sooner work for the Russians, if he thinks he is working for peace, than for his own people, if he knows he is working for war. Which makes him all the more difficult to move—and which, in turn, makes necessary the use of every lever that comes to hand."

"The fate of his young son is, of course, a matter of indifference." The Count waved an airy hand. "Where such tremendous stakes are at issue——"

"Brian, his son, was in Poznań all day yesterday," Reynolds interrupted. "Some exposition or other, mainly for youth organisations. Two men shadowed him from the moment he got up. By noon tomorrow—today, that is— he'll be in Stettin. Twenty-four hours later he'll be in Sweden."

"Ah, so. But you are too confident, Reynolds, you underestimate Russian vigilance." The Count was regarding him thoughtfully over the rim of his brandy glass. "Agents have been known to fail."

"These two agents have never failed. They are the best in Europe. Brian Jennings will be in Sweden tomorrow. The call-sign comes from London on a regular European transmission. Then, and not till then, we approach Jennings."

"So." The Count nodded. "Perhaps you have some humanity after all."

"Humanity!" Jansci's voice was cold still, almost contemptuous. "Just another lever to use against the poor old man—and Reynolds' people know very well that if they left the boy to die in Russia, Jennings would never work for them again."

The Count lit another in his interminable chain of brown cigarettes.

"Perhaps we are being too harsh. Perhaps, here, self-interest and humanity go hand in hand. 'Perhaps,' I said . . . And what if Jennings still refuses to go?"

"Then he'll just have to go whether he wants to or not."

"Wonderful! Just wonderful!" The Count smiled wryly. "What a picture for *Pravda*. Our friends here lugging Jennings by the heels across the border and the caption, 'British Secret Agent Liberates Western Scientist.' Can't you just see it, Mr. Reynolds?"

Reynolds shrugged and said nothing. He was only too keenly aware of the change of atmosphere in the past five minutes, the undercurrent of hostility that now ran strongly towards himself. But he had had to tell Jansci everything—Colonel Mackintosh had been insistent on that point—and it had been inevitable if they were to have Jansci's help. The offer of help, if it were to be made at all, now hung in the balance—and without it, Reynolds knew, he might as well have saved himself the trouble of coming at all. . . . Two minutes passed in silence, then Jansci and the Count looked at one another and exchanged an almost imperceptible nod. Jansci looked squarely at Reynolds.

"If all your countrymen were like you, Mr. Reynolds, I wouldn't lift a finger to help you—cold-blooded, emotionless people to whom right and wrong, justice and injustice and suffering are matters of academic disinterest are as guilty, by silence of consent, as the barbarous murderers of whom you so recently spoke—but I know they are not all like you. Neither would I help if it were only to enable your scientists to make machines of war. But Colonel Mackintosh was—is—my friend, and I think it inhuman, no matter what the cause, that an old man should die in a foreign land, among uncaring strangers, far from his family and those he loves. If it lies in our power, in any way at all, we will see to it, with God's help, that the old man comes safely home again."

4

THE inevitable cigarette holder clipped between his teeth, the inevitable Russian cigarette well alight, the Count leaned a heavy elbow on the buzzer and kept on leaning until a shirt-sleeved little man, unshaven and still rubbing the sleep from his eyes, came scurrying out from the little cubicle behind the hotel's reception desk. The Count eyed him with disfavour.

"Night porters should sleep in the daytime," he said coldly. "The manager, little man, and at once."

"The manager? At this hour of the night?" The night porter stared with ill-concealed insolence at the clock above his head, transferred his stare to the Count, now innocuously dressed in a grey suit and grey raglan raincoat, and made no effort at all to conceal the truculence in his voice. "The manager is asleep. Come back in the morning."

There came a sudden sound of ripping linen, a gasp of pain, and the Count, his right hand gripping the bunched folds of the porter's shirt, had him halfway across the desk: the bloodshot, sleep-filmed eyes, widening first with surprise and then with fear, were only inches away from the wallet that had magically appeared in the Count's free hand. A moment of stillness, a contemptuous shove, and the porter was scrabbling frantically at the pigeonholed mail racks behind him in an attempt to keep his balance.

"I'm sorry, comrade, I'm terribly sorry!" The porter licked his lips, suddenly dry and stiff. "I—I didn't know——"

"Who else do you expect to come calling this hour of night?" the Count demanded softly.

"No one, comrade, no one! No—no one at all. It's just that—well, you were here only twenty minutes ago——"

"*I* was here?" It was the raised eyebrow as much as the inflection of the voice that cut short the frightened stammering.

"No, no, of course not! Not you—your people, I mean. They came——"

"I know, little man. I sent them." The Count waved a weary hand in bored dismissal and the porter hurried off across the hall. Reynolds rose from the wall bench where he had been sitting and crossed the room.

"Quite a performance," he murmured. "You even had me scared."

"Just practice," the Count said modestly. "Sustains my reputation and doesn't do them any permanent harm, distressing though it is to be addressed as 'comrade' by such a moron . . . You heard what he said?"

"Yes. They don't waste much time, do they?"

"Efficient enough in their own unimaginative way," the Count conceded. "They'll have checked most of the hotels in town by morning. Only a slim chance, of course, but one that they can't afford to neglect. Your position is now doubly safe, three times as safe as it was at Jansci's house."

Reynolds nodded and said nothing. Only half an hour had elapsed since Jansci had agreed to help him. Both Jansci and the Count had decided that he must leave there at once: it was too inconvenient, too dangerous. It was inconvenient not so much because of the cramped accommodations but because it was in a lonely and out-of-the-way place. Movements of a stranger at any hour of the day or night, such as Reynolds might be compelled to make, would be sure to draw unfavourable attention; it was too remote from the centre of the town, from the big hotels of Pest, where Jennings might be expected to be staying; and, biggest drawback of all, it had no telephone for instant communications.

And it was dangerous because Jansci was becoming increasingly convinced that the house was being watched: in the past day or two both Sandor and Imre had seen two people, singly and on several different occasions, walking slowly by the house on the other side of the street. It was unlikely that they were police or agents of the police, just as it was unlikely that they were innocent passers-by: like every city under a police-state rule, Budapest had its hundreds of paid informers, and probably they were just confirming their suspicions and gathering their facts before going to the police and collecting their blood money. Reynolds had been surprised by the casual, almost indifferent way Jansci had treated this danger, but the Count had explained as he had driven the Mercedes through the snow-filled street to this hotel on the banks of the Danube. The changing of their hideouts because of suspicious neighbors had become so frequent as to be almost routine, and Jansci had a sixth sense which, so far, had always led them to pull out in good time. Annoying, the Count said, but no serious inconvenience; they knew of half a dozen bolt holes just as good, and their permanent headquarters, a place known to Jansci, Julia, and himself, was in the country.

Reynolds' thoughts were interrupted by the sound of the door across the hall opening. He looked up to see a man hurrying across the parquet floor, the tap-tap of his metalled heels urgent and almost comically hurried; he was shrugging a jacket over a crumpled shirt, and the thin, bespectacled face was alive with fear and anxiety.

"A thousand apologies, comrade, a thousand apologies!" He wrung white-knuckled hands in his distress, then glared at the porter following more slowly behind him. "This oaf here——"

"You are the manager?" the Count interrupted curtly.

"Yes, yes, of course."

"Then dismiss the oaf. I wish to talk to you privately." He waited till the porter had gone, drew out his gold cigarette case, selected a cigarette with due care, examined it minutely, inserted it with much deliberation in his holder, took his time about finding his matchbox and removing a match, finally lit the cigarette. A beautiful performance, Reynolds thought dispassionately: the manager, already on the tenterhooks of fright, was now almost in hysterics.

"What is it, comrade, what has gone wrong?" In his attempt to keep his voice steady, it had been louder than intended, and it now dropped to almost a whisper. "If I can help the AVO in any way, I assure you——"

"When you speak, you will do so only to answer my questions." The Count hadn't even raised his voice, but the manager seemed to shrink visibly, and his mouth closed tightly in a white line of fear. "You spoke to my men some little time ago?"

"Yes, yes, a short time ago. I wasn't even asleep just now——"

"Only to answer my questions," the Count repeated softly. "I trust I do not have to say that again. . . . They asked if you had any new arrival staying here, any fresh bookings, checked the register and searched the rooms. They left, of course, a typed description of the man they were looking for?"

"I have it here, comrade." The manager tapped his breast pocket.

"And orders to phone immediately if anyone resembling that description appeared here?"

The manager nodded.

"Forget all that," the Count ordered. "Things are moving quickly. We have every reason to believe that the man is either coming here or that his contact is already living here or will be coming here in the course of the next twenty-four hours." The Count exhaled a long, thin streamer of smoke and looked speculatively at the manager. "To our certain knowledge, this is the fourth time in three months that you have harboured enemies of the state in your hotel."

"Here? In this hotel?" The manager had paled visibly. "I swear to God, comrade——"

"God?" The Count creased his forehead. "What God? Whose God?"

The manager's face was no longer pale, it was ashen grey: good Communists never made fatal blunders of this kind. Reynolds could almost feel sorry for him, but he knew what the Count was after: a state of terror, instant compliance, blind, unreasoning obedience. And already he had it.

"A—a slip of the tongue, comrade." The manager was now stuttering in his panic, and his legs and hands were trembling. "I assure you, comrade——"

"No. No, let me assure _you_, comrade." The Count's voice was almost a purr. "One more slip-up and we must see to a little re-education, an elimination of these distressing bourgeois sentiments, of your readiness to give refuge to people who would stab our mother country in the back." The manager opened his mouth to protest, but his lips moved soundlessly, and the Count went on, his every word now a cold and deadly menace. "My instructions will be obeyed and obeyed implicitly, and you will be held directly responsible for any failure, however inavoidable that failure. That, my friend, or the Black Sea Canal."

"I'll do anything, anything!" The manager was begging now, in a state of piteous terror, and he had to clutch the desk to steady himself. "Anything, comrade. I swear it!"

"You will have your last chance." The Count nodded towards Reynolds. "One of my men. Sufficiently like the spy we are after, in build and appearance, to pass muster, and we have disguised him a little. A shadowed corner of your lounge, say, an incautious approach, and the contact is ours. The contact will sing to us, as all men sing to the AVO, and then the spy himself will be ours also."

Reynolds stared at the Count, only the years of professional training keeping his face expressionless, and wondered if there was any limit to this man's effrontery. But in that same insolent audacity, Reynolds knew, the best hope of safety lay.

"However, all that is no concern of yours," the Count

continued. "These are your instructions. A room for my friend here—let us call him, for the sake of convenience, say, Mr. Rakosi—the best you have, with a private bathroom, fire escape, short-wave radio receiver, telephone, alarm clock, duplicates of all master keys in the hotel, and absolute privacy. No switchboard operator eavesdropping on Mr. Rakosi's room telephone—as you are probably aware, my dear manager, we have devices that tell us instantly when a line is being monitored. No chambermaid, no floor waiters, no electricians, plumbers, or any other tradesmen to go near his room. All meals will be taken up by yourself. Unless Mr. Rakosi chooses to show himself, he doesn't exist. No one knows he exists; even you have never seen him, you haven't even seen me. All that is clearly understood?"

"Yes, of course, of course." The manager was grasping frantically at this straw of a last chance. "Everything will be exactly as you say, comrade, exactly. You have my word."

"You may yet live to mulct a few thousand more guests," the Count said contemptuously. "Warn that oaf of a porter not to talk, and show us this room immediately."

Five minutes later they were alone. Reynolds' room was not large, but comfortably furnished, complete with radio and telephone and a fire escape conveniently placed outside the adjoining bathroom. The Count glanced round approvingly.

"You'll be comfortable here for a few days, two or three, anyway. Not more, it's too dangerous. The manager won't talk, but you'll always find some frightened fool or mercenary informer who will."

"And then?"

"You'll have to become somebody else. A few hours' sleep, then I go to see a friend of mine who specialises in such things." The Count thoughtfully rubbed a blue and bristly chin. "A German, I think will be best for you, preferably from the Ruhr—Dortmund, Essen, or thereabouts. Much more convincing than your Austrian, I assure you. East-West contraband trade is becoming so big that the deals are now being handled by the principals themselves, and the Swiss and Austrian middlemen who used to handle these transactions are having a thin time of it. Very rare birds now, and hence an object of suspicion. You can be a supplier of, let us say, aluminium and copper goods. I'll get you a book on it."

"These, of course, are banned goods?"

"Naturally, my dear fellow. There are hundreds of banned goods, absolutely proscribed by the governments of the West, but a Niagara of the stuff flows across the Iron Curtain every year—£100,000,000 worth, £200,-000,000—no one knows."

"Good lord!" Reynolds was astonished but recovered quickly. "And I'll contribute my quota to the flow?"

"Easiest thing imaginable, my boy. Your stuff is sent to Hamburg or some other free port under false stencils and manifests: these are changed inside the factory and the stuff embarked on a Russian ship. Or, easier still, just send them across the border to France, break up, repack, and send to Czechoslovakia—by the 1921 'In transit' agreement goods can be shipped from countries A to C clear across B without benefit of any customs examinations. Beautifully simple, is it not?"

"It is," Reynolds admitted. "The governments concerned must be at their wit's end."

"The governments!" The Count laughed. "My dear Reynolds, when a nation's economy booms, governments become afflicted with an irremediable myopia. Some time ago an outraged German citizen, a Socialist leader by the name of, I think, Wehner—that's it, Herbert Wehner—sent to the Bonn Government a list of six hundred firms—six hundred, my dear fellow!—actively engaged in contraband trade."

"And the result?"

"Six hundred informants in six hundred factories sacked," the Count said succinctly. "Or so Wehner said, and no doubt he knew. Business is business, and profits are profits the world over. The Communists will welcome you with open arms, provided you have what they want. I'll see to that. You will become a representative, a partner, of some big metal firm in the Ruhr."

"An existing firm?"

"But of course. No chances—and what that firm doesn't know won't hurt them." The Count pulled a stainless-steel hip flask from his pocket. "You will join me?"

"Thank you, no." To Reynolds' certain knowledge the Count had drunk three quarters of a bottle of brandy that night already, but its effects, outwardly at least, were negligible: the man's tolerance to alcohol was phenomenal. In fact, Reynolds reflected, a phenomenal character in many ways, an enigma if ever he had known one. Though normally the Count was a coldly humorous man with a quick, sardonic wit, his face, in its rare moments of repose, held a withdrawn remoteness, almost a sadness that was in sharp, baffling contrast to his normal self. Or maybe his remote self *was* his normal self. . . .

"Just as well." The Count fetched a glass from the bathroom, poured a drink, and swallowed it in one gulp. "A purely medicinal precaution, you understand, and the less you have the more I have and thus the more adequately is my health safe-guarded. . . . As I say, first thing this morning I fix your identity. Then I'll go to the Andrassy Ut and find out where the Russian delegates to this conference are staying. The Three Crowns, probably—staffed entirely by our people—but it may be elsewhere." He brought out paper and pencil and scribbled on it for a minute. "Here are the names and the addresses of seven or eight hotels—it's bound to be one of these. Listed A-H, you observe. When I call you on the phone, I'll first of all address you by the wrong name. The first letter of that name will correspond to the hotel. You understand?"

Reynolds nodded.

"I'll also try to get you Jennings' room number. That will be more difficult. I'll reverse it on the phone—in the form of some financial quotations in connection with your export business." The Count put away his brandy flask and stood up. "And that, I'm afraid, is about all I can do for you, Mr. Reynolds. The rest is up to you. I can't possibly go near any hotel where Jennings is staying, because our own men will be there watching, and besides, I expect to be on duty this coming afternoon and evening till ten o'clock at least. Even if I could approach him, it would be useless. Jennings would know me for a foreigner right away and be instantly suspicious, and, apart from that, you are the only person who has seen his wife and can bring all the facts and necessary arguments to bear."

"You've already done more than enough," Reynolds assured him. "I'm alive, aren't I? And I won't leave this room till I hear from you?"

"Not a step. Well, a little sleep, then on with the

uniform and my daily stint of terrorising all and sundry."
The Count smiled wryly. "You cannot imagine, Mr. Reynolds, what it feels like to be universally beloved. *Au revoir.*"

Reynolds wasted no time after the Count had gone. He felt desperately tired. He locked his room door, securing the key so that it could not be pushed clear from the outside, placed a chair back under the handle as additional security, locked his room and bathroom windows, placed an assortment of glasses and other breakable articles on the window sills—a most efficient burglar alarm, he had found from past experience—slipped his automatic under his pillow, undressed, and climbed thankfully into bed.

For a minute or two only, his thoughts wandered over the past few hours. He thought of the patient and gentle Jansci, a Jansci whose appearance and philosophies were at such wild variance with the almost incredible violence of his past; of the equally enigmatic Count; of Jansci's daughter, so far only a pair of blue eyes and golden hair without any personality to go with them; of Sandor, as gentle in his own way as his master, and of Imre with the nervous, shifting eyes.

He tried, too, to think of tomorrow—today, it was now—of his chances of meeting the old professor, of the best method of handling the interview, but he was far too tired really, his thoughts were no more than a kaleidoscopic pattern without either form or coherence, and even that pattern blurred and faded swiftly into nothingness as he sank into the sleep of exhaustion.

The harsh jangling of the alarm clock roused him only four hours later. He woke with that dry, stale feeling of one who has only half slept, but nonetheless he woke instantly, cutting off the alarm before it had rung for more than a couple of seconds. He rang down for coffee, put on his dressing gown, lit a cigarette, collected the coffeepot at the door, locked it again, and clamped the radio's headphones to his ears.

The password announcing Brian's safe arrival in Sweden was to consist of a planned mistake on the announcer's part: it had been agreed that he would say, ". . . tonight—I beg your pardon, that should read 'tomorrow' night . . ." But the BBC's shortwave European news transmission that morning was innocent of any such deliberate slip, and Reynolds took off the headphones without any feeling of disappointment. He hadn't really expected it as early as this, but even so remote a chance was not to be neglected. He finished the rest of the coffee and was asleep again within minutes.

When he woke again he did so naturally, feeling completely rested and refreshed. It was just after one o'clock. He washed, shaved, rang down for lunch, dressed, and then pulled apart his window curtains. It was so cold outside that his windows were still heavily frosted, and he had to open them to see what the weather was like. The wind was light, but it struck through his thin shirt like a knife, and it had all the makings, he thought grimly, of an ideal night for a secret agent at large—provided, that was, that the secret agent didn't freeze to death. The snowflakes, big, lazy, feathery snowflakes, were swirling down gently out of a dark and leaden sky. Reynolds shivered and hastily closed the window just as the knock came on the door.

He unlocked the door and the manager carried in a tray with Reynolds' lunch under covers. If the manager resented what he must have regarded as menial work, he showed no signs of it: on the contrary, he was obsequiousness itself, and the presence on the tray of a bottle of Imperial Aszu, a mellow and golden tokay with, Reynolds rightly judged, the scarcity value of gold itself, was proof enough of the manager's almost fanatical desire to please the AVO in every conceivable way. Reynolds refrained from thanking him—the AVO, he fancied, were not given to such little courtesies—and waved a hand in dismissal. But the manager dug into his pocket and brought out an envelope, blank on both sides. "I was told to deliver this to you, Mr. Rakosi."

"To me?" Reynolds' voice was sharp, but not with anxiety. Only the Count and his friends knew his new assumed name. "When did it arrive?"

"Only five minutes ago."

"Five minutes ago!" Reynolds stared coldly at the manager, and his voice dropped a theatrical octave: melodramatic tones and gestures that would have led only to ridicule back home were, he was beginning to discover, all too readily accepted as genuine in this terror-ridden country. "Then why wasn't it brought to me five minutes ago?"

"I'm sorry, comrade." The quaver was back in the voice once more. "Your—your lunch was almost ready, and I thought——"

"You're not required to think. Next time a message arrives for me deliver it immediately. Who brought this?"

"A girl—a young woman."

"Describe her."

"It is difficult. I am not good at this." He hesitated. "You see, she wore a belted raincoat with a big hood attached. She wasn't tall, short almost, but well built. Her boots——"

"Her face, idiot! Her hair."

"The hood covered her hair. She had blue eyes, very blue eyes." The manager seized eagerly on this point, but then his voice trailed away. "I'm afraid, comrade——" Reynolds cut him off and dismissed him. He had heard enough and the description tallied sufficiently well with Jansci's daughter. His first reaction, surprising even to himself, was a faint stirring of anger that she should be risked in this fashion, but on the heels of the thought came the awareness of its injustice: it would have been highly dangerous for Jansci himself, with a face that must have been known to hundreds, to move abroad in the streets, and Sandor and Imre, conspicuous figures as they must have been in the October rising, would be remembered by many: but a young girl would rouse neither suspicion nor comment, and even if enquiries were made later, the manager's description would have fitted a thousand others.

He slit open the envelope. The message was brief, printed in block capitals: "Do not come to the house tonight. Meet me in the White Angel Café between eight and nine." It was signed "J." Julia, of course, not Jansci— if Jansci wouldn't take the chance of walking through the streets, he certainly wouldn't go near a crowded café. The reason for the change in plan—he had been supposed to report to Jansci's house after his meeting with Jennings— he couldn't guess. Police or informer surveillance, probably, but there could be half a dozen other reasons. Typically, Reynolds wasted no time in worry about it: guessing would get nowhere, and he would find out from the girl in due time. He burnt letter and envelope in the bathroom washbasin, flushed away the ashes, and sat down to an excellent dinner.

The hours came and went. Two o'clock, three o'clock, four o'clock, and still no word from the Count. Either he was having difficulty in getting the information or, more likely, he could find no opportunity of passing it on. Reynolds, interrupting his pacing of the room only for an occasional glance through the window at the snow sifting down soundlessly, more heavily than ever, on the houses and streets of the darkening city, was beginning to grow anxious: if he was to find out where the professor was staying, interview him, persuade him to make the break for the Austrian frontier, and himself be at the White Angel Café—he had found its address in the directory— by nine o'clock, time was growing very short indeed.

Five o'clock came and passed. Half-past. Then, at twenty minutes to six the telephone bell jangled shrilly in the silence of the room. Reynolds reached the phone in two strides and picked up the receiver.

"Mr. Buhl? Mr. Johann Buhl?" The Count's voice was low and hurried, but it was unmistakably the Count's voice.

"Buhl speaking."

"Good. Excellent news for you, Mr. Buhl. I've been to the Ministry this afternoon, and they're very interested in your firm's offer, especially in the rolled aluminium. They'd like to discuss it with you right away—provided you're willing to accept their top price—ninety-five."

"I think my firm would find that acceptable."

"Then they will do business. We can talk over dinner. Six-thirty too early for you?"

"Not at all. I'll be there. Third floor, isn't it?"

"Second. Until six-thirty, then. Good-bye." The receiver clicked, and Reynolds replaced his own phone. The Count had sounded pushed for time and in danger of being overheard, but he had got all the information through. B for Buhl—that was indeed the Three Crowns Hotel, the one exclusively staffed by the AVO and its creatures. A pity, it made everything trebly dangerous, but at least he would know where he stood there—every man's hand would be against him. Room fifty-nine second floor, and the professor dined at six-thirty, when his room would be presumably empty. Reynolds looked at his watch and wasted no more time. He belted on his trench coat, pulled his trilby well down, screwed the special silencer on to his Belgian automatic, and stuck the gun in his right-hand pocket, a rubberised torch in the other, and two spare clips for the gun in an inside jacket pocket. Then he rang the switchboard, told the manager that he was on no account to be disturbed by visitors, telephone calls, messages, or meals during the next four hours, secured the key in the lock, left the light burning to mislead any person inquisitive enough to peep through the keyhole, unlocked the bathroom window and left by the fire escape.

The night was bitterly cold, the thick, soft snow more than ankle-deep, and before he had covered two hundred yards Reynolds' coat and hat were as white, almost, as the ground beneath his feet. But he was grateful for both the cold and the snow: the cold would discourage even the most conscientious of the police and Secret Police from prowling the streets with their ususal vigilance, and the snow—apart from shrouding him in the protective anonymity of its white cocoon—also muffled every noise, reducing even the sound of his footfalls to the merest whisper. A night for a hunter, Reynolds thought grimly.

He arrived at the Three Crowns in less than ten minutes—even in the snow-filled gloom he had found his way there as unerringly as if he had lived in Budapest all his days—and made his first circumspect inspection of the place, keeping to the far side of the street.

It was a big hotel, occupying a city block to itself. The entrance, big double glass doors open to the night with a revolving door behind the vestibule, was bathed in a harsh fluorescent light. Two uniformed doormen, occasionally stamping their feet and beating their arms against the cold, guarded the entrance: both men, Reynolds could see, were armed with revolvers in buttoned-down holsters and carried a baton or night stick apiece. They were no more doormen than he was himself, Reynolds guessed, but almost certainly regular members of the AVO. One thing was certain: no matter how he was going to effect an entry, it wasn't going to be through that front door. All this Reynolds saw out of the corner of his eyes as he hurried along the other side of the street, head bent against the snow, to all appearances a man homeward bound with all speed to the comforts of his own fireside. As soon as he was out of their sight he doubled in his tracks and made a quick examination of the sides of the Three Crowns. There was no more hope here than there had been at the front: all the ground-floor windows were heavily barred, and the windows of the story above might as well have been on the moon as far as accessibility was concerned. That left only the back.

The trade and staff entrance to the hotel lay through a deep archway in the middle of the wall, wide enough and high enough to take a big delivery truck. Through the archway Reynolds caught a glimpse of the snow-covered courtyard beyond—the hotel was built in the form of a hollow square—an entrance door at the far side, opposite the main doors, and one or two parked cars. Above the entrance door to the main block, a hooded electric lantern burned brightly and light shone from several of the ground- and first-floor windows. The total illumination was not much, but enough to let him see the angular shapes of three fire escapes zigzagging upwards before being lost in the snow and the darkness.

Reynolds walked to the corner, glanced quickly round him, crossed the street at a fast walk, and made his way back towards the entrance, hugging the hotel wall as closely as he could. Approaching the opening of the archway, he slowed down, stopped, pulled the brim of his hat further over his eyes, and peered cautiously round the corner.

For the first moment he could see nothing, for his eyes, so long accustomed and adjusted to the darkness, were momentarily dazzled, blinded by the beam from a powerful torch, and in that sickening instant he was certain he had been discovered. His hand was just coming out of his pocket, the butt of the automatic cradled in his hand, when the beam left him and went round the inside of the courtyard.

The pupils of his eyes slowly widening again, Reynolds could see now what had happened. A man, a soldier armed with a shoulder-slung carbine, was making his rounds of the perimeter of the courtyard, and the carelessly swinging torchlight had illuminated Reynolds' face for an instant, but the guard, his eyes obviously not following the beam, had missed it.

Reynolds turned into the archway, took three silent paces foward, and stopped again. The guard was going away from him now, approaching the main block, and

Reynolds could clearly see what he was doing. He was making a round of the fire escapes, shining his light on the bottom, snow-covered flight of steps of each. Reynolds wondered ironically whether he was guarding against the possibility of outsiders going in—or insiders going out. Probably the latter—from what the Count had told him, he knew that quite a few of the guests at this forthcoming conference would willingly have passed it up in exchange for an exit visa to the West. A rather stupid precaution, Reynolds thought, especially when it was made so obvious: any reasonably fit person, forewarned by the probing torch, could go up or down the first flight of a fire escape without his feet making any tell-tale tracks on the steps.

Now, Reynolds decided, now's my chance. The guard, passing under the electric storm lantern at the far entrance, was at his maximum distance, and there was no point in waiting until he had made another circuit. Soundlessly, a shadowy ghost in the white gloom of the night, Reynolds flitted across the cobbled stones of the archway, barely checked an exclamation, halted abruptly in midstep, and shrank into the wall beside him—legs, body, arms, and widespread, stiff-fingered hands pressing hard against the cold, clammy stone of the wall behind, the brim of his hat crushed flat between the side of his head and the archway. His heart was thumping slowly, painfully in his chest.

You fool, Reynolds, he told himself savagely, you bloody kindergarten idiot. You almost fell for it; but for the grace of God and the red arc of that carelessly flung cigarette now sizzling to extinction in the snow not two feet from where you stood, rock-still, not even daring to breathe, you would have fallen for it. He should have known; he should have done the intelligence of the AVO the elementary courtesy of guessing that they wouldn't make things so childishly simple for anyone hoping to break in or out.

The sentry box just inside the courtyard stood only a few inches back from the archway, and the sentry himself, half in, half out of the box, his shoulders leaning against the corners both of the box and the archway, was less than thirty inches from where Reynolds stood. Reynolds could hear him breathing, slowly, distinctly, and the occasional shuffling of his feet on the wooden floor of the box was almost thunderous in his ears.

He had barely seconds left, Reynolds knew, half a dozen at the most. The sentry had only to stir, to turn his head a couple of lazy inches to the left, and he was lost. Even if he didn't so stir, his companion, now only yards away, would be bound to catch him in the sweep of his torch as he came by the entrance. Three courses, Reynolds' racing mind calculated, three courses only lay open to him. He could turn and run, and stood a good chance of escape in the snow and the darkness, but the guard would be then so strengthened that his last chance of seeing old Jennings would have gone forever. He could kill both men—he never questioned his own ability to do this and would have destroyed them ruthlessly if the necessity were there—but the problem of the disposal of the bodies would be insuperable, and if the hue and cry over their discovery were raised while he was still inside the Three Crowns, he knew he would never come out alive. There was only the third way that offered any chance of success, and there was time for neither further thought nor delay.

The automatic was out now, the butt firmly clasped in both hands, the back of his right wrist pressed hard against the archway wall for maximum steadiness. The bulk of the silencer made sighting difficult, the swirling snow made it doubly so, but the chance had to be taken. The soldier with the torch was perhaps ten feet away, the guard in the box clearing his throat to make some remark to his companion when Reynolds slowly squeezed the trigger.

The soft "plop" of the silencer muffling the escaping gases was lost in the sudden crash as the storm lantern above the entrance door shattered into a hundred pieces, the broken fragments tinkling against the wall behind before falling into the cushioning silence of the snow. To the ears of the man at the sentry box the dull report of the silencer must have come a fraction of a second before the smashing of the glass, but the human ear is incapable of making such fine distinctions in time, and only the vastly louder sound could have registered. Already he was pounding across the courtyard towards the far entrance, the man with the torch close by his side.

Reynolds wasn't far behind them. He passed the sentry box, turned sharply right, ran lightly along the track the circling sentry had beaten in the virgin snow, passed the first fire escape, turned, launched himself sideways and upwards, and caught the stanchion supporting the handrail on the first platform at the full extent of his arms. For one bad moment he felt his fingers slipping on the cold, smooth steel, tightened his grip desperately, held, then overhanded himself upwards till he caught the rail. A moment later he was standing securely on the first platform, and neither the snow round the three outer edges of the platform nor that on any of the steps leading up to it showed any signs of having been disturbed.

Five seconds later, taking two steps at a time, with his feet placed sideways in the middle of each step so as to leave no visible trace from below, he had reached the second platform, on a level now with the first floor. Here he crouched, kneeling so as to reduce his bulk to the smallest dimensions possible, for the two soldiers were returning to the archway in no great hurry, talking to one another. They were convinced, Reynolds could hear, that the hot glass had shattered because of the extreme cold, and were not disposed to worry unduly about it. Reynolds felt no surprise: the spent bullet reflected by these granite-hard walls would leave scarcely a mark, and it might lie undisturbed, undiscovered for days under the thick carpet of snow. In their position he would probably have come to the same conclusion himself. For form's sake, the two men walked round the parked cars and shone their torches over the lower flights of the fire escapes, and by the time their cursory inspection was over Reynolds was on the platform level with the second floor, standing outside a set of double glass doors.

He tried them, cautiously, firmly. They were locked. He had expected nothing else. Slowly, with the utmost care—for his hands were now almost numbed with the cold and the slightest fumble could be his undoing—he had brought out his knife, eased the blade open without a click, slid it into the crack between the doors, and pressed upwards. Seconds later he was inside locking the glass doors behind him.

The room was pitch-dark, but his outstretched, enquiring hands soon told him where he was. The hard smoothness all around, the glazed feel of wall tiles, marble washbasins, and chromed rails could belong only to a bathroom. He pulled the door curtains carelessly together —as far as the men below were concerned, there was no reason why a light should not appear in that room more than in any other room—fumbled his way across to the door and switched on the light.

It was a large room with an old-fashioned bath, three of the walls tiled and the other given up to a couple of big linen cupboards, but Reynolds wasted no time in examining it. He crossed to the washbasin, ran the water till the basin was almost full of hot water, and plunged his hands in—a drastic method of restoring circulation to numbed and frozen hands and an exquisitely painful one, but what it lacked in finesse it more than compensated for in speed, and Reynolds was interested in that alone. He dried his tingling fingers, took his automatic out, switched off the light, cautiously opened the door, and eased an eye round the corner of the jamb.

He was standing, he found, at the end of a long corridor, luxuriously carpeted as he would have expected of any hotel run by the AVO. Both sides of the corridor were lined with doors, the one opposite him bearing the number 56 and the next but one 57: luck was beginning to break his way and chance had brought him directly into the wing where Jennings and probably a handful of other top scientists were quartered. But as his glance reached the end of the corridor, his mouth tightened and he drew back swiftly, noiselessly inside the door, shutting it softly behind him. Self-congratulations were a trifle premature, he thought grimly. There had been no mistaking the identity of that uniformed figure standing at the far end of the corridor, hands clasped behind his back and staring out through a frost-rimed window: there was no mistaking an AVO guard anywhere.

Reynolds sat on the edge of the bath, lit a cigarette, and tried to figure out his next move. The need for haste was urgent, but not desperate enough for rashness: at this stage, rashness could ruin everything.

The guard, obviously, was there to stay—he had that curiously settled look about him. Equally obviously he, Reynolds, could not hope to break his way into number 59 as long as the guard remained there. Problem, remove the guard. No good trying to rush him or even stalk him down the brightly lit length of the 120-foot corridor: there were other ways of committing suicide but few more foolish. The guard would have to come to him, and he would have to come unsuspectingly. Suddenly Reynolds grinned, crushed out his cigarette, and rose quickly to his feet. The Count, he thought, would have appreciated this.

He stripped off coat, hat, jacket, tie, and shirt, tossing them into the bath, ran hot water into the basin, took a bar of soap, and lathered his face vigorously till it was covered in a deep white film up to his eyes: for all he knew, his description had been issued to every policeman and AVO man in Budapest. Then he dried his hands thoroughly, took the gun in his left hand, draped a towel over it and opened the door. His voice, when he called, was low-pitched enough but it carried down the length of the corridor with remarkable clarity.

The guard whirled round at once, his hand automatically reaching down for his gun, but he checked the movement as he saw the harmless appearance of the singlet-clad, gesticulating figure at the other end of the corridor. He opened his mouth to speak, but Reynolds urgently gestured him to silence with the universal dumb show of a forefinger raised to pursed lips. For a second the guard hesitated, saw Reynolds beckoning him frantically, then came running down the corridor, his rubber soles silent on the deep pile of the carpet. He had his gun in his hand as he drew up alongside Reynolds.

"There's a man on the fire escape outside," Reynolds whispered. His nervous fumbling with the towel concealed the transfer of the gun, barrel foremost, to his right hand. "He's trying to force the doors open."

"You are sure of this?" The man's voice was no more than a hoarse, guttural murmur. "You saw him?"

"I saw him." Reynolds' whisper was shaking with nervous excitement. "He can't see in, though. The curtains are drawn."

The guard's dark eyes narrowed and the thick lips drew back in a smile of almost wolfish anticipation. Heaven only knew what wild dreams of glory and promotion were whirling through his mind. Whatever his thoughts, none was of suspicion or caution. Roughly he pushed Reynolds to one side and pushed open the bathroom door, and Reynolds, his right hand coming clear of the towel, followed on his heels.

He caught the guard as he crumpled and lowered him gently to the floor. To open up the linen cupboard, rip up a couple of sheets, bind and gag the unconscious guard, lift him into the cupboard, and lock the door on him took Reynolds' trained hands only two minutes.

Two minutes later, hat in hand and overcoat over his arm, very much in the manner of a hotel guest returning to his room, Reynolds was outside the door of number 59. He had half a dozen skeleton keys, together with four masters the manager of his own hotel had given him—and not one of them fitted.

Reynolds stood quite still. This was the last thing he had expected—he would have guaranteed the entry to any hotel door with these keys. And he couldn't risk forcing the door—breaking it open was out of the question, and a lock tripped by force can't be closed again. If a guard accompanied the professor back to his room, as might well happen, and found unlocked a door he had left locked, suspicion and immediate search would follow.

Reynolds moved on to the next door. On both sides of this corridor only every other door bore a number, and it was a safe assumption that the numberless doors were the corridor entrances to the private bathrooms adjoining each room—the Russians accorded to their top scientists facilities and accommodation commonly reserved in other and less realistic countries for film stars, aristocracy, and the leading lights of society.

Inevitably this door too was locked. So long a corridor in so busy a hotel couldn't remain empty indefinitely, and Reynolds was sliding the keys in and out of the lock with the speed and precision of a sleight-of-hand artist. Luck was against him again. He pulled out his torch, dropped to his knees, and peered into the crack between the door and the jamb; this time luck was with him. Most continental doors fit over a jamb, leaving the lock bolt inaccessible, but this one fitted into the jamb. Reynolds quickly took from his wallet a three-by-two oblong of fairly stiff celluloid—in some countries the discovery of such an article on a known thief would be sufficient to bring him before a judge on a charge of being in possession of a burglarious implement—and slipped it between door and jamb. He caught the door handle, pulling towards himself and in the direction of the hinges, worked the celluloid in behind the bolt, eased the door, and jerked it back again. The bolt slid back with a loud click, and a moment later Reynolds was inside.

The bathroom, for such it was, resembled the one he

had just left in every detail, except for the positioning of the doors. The double cupboard was to his right as he entered, between the two doors. He opened the cupboard, saw that one side was given over to shelves and the other, with a full-length mirror to its door, empty, then closed them again. A convenient bolt hole, but one that he hoped he would have no occasion to use.

He crossed to the bedroom connecting door and peered through the keyhole. The room beyond was in darkness. The door yielded to his touch on the handle and he stepped inside, the pencil beam of his torch swiftly circling the room. Empty. He crossed to the window, saw that no chink of light could possibly escape through the shutters and heavy curtains, crossed over to the door, switched on the light, and hung his hat over the handle to block off the keyhole.

Reynolds was a trained searcher. It took only a minute's meticulous examination of walls, pictures, and ceilings to convince him that there was no spy hole into the room, and less than twenty seconds thereafter to find the inevitable microphone, concealed behind the ventilation grille above the window. He transferred his attention to the bathroom, and the examination there took only seconds. The bath was built in, so there could be nothing there. There was nothing behind the washbasin or the water closet, and behind the shower curtains were only the brass handgrip and the old-fashioned spray nozzle fixed to the ceiling.

He was just pulling back the curtains when he heard footsteps approaching in the corridor outside—only feet away, the deep carpet had muffled their approach. He ran through the connecting door into the bedroom, switched off the light—there were two people coming, he could hear them talking and could only hope that their voices drowned the click of the switch—picked up his hat, moved swiftly back into the bathroom, had the door three parts shut and was peering through the crack between jamb and door when the key turned in the lock and Professor Jennings walked into the room. And hard on his heels a tall, bulky man in a brown suit followed him through the doorway. Whether he was some AVO-appointed guard or just a colleague of Jennings, it was impossible to say. But one thing was clear enough: he

carried with him a bottle and two glasses and he intended
to stay.

5

REYNOLDS' gun was in his hand, almost without
his being aware of it. If Jennings' companion chose to
make an inspection of the bathroom, there was no time for
him, Reynolds, to move into the shelter of the big cupboard. And if he was discovered, then Reynolds would be
left without any option; and with the guard—and for
safety's sake he had to assume that it was a guard—
unconscious or dead, his boats would have been burnt
behind him. There would never then be another chance of
contacting Jennings; the old professor would have to come
with him that night whether he liked it or not, and Reynolds rated as almost nonexistent his chances of escaping
unobserved from the Three Crowns with an unwilling
prisoner at the point of a gun and getting any distance at
all through the hostile dark of Budapest.

But the man with Jennings made no move to enter the
bathroom, and it soon became apparent that he was no
guard. Jennings appeared to be on friendly enough terms
with the man, called him Jozef, and discussed with him in
English some highly technical subjects that Reynolds
couldn't even begin to understand. A scientific colleague,
beyond doubt. For a moment Reynolds was conscious of
astonishment that the Russians should allow two scientists, one a foreigner, to discuss so freely: then he remembered the microphone, and he wasn't astonished any
more. It was the man in the brown suit who was doing
most of the talking, and this was at first surprising, for
Harold Jennings had the reputation of being talkative to
the point of garrulousness, forthright to the point of indiscretion. But Reynolds, peering through the jamb of the
door, could see that Jennings was a vastly changed Jennings from the person whose figure and face he had
memorised from a hundred photographs. Two years in
exile had added more than ten in age to his appearance.
He seemed smaller, somehow, curiously shrunken, and in
place of a once splendid mane of white hair were now
only a few straggling locks across a balding head: his face
was unhealthily pale, and only his eyes, dark, sunken

pools in a deeply lined and etched face, had lost none of their fire and authority. Reynolds smiled to himself in the darkness. Whatever the Russians had done to the old man, they hadn't broken his spirit: that would have been altogether too much to expect.

Reynolds glanced down at the face of his luminous watch, and his smile vanished. Time was running out. He must see Jennings, see him alone, and soon. Half a dozen different ideas occurred to him within the space of a minute, but he dismissed them all as unpractical or too dangerous. He must take no chances. For all the apparent friendliness of the man in the brown suit, he was a Russian and must be treated as an enemy.

Finally he came up with an idea that carried with it at least a fair chance. It was far from foolproof, it could fail as easily as it could succeed, but the chance had to be taken. He crossed the bathroom on noiseless feet, picked up a piece of soap, made his silent way back to the big cupboard, opened the door with the long mirror inside, and started to write on the glass.

It was no good. The dry soap slid smoothly over the smooth surface and made scarcely a mark. Reynolds swore softly, as softly recrossed to the washbasin, turned the tap with infinite care till a little trickle of water came out, then wet the soap thoroughly. This time the writing on the glass was all he could have wished for, and he wrote in clear block letters:

I AM FROM ENGLAND—GET RID OF YOUR FRIEND AT ONCE. Then gently, careful to guard against even the smallest metallic sound or creak of hinges, he eased open the bathroom corridor door and peered out. The corridor was deserted. Two long paces took him outside Jennings' bedroom door, a very soft, quick tap-tap on the wood and he was back inside the bathroom as noiselessly as he had gone, picking his torch up from the floor.

The man in the brown suit was already on his feet, walking towards the door, when Reynolds stuck his head through the partly open bathroom door, one finger in urgent warning at his lips, another pressing down on the morse button of his torch, the beam striking Jennings' eyes—a fraction of a second only, but long enough. Jennings glanced up, startled, saw the face at the door, and not even Reynolds' warning forefinger could stifle the exclamation that leapt to his lips. The man in the brown suit, with the door open now and glancing uncomprehendingly along the length of the corridor, swung round.

"Something is wrong, Professor?"

Jennings nodded. "This damned head of mine—you know how it troubles me . . . No one there?"

"No one—no one at all. I could have sworn—— You do not look well, Professor Jennings."

"No. Excuse me." Jennings smiled wanly and rose to his feet. "A little water, I think, and some of my migraine tablets."

Reynolds was standing inside the big cupboard, the door just ajar. As soon as he saw Jennings come into the bathroom, he pushed the door wide open. Jennings couldn't fail to see the mirror with its message: he nodded almost imperceptibly, glanced warningly at Reynolds, and continued towards the washbasin without breaking his stride. For an old man unaccustomed to this sort of thing, it was a remarkable performance.

Reynolds interpreted the warning glance correctly, and the cupboard door had hardly closed before the professor's companion was in the room.

"Perhaps I should get the hotel doctor," he said worriedly. "He would be only too willing."

"No, no." Jennings swallowed a tablet and washed it down with a gulp of water. "I know these damned migraines of mine better than any doctor. Three of these tablets, three hours lying down in absolute darkness. I'm really terribly sorry, Jozef, our discussion was just beginning to become really interesting, but if you would excuse me——"

"But of course, of course." The other was cordiality and understanding itself. "Whatever else happens, we must have you fit and well for the opening speech on Monday." A few platitudes of sympathy, a word of farewell, and the man in the brown suit was gone.

The bedroom door clicked shut and the soft sound of his footfalls faded in the distance. Jennings, his face a nice mixture of indignation, apprehension, and expectation, made to speak, but Reynolds held up his hand for silence, went to the bedroom door, locked it, withdrew the key, tried it in the bathroom corridor door, found to his relief that it fitted, locked it, and closed the communicating door leading to the bedroom. He produced his cigarette case and offered it to the professor, only to have it waved aside.

"Who are you? What are you doing in my room?" The professor's voice was low, but the asperity in it, an asperity just touched with fear, was unmistakable.

"My name is Michael Reynolds." Reynolds puffed a cigarette alight: he felt he needed it. "I left London only forty-eight hours ago, and I would like to talk to you, sir."

"Then, dammit, why can't we talk in the comfort of my bedroom?" Jennings swung round, then was brought up abruptly as Reynolds caught him by the shoulder.

"Not in the bedroom, sir." Reynolds shook his head gently. "There's a concealed microphone in the ventilation grille above your window."

"There's a what——— How did *you* know, young man?" The professor walked slowly back towards Reynolds.

"I had a look around before you came," Reynolds said apologetically. "I arrived only a minute before you."

"And you found a microphone in that time?" Jennings was incredulous and not even politely so.

"I found it right away. It's my job to know where to look for such things."

"Of course, of course! What else could you be? An espionage agent, counterespionage—damned things mean the same to me. Anyway, the British Secret Service."

"A popular if erroneous———"

"Bah! A rose by any other name." Whatever of fear there was in the little man, Reynolds thought drily, it certainly wasn't for himself: the fire of which he had heard so much burned as brightly as ever. "What do you want, sir? What do you want?"

"You," Reynolds said quietly. "Rather, the British Government wants you. I am asked by the government to extend to you a most cordial invitation———"

"Uncommonly civil of the British Government, I must say. Ah, I expected this, I've been expecting it for a long time now." If Jennings had been a dragon, Reynolds mused, everything within ten feet of him would have been incinerated. "My compliments to the British Government, Mr. Reynolds, and tell them from me to go to hell. Maybe when they get there, they'll find someone who'll help them build their infernal machines, but it isn't going to be me."

"The country needs you, sir, and needs you desperately."

"The last appeal and the most pathetic of all." The old man was openly contemptuous now. "The shibboleths of outworn nationalism, the catchpenny phrase words of the empty-headed flag wavers of your bogus patriotism are only for the children of this world, Mr. Reynolds, the morons, the self-seekers, and those who live entirely for war. I care only to work for the peace of the world."

"Very good, sir." The people at home, Reynolds thought wryly, had badly underestimated either Jennings' credulity or the subtlety of Russian indoctrination: even so, his words had seemed a far-off echo of something Jansci had said. He looked at Jennings. "The decision, of course, must rest entirely with you."

"What!" Jennings was astonished and could not conceal his astonishment. "You accept it? You accept it as easily as that—and you have come so far?"

Reynolds shrugged. "I am only a messenger, Dr. Jennings."

"A messenger? And what if I had agreed to your ridiculous suggestion?"

"Then, of course, I would have accompanied you back to Britain."

"You would have—— Mr. Reynolds, do you realise what you are saying? Do you realise what—— You—you would have taken me out of Budapest, through Hungary and across the frontier . . ." Jennings' voice slowly trailed away into nothingness, and when he looked up at Reynolds again, the fear was back in his eyes.

"You are no ordinary messenger, Mr. Reynolds," he whispered. "People like you are never messengers." All of a sudden certainty struck home at the old man, and a thin white line touched the edges of his mouth. "You were never told to invite me back to Britain—you were told to bring me back. There were to be no 'ifs' or 'maybes,' were there, Mr. Reynolds?"

"Isn't that rather silly, sir?" Reynolds said quietly. "Even if I were in position to use compulsion, and I'm not, I wouldn't be such a fool as to use it. Supposing you were to be dragged back to Britain bound hand and foot, there's still no way of keeping you there or making you work against your own will. Let's not confuse flag wavers with the secret police of a satellite state."

"I don't for a moment think you'd use direct force to get me home." The fear was still in the old man's eyes, fear and sickness of heart. "Mr. Reynolds, is—is my wife still alive?"

"I saw her two hours before I left London Airport." There was a quiet sincerity in every word that Reynolds spoke, and he had never seen Mrs. Jennings in his life. "She was holding her own, I think."

"Would you say—would you say she is still critically ill?"

Reynolds shrugged. "That is for the doctors to say."

"For God's sake, man, don't try to torture me! What *do* the doctors say?"

"Suspended animation. Hardly a medical term, Dr. Jennings, but that's what Mr. Bathurst—he was her surgeon—calls it. She's conscious all the time, and in little pain, but very weak: to be brutally frank, she could go at any moment. Mr. Bathurst says she's just lost the will to live."

"My God, my God!" Jennings turned away and stared unseeingly through the frosted window. After a moment he swung round, his face contorted, his dark eyes blurred with tears. "I can't believe it, Mr. Reynolds, I just *can't*. It's not possible. My Catherine was always a fighter. She was always——"

"You don't *want* to believe it," Reynolds interrupted. His voice was cold to the point of cruelty. "Doesn't matter what the self-deception is, does it, as long as it satisfies your conscience, this precious conscience that would let you sell your own people down the river in exchange for all this claptrap about coexistence. You know damned well your wife has nothing to live for—not with her husband and son lost for ever to her beyond the Iron Curtain."

"How dare you talk——"

"You make me sick!" Reynolds felt a momentary flash of distaste for what he was doing to this defenceless old man, but crushed it down. "You stand here making noble speeches and standing upon all these wonderful principles of yours, and all the time your wife is in a London hospital, dying: she's dying, Dr. Jennings, and you are killing her as surely as if you were standing by her side and throttling——"

"Stop! Stop! For God's sake stop!" Jennings had his

hands to his ears and was shaking his head like a man in agony. He drew back his hands across his forehead. "You're right, Reynolds, heaven only knows you're right. I'd go to her tomorrow, but there's more to it than that." He shook his head in despair. "How can you ask any man to choose between the lives of his wife, who may be already beyond hope, and his only son. My situation is impossible! I have a son——"

"We know all about your son, Dr. Jennings. We are not inhuman altogether." Reynolds' voice had dropped to a gentle, persuasive murmur. "Yesterday Brian was in Poznań. This afternoon he will be in Stettin, and tomorrow morning he will be in Sweden. I have only to receive radio confirmation from London, and then we can be on our way. Certainly inside twenty-four hours."

"I don't believe it, I don't believe it." Hope and disbelief struggled pitifully for supremacy in the old, lined face. "How can you say——"

"I can't prove a thing, I don't have to prove a thing," Reynolds said wearily. "With all respect, sir, what the hell's happened to this mighty intellect? Surely you know that all the government wants of you is that you should work for them again, and you also know *they* know what you're like: they know damned well if you returned home and found your son still a prisoner in Russia that you'd never work for them as long as you lived. And that's the last thing in the world they'd ever want."

Conviction had come slowly to Jennings, but now that it had come, it had come for keeps. Reynolds, seeing the new life come into the professor's face, the determination gradually replacing the worry and the sorrow and the fear, could have laughed aloud from sheer relief: even on himself the strain had been greater than he had realised. Another five minutes, a score of questions tumbling out one after the other, and the professor, afire now with the hope of seeing his wife and son in the course of the next few days, was all for leaving that very night, at that very instant, and had to be restrained. Plans had to be made, Reynolds explained gently, and much more important, they had first to get news of Brian's escape, and this had brought Jennings to earth immediately. He agreed to await further instructions, repeated aloud several times the address of Jansci's house until he had completely memorised it, but agreed never to use it except in extreme emergency—the police might have already moved in as far as Reynolds knew—and promised, in the meantime, to carry on working and behaving exactly as he had been doing.

So completely had his attitude towards Reynolds changed that he tried to persuade him to share a drink, but Reynolds declined. It was only half-past seven, he had plenty of time before his appointment in the White Angel, but he had already pushed his luck to the limit: at any moment now the imprisoned guard might recover consciousness and start to kick the door down, or a supervisor might make his rounds and find him missing. He left immediately by way of the professor's bedroom window and by means of a couple of sheets which let him climb down far enough to catch the barred grilles of a window on the ground story. Even before Jennings had had time to reel in the sheets and close his windows, Reynolds had dropped silently to the ground and vanished wraithlike into the darkness and the snow.

The White Angel Café lay just back from the east bank of the Danube on the Pest side, opposite St. Margit Island, and Reynolds passed through its frosted swing doors just as a nearby church bell, muffled and faint through the curtaining snow, struck the hour of eight o'clock.

The contrast between the world outside these swing doors and the one inside was as abrupt as it was complete. One step across the threshold and the snow, the cold, the chill dark silent loneliness of the lifeless streets of Budapest were magically transformed into warmth and brightness and the gaiety of laughing, babbling voices as men and women found outlet for their natural gregariousness in the cramped and smoky confines of the little café and sought to make their escape, however artificial and ephemeral such escape might be, from the iron realities of the world outside. Reynolds' first and immediate reaction was that of surprise, shock almost, to find such an oasis of color and light in the grim, drab greyness of a police state, but that reaction was brief: it was inevitable that the Communists, no mean psychologists, should not only permit such places but positively encourage them. If people were to gather in the company of one another, as people would no matter what the prohibitions, how much better that they should do it in the open and drink their coffee and wine and porter under the watchfully benevolent eye of some trusted servants of the state rather than gather in dark and huddled corners and plot against the regime. Excellent safety valves, Reynolds thought drily.

He had broken step and paused just inside the door, then moved on again almost at once but without haste. Two tables near the doors were crowded with Russian soldiers, laughing, singing, and banging their glasses on the table in high good humour. Harmless enough, Reynolds judged, and doubtless that was why the café had been chosen as a rendezvous: no one was going to look for a Western spy in the drinking haunt of Russian soldiers. But these were Reynolds' first Russians, and he preferred not to linger.

He moved in to the back of the café and saw her almost at once, sitting alone at a tiny table for two. She was dressed in the belted, hooded coat the manager had described to Reynolds earlier in the day, but now the hood was down and the coat open at the throat. Her eyes caught his without a flicker of recognition, and Reynolds took his cue at once. There were half a dozen tables nearby with one or two vacant places, and he stood there hesitating over which seat to choose long enough for several people to notice his presence. Then he moved across to Julia's table.

"Do you mind if I share your table?" he asked.

She stared at him, turned her head to look pointedly at a small empty table in the corner, glanced at him again, then pointedly shifted her body until her shoulder was turned to him. She said nothing, and Reynolds could hear the stifled sniggers behind him as he sat down. He edged his chair closer to hers, and his voice was only a murmur.

"Trouble?"

"I'm being followed." She had turned towards him again, her face hostile and aloof. She's no fool, Reynolds thought, and by heavens she knew how to act.

"He's here?"

A millimetric nod, but nod nevertheless.

"Where?"

"Bench by the door. Near the soldiers."

Reynolds made no move to turn his head. "Describe him."

"Medium height, brown raincoat, no hat, thin face, and

black moustache." The disdain still registering on her face was in almost comical contrast with the words.

"We must get rid of him. Outside. You first, me last." He stretched out his hand, squeezed her forearm, bent forward, and leered at her. "I've been trying to pick you up. In fact, I've just made a most improper suggestion. How do you react?"

"Like this." She swung back her free hand and caught Reynolds across the face with a slap so loud that it momentarily stopped all the hubbub and conversation and turned every eye in their direction. Then Julia was on her feet, gathering up her handbag and gloves and walking haughtily towards the door, looking neither to her left nor right. As if by a signal, the talk and the laughter broke out again—and most of the laughter, Reynolds knew, was directed against himself.

He lifted a hand and gingerly caressed a tingling cheek. The young lady, he thought ruefully, carried realism to quite unnecessary lengths. A scowl on his face, he swivelled in his seat in time to see the glass doors swinging to behind her and to see a man in a brown raincoat rise unobtrusively from his seat by the door, throw some money on his table, and follow close behind her even before the door had stopped swinging.

Reynolds was on his feet a moment later, shamefaced and with his eyes on the floor at his feet, a man obviously bent on leaving the scene of his discomfiture and mortification with all possible speed. Everybody, he knew, was looking at him, and when he pulled his coat collar up and his hatbrim down, a renewed chorus of sniggers broke out. Just as he approached the door, a burly Russian soldier, his face red with laughter and drink, heaved himself to his feet, said something to Reynolds, thumped him on the back hard enough to send him staggering against the counter, then doubled up, convulsed with laughter over his own wit. A stranger to Russians and Russian ways, Reynolds had no idea whether anger or fear would be the safer reaction in the circumstances: he contented himself with a grimace that was compounded of a sullen scowl and sheepish grin, side-stepped nimbly, and was gone before the humorist could renew the assault.

The snow was very light now, and he had little difficulty in locating both the girl and the man. They were walking slowly up the street to the left, and he followed, keeping the man at the very limit of observation. Two hundred yards, four hundred, a couple of corners, and Julia had halted in a streetcar shelter outside a row of shops. Her shadow slid silently into a doorway behind the shelter, and Reynolds went past the man, joining Julia in the glass-fronted shelter.

"He's behind us in a doorway," Reynolds murmured. "Do you think you could put up a desperate fight for your honour?"

"Could I——" She broke off and glanced nervously over her shoulders. "We must be careful. He's AVO, I'm certain, and all AVO men are dangerous."

"Dangerous, fiddlesticks," Reynolds said roughly. "We haven't all night." He looked at her speculatively, then lifted his hands and caught her by the coat lapels. "Strangulation, I think. Must account for the fact that you're not screaming for help. We have enough company as it is!"

The shadow fell for it; he would have been less than human not to fall for it. He saw the man and woman come staggering out of the streetcar shelter, the woman fighting desperately to tear away the hands encircling her throat, and didn't hesitate. His feet silent on the hard-packed snow, he came running lightly across the pavement, a weapon raised high in his right hand ready to strike—then collapsed soundlessly as Reynolds, at a warning exclamation from the girl, swung round, elbowed him viciously in the solar plexus, and chopped him with the edge of his open hand across the side of the neck. It took only seconds thereafter for Reynolds to stuff the man's blackjack—a canvas tube filled with lead shot—in his pocket, bundle the man himself into the streetcar shelter, take the girl's arm, and hurry away along the street.

The girl shivered violently, and Reynolds peered at her in surprise in the almost total darkness of the watchman's box. Confined as they were in a narrow space and sheltered from the snow and the bitter wind, they were relatively comfortable, and even through his coat he could feel the warmth of the girl's shoulder against his own. He reached for her hand—she had taken off her gloves to rub the circulation into life when they had arrived ten minutes previously—but she snatched it away as from the touch of flame.

"What's the matter?" Reynolds' voice was puzzled. "Still feeling frozen?"

"I don't know. I—yes, I do know. I'm not cold." She shivered again. "It's—it's you. You're too inhuman. I'm afraid of people who are inhuman."

"Afraid of me?" Reynolds sounded incredulous and felt that way. "My dear child, I wouldn't harm a hair of your head."

"Don't you 'child' me!" A sudden flash of spirit, then a quiet, small voice, "I know you wouldn't."

"Then what the devil am I supposed to have done?"

"Nothing. That's the whole point. It's not what you do, it's what you don't do, it's what you don't *show*. You show no feelings, no emotions, no interest or concern in anything. Oh yes, you're interested enough in the job to be done, but the method, the how of it, is a matter of absolute indifference, just so long as the job is done.

"The Count says you're only a machine, a mechanism designed to carry out a certain piece of work, but without any life or existence as an individual. He says you're about the only person he knows who cannot be afraid, and he is afraid of people who cannot be afraid. Imagine! The Count afraid!"

"Imagine," Reynolds murmured politely.

"Jansci says the same. He says you're neither moral nor immoral, just amoral, with certain conditioned pro-British, anti-Communist reactions that are valueless in themselves. He says whether you kill or not is decided not on a basis of wrong or right but simply of expediency. He says that you are the same as hundreds of young men he has met in the NKVD, the Waffen SS, and other such organisations, men who obey blindly and kill blindly without ever asking themselves whether it is right or wrong. The only difference, my father says, is that you would never kill wantonly. But that is the only difference."

"I make friends wherever I go," Reynolds murmured.

"There! You see what I mean? One cannot touch you. And now tonight. You bundle a man into a hotel cupboard, bound and gagged, and let him suffocate—he probably did. You hit another and leave him to freeze to death in the snow—he won't last twenty minutes in this. You——"

"I could have shot the first man," Reynolds said quietly. "I have a silencer, you know. And do you think that lad with the blackjack wouldn't have left *me* to freeze to death if he'd got in first?"

"You're just quibbling ... And, worst of all, that poor old man. You don't care what you do as long as he goes back to Britain, do you? He thinks his wife is dying, and yet you'd torture him till he must be almost insane with worry and grief. You encourage him to believe, you *make* him believe that if she dies he'll be her murderer. Why, Mr. Reynolds, why?"

"You know why. Because I'm a nasty, amoral, emotionless machine of a Chicago gangster just doing what I'm told. You just said so, didn't you?"

"I'm just wasting my breath, am I not, Mr. Reynolds?" The tone was flat and dull.

"By no means." Reynolds grinned in the darkness. "I could listen all night to your voice, and I'm sure you wouldn't preach so earnestly unless you thought there was some hope of conversion."

"You're laughing at me, aren't you?"

"A nasty, superior sort of smirk," Reynolds admitted. Suddenly he caught her hand and lowered his voice. "Keep quiet—and keep still!"

"What——" Only the one word had escaped before Reynolds clamped his hand tightly over her mouth. She started to struggle, then relaxed almost immediately. She, too, had heard it—the crunch of footsteps in the snow. They sat without moving, hardly daring to breathe while three policemen walked slowly past them, past the abandoned café terraces further on, and disappeared along a winding path beneath the bare, snow-laden beeches, planes, and oaks that lined the perimeter of a great lawn.

"I thought you told me this part of Margit Island was always deserted?" His voice was a savage whisper. "That no one ever came here in the winter?"

"It always has been before," she murmured. "I knew the policemen made a round, but I didn't know they came that way. But they won't be back for another hour, I'm sure of that. The Margit Sziget is big, and they will take time to go round."

It had been Julia, teeth chattering with the cold and desperate for a place where they could talk in privacy—the White Angel had been the only café in the area which was open—who, after a fruitless search elsewhere, had suggested Margit Island. Parts of it, she had said, were banned and under curfew after a certain hour, but the curfew wasn't treated too seriously. The patrolling guards were members of the ordinary police forces, not the Secret Police, and were as different from the AVO as chalk from cheese. Reynolds, himself almost as cold as the girl, had readily agreed, and the watchman's hut, surrounded by the granite sets, chips, and tar barrels of road repairers who had vanished with the onset of the cold weather, had seemed an ideal place.

There Julia had told of the latest happenings at Jansci's house. The two men who had been watching the house so assiduously had made an error—only one, admittedly, but their last. They had grown overconfident and had taken to walking past on the same side of the street as the garage instead of the opposite side, and on one occasion, finding the garage door open, had gone so far as to let their curiosity get the better of them and peer in, which was a mistake, as Sandor had been waiting for them. Whether they had been informers or AVO men was not yet known, as Sandor had cracked their heads together rather harder than was necessary. All that mattered was that they were under lock and key and that it would now be safe for Reynolds to visit the house to make final plans for the abduction of the professor. But not before midnight, Jansci had insisted on that.

Reynolds in his turn had told her of what had happened to him, and now, just after the departure of the three policemen, he looked at her in the gloom of the shelter. Her hand was still in his, she was quite unaware of it: and her hand was tense and rigid and unyielding.

"You're not really cut out for this sort of thing, Miss Illyurin," he said quietly. "Very few people are. You don't stay here and lead this life because you like it?"

"Like it! Dear God, how could anyone ever like this life? Nothing but fear and hunger and repression and, for us, always moving from place to place, always looking over our shoulders to see if anyone is there, afraid to look over our shoulder in case someone *is* there. To speak in the wrong place, to smile at the wrong time——"

"You'd go over to the West tomorrow, wouldn't you?"

"Yes. No, no, I can't. I can't. You see——"

"Your mother, isn't that it?"

"My mother!" He could feel her shift against him as she turned to stare in the darkness. "My mother is dead, Mr. Reynolds."

"Dead?" His voice inflected in surprise. "That's not what your father says."

"I know it's not." Her voice softened. "Poor, dear Jansci, he'll never believe that Mother is dead. She was dying when they took her away—one lung was almost gone—she couldn't have lived a couple of days. But Jansci will never believe it. He'll stop hoping when he stops breathing."

"But you tell him you believe it too?"

"Yes. I wait here because I am all Jansci has left in the world, and I cannot leave him. But if I told him that, he would have me across the Austrian frontier tomorrow—he would never have me risk my life for him. And so I tell him I wait for Mother."

"I see." Reynolds could think of nothing else to say, wondered if he himself could have done what this girl was doing if he felt as she did. He remembered something, his impression that Jansci had seemed indifferent to the fate of his wife. "Your father—he has looked for your mother, searched for her, I mean?"

"You don't think so, do you? He always gives that impression, I don't know why." She paused for a moment, then went on, "You will not believe this, no one believes this, but it is true: there are nine concentration camps in Hungary, and in the past eighteen months Jansci has been inside five of them, just looking for Mother. Inside and, as you can see, out again. It's just not possible, is it?"

"It's just not possible," Reynolds echoed slowly.

"And he'd combed a thousand, over a thousand collective farms—or what were collective farms before the October rising. He has not found her, he never will find her. But always he looks, always he will keep on looking, and he will never find her."

Something in her voice caught Reynolds' attention. He reached up a gentle hand and touched her face: her cheeks were wet, but she did not turn away, she didn't resent the touch.

"I told you this life wasn't for you, Miss Illyurin."

"Julia, always Julia. You mustn't say that name, you

mustn't even think that name. . . . Why am I telling you all these things?"

"Who knows? But tell me more—tell me about Jansci. I have heard a little, but only a little."

"What can I tell you? 'A little,' you say, but that's all I, too, know about my father. He will never talk about what is gone, he will not even say why he will not talk. I think it is because he lives now only for peace and the making of peace, to help all those who cannot help themselves. That is what I heard him say once. . . . I think his memory tortures him. He has lost so much, and he has killed so many."

Reynolds said nothing, and after a time the girl went on, "Jansci's father was a Communist leader in the Ukraine. He was a good Communist, and he was also a good man—you can be both at the same time, Mr. Reynolds. In 1938 he—and practically every leading Communist in the Ukraine—died in the Secret Police torture cellars in Kiev. That was when it all started. Jansci executed the executioners and some of the judges, but too many hands were against him. He was taken to Siberia and spent six months in an underground cell in the Vladivostok transit camp waiting for ice to melt and the steamer to come to take them away. He saw no daylight for six months, he didn't see another human being for six months—his crusts and the slops that passed for food were lowered through a hatch. They all knew who he was, and he was to take a long time dying. He had no blankets, no bed, and temperature was far below zero. For the last month they stopped all supplies of water also, but Jansci survived by licking the hoarfrost off the iron door of his cell. They were beginning to learn that Jansci was indestructible."

"Go on, go on." Reynolds still held the girl's hand tightly in his own, but neither of them was aware of it. "And after that?"

"After that the freighter came and took him away, to the Kolyma Mountains. No one ever comes back from the Kolyma Mountains—but Jansci came back." He could hear the awe in the girl's voice even as she spoke, even as she repeated something she must have said or thought a thousand times. "These were the worst months of his life. I don't know what happened in those days, I don't think there is anyone still alive who knows what happened then. All I know is that he sometimes still wakes up from his sleep, his face grey, whispering, *'Davai, davai!'*—get going, get going!—and *'Bystrey, bystrey'*—faster, faster! It's something to do with driving or pulling sledges, I don't know what. I know, too, that till this day he cannot bear to hear the sound of sleigh bells. You've seen the missing fingers on his hands—it was a favourite sport to drag prisoners along behind the NKVD's—or OGPU's, as it was then—propeller-driven sledges and see how close they could be brought to the propeller. . . . Sometimes they were jerked too close, and their faces . . ." She was silent for a moment, then went on, her voice unsteady. "I suppose you could say Jansci was lucky. His fingers, only his fingers . . . and his hands, those scars on his hands. Do you know how he came by those, Mr. Reynolds?"

He shook his head in the darkness, and she seemed to sense the movement.

"Wolves, Mr. Reynolds. Wolves mad with hunger. The guards trapped them, starved them, and then flung a man and a wolf into the same pit. The man would have only his hands: Jansci had only his hands. His arms, his entire body is a mass of those scars."

"It's not possible, all this is not possible." Reynolds' low-pitched mutter was that of a man trying to convince himself of something which must be true.

"In the Kolyma Mountains all things are possible. That wasn't the worst, that was nothing. Other things happened to him there, degrading, horrible, bestial things, but he has never spoken of them to me."

"And the palms of his hands, the crucifixion marks on his hands?"

"These aren't crucifixion marks. All the biblical pictures are wrong—you can't crucify a man by the palms of his hands. . . . Jansci had done something terrible, I don't know what it was, so they took him out to the taiga, the deep forest, in the middle of winter, stripped him of all his clothes, nailed him to two trees that grew close together, and left him. They knew it would be only a few minutes, the fearful cold or the wolves . . . He escaped—God knows how he escaped—Jansci doesn't, but he escaped, found his clothes where they had thrown them away, and left the Kolyma Mountains. That was when all his fingers—his fingertips and nails—went, that's when he lost all his toes—— You have seen the way he walks?"

"Yes." Reynolds remembered the strange stiff-legged gait. He thought of Jansci's face, its kindness and its infinite gentleness, and tried to see that face against the background of its history, but the gap was too great; his imagination baulked at the attempt. "I would not have believed this of any man, Julia. To survive so much ... He *must* be indestructible."

"I think so too. . . . It took him four months to arrive at the Trans-Siberian Railway where it crosses the Lena, and when he stopped a train he was quite insane. He was out of his mind for a long time, but he finally recovered and made his way back to the Ukraine.

"That was in 1941. He joined the army and became a major inside a year. Jansci joined for the reason that most Ukrainians joined—to wait his chance, as they are still waiting their chance, to turn their regiments against the Red Army. And the chance came soon, when Germany attacked."

There was a long pause, then she went on quietly.

"We know now, but we didn't know then, what the Russians told the world. We know what they told of the long bloody battle as we fell back on the Dnieper, the scorched earth, the desperate defence of Kiev. Lies, lies, all lies—and still most of the world doesn't know it." He could hear her voice softening in memory. "We welcomed the Germans with open arms. We gave them the most wonderful welcome any army has ever had. We gave them food and wine, we decorated our streets, we garlanded the storm troopers with flowers. Not one shot was fired in defence of Kiev. Ukrainian regiments, Ukrainian divisions deserted en masse to the Germans—Jansci said there's never been anything like it in history—and soon the Germans had an army of a million Russians fighting for them under the command of the Soviet General Andrei Vlassov. Jansci was with this army; he rose to be major general and one of Vlassov's right-hand men, and fought with this army until the Germans fell back on his home town of Vinnitsa in 1943." Her voice trailed away, came again after a long silence. "It was after Vinnitsa that Jansci changed. He swore he would never fight again; he swore he would never kill again. He has kept his promise."

"Vinnitsa?" Reynolds' curiosity was aroused. "What happened at Vinnitsa?"

"You—you've never heard of Vinnitsa?"

"Never."

"Dear God," she whispered. "I thought the whole world had heard of Vinnitsa."

"Sorry, no. What happened there?"

"Don't ask me, don't ask me!" Reynolds heard the long, quivering sigh. "Someone else, but *please* don't ask me."

"Okay, okay," Reynolds' voice was quick, surprised. He could feel her whole body shaking with silent sobs, and he patted her shoulder awkwardly. "Skip it. It doesn't matter."

"Thank you." Her voice was muffled. "That's just about all, Mr. Reynolds. Jansci went to visit his old home in Vinnitsa, and the Russians were waiting for him—they had been waiting a long time. He was put in command of a Ukrainian regiment—all deserters who had been recaptured—given obsolete weapons and no uniforms at all, and forced into a suicide position against the Germans. That happened to tens of thousand of Ukrainians. He was captured by the Germans—he had thrown away his weapons and walked across to their lines, was recognised, and spent the rest of the war with General Vlassov. After the war the Ukrainian Liberation Army broke up into sections—some of them, believe it or not, are still operating —and it was there that he met the Count. They have never parted since."

"He *is* a Pole, isn't he—the Count, I mean?"

"Yes, that's where they met—in Poland."

"And who is he really? Do you know?"

He sensed rather than saw the shake of the head in the darkness.

"Jansci knows, but only Jansci. I only know that next to my father he is the most wonderful person I have ever known. And there's some strange bond between them. I think it's because they both have so much blood on their hands and because neither of them has killed for years. They are dedicated men, Mr. Reynolds."

"Is he really a count?"

"He is indeed. So much I know. He owned huge estates, lakes and forests and great pastures at a place called Augustow up near the borders of East Prussia and Lithuania—or what used to be the borders. He fought the Germans in 1939, then took to the underground. After a long time he was captured, and the Germans thought that it would be very amusing to make a Polish aristocrat earn his living by forced labour. You know the kind of labour, Mr. Reynolds—clearing the thousands of corpses out of the Warsaw ghetto after the Stukas and the tanks had finished with it. He and a band of others killed their gaolers and joined General Bor's Polish Resistance Army. You will remember what happened—Marshal Rossokovsky halted his Russian armies outside Warsaw and let the Germans and the Polish resistance fight it out to the death in the sewers of Warsaw."

"I remember. People speak of it as the bitterest battle of the war. The Poles were massacred, of course."

"Nearly all. The remnants, the Count among them, were taken off to the Auschwitz gas chambers. The German guards let them nearly all go, no one yet knows why—but not before they branded them. The Count has his number inside his forearm, running from wrist to elbow, all scarred, raised lumps." She shivered. "It's horrible."

"And then he met your father?"

"Yes. They were both with Vlassov's men, but they didn't stay long. The endless, senseless killings sickened them both. These bands used to disguise themselves as Russians, stop and board the Polish trains, make the passengers get out, and shoot all who held Communist Party cards—and many of the holders had no option but to have those cards if they and their families were to survive; or they would move into towns, ferret out the Stakhanovites or would-be Stakhanovites, and throw them among the ice blocks of the Vistula. So they left for Czechoslovakia and joined the Slovak partisans in the High Tatras."

"I've heard of them, even in England," Reynolds acknowledged. "The fiercest and most independent fighters in Central Europe."

"I think Jansci and the Count would agree," she said feelingly. "But they left very soon. The Slovaks weren't really interested in fighting for something, they were just interested in fighting, and when things were dull they were just as happy to fight among themselves. So Jansci and the Count came to Hungary—they've been here over seven years now, most of the time outside of Budapest."

"And how long have you been here?"

"The same time. One of the first things Jansci and the Count did was to come to the Ukraine for us, and they took my mother and me here by way of the Carpathians and the High Tatra. I know what it must sound like, but it was a wonderful journey. It was high summer, the sun shone, they knew everybody, they had friends everywhere. I never saw my mother so happy."

"Yes." Reynolds steered her away from the topic. "The rest I know. The Count tips off who's next for the axe, and Jansci gets them out. I've talked to dozens in England alone who were taken out by Jansci. The strange thing was that none of them hated the Russians. They all want peace; Jansci has talked them all into preaching for peace. He even tried to talk to me!"

"I told you," she said softly. "He's a wonderful man." A minute passed in silence, two minutes, then she said suddenly, surprisingly: "You're not married, are you, Mr. Reynolds?"

"What's that again?" Reynolds was startled at the sudden switch.

"You haven't a wife, have you, or a sweetheart or any girls at all? And please don't say 'No, and don't bother applying for the vacancy,' for that would be harsh and cruel and just a little cheap, and I don't really think you are any of these things."

"I never opened my mouth," Reynolds protested. "As to the question, you guessed the answer. Anybody could. Women and my kind of life are mutually exclusive. Surely you can see that."

"I know it," she murmured. "I also know that two or three times this evening you have turned me away from—from unpleasant subjects. Inhuman monsters just don't bother about that kind of thing. I'm sorry I called you that, but I'm glad I did, for I found out I was wrong before Jansci and the Count did. You don't know what it's like for me—those two—they're always right, and I'm always wrong. But this time I'm right before they are."

"I've no doubt you know what you're talking about ——" Reynolds began politely.

"And can't you just see their expressions when I tell them that I sat for ten minutes tonight with Mr. Reynolds' arm around me?" The voice was demure, but with bubbling undertones of laughter. "You put it round me when you thought I was crying—and so I was crying," she admitted. "Your wolf's clothing is getting a little threadbare, Mr. Reynolds."

"Good lord." Reynolds was genuinely astonished. For the first time he realised that his arm lay along her shoulders; he could just feel the touch of her hair on the back of his almost numbed hand. He muttered some discomfited apology and was just starting to lift his arm when he froze into perfect stillness. Then his arm fell back slowly and tightened round her shoulder as he put his lips to her ear.

"We have company, Julia," he murmured.

He looked out of the corner of his eye, and his eye confirmed what his abnormally keen ear had already told him. The snow had stopped, and he could clearly see three people advancing softly towards them. He would have seen them a hundred feet away if his vigilance hadn't slipped. For the second time that night Julia had been wrong about the policemen, and this time there was no escaping them. That soft-footed advance was a sure acknowledgment of the policemen's awareness of their presence in the little hut.

Reynolds didn't hesitate. He brought his right hand over, caught her by the waist, bent down, and kissed her. At first, as if by reflex instinct she tried to push him off, to turn her face away, her whole body stiff in his arms. Then all at once she relaxed, and Reynolds knew that she understood. She was her father's daughter, and she caught on fast. Her arm came up around his neck.

Ten seconds passed, then as many again. The policemen, Reynolds thought—and it was becoming difficult to keep his thoughts on the policemen—were in no hurry to make their presence known, but it was no punishment, and he could have sworn that the pressure of her arm around his neck was beginning to tighten when a powerful flashlight clicked on and a deep, cheerful voice spoke.

"By heaven, Stefan, I don't care what people say, there's nothing wrong with the young generation. Here they are, the thermometer twenty degrees below zero, and you'd think they were lying on the beaches of Balaton in a heat wave. Now, now, not so fast, young man." A large hand reached out of the darkness behind the torch beam and pushed Reynolds, who had been struggling to his feet, back down again. "What are you doing here? Don't you know this place is forbidden at night?"

"I know it is," Reynolds muttered. His face was a nice mixture of fear and embarrassment. "I'm sorry. We had nowhere else to go."

"Nonsense!" the hearty voice boomed. "When I was your age, young man, there was nothing better in wintertime than the little curtained alcoves of the White Angel. Only a few hundred metres from here."

Reynolds began to relax. There was little to fear from this man. "We were at the White Angel——"

"Show us your papers," another voice demanded, a cold, hard, mean little voice. "You have them?"

"Of course I have them." The man behind that voice was a different proposition altogether. Reynolds reached inside his coat, his fingers folding over the butt of his automatic, when the first policeman spoke again.

"Don't be silly, Stefan. You really will have to be careful—all those terrible thrillers you read. Or maybe you think he's a Western spy sent to find out how much co-operation they can expect from the young ladies of Budapest when the next rising comes." He roared with laughter, bent over, and slapped his thigh, all but overcome by his own wit, then slowly straightened. "Besides, he's as Budapest born-and-bred as I am. The White Angel, you said," his voice suddenly thoughtful. "Come out of there, the two of you."

They rose stiffly, and the torch shone so close to Reynolds' face that he screwed his eyes shut.

"This is him, all right," the policeman announced jovially. "This is the one we heard about. Look—you can still see the mark of every finger on his cheek. No wonder he wouldn't go back. It's a wonder his jaw wasn't dislocated." He swung his torch onto a blinking Julia. "Looks as if she could do it too. Built like a boxer." He ignored the outraged gasp and turned to Reynolds, waving a warning forefinger, his voice solemn with the solemnity of a comic vastly enjoying himself. "You want to be careful, young man. Beautiful, but—well, you can see for yourself. If she's as plump as this in her twenties, what's she going to be like in her forties? You should see my wife!" His laugh boomed out again, and he waved a hand in dismissal. "Be off, my children. Next time it's the dungeon for you."

Five minutes later they parted on the shore side of the

bridge, just as the snow began to fall again. Reynolds glanced at his luminous watch.

"Just after nine o'clock. I'll be there in three hours."

"We will be expecting you then. That should give me just about enough time to describe in detail how I almost dislocated your jaw and how the ice-cold calculating machine had his arm round me and kissed me for a whole minute without coming up for air once!"

"Thirty seconds," Reynolds protested.

"A minute and a half at least. And I won't tell them why. I can hardly wait to see their faces!"

"I'm at your mercy." Reynolds grinned. "But don't forget to tell them what you're going to look like by the time you're forty."

"I won't," she promised. She was standing close to him now, and he could see the mischief in her eyes. "After what has passed between us," she went on solemnly, "this counts even less than a handshake." She reached up on tiptoe, brushed her lips lightly across his cheek, and hurried away into the darkness. For a full minute Reynolds stood looking after her, long seconds after she had vanished, thoughtfully rubbing his cheek: then he swore softly to himself and made off in the opposite direction, head bent forward and hatbrim pulled far down against the snow in his eyes.

When Reynolds reached his room in the hotel, unobserved and by way of the fire escape, it was twenty minutes to ten and he was very cold and very hungry. He switched on the central heating, satisfied himself that no one had been in the room during his absence, then called the manager on the phone. There had been no messages for him, no callers. Yes, he would be delighted to provide dinner even at this late hour: the chef was just going to bed but would consider it an honour to show Mr. Rakosi just what he could do in the way of an impromptu meal. Reynolds rather ungraciously said that speed was of the essence and that the culinary masterpieces could wait till another day.

He finished an excellent meal and the best part of a bottle of Soproni just after eleven o'clock and prepared to depart. Almost an hour yet to his appointment, but what had taken only six or seven minutes in the Count's Mercedes would take far longer by foot, the more so as his route would be wandering and devious. He changed a damp shirt, tie, and socks and folded them neatly away—for he did not then know that he was never to see either that room or its contents again—jammed the key in the door, dressed against the winter night, and left once more by the fire escape. As he reached the street, he could hear a telephone ringing faintly, insistently, but he ignored it; the sound could have come from a hundred rooms other than his own.

By the time he had arrived at the street of Jansci's house it was a few minutes after twelve. Despite the brisk pace he had kept up throughout, he was half frozen, but satisfied enough for all that; he was certain that he had neither been followed nor observed since he had left the hotel. Now, if only the Count still had some of that *barack* left . . .

The street was deserted and the garage door, when he came to it, was, as by arrangement, open. He turned into the darkness of its interior without breaking step, angled confidently across to the corridor door at the other end, and had taken perhaps four paces when the garage was flooded with light at the touch of a switch and the iron doors clanged shut behind him.

Reynolds stood perfectly still, keeping both hands well clear of his clothes, then looked slowly around him. In each corner of the garage, a submachine gun cradled under his arm, stood a watchful, smiling AVO man, each in his high peaked cap and long, sweeping belted trench coat. There was no mistaking these men, Reynolds thought dully, there was no mistaking the real thing when you saw it, the coarsened brutality, the leering, expectant sadism of the lowermost dregs of society which automatically find their ways into the Secret Police of Communist countries the world over.

But it was the fifth man, the little man by the corridor door with the dark, thin, intelligent Jew's face, that caught and held his attention. Even as Reynolds looked at him, he put away and buttoned up his pistol, took two steps forward, smiled, and bowed ironically.

"Captain Michael Reynolds of the British Secret Service, I believe. You are very punctual, and we sincerely appreciate it. We of the AVO do not like to be kept waiting."

6

WITHOUT moving, without speaking, Reynolds stood in the middle of the floor. He stood there, it seemed to him, for an eternity of time, while his mind first of all absorbed the shock, then the bitter realisation, then hunted frantically for the reason for this, for the presence of the AVO and the absence of his friends. But it was no eternity, it was probably no more than fifteen seconds altogether, and even as the seconds passed Reynolds let his jaw fall lower and lower in shock while his eyes slowly widened in fear.

"Reynolds," he whispered, the word coming awkwardly with difficulty as it would to a Hungarian. "Michael Reynolds? I—I do not know what you mean, comrade. What—what is wrong? Why are these guns—I swear I have done nothing, comrade, nothing! I swear it!" His hands were clasped together now, wringing each other till the knuckles stood white, and the tremor in his voice was the quaver of fear.

The two guards that Reynolds could see wrinkled their heavy brows and stared at each other in slow, puzzled wonder, but not even a shadow of doubt touched the dark, amused eyes of the little Jew.

"Amnesia," he said kindly. "The shock, my friend, that is why you forget your own name. A remarkable effort, nonetheless. and had I not known your identity beyond any doubt, I too—like my men here who do not yet know who you are—would have been more than halfway toward belief. The British Espionage Service do us a great compliment; they send us only their best. But then I would have expected nothing else but the best when the—ah—recovery, shall we say?—of Professor Harold Jennings is concerned."

Reynolds could feel the sickness deep down in his stomach, the bitter taste of despair in his mouth. God, this was even worse than he had feared; if they knew this, they knew everything, it was the end of everything. But the stupid, fearful expression remained on his face: it might have been pinned there. Then he shook himself, a person throwing off the dark terror of a nightmare, and looked wildly around him.

"Let me go, let me go!" His voice was high-pitched now, almost a scream. "I've done nothing, I tell you, nothing, nothing! I am a good Communist, I am a member of the party." His mouth was working uncontrollably in a strained face. "I am a citizen of Budapest, comrade, I have my papers, my membership cards! I will show you, I will show you!" His hand was reaching up to go inside his coat, when he froze at a single word from the AVO officer, a soft-pitched word, but cold and dry and cutting like the lash of a whip.

"Stop!"

Reynolds arrested his hand just at the lapels of his coat, then let it fall slowly to his side. The little Jew smiled.

"A pity you will not live to retire from your country's secret service, Captain Reynolds. A pity, indeed, that you ever joined it— I feel convinced that a notable Thespian has been thereby lost to the boards and the silver screen." He looked over Reynolds' shoulder at a man standing by the garage door. "Coco, Captain Reynolds was about to produce a pistol or some such offensive weapon. Relieve him of the temptation."

Reynolds heard the tread of heavy boots on the concrete floor behind him, then grunted in agony as a rifle butt smashed into the small of his back just above the kidney. He swayed dizzily on his feet, and through the red haze of pain he could feel trained hands searching his clothes, could hear the little Jew's apologetic murmur.

"You must excuse Coco, Captain Reynolds. A singularly direct fellow in his approach to these matters, always the same. However, experience has taught him that a sample of what misbehaviour will inevitably bring, when he is searching a prisoner, is much more effective than even the direst threats." His voice changed subtly. "Ah, Exhibit A, and most interesting. A Belgian 6.35 automatic —and a silencer—neither of which is obtainable in this country. No doubt you found them lying in the streets. . . . And does anyone recognise this?"

Reynolds focussed his eyes with difficulty. The AVO officer was tossing in his hand the blackjack Reynolds had taken from his assailant earlier in the evening.

"I think so, I think I do, Colonel Hidas." The AVO man his superior called Coco moved into Reynolds' line of sight—a mountain of a man, Reynolds could now see, six foot four if an inch, and built accordingly, with a broken-nosed, seamed, and brutalised face—and took the black-jack, almost engulfing it in his huge, black-haired paw. "This is Herped's, Colonel. Without a doubt. See, it has his initials on the base. My friend Herped. Where did you get this?" he snarled at Reynolds.

"I found it along with the gun," Reynolds said sullenly. "In a parcel at the corner of Brody Sandor Street and ———"

He saw the blackjack whipping across, but too late to duck. It smashed him back against a wall, and he slipped down to the floor and pushed himself groggily to his feet. In the silence he could hear the blood from his smashed lips dripping on the floor, could feel teeth loose in the front of his mouth.

"Now, now, Coco." Hidas spoke soothingly, reprovingly. "Give that back to me, Coco. Thank you. Captain Reynolds, you have only yourself to blame—we do not know yet whether Herped *is* Coco's friend or *was* Coco's friend: he was at death's door when he was found in that streetcar shelter where you left him." He reached up and patted the shoulder of the scowling giant by his side. "Do not misjudge our friend here, Mr. Reynolds. He is not always thus, as you can judge from his name—not his own, but that of a famous clown and comic of whom you have doubtless heard. Coco can be most amusing, I assure you, and I have seen him convulsing his colleagues down in the Stalin Street cellars with the interesting variations in his—ah—techniques."

Reynolds said nothing. The reference to the AVO torture chambers, the free hand Colonel Hidas was allowing this sadistic brute were neither unconnected nor accidental. Hidas was feeling his way, shrewdly assessing Reynolds' reaction and resistance to this line of approach. Hidas was interested only in certain results to be achieved by the swiftest means, and if he became convinced that brutality and violence were a waste of time with a man like Reynolds, he would desist and seek out more subtle methods. Hidas looked a dangerous man, cunning and embittered, but there was no sadism that Reynolds could see in the dark, thin features. Hidas beckoned to one of his men.

"Go to the bottom of the street—there's a telephone there. Have a van come round here right away. They know where we are." He smiled at Reynolds. "We could not, unfortunately, park it outside the front door. Might have aroused your suspicion, eh, Captain Reynolds?" He glanced at his watch. "The van should be here in ten minutes, no more, but that ten minutes can be passed profitably. Captain Reynolds might be interested in writing—and signing—an account of his recent activities. Nonfiction, of course. Bring him inside."

They brought him inside and stood him facing the desk while Hidas sat behind it and adjusted the lamp so that it shone strongly into Reynolds' face from a distance of less than two feet.

"We will sing, Captain Reynolds, then we will record the words of the song for a grateful posterity—or at least for the People's Court. A fair trial awaits you. Equivocation, outright lies, or even delay will serve you nothing. A speedy confirmation of what we already know may yet spare your life—we would prefer to dispense with what would inevitably become an international incident. And we know everything, Captain Reynolds, *everything.*" He shook his head, a man remembering and wondering. "Who would have thought that your friend"—he snapped his fingers—"I forget his name, the squat fellow with the shoulders like a barn door, would have had such a beautiful singing voice?" He pulled a paper out from a drawer in front of him, and Reynolds could see that it was covered with writing. "A somewhat unsteady hand, understandable perhaps in the circumstances, but it will serve: I think the judge will have little difficulty in deciphering it."

In spite of the deep-seated, tearing pain in his side and puffing agony of his smashed mouth, Reynolds felt a wave of elation wash over him and spat blood on the floor to conceal the expression on his face. He knew now that no one had talked, because the AVO had caught none of them. The nearest they had come to Jansci and his men, probably, was a glimpse some informer had had of Sandor working about the garage. . . . There were far too many things wrong with what Hidas had said.

Sandor, Reynolds was sure, did not know enough to tell Hidas everything he wanted to know. They wouldn't have started on Sandor anyway, not with the girl and Imre around. Nor was Hidas the man to forget the name of any person, especially a name that he had only that evening learned. Besides, the whole idea of Sandor talking under physical torture—there had been time for nothing else—was incomprehensible. Hidas, Reynolds reflected grimly, had never been crushed in Sandor's grip and gazed into those gentle, implacable eyes from a range of six inches. Reynolds stared at the document on the table, then looked slowly around him. If they had tried to torture Sandor in that room, he doubted very much whether even the walls would be still standing.

"Suppose you begin by telling us how you entered the country," Hidas suggested. "Were the canals frozen, Mr. Reynolds?"

"Entered the country? Canals?" Reynolds' voice came thick and blurred through his swollen lips, and he shook his head slowly. "I'm afraid I don't know——"

He broke off, jumped sideways, and twisted round in one convulsive movement, a movement that sliced fresh agony through his side and back: even in the relative gloom where Hidas was sitting he had caught the sudden shift of eyes, the tiny nod to Coco, and it was not until afterward that Reynolds realised that he had probably been meant to catch both. Coco's downward clubbing fist missed him almost completely, the burred edge of a signet ring burning a thin line from temple to jaw, but Reynolds, with the giant guard completely off balance, made no mistake.

Hidas was on his feet now, his pistol showing. His eyes moved over the tableau: the other two guards moving in with carbines ready, Reynolds leaning heavily on one foot—the other felt as if it were broken—and Coco rolling about the floor, writhing in a silent agony; then he smiled thinly.

"You condemn yourself, Captain Reynolds. A harmless citizen of Budapest would have been where the unfortunate Coco now lies: the *savate* is not taught in the schools hereabouts." Reynolds realised with a chill wonder that Hidas had deliberately provoked the incident, indifferent to the consequences to his subordinate. "I know all I want—and I do you the compliment of realising that breaking your bones is just a waste of time. Stalin Street for us, Captain Reynolds, and some gentler forms of persuasion."

Three minutes later they were all inside the lorry that had just drawn up outside the garage. The giant Coco, grey-faced and still breathing stertorously, was stretched his length on one fore-and-aft bench seat, while Colonel Hidas and two of the guards sat on the opposite bench, with Reynolds sitting on the floor between with his back to the cab: the fourth AVO man was in the cab with the driver.

The smash, the grinding crash that flung all the men in the back of the lorry off their seats and catapulted one of the guards on top of Reynolds, came within twenty seconds of starting off, just as they were rounding the first corner. There was no warning, not even a split second in which to prepare themselves, just a squealing of brakes and tearing of metal as the truck's tires slithered across the hard-packed snow of the street and bumped softly into the opposite curb.

They were still sprawled anyhow across the floor of the truck, still recovering their wits to make the first move, when the doors of the back of the truck were flung open, the light switched off, and the suddenly darkened interior illuminated a moment afterward by the white, blinding light from a pair of powerful torches. The long slender snouts of two gun barrels, gleaming evilly, slid forward into the narrow arcs of the torch beams, and a deep, hoarse-sounding voice ordered them to clasp their hands above their heads. Then, at some low murmur from the road outside, the two torches and guns moved further apart and a man—Reynolds recognised him as the fourth AVO man—came stumbling into the pool of light, followed almost at once by an unconscious form that was bundled unceremoniously on the floor. Then the doors slammed shut, the truck engine revved furiously in reverse, there came a thin, screeching sound as if the truck were freeing itself from some metal obstruction, and a moment later they were on their way again. The whole operation hadn't taken twenty seconds from first to last, and Reynolds mentally saluted the high-speed, smoothly functioning efficiency of a group of experts.

The identity of the experts he did not for a moment doubt, but even so it was not until he had caught a momentary glimpse of the hand that held one of the guns—a gnarled, scarred hand with a curious bluish-purple mark in the middle, a hand that no sooner appeared than it was snatched back again—that the relief of certainty swept over him like a warm and releasing wave: only then, and not till then, could he appreciate how tense and how keyed up he had been, how steeled his every nerve and thought against the nameless horrors that awaited all the luckless beings who were ever interrogated in the cellars of Stalin Street.

The agony in his side and mouth was back again, redoubled in its acuteness now that the dread of the future was removed and he could think again of the present. Waves of nausea swept over him; he could feel the blood pounding in his dizzily swimming head, and he knew that it required only the slightest deliberate relaxation of his will for the grateful oblivion of unconsciousness to sweep over him. But there would come a time for that later.

Grey-faced with the pain, setting his teeth against the groan that came to his mouth, he pushed away the guard who was leaning against and on top of him, bent over, and took his carbine away: this he placed on the bench by his left and sent sliding down to the rear where an unseen hand drew it into the darkness. Another two carbines went the same way, followed by Hidas' pistol: his own gun Reynolds retrieved from Hidas' tunic, thrust it under his coat, and sat up on the bench opposite Coco.

After a few minutes they heard the truck engine slowing down and felt the truck itself braking to a stop. The guns at the back of the truck poked forward a few suggestive inches, and a hoarse voice warned them to keep absolute silence. Reynolds took out his automatic, screwed on the silencer, and pressed the barrel none too softly into the base of Hidas' neck: the faint, appreciative murmur from the rear reached him just as the truck ground to a halt.

The halt was brief. A question from some unknown person, a quick, harsh authoritative reply—tones, only, could be distinguished inside the back of the lorry; the words were quite undistinguishable—an acknowledgment, the hiss of releasing air brakes, and they were on their way once more, Reynolds leaning back in his seat with a long, soundless sigh and pocketing his gun again. The mark gouged out on Hidas' neck by his silencer was deep and red and angry: it had been a tense, nerve-racking moment.

Once again they came to a halt, and once again Reynolds' automatic found the selfsame spot in the AVO officer's neck, but the halt was this time, if anything, even briefer. After that there were no more stops, and from the gently undulating and curving nature of the road, together with the lack of exhaust echo beating back from encompassing walls and buildings, Reynolds realised that they were clear of Budapest's suburbs and running into the country. He forced himself to stay awake, to cling grimly to the thread of consciousness, and he did so by constantly shifting his gaze round the interior of the truck. His eyes were now accustomed to the gloom in the rear end and in the faint backwash of light he could just make out two figures with hats pulled low over their eyes, sitting hunched and motionless over guns and torches that never wavered: there was something almost inhuman in the intensity of that vigilance, in its unflagging concentration, and Reynolds began to have his first inkling of how Jansci and his friends had come to survive so long. Now and again Reynolds' eyes would come back to the men at his feet, and he could see the uncomprehending, fearful play of expression on their faces, the trembling of their arms as their shoulder muscles ached from the long strain of holding their arms clasped above their heads: only Hidas remained immobile throughout, his features composed and empty of all expression. For all the man's cold-blooded indifference to the suffering of others, Reynolds had to admit to himself that there was something admirable about him: with no hint of either fear or self-pity he accepted defeat with the same detached remoteness that characterised him in the moment of victory.

One of the men at the back of the truck flashed a light at his wrist—a watch, probably, though Reynolds couldn't see it at that distance—then spoke. A deep, gruff voice, muffled by the swathes of the handkerchief, it could have belonged to anyone.

"Boots and shoes off, all of you, but one at a time. Place them on the right-hand bench." For a moment it seemed that Colonel Hidas was going to refuse—and there was no doubt that the man had sufficient courage to do just that—but the urgent jab from Reynolds' gun made all too apparent the uselessness of any resistance. Even Coco, now sufficiently recovered to lean on an elbow and help himself, had his boots off within thirty seconds.

"Excellent," came the dry voice from the rear. "Now the overcoats, gentlemen, and that will be all." A pause. "Thank you. Now listen carefully. We are at present driving along a very quiet and deserted road and will stop soon at a tiny hut by the wayside. The nearest house in any direction—and I'm not telling you which direction—is over three miles away. If you try to find it tonight in the darkness, in your stockinged feet, you will probably be frozen before you find it—and you will almost certainly have to have both feet amputated: that is not a melodramatic threat, but a warning. If you want to find out the hard way, do so by all means.

"On the other hand," the voice went on, "the hut is dry, windproof, and is provided with a good stock of wood. You can keep warm, and a passing farmer's cart or truck will doubtless come your way in the morning."

"Why are you doing all this?" Hidas' voice was quiet, almost bored.

"Leaving you in the middle of nowhere, you mean—or just sparing your worthless lives?"

"Both."

"You should guess easily enough. No one knows we have an AVO truck, and provided you're not let loose near a telephone box, no one will know until we reach the Austrian frontier—and this truck in itself should grant us a safe passport all the way. As to your lives, the question is natural enough from you: those who live by the sword must expect to die by it. But we are no murderers."

Almost as the man behind the torch finished speaking the truck drew up. A few seconds passed in complete silence, then the crunch of feet in the snow was heard and the rear doors were flung wide. Reynolds caught a glimpse of two figures standing in the road, outlined against the snow-covered walls of a tiny hut just behind them, then at a gruff order Hidas and his men filed out, one of them helping a still crippled Coco. Reynolds heard a faint click as the inspection hatch behind the driver's cab was opened, but the face of the man peering through was only a grey blur in the gloom. He looked out again through the rear of the truck, saw the last of the AVO men being bundled into the hut and the door shut behind them, again heard a click, this time as the hatch was closed, and almost at once three figures piled into the back of the truck, the doors slammed, and the truck was under way again.

The light clicked on, fumbling hands were busily undoing handkerchiefs that concealed their faces, then Reynolds heard a girl's gasp of horror—understandable enough, Reynolds thought wryly, if his face looked anything like it felt—but it was the Count who spoke first.

"You would appear to have fallen under a bus, Mr. Reynolds. Either that or spent an entertaining half hour with our good friend Coco."

"You know him?" Reynolds' voice was hoarse and indistinct.

"Everybody in the AVO knows him—and half of Budapest, to their cost. Makes friends wherever he goes. What happened to our vast friend, incidentally? He did not seem to be in his usual high spirits?"

"I hit him."

"You hit him!" The Count raised an eyebrow—a gesture equivalent to blank astonishment in any other man. "Even to lay a finger on Coco is itself a feat, but to render him *hors de combat*——"

"Oh, will you stop talking!" Julia's voice held a mixture of exasperation and distress. "Look at his face! We must do something."

"It isn't pretty," the Count admitted. He reached for his hip flask. "The universal specific."

"Tell Imre to stop." It was Jansci speaking, his voice deep and low and authoritative. He looked closely at Reynolds, who was coughing and spluttering as the fiery liquid burnt his mouth and throat, and screwing his eyes tight with every cough. "You are badly hurt, Mr. Reynolds. Where?"

Reynolds told him, and the Count swore. "My apologies, my boy. I should have realised. That damned Coco . . . Come, some more *barack*. It hurts, but it helps."

The truck stopped; Jansci jumped out and returned a minute later with one of the AVO's overcoats packed with snow.

"Woman's work, my dear." He handed Julia the coat and a handkerchief. "See if you can't make our friend look a bit more presentable."

She took the handkerchief from Jansci and turned toward Reynolds. Her touch was as gentle as her face was concerned, but even so the freezing snow stung cruelly at the open cuts on cheek and lips as she washed the matted blood away, and Reynolds winced in spite of himself. The Count cleared his throat.

"Perhaps you should try the more direct method, Julia," he suggested. "Like when the policemen were watching you tonight in the Margit Sziget. For almost three minutes, Mr. Reynolds, she told us——"

"A lying minx." Reynolds tried to smile, but it hurt too much. "Thirty seconds, and in self-defence only . . ." He looked at Jansci. "What happened tonight? What went wrong?"

"You may well ask," Jansci said quietly. "What went wrong? Everything, my boy, just everything. Blunders everywhere, by everyone—by you, by us, by the AVO. The first mistake was ours. You know that the house was being watched and that we had assumed that the watchers were just common informers. A bad mistake on my part— they were nothing of the sort. They were AVO, and the Count here recognised the two men Sandor had caught as soon as he came off duty tonight and came to the house. But by that time Julia had gone to meet you, we couldn't get word to you by her, and later we decided not to bother anyway: the Count knows the ways of the AVO as well as any man and was certain that if they were going to move in on us they wouldn't do it until the early hours of the morning. . . . That's how they invariably work. We were going to leave in the middle of the night."

"So the man who had followed Julia to the White Angel had probably trailed her from the house?"

"Yes. An efficient job of disposal on your part, by the way, but not more than I have come to expect. . . . But the worst mistake of the night had come earlier, when you were talking to Dr. Jennings."

"When I was—— I don't understand."

"It was as much my fault as his," the Count said heavily. "I knew— I should have warned him."

"What are you talking about?" Reynolds demanded.

"This." Jansci looked down on his hands, then raised his eyes slowly. "Did you look for microphones in his room?"

"Yes, I did. It was behind the ventilation grille."

"And the bathroom?"

"Nothing there."

"There was, I'm afraid. Built into the shower. The Count says there's one in the shower in every bathroom in the Three Crowns. None of the showers works: you should have tried it."

"In the shower!" Oblivious of the shooting pain in his

119

back, Reynolds jerked upright, brushing the startled girl to one side. "A microphone! Oh, my God!"

"Exactly," Jansci said heavily.

"Then every word, everything I said to the professor ——" Reynolds broke off and leaned back against the side of the truck, overcome for the moment by the enormity of the implications, the surely fatal blunder he had made. No wonder Hidas had known who he was and why he was there. Hidas knew everything now. As far as any hope that now remained of rescuing the professor was concerned, he might as well have remained in London. He had suspected as much, had almost known as much from what Hidas had said to him in Jansci's garage, but the confirmation that Hidas knew, why he knew, and how he came to have proof seemed to set the final seal of inevitability and defeat on everything.

"It is a bitter blow," Jansci said gently.

"You did all you could," Julia murmured. She brought his head forward to be sponged again, and he made no resistance. "You are not to blame yourself."

A minute passed in silence, while the truck bumped and jounced along the snow-rutted road. The pain in Reynolds' side and head was lessening now, dulling down to a nagging, throbbing ache, and he was beginning to think clearly for the first time since Coco had hit him.

"The security guard will have been clamped on Jennings—he may already be on his way back to Russia," he said to Jansci. "I spoke to Jennings of Brian, so the word will have already gone to Stettin to try to stop him. The game is lost." He stopped, probed two loose teeth in his lower jaw with an exploring tongue. "The game is lost, but otherwise I don't think any great harm has been done. I didn't mention the name—or the activities—of any person in your house, although I did give the professor the address. Not that that makes them any the wiser—they knew anyway. But so far as you people, personally, are concerned, the AVO don't know you exist. A couple of points trouble me."

"Yes?"

"Yes. First, why, if they were listening in the hotel, didn't they nail me there and then?"

"Simple. Almost every microphone in the place is wired to tape recorders." The Count grinned. "I'd have given a fortune to see their faces when they ran off that reel."

"Why didn't you phone to stop me? You must have known from what Julia said that the AVO would come round to your place right away."

"They did—almost. We got out only ten minutes before them. And we did phone you—but there was no reply."

"I had left my room early." Reynolds remembered the ringing of the telephone bell as he had reached the bottom of the fire escape. "You could still have stopped me on the street."

"We could." It was Jansci speaking. "You'd better tell him, Count."

"Very well." For a moment the Count looked almost uncomfortable—so unexpected an expression to find on his face that Reynolds for a moment doubted he had read it correctly. But he had.

"You met my friend Colonel Hidas tonight," the Count began obliquely. "Second-in-command of the AVO, a dangerous and clever man—no more dangerous and clever man in all Budapest. A dedicated man, Mr. Reynolds, who has achieved more—and more remarkable—success than any police officer in Hungary. I said he was clever—he's more; he's brilliant, an ingenious, resourceful man, entirely without emotion, who never gives up. A man, obviously, for whom I have the highest respect—you will observe that I was at considerable pains not to let him see me tonight, even though I was disguised. And that Jansci was at even more pains to direct his line of thinking toward the Austrian border, where, I assure you, we have no intention of going."

"Get to the point," Reynolds said impatiently.

"I have arrived. For several years past our activities have been far the greatest thorn in his flesh, and lately I have had just the tiniest suspicion that Hidas was taking just a little too much interest in me." He waved a deprecatory hand. "Of course we officers at the AVO expect ourselves to be checked and shadowed from time to time, but perhaps I have become just a trifle hypersensitive about these things. I thought perhaps that my trips to police blocks had not been so unobserved as I would have wished and that Hidas had deliberately planted you on me to break us up." He smiled slightly, ignoring the astonishment on the faces of both Reynolds and Julia. "We survive by never taking a chance, Mr. Reynolds—it was really too opportune, a Western spy so ready to hand. We thought, as I say, you were a plant. The fact that you knew—or said Colonel Mackintosh knew—that Jennings was in Budapest while we didn't was another point against you: all the questions you asked Julia tonight about us and our organisation might have been friendly interest—but it might equally well have been from a more sinister reason, and the policemen might have left you alone because they knew who you were, not because of your—ah—activities in the watchman's box."

"You never told any of this to me!" Julia's face was flushed, the blue eyes cold and angry.

"We seek," said the Count gallantly, "to shelter you from the harsher realities of this life. . . . Then, Mr. Reynolds, when there was no reply to our telephone call, we suspected you might be elsewhere—the Andrassy Ut, for example. We weren't sure, not by a long way, but suspicious enough to take no chances. So we let you walk into the spider's web—I regret to say that we actually saw you walking. We weren't a hundred yards away, lying low in the car—not mine, I'm glad to say—which Imre later crashed into the truck." He looked regretfully at Reynolds' face. "We did not expect you to get the full treatment right away."

"Just so long as you don't expect me to go through it all again." Reynolds pulled at a loose tooth, winced as it came out, and threw it on the floor. "I trust you're satisfied now."

"Is that all you've got to say?" Julia demanded. Her eyes, hostile as they looked at both the Count and Jansci, softened as she looked at the battered mouth. "After all that's been done to you?"

"What do you expect me to do?" Reynolds asked mildly. "Try to knock out a few of the Count's teeth? I'd have done the same in his position."

"Professional understanding, my dear," Jansci murmured. "Nevertheless we are extremely sorry for what has happened. And the next move, Mr. Reynolds—now that that tape recording will have started off the biggest man hunt for months? The Austrian frontier, I take it, with all speed."

"The Austrian frontier, yes. With all speed—I don't know." Reynolds looked at the two men sitting there, thought of their fantastic histories as Julia had recounted them, and knew there was only one possible answer to

Jansci's question. He gave another tentative wrench, sighed with relief as a second tooth came clear, and looked at Jansci. "It all depends how long I take to find Professor Jennings."

Ten seconds, twenty, half a minute passed, and the only sounds were the whirr of the snow tires on the road, the low murmur from the cab of Sandor's and Imre's voices above the steady roar of the engine, then the girl reached out and turned Reynolds' face toward her, her fingertips gentle against the cut and swollen face.

"You're mad." She stared at him, her eyes empty of belief. "You must be mad."

"Beyond all question." The Count unstopped his flask, gulped, and replaced the stopper. "He has been through a great deal tonight."

"Insanity," Jansci agreed. He gazed down at his scarred hands, and his voice was very soft. "There is no disease half so contagious."

"And very sudden in its onset." The Count gazed down sadly at his hip flask. "The universal specific, but this time I left it too late."

For a long moment the girl stared at the three men, her face a study of bewildered incomprehension, then understanding came and with it some certainty of foreknowledge, some evil vision that drained all the colour from her cheeks, darkened the cornflower blue of her eyes, and left them filled with tears. She made no protest, no slightest gesture of dissent—it was as if the same foreknowledge had warned her of the uselessness of dissent—and as the first tears brimmed over the edge of her eyes, she turned away so that they could not see her face.

Reynolds reached out a hand to comfort her, hesitated, caught Jansci's troubled eye and the slow shake of the white head, nodded, and withdrew his hand.

He drew out a pack of cigarettes, placed one between his smashed lips, and lit it. It tasted like burnt paper.

7

IT was still dark when Reynolds awoke, but the first grey tinges of dawn were beginning to steal through the tiny window facing the east. Reynolds had known that the room had a window, but until then he hadn't known where it was: when they had arrived in the abandoned farmhouse last night—or early that morning, it had been almost two o'clock—after a mile-long, freezing trudge in the snow, Jansci had forbidden lights in all rooms without shutters, and Reynolds' had been in one of these.

He could see the whole of the room from where he lay without even moving his head. It wasn't difficult—the entire floor area was no more than twice that of the bed, and the bed only a narrow canvas cot. A chair, a washbasin, and a mildewed mirror, and the furnishings of the room were complete: there would have been no room for more.

The light was beginning to filter in more strongly now through the single pane of glass above the washbasin, and Reynolds could see in the distance, perhaps a quarter of a mile away, the heavily snow-weighted branches of pine trees: the trees must have been well downhill, the feathery white tops appeared to be almost on level with his eyes. The air was so clear that he could make out every tiny detail of the branches. The greying sky was changing to a very pale blue hue, empty of all snow and clouds: the first cloudless sky—indeed the first patch of blue sky—he had seen at all since he had come to Hungary: perhaps it was a good omen, he needed all the good omens he could get. The wind had dropped, not the slightest zephyr stirring across the great plains, and the silence everywhere was profound with that frozen stillness that comes only with a sub-zero dawn and the snow lying deeply across the land.

The silence was interrupted—one could not say ended, for afterwards it seemed even deeper than before—by a thin, whiplike crack, like a distant rifle shot, and now that Reynolds searched back through his memory he knew that was what had waked him in the first place. He waited, listening, then after a minute or so he heard it again, perhaps closer this time. After even a shorter interval, he heard it a third time and decided to investigate. He flung back the bedclothes and swung his legs out of bed.

Only seconds afterwards he decided not to investigate and that flinging his legs over the side of the cot without due forethought was not to be recommended; with the sudden movement his back felt as if somebody had stuck in a giant hook and pulled with vicious force. Gently, carefully, he pulled his legs back into the cot and lay down with a sigh: most of the trouble, he thought, came from the large area of stiffness that extended even up past his shoulder blades, but the sudden jerking of stiffened muscles could be as agonising as any other pain. The noise outside could wait, no one else appeared unduly worried, and even his brief contact with the outer air—all he wore was a pair of borrowed pyjama trousers—had convinced him that a further acquaintance should be postponed as long as possible. There was no heating of any kind and the little room was bitterly cold.

He lay back, staring at the ceiling, and wondered if the Count and Imre had made it safely back to Budapest last night after they had dropped the others. It had been essential that the truck be abandoned in the anonymity of the big city: just to park it in some empty lane near at hand would have invited disaster. As Jansci had said, the hunt would be up for that truck this morning over all western Hungary, and no better place could be found for it than some deserted alley in a large town.

Further, it had been essential that the Count return also. The Count was now as near certain as he could be that no suspicion had fallen on him, and if they were ever to find out where Dr. Jennings had been taken—it was unlikely that the Russians would risk keeping him in a hotel no matter how heavy a guard they mounted—he would have to return to the AVO offices, where he was due on duty anyway after lunch time. There was no other way they could find out. There was always an element of risk in his going there, but then there always had been.

Reynolds did not deceive himself. With the finest help in the world—and with Jansci and the Count he believed that he had just that—the chances of ultimate success were still pretty poor. Forewarned was forearmed, and the Communists—he thought of the tape recorder with a deep chagrin that would long remain with him—had been well and truly forewarned. They could block all the roads; they could stop all traffic in and out of Budapest. They could remove the professor to the security of the most remote and impregnably fortified prison or concentration camp in the country; they might even ship him back to Russia. And, over and above all that, there was the keystone to the whole conjectural edifice, the overriding question of what had happened to young Brian Jennings in Stettin: the

Baltic port, Reynolds was grimly aware, would be combed that day as it had seldom been combed before, and it required only one tiny miscalculation, the slightest relaxation of vigilance by the two agents responsible for the boy's safety—and they had no means of knowing that the alarm call was out, that hundreds of the Polish UB would be searching every hole and corner in the city—for everything to be lost. It was frustrating, maddening, to have to lie there, to wait helplessly while the net closed a thousand miles away.

The fire in his back gradually ceased, the sharp, stabbing pains finally stopping altogether. Not so, however, the whiplike cracks from just outside the window: they were becoming clearer and more frequent with the passing of every minute. Finally Reynolds could restrain his curiosity no longer, and, moreover, a wash was urgently needed—on arrival that night he had just tumbled, exhausted, into bed and had been asleep in a moment. With infinite care he slowly levered his legs over the side of the bed, sat on its edge, pulled on the trousers of his grey suit—now considerably less immaculate than when he had left London three days previously—pushed himself gingerly to his feet, and hirpled across to the tiny window above the washbasin.

An astonishing spectacle met his eyes—not so much the spectacle, perhaps, as its central figure. The man below his window, no more than a youngster really, looked as if he had stepped directly from the stage of some Ruritanian musical comedy: with his high-plumed velvet hat, long, flowing cloak of yellow blanket cloth, and magnificently embroidered high boots fitted with gleaming silver spurs all so sharply limned against and emphasised by the dazzling white background of snow, he was a colourful figure indeed in that drab, grey Communist country, colourful even to the point of the bizarre.

His pastime was no less singular than his appearance. In his gauntleted hand he held the grey-horned stock of a long, thin whip, and even as Reynolds watched he flicked his wrist with casual ease and a cork lying on the snow fifteen feet away jumped ten feet to one side. With the next flick it jumped back to exactly where it had lain before. A dozen times this was repeated, and not once did Reynolds see the whip touch the cork, or go anywhere near the cork; the lash was too fast for his eyes to follow.

The youngster's accuracy was fantastic, his concentration absolute.

Reynolds, too, became absorbed in the performance, so absorbed that he failed to hear the door behind him open softly. But he heard the startled "Oh!" and swung round away from the window, the sudden jerk screwing up his face as the pain knifed sharply across his back.

"I'm sorry." Julia was confused. "I didn't know——"

Reynolds cut her off with a grin.

"Come in. It's all right— I'm quite respectable. Besides, you ought to know that we agents are accustomed to entertaining all sorts of feminine company in our bedrooms." He glanced at the tray she had laid on his bed. "Sustenance for the invalid? Very kind of you."

"More of an invalid than he'll admit." She was dressed in a belted blue woolen dress with white at the wrists and throat, her golden hair had been brushed till it gleamed, and her face and eyes looked as if they had just been washed in the snow. Her fingertips, as they touched the tender swelling on his back, were as fresh and cool as her appearance. He heard the quick indrawn breath.

"We must get a doctor, Mr. Reynolds. Red, blue, purple—every colour you could think of. You can't leave this as it is—it looks terrible." She turned him round gently and looked up at his unshaven face. "You should go back to bed. It hurts badly, doesn't it?"

"Only when I laugh, as the bloke said with the harpoon through his middle." He moved back from the washbasin and nodded through the window. "Who's the circus artist?"

"I don't have to look," she laughed. "I can hear him. That's the Cossack—one of my father's men."

"The Cossack?"

"That's what he calls himself. His real name is Alexander Moritz—he thinks we don't know that, but my father knows everything about him, the same way he knows everything about nearly everybody. He thinks Alexander is a sissy's name, so he calls himself the Cossack. He's only eighteen."

"What's the comic-opera getup for?"

"Insular ignorance," she reproved. "Nothing comic about it. Our Cossack is a genuine *csikós*—a cowboy, you would say, from the *puszta*, the prairie land to the east, round Debrecen, and that's exactly how they dress. Even to the whip. The Cossack represents another side to Jansci's activities that you haven't heard of yet—feeding starving people." Her voice was quiet now. "When winter comes, Mr. Reynolds, many people of Hungary starve. The government takes away far too much meat and potatoes from the farms—they have to meet terribly high surrender quotas—and it's worst of all in the wheat areas, where the government takes all. It was so bad at one time that the people of Budapest were actually sending bread to the country. And Jansci feeds these hungry people. He decides from which government farm the cattle shall be taken and where they'll be taken: the Cossack takes them there. He was across the border only last night."

"Just as simple as that?"

"It is for the Cossack: he has a strange gift for handling cattle. Most of them come from Czechoslovakia—the border is only twenty kilometres from here. The Cossack just chloroforms them or gives them a good drink of bran mash laced with cheap brandy. When he's got them half drunk or half anesthetised, he just walks across the border with them with as little trouble as you or I would cross a street."

"Pity you can't handle humans the same way," Reynolds said drily.

"That's what the Cossack wants—to help Jansci and the Count with people, I mean, not to chloroform them. He will soon." She lost interest in the Cossack, gazed unseeingly out of the window for some moments, then looked up at Reynolds, the remarkable blue eyes grave and still. She said tentatively, "Mr. Reynolds, I——"

Reynolds knew what was coming and hastened to forestall her. It had needed no perspicuity last night to see that her acceptance of their decision not to give up the search for Jennings was a token one and only for the moment: he had been waiting for this, for the inevitable appeal, had known it was in her mind from the moment she had entered the room.

"Try Michael," he suggested. "I find it difficult to be formal and stand on my dignity with my shirt off."

"Michael." She said the name slowly, pronouncing it "Meechail." "Mike?"

"I'll murder you," he threatened.

"Very well. Michael."

"Meechail," he mimicked, and smiled down at her. "You were going to say something?"

For a moment the dark brown eyes and the blue ones met and held mute understanding. The girl knew the answer to her question without ever having to ask it, and the slender shoulders drooped fractionally in defeat as she turned away.

"Nothing." The life had gone out of her voice. "I'll see about a doctor. Jansci says to be down in twenty minutes."

"Good lord, yes!" Reynolds exclaimed. "The broadcast. I'd forgotten all about it."

"That's something anyway." She smiled faintly and closed the door behind her.

Jansci rose slowly to his feet, turned off the radio, and looked down at Reynolds.

"It is bad, you think?"

"It's bad enough." Reynolds stirred in his chair to try to ease his aching back: even the effort of washing, dressing, and coming downstairs had taken more out of him than he cared to admit, and the pain was constant now. "The call word was definitely promised for today."

"Perhaps they have arrived in Sweden and haven't yet been able to get word through to your people?" Jansci suggested.

"I'm afraid not." Reynolds had banked heavily on the call word coming through that morning, and the disappointment ran deep. "Everything was laid on for that: a contact from the consul's office at Hälsingborg is waiting all the time."

"Ah, so ... But if these agents are as good as you said they were, they may have become suspicious and are lying low in Stettin for a day or two. Till—how do you say?—the heat is off."

"What else can we hope for? My God, to think I should have fallen for that mike in the shower," he said bitterly. "What's to be done now?"

"Nothing except possess our souls in patience," Jansci counselled. "Us, that is. For you, bed—and no arguments. I've seen too much sickness not to know a sick man when I see one. The doctor has been sent for. A friend of mine for years," he smiled, seeing the question in Reynolds' face. "We can trust him completely."

The doctor came up to Reynolds' room with Jansci twenty minutes later. A big, burly, red-faced man with a clipped moustache, he had the professionally cheerful voice that invariably made patients suspect the worst, and radiated a magnificent self-confidence—in fact, Reynolds thought drily, he was very much like doctors the world over. Like many doctors also, he was a man of strong opinions and not unduly backward about expressing them: he roundly cursed those damned Communists half a dozen times within the first minute of entering the room.

"How have you managed to survive so long?" Reynolds smiled. "I mean, if you express your opinions——"

"Tchah! Everybody knows what I think of these damned Communists. Daren't touch us quacks, my boy. Indispensable. Especially the good ones." He clamped a stethoscope to his ears. "Not that I'm any damned good. The whole trick lies in making them think you are."

The doctor did himself considerably less than justice. The examination was skilled, thorough, and swift.

"You'll live," he announced. "Probably some internal haemorrhaging, but very slight. Considerable inflammation and really magnificent bruising. A pillowcase, Jansci, if you please. The effectiveness of this remedy," he continued, "is in direct proportion to the pain it inflicts. You'll probably go through the roof, but you'll be better tomorrow." He spooned a liberal amount of a greyish paste on to the pillowcase and spread it evenly. "A form of horse liniment," he explained. "Centuries-old recipe. Use it everywhere. Not only do patients have trust in the doctor that sticks to the good old-fashioned remedies, but it also enables me to dispense with the tedious and laborious necessity of keeping abreast of all the latest developments. Besides, it's just about all these damned Communists have left us."

Reynolds winced as the liniment burned in through his skin, and he could feel the sweat coming to his brow. The doctor seemed pleased.

"What did I tell you? Fit as a fiddle tomorrow! Just swallow a couple of these white tablets, my boy—they'll ease the pain internally—and the blue one. Make you sleep—if you don't, you'll have that poultice off in ten minutes. Quick-acting, I assure you."

They were indeed, and Reynolds' last conscious recollection was of hearing the doctor loudly declaiming against those damned Communists as he went down the stairs. After that he remembered nothing more for almost twelve hours.

When he awoke night had come again, but this time his window had been curtained and a small oil lamp was burning. He awoke quickly and completely, as he had long trained himself to do, without movement or change in his rate of breathing, and his eyes were on Julia's face, a face with an expression he had not seen on it before, for a full second before she was aware he was awake and looking at her. He could see the dull colour touching throat and face as she slowly withdrew from his shoulder the hand that had been shaking him awake, but he twisted his wrist and glanced at his watch, a man who had observed nothing unusual.

"Eight o'clock!" He sat up abruptly in bed, and it was only after he had done so that he remembered the agony that had followed the last precipitate move he had made. The surprise on his face was obvious.

"How does it feel?" she smiled. "Better, isn't it?"

"Better? It's miraculous!" His back felt almost as if it were on fire, but the pain was quite gone. "Eight o'clock!" he repeated incredulously. "I've been asleep for twelve hours?"

"You have indeed. Even your face looks better." Her composure was back again. "The evening meal is ready. Shall I bring it up?"

"I'll be down in a couple of minutes," Reynolds promised.

He was as good as his word. A cheerful wood fire was burning in the small kitchen, and the table, set for four, was over against the fire. Sandor and Jansci greeted him, were pleased to hear of the progress made in his recovery, and introduced him to the Cossack. The Cossack shook hands briefly, nodded, scowled, sat down to his bread soup, and said nothing, not a word throughout the course of the meal; he kept his head lowered all the time so that though Reynolds had an excellent view of his thick, black Magyar hair, brushed straight back from the forehead, it was not until the Cossack rose with his last mouthful and left, with a muttered word to Jansci, that Reynolds caught his first sight of the open, good-looking, boyish face with its ill-concealed expression of truculence. That the expression was meant for him, Reynolds was left in no doubt.

131

Seconds after the door was slammed, they heard the roar of what seemed to be a powerful motorcycle that swept past the house and faded swiftly away in the distance, soon to be lost in silence. Reynolds looked round the others at table.

"Will somebody please tell me what I'm supposed to have done? Your young friend just tried to incinerate me by will power alone."

He looked at Jansci, but Jansci was having trouble in getting his pipe to light. Sandor was staring into the fire, lost apparently in his own thoughts. When the explanation finally came, it came from Julia, her voice edged with an irritation and annoyance so foreign to her that Reynolds glanced at her in surprise.

"Very well, if these two cowards won't tell you, it seems I must. The only thing about you that annoys the Cossack is the fact that you're here at all. You see, he—well, he fancies he's in love with me—*me*, six years older than he is."

"What's six years, after all," Reynolds began judicially, "if you——"

"Oh, do be quiet! Then one night he got hold of the remains of a bottle of *szilvorium* the Count had left lying around and he told me. I was surprised and confused, but he's such a nice boy and I was wanting to be kind, so like a fool I said something about waiting until he was grown up. He was furious . . ."

Reynolds wrinkled his brow. "What has all this——"

"Don't be so dense! He thinks you are a—well, a rival for my affections!"

"May the best man win," Reynolds said solemnly. Jansci choked on his pipe, Sandor covered his face with one massive hand, and the stony silence from the head of the table made Reynolds think that he himself had better look elsewhere. But the silence stretched out; he felt compelled to look eventually, and when he did so he found neither the anger nor the blushing confusion he had expected, but a composed Julia, chin on hand, regarding him with a thoughtfulness and just possibly the faintest trace of mockery that he found vaguely disquieting. Not for the first time he had to remind himself that underestimating the daughter of such a man as Jansci might be foolish in the extreme.

Finally she rose to clear away the dishes and Reynolds turned to Jansci.

"I take it that was the Cossack we heard departing. Where has he gone?"

"Budapest. He has a rendezvous with the Count on the outskirts of the town."

"What! On a big powerful motorbike you can hear miles away—and in those clothes that can be seen from about the same distance?"

"A small motorbike only—the Cossack removed the silencer some time ago because not enough people could hear him coming. . . . He has the vanity of extreme youth. But the loudness of both machine and clothes is his surest safeguard. He is so conspicuous that no one would ever dream of suspecting him."

"How long?"

"On good roads, he'd be there and back in just over half an hour—we're only about fifteen kilometres from the town. But tonight?" Jansci thought. "Perhaps an hour and a half."

It took in fact two hours—two of the most unforgettable hours Reynolds had ever spent. Jansci talked nearly all the time, and Reynolds listened with the intentness of a man aware that he was being accorded a rare privilege which might never come his way again. The mood of expansiveness, Reynolds divined, came seldom to this man; so much the most remarkable, the most extraordinary man Reynolds had ever met in a chequered and dangerous lifetime that all others, with the possible exception of Jansci's alter ego, the Count, seemed to fade away into insignificance. And for two unbroken hours Julia sat on a cushion by his side: the mischief and laughter that were never long absent from her eyes were gone as if they had never been, and she was grave and unsmiling as Reynolds had imagined she could never be: during these hours her eyes left her father's face hardly at all, and even then, before seeking his face again, only to gaze at the scarred and shattered ruins that were Jansci's hands. It was as if she, too, shared Reynolds' irrational presentiment that this privilege would never come her way again, as if she were seeking to memorise every detail of her father's face and hands so that she would never forget them: and Reynolds, remembering the strange, fey look in her eyes in the truck the previous night, felt queerly, unaccountably cold. It cost him almost physical effort to shake off this abnormal feeling, to dismiss from his mind what he knew could only be the first tentative stirrings of superstitious nonsense.

Jansci spoke of himself not at all, and of his organisation and its method of operation only where necessary: the only concrete fact that Reynolds gathered in the course of the evening was that his H.Q. was not here but in a farmhouse that lay in the low hills between Szombáthely and the Neusiedler See, not far from the Austrian frontier —the only frontier of any interest to the great majority of those escaping to the West. He talked instead of people, hundreds of people whom he and the Count and Sandor had helped to safety, of their hopes and fears and terrors of this world. He talked of peace, of his hope for the world, of his conviction that that peace would ultimately come for the world if only one good man in a thousand worked for it, of the folly of imagining that there was anything else in the world worth working for, not even the ultimate peace, for that could only come from this. He spoke of Communists and non-Communists, and of the distinctions between them that existed only in the tiny minds of men, of the intolerance and the infinite littleness of minds that knew beyond question that all men were inescapably different by virtue of their births and beliefs, their creeds and religions, and that the God who said that every man was the brother of the next was really a pretty poor judge of these things. He spoke of the tragedies of the various creeds that knew beyond doubt that theirs was the only way that was the right way, of the religious sects that usurped the gates of heaven against all comers, of the tragedy of his own Russian people who were perfectly willing to let others do this, for there were no gates anyway.

Jansci was wandering, not arguing, and he drifted from his own people to his youth among them. The transition seemed pointless, inconsequential at first, but Jansci was not an aimless wanderer, almost everything he did or said or thought was concerned with reinforcing and consolidating, both in himself and all his listeners, his almost obsessive faith in the oneness of humanity. When he spoke of his boyhood and young manhood in his own country, it could have been any person, of any creed, remembering with a fond nostalgia the happiest hours of a happy land.

The picture he painted of the Ukraine was one touched perhaps with the sentimentality felt for that which is irrecoverably lost, but nonetheless Reynolds felt it to be a true picture, for the sadly remembered gladness in those tired and gentle eyes could never have arisen from self-deception, however unaware. Jansci did not deny the hardships of the life, the long hours in the fields, the occasional famines, the burning heat of summer, and the bitter cold when the Siberian wind blew across the steppes: but it was essentially a picture of a happy land, a golden land untouched by fear or repression, a picture of far horizons with the golden wheat waving into the blurred and purpling distance, a picture of laughter and singing and dancing, of jingling horse-drawn, fur-collared troika rides under the frozen stars, of a steamboat drifting gently down the Dnieper in the warmth of a summer's night, and the soft music dying away across the water. And it was then, when Jansci was talking wistfully of the nighttime scents of honeysuckle and wheat, of jasmine and new-mown hay drifting across the river, that Julia rose quickly to her feet, murmured something about coffee, and hurried from the room. Reynolds caught only a glimpse of her face as she went, but he saw her eyes were dimmed with tears.

The spell was broken, but somehow a trace of its magic lingered on. Reynolds was under no illusion. For all his apparently aimless generalisations, Jansci had been talking directly at him, trying to undermine beliefs and prejudices, trying to make him see the glaringly tragic contrasts between the happy people whose portrait he had just drawn and the sinister apostles of world revolution, making him question whether so complete reversal lay within the bounds of credulity or even possibility, and it had been no accident, Reynolds thought wryly, that the first part of Jansci's ramblings had been devoted to the intolerance and wilful blindness of humanity at large. Jansci had deliberately intended that Reynolds should see in himself a microcosm of that humanity, and Reynolds was uncomfortably aware that he had not entirely failed. He did not like the unsettling, questioning half doubts that were beginning to trouble him, and pushed them deliberately aside. For all his old friendship with Jansci, Colonel Mackintosh, Reynolds thought grimly, would not have approved of tonight's performance: Colonel Mackintosh did not like to have his agents unsettled, they were to keep their thoughts on the ultimate objective, the job on hand and only the job on hand, and not concern themselves with side issues. Side issues, Reynolds thought incredulously, then pushed the matter from his mind.

Jansci and Sandor were talking now in low friendly tones, and as he listened Reynolds realised that he had misjudged the relationship between these two men. There was nothing of the master and the man, the employer and the employed about it; the atmosphere was too easy, too informal for that, and Jansci listened as carefully and considerately to what Sandor had to say as Sandor did to him. There was a bond between them, Reynolds realised, unseen but no less powerful for that, the bond of a devotion to a common ideal, a devotion which, on Sandor's side, made no distinction between the ideal and the man who was the inspiration of it. Jansci, Reynolds was slowly beginning to discover, had the unconscious gift of inspiring a loyalty which barely stopped this side of idolatry, and even Reynolds himself, uncompromising individualist that nature and training had inescapably made him, could feel the magnetism of its subtle pull.

It was exactly eleven o'clock when the door was flung open and the Cossack strode in, bringing with him a snow-laden flurry of freezing air, dropped a large paper parcel in one corner, and clapped his gauntlets vigorously together. His face and hands were blue with cold, but he affected to be unaware of it, not even seeking the warmth of the fire. Instead he sat at the table, lit a cigarette, rolled it into the corner of his mouth, and let it stay there. Reynolds noted with amusement that though the smoke laced upward and brought tears to one eye, the Cossack made no attempt to remove it: there he had placed it and there it would stay.

His report was brief and to the point. He had met the Count as arranged. Jennings was no longer in his hotel, and already a precautionary rumour was circulating to the effect that he was unwell. The Count did not know where he was—he certainly had not been removed to the AVO H.Q. or any of their known centres in Budapest; he had either been taken directly back to Russia, the Count thought, or to some place of safety outside the city. He would try to find out where, but he had little hope. The Count, the Cossack said, was almost certain that they would not be taking him directly home, he was much too important a figure at the conference; they were probably hiding him in a place of absolute security until they heard from Stettin, and if Brian was still there the Russians would still let Jennings participate in the conference—after letting him hear his son on the phone. But if his son had escaped, then Jennings himself would almost certainly be immediately removed to Russia. Budapest was too near the frontier, and the Russians couldn't afford the incalculable prestige loss of having him escape. . . . And there was one other extremely disquieting bit of information. Imre had disappeared, and the Count could not find him anywhere.

The day that followed, an interminable, wonderful Sunday with an azure, cloudless, windless sky and a dazzling white sun turning the undulating plains and heavy-laden pines into an impossibly lovely Christmas card, was never afterwards clear in Reynolds' mind. It was as if everything that day had been seen through a haze or in a dimly remembered dream: it was almost as if it had been a day lived by someone else, so remote it was, so detached from all reality, whenever he later tried to recall it.

And it wasn't because of his health, the injuries he had received, that all this was so: the doctor had claimed no more than the truth for the effectiveness of his liniment, and though Reynolds' back was still stiff, the pain had gone: his mouth and jaw, too, were healing fast, with only an occasional throb to remind him of where his teeth had been before he had run foul of the giant Coco. He knew himself, and admitted to himself, that it all stemmed from the tearing anxiety in his mind, a savage restlessness that would not let him be still a moment but led him to pacing through the house and over the hard frozen snow outside the house until even the phlegmatic Sandor begged him to take a rest.

Once again that morning they had listened to the BBC seven o'clock broadcast, and once again the message had failed to come through. Brian Jennings had failed to arrive in Sweden, and Reynolds knew that there could be little hope left: but he had been on missions before that had ended in failure, and the failure had never troubled him. What troubled him was Jansci, for he knew that that gentle man, having given his promise of help, meant to carry it out at all costs, even though he must have known, more clearly even than Reynolds himself, just what the cost of trying to rescue the most heavily guarded man in Communist Hungary must almost inevitably be. And then, beyond that again, he knew that his worry wasn't solely on Jansci's behalf—deep as was his admiration and respect for the man, it wasn't even mainly on his behalf—it was on account of his daughter, who worshipped her father and would be brokenhearted and inconsolable at the loss of the last member of her family left alive. And worse still, she would regard him as the sole instrument of her father's death, the barrier between them would forever remain, and Reynolds looking for the hundredth time at the smiling curve of the mouth and the grave, troubled eyes above that belied the smile realised with a slow wonder and a profound sense of shock that that was what he feared above all. They were together much of the day, and Reynolds came to love the slow smile and the outlandish way she pronounced his name, but once when she said "Meechail" and smiled with her eyes as well as her lips, he had been brusque to her, even rude, and he had seen the uncomprehending hurt in her eyes as the smile faded and vanished, and he himself had felt sick to his heart and more confused than he had been all day. . . . Reynolds could only feel profoundly thankful that Colonel Mackintosh could not see him, could not see just then the man whom he regarded as the person most likely to succeed himself someday; but the colonel probably wouldn't have believed it anyway.

The interminable day wheeled slowly to its close, the sun setting over the distant hills to the west burnished the snow-capped pine tops with a brush of flame and gold, and darkness fell swiftly over the land as the stars stood white in the frozen sky. The evening meal came and went almost in complete silence, then Jansci and Reynolds tried on, and altered with Julia's help, the contents of the parcel the Cossack had brought home the previous night—a couple of AVO uniforms. There had been no question of the Count's gambling that these might prove useful when he had sent them; no matter where old Jennings was, they would be essential: they were the "open sesame" to every door in Hungary. And they could only be for Jansci and Reynolds: no uniform Reynolds had ever seen could have stretched across the width of Sandor's shoulders.

The Cossack departed on his motorbicycle shortly after nine o'clock. He departed dressed in his usual flamboyant clothes, a cigarette over each ear and another unlit in the corner of his mouth, and in high good humour; he could not have failed to observe the strain between Reynolds and Julia during the course of the evening and had reason for his cheerful smile.

He should have been back by eleven o'clock, by midnight at the latest. Midnight came and went, but there was no sign of the Cossack. One o'clock struck, half-past one; anxiety had changed to tension and almost to despair when he made his appearance a few moments before two o'clock. He arrived not on his motorbike, but at the wheel of a big grey Opel Kapitan, braked, stopped the engine, and climbed out with the unconcerned indifference of one who was accustomed to this sort of thing to the point of boredom. It was not until later that they discovered that this was the first time in his life that the Cossack had ever driven a car, a fact which wholly accounted for his delay in arrival.

The Cossack brought with him good news, bad news, papers, and instructions. The good news was that the Count had discovered Jennings' whereabouts with almost ridiculous ease—Furmint, the chief of the AVO had told him personally in the course of conversation. The bad news was twofold: the place where the professor had been taken was the notorious Szarháza prison about one hundred kilometres south of Budapest, considered the most impregnable fortress in Hungary and generally reserved for such enemies of the state as were destined never to be seen again. And the Count himself, unfortunately, could not help them: Colonel Hidas himself had personally put him in charge of a loyalty investigation in the town of Gödöllö, where disaffected elements had been giving trouble for some time. Also on the debit account was the fact that Imre was still missing: the Count feared that his nerve had gone altogether and that he had run out on them.

The Count, the Cossack said, regretted that he could provide them with practically no details at all of the Szarháza, as he himself had never been there, his sphere of operations being limited to Budapest and northwest Hungary. The internal geography and routine of the prison, the Count had added, were unimportant anyway:

only complete and brazen bluff could hope to serve their purposes. Hence the papers.

The papers were for Jansci and Reynolds, and master-pieces of their kind. Complete AVO identity cards for both, and a document, on the Allam Védelmi Hátoság's own headed, unreproduceable notepaper, signed by Fur-mint and countersigned by a cabinet minister, with the appropriate and correct stamps for each office, authorising the commandant of the Szarháza prison to hand over Professor Harold Jennings to the bearers of the document.

It was the Count's suggestion that, should the rescue of the professor still be on the cards, they stood a fair chance: no higher authority could be produced for the release of a prisoner than the document he had provided; and the idea of anyone willingly penetrating the walls of the dreaded Szarháza was so fantastic as to be beyond sane contempla-tion.

It was the Count's further suggestion that the Cossack and Sandor should accompany them as far as the inn of Koteli, a small village about five miles north of the prison, and wait there by the telephone: that way all members of the organisation could keep in touch with each other. And to complete a magnificent day's work, the Count had provided the essential transport. He had omitted to say where he had obtained it.

Reynolds shook his head in wonder.

"The man's a marvel! Heaven only knows how he managed to do all this in one day—you'd think they'd given him a holiday just to concentrate on our business." He gazed at Jansci, his face carefully empty of expression. "What do you think?"

"We will go in," Jansci said quietly. He was looking at Reynolds, but Reynolds knew he was talking to Julia. "If there is any hope left of good news from Sweden, we will go in. He is an old man, and it is inhuman that he should die so far from his wife and from his homeland. If we did not go in——" He broke off and smiled. "You know what the good Lord—or maybe I would only get the length of St. Peter—do you know what St. Peter would say to me? He'd say, 'Jansci, we have no place for you here. You cannot expect kindness and mercy from us— what kindness and mercy had you in your heart for Harold Jennings?' "

Reynolds looked at him and thought of the man he had revealed himself to be last night, a man to whom compassion in and for his fellow man and a belief in all-embracing supernatural compassion were the keystones of existence, and knew that he lied. He glanced at Julia and saw the smile of understanding on her face, then he saw below the shadowing hand and knew that she too had not been deceived, for her eyes were dark and stricken and numb.

". . . the conference in Paris ends this evening, when an official statement will be issued. It is expected that the Foreign Minister will fly home tonight—I beg your pardon, that should read tomorrow night—and report to the Cabinet. It is not yet known . . ."

The announcer's voice trailed away into silence and died away altogether as the radio switch clicked off, and for a long moment no one looked at anyone else. It was Julia who finally broke the silence, her voice unnaturally calm and matter-of-fact.

"Well, that's it, isn't it? That's the password that's been so long in coming. 'Tonight—tomorrow night.' The boy is free; he's safe in Sweden. You had better go at once."

"Yes." Reynolds rose to his feet. He felt none of the relief, none of the elation that he had expected when the green light had been given them at last, just a numbness, such as he had seen in Julia's eyes that night, and a strange heaviness of heart. "If we know, the Communists are bound to know by this time also; he may be leaving for Russia at any hour. We have no time to waste."

"Indeed we haven't." Jansci pulled on his greatcoat—like Reynolds, he was already dressed in his borrowed uniform—and pulled his military gauntlets on. "Please don't worry about us, my dear. Just be at our H.Q. twenty-four hours from now—and don't go through Budapest." He kissed her and went out into the dark bitter morning. Reynolds hesitated, half turned towards her, saw her avert her head and stare into the fire, and left without a word. As he climbed into the back seat of the Opel, he caught a glimpse of the Cossack's face following him into the car; he was beaming from ear to ear.

Three hours later, under a dark and lowering sky heavy with its burden of unshed snow, Sandor and the Cossack were dropped at the roadside not far from the Koteli Inn.

The journey had been completely uneventful, and although they had been prepared for roadblocks, there had been none. The Communists were very sure of themselves; they had no reason to be anything else.

Ten minutes later the great grey forbidding mass of the Szarháza came into sight, an old, impregnably walled building surrounded now by three concentric rings of barbed wire with ploughed earth between, the wire no doubt electrified and the earth heavily sown with fragmentation mines. The inner and outer rings were dotted with manned machine-gun towers raised high on wooden stilts, and, gazing at it for the first time, Reynolds felt the first touch of fear, the realisation of the madness of what they were doing.

Jansci might well have divined his feelings, for he made no comment, increased speed over the last half mile, and skidded to a stop outside the great arched gateway. One of the guards came rushing forward, gun in hand, demanding to know their identity and see their papers, but stepped back respectfully as Jansci emerged in his AVO uniform, froze him with a single contemptuous glance, and demanded to see the commandant. It spoke well for the terror inspired by that uniform even among those who had no reasonable cause to fear it that Jansci and Reynolds were inside the commandant's office in five minutes' time. The commandant was the last kind of person Reynolds would have expected to see in that position. He was a tall, slightly stooped man in a well-cut dark suit, with a high-domed, thin, intellectual face. He wore a pince-nez, had lean capable hands, and looked to Reynolds more like an outstanding surgeon or scientist. In point of fact he was both, and reckoned the greatest expert on psychological and physiological breakdown procedures outside the Soviet Union.

He had no suspicions as to their genuineness, Reynolds could see. He offered them a drink, smiled when they refused it, gestured them to a seat, and took the release paper that Jansci handed him.

"Hm! No doubt about the validity of this document, is there, gentlemen?" "Gentlemen," Reynolds noted. A man had to be very sure of himself before he used that word in place of the ubiquitous "comrade." "I have been expecting this from my good friend Furmint. After all, the conference opens today, does it not? We cannot afford to have

Professor Jennings absent. The brightest jewel in our crown, if one may use a somewhat—ah—outmoded expression. You have your own personal papers, gentlemen?"

"Naturally." Jansci produced his, Reynolds did the same, and the commandant nodded, apparently satisfied. He looked at Jansci, then nodded at his phone.

"You know of course that I have a direct line into the Andrassy Ut. I can take no chances with a prisoner of Jennings—ah—magnitude. You will not be offended if I phone for confirmation of this release—and of your identity papers?"

Reynolds felt his heart miss a beat, felt the skin on his face tighten till it seemed like waxed paper. God, how could they possibly have overlooked so obvious a precaution? Their pistols—there was only the one chance, their pistols, the commandant as hostage . . . His hand was actually beginning to move when Jansci spoke, his voice magnificent in its assured confidence, his face unclouded by the slightest trace of worry.

"But of course, Commandant! A prisoner of Jennings' importance? We should have expected nothing else."

"In that case, there is no need." The commandant smiled, pushed the papers across the desk, and Reynolds could feel every stiffened muscle in his body relax as relief poured over him, flooded him like a great wave. He was beginning to realise, just vaguely realise, what manner of man Jansci really was; in comparison, he himself had not yet started to learn.

The commandant reached for a sheet of paper, scribbled on it, and stamped it with an official seal. He rang a bell, handed it to a warder, and dismissed the man with a wave of his hand.

"Three minutes, gentlemen, no more. He is not far from here."

But the commandant overestimated. It was not three minutes, it was less than thirty seconds before the door opened, and it opened to admit not Jennings but half a dozen armed swift-moving guards who had Jansci and Reynolds pinned helplessly to their seats before they had recovered from their state of lulled security and could properly begin to realise what was happening. The commandant shook his head and smiled sadly.

"Forgive me, gentlemen. A subterfuge, I fear—

unpleasant as are all subterfuges, but essential. That document I signed was not for the professor's release but your arrest." He took off his pince-nez, polished them, and sighed. "Captain Reynolds, you are an uncommonly persistent young man."

8

REYNOLDS, in those first few moments of shock, was conscious of nothing but the entire absence of all emotion, of all feeling, as if the touch of the metal fetters on his wrists and ankles had somehow deprived him of all capacity to react. But then came the first slow wave of numbed disbelief, then the shocked disbelief and chagrin that this should have happened to him again, then the bitter, intolerable realisation that they had been effortlessly and absolutely trapped, that the commandant had been toying with them and had deceived them completely, that they were prisoners now within the dreaded Szarházan, and that if they ever emerged they would do so only as unrecognisable zombies, as the broken, empty husks of the men they had once been.

He looked across at Jansci to see how the older man was taking his crushing blow, the final defeat of all their plans, the virtual sentence of death on themselves, to see what his reaction was. As far as he could judge, Jansci wasn't reacting at all. His face was quiet and he was looking at the commandant with a thoughtful, measuring gaze—a gaze, Reynolds thought, curiously like the one with which the commandant was regarding Jansci.

As the last metal shackle clipped home around a chair leg, the leader of the guards looked questioningly at the commandant. The latter waved a hand in dismissal.

"They are secure?"

"Completely."

"Very well, then. You may go."

The guard hesitated. "They are dangerous men——"

"I am aware of that," the commandant said patiently. "Why else do you think I deemed it necessary to summon so many to secure them? But they are shackled to chairs that are bolted to the floor. It is unlikely that they will merely evaporate."

He waited until the door had closed, steepled his thin fingers, and went on in his quiet, precise voice.

"This, gentlemen, is the moment, if ever there was a moment, for gloating: a self-confessed British spy—that recording, Mr. Reynolds, will create an international sensation in the People's Court—and the redoubtable leader of the best organised escape group and anti-Communist ring in Hungary, both in one fell swoop. We shall, however, dispense with the gloating: it is useless and time-wasting, a fit pastime only for morons and imbeciles." He smiled faintly. "Speaking of such, it is, incidentally, a pleasure to deal with intelligent men who accept the inevitable and who are sufficiently realistic to dispense with the customary breast-beating lamentations, denials, and outraged expostulations of innocence.

"Nor do theatricalism, prolonged climaxes, the creation of suspense or unnecessary secrecy interest me," he continued. "Time is the most valuable gift we have and its waste an unforgiveable crime. . . . Your first thought, naturally—Mr. Reynolds, be so good as to follow your friend's example and refrain from doing yourself an unnecessary injury in testing these shackles—your first thought, I say, is how has it come about that you find yourself in this melancholy position? There is no reason why you should not know, and at once." He looked at Jansci. "I regret to inform you that your brilliantly gifted and quite incredibly courageous friend who has been masquerading so long and with such fantastic success as a major in the Allam Védelmi Hátoság has finally betrayed you."

There was a long moment's silence. Reynolds looked expressionlessly at the commandant, then at Jansci. Jansci's face was quite composed.

"That is always possible." He paused. "Inadvertently, of course. Completely so."

"It was," the commandant nodded. "Colonel Josef Hidas, whose acquaintance Captain Reynolds here has already made, has had a feeling—he could call it no more than that, it was not even a suspicion—about Major Howarth for some little time." It was the first time Reynolds heard the name by which the Count was known in the AVO. "Yesterday the feeling became suspicion and certainty, and he and my good friend Furmint prepared a trap baited with the name of this prison and convenient access to Furmint's room for a length of time sufficient to secure certain documents and stamps—these now on the table before me. For all his undoubted genius, your friend walked into the trap. We are all human."

"He is dead?"

"Alive, in the best of health and, as yet, in blissful ignorance of what is known. He was dispatched on a wild-goose chase to keep him out of the way during the course of today: I believe that Colonel Hidas wishes to make the arrest personally. I expect him here this morning—later in the day. Howarth will be seized, given a midnight court-martial at the Andrassy Ut, and executed —but not, I fear, summarily."

"Of course." Jansci nodded heavily. "With every AVO officer and man in the city present he will die only a little at a time, so that no one else will be tempted to emulate him. The fools, the blind, imbecilic fools! Do they not know that there can never be another?"

"I'm afraid I agree with you. But it is no direct concern of mine. Your name, my friend?"

"Jansci will serve."

"For the moment." He removed his pince-nez and tapped them thoughtfully on the table. "Tell me, Jansci, what do you know of us members of the Political Police— of our composition, I mean?"

"You tell me. It is obvious that you wish to."

"Yes, I'll tell you, though I think you must already know. Of our members, all but a negligible fraction are composed of power-seekers, morons who find our service intellectually undemanding, the inevitable sadists whose very nature bans them from all normal civilian employment, the long-time professionals—the very people who dragged screaming citizens from their beds in the service of the Gestapo are still doing precisely the same thing for us—and those with a corroding grievance against society. Of the last category, Colonel Hidas, a Jew whose people have suffered in Central Europe agonies beyond all imagining, is the prime example in the AVO today. There are also, of course, those who believe in communism, a tiny minority only, but nevertheless certainly the most feared and dangerous of all inasmuch as they are automats pervaded by the whole idea of the state, with their own moral judgments either in a state of permanent suspension or completely atrophied. Furmint is one such. So, also, strangely enough, is Hidas."

"You must be terribly sure of yourself." Reynolds was speaking for the first time, slowly.

"He is the commandant of the Szarháza prison." Jansci's words were answer enough. "Why do you tell us this? Did you not say waste of time was abhorrent to you?"

"It still, is, I assure you. Let me continue. When it comes to the delicate question of gaining another's confidence, all the various categories in the list I have given you have one thing in common. With the exception of Hidas, they are all victims of the *idée fixe,* of the hidebound conservatism—and somewhat biased dogmatism— of their unshakeable convictions that the way to a man's heart——"

"Spare us the fancy phrases," Reynolds growled. "What you mean is, if they want the truth from a man they batter it out of him."

"Crude, but admirably brief," the commandant murmured. "A valuable lesson in time saving. To continue in the same curt fashion, I have been entrusted with the task of gaining *your* confidence, gentlemen: to be precise, a confession from Captain Reynolds and, from Jansci, his true name and the extent and *modus operandi* of his organisation. You know yourselves the almost invariable methods as practised by the—ah—colleagues I have mentioned? The whitewashed walls, the brilliant lights, the endless, repetitive, trip-hammering questions, all judiciously interspersed with kidney beatings, teeth and nail extraction, thumbscrews, and all the other revolting appurtenances and techniques of the medieval torture chamber."

"Revolting?" Jansci murmured.

"To me, yes. As an ex-professor of neural surgery in Budapest's university and leading hospitals, the whole medieval conception of interrogation is intensely distasteful. To be honest, interrogation of any kind is distasteful, but I have found in this prison unsurpassed opportunities for observation of nervous disorders and for probing more deeply than ever before possible into the intensely complicated workings of the human nervous system. For the moment I may be reviled: future generations may differ in their appraisal . . . I am not the only medical man in charge of prisons or prison camps, I assure you. We are

147

extremely useful to the authorities: they are no less so to us."

He paused, then smiled, almost diffidently.

"Forgive me, gentlemen. My enthusiasm for my work at times quite carries me away. To the point. You have information to give, and it will not be extracted by medieval methods. From Colonel Hidas I have already learned that Captain Reynolds reacts violently to suffering and is likely to prove difficult to a degree. As for you"—he looked slowly at Jansci—"I do not think I have ever seen in any human face the shadows of so many sufferings; suffering for you can now itself be only a shadow. I have no wish to flatter when I say that I cannot conceive of a physical torture which could even begin to break you."

He sat back, lit a long, thin cigarette, and looked at them speculatively. After the lapse of over two minutes he leaned forward again.

"Well, gentlemen, shall I call a stenographer?"

"Whatever you wish," Jansci said courteously. "But it would grieve us to think of wasting any more of your time than we have already done."

"I expected no other answer." He pressed a switch, talked rapidly into a boxed microphone, then leaned back. "You will, of course, have heard of Pavlov, the Russian medical psychologist?"

"The patron saint of the AVO, I believe," Jansci murmured.

"Alas, there are no saints in our Marxist philosophy— one to which, I regret to say, Pavlov did not subscribe. But you are right insofar as your meaning goes. A bungler, a crude pioneer in many ways, but nevertheless one to whom the more advanced of us—ah—interrogators owe a considerable debt and——"

"We know all about Pavlov and his dogs and his conditioning and breakdown processes," Reynolds said roughly. "This is the Szarháza prison, not the University of Budapest. Spare us the lecture on the history of brainwashing."

For the first time the commandant's studied calm cracked, a flush touched the high cheekbones, but he was immediately under control again. "You are right, of course, Captain Reynolds. One requires a certain, shall we say, philosophical detachment to appreciate—but there I go again. I merely wished to say that with the combination of the very advanced developments we have made of Pavlov's physiological techniques and certain—ah—psychological processes that will become apparent to you in the course of time, we can achieve quite incredible results." There was something about the man's detached enthusiasm that was chilling, frightening. "We can break any human being who ever lived—and break him so that never a scar shows. With the exception of the incurably insane, who are already broken, *there are no exceptions*. Your stiff-upper-lipped Englishman of fiction—and, for all I know, fact—will break eventually like everyone else; the efforts of the Americans to train their serviceman to resist what the Western world so crudely calls brainwashing—let us call it rather a reintegration of personality—are as pathetic as they are hopeless. We broke Cardinal Mindszenty in eighty-four hours: we can break anyone."

He broke off as three men, white-coated and carrying a flask, cups, and a small metal box, entered the room and waited until they had poured out two cups of what was indubitably coffee.

"My assistants, gentlemen. Excuse the white coats—a crude psychological touch which we find effective with a large majority of our—ah—patients. Coffee, gentlemen. Drink it."

"I'll be damned if I will," Reynolds said coldly.

"You will have to undergo the indignity of nose clips and a forcible tube feed if you don't," the commandant said wearily. "Do not be childish."

Reynolds drank and so did Jansci. It tasted like any other coffee, but perhaps stronger and more bitter.

"Genuine coffee." The commandant smiled. "But it also contains a chemical commonly known as actedron. Do not be deceived by its effects, gentlemen. For the first minutes you will feel yourself stimulated, more determined than ever to resist: but then will come somewhat severe headaches, dizziness, nausea, inability to relax, and a state of some mental confusion—the dose, of course, will be repeated." He looked at an assistant with a syringe in his hands, gestured at it, and went on to explain. "Mescaline—produces a mental state very akin to schizophrenia, and is becoming increasingly popular, I believe, among writers and other artists of the Western world: for their own sakes, I trust, they do not take it with actedron."

149

Reynolds stared at him and had to force himself not to shiver. There was something evil, something abnormally wrong and inhuman about the quiet-talking commandant with the gently humorous professorial talk, all the more evil, all the more inhuman because it was deliberately neither, just the chillingly massive indifference of one whose utter and all-exclusive absorption in an insatiable desire for the furthering of his own particular life's work left no possible room for any mere considerations of humanity . . . The commandant was speaking again.

"Later I shall inject a new substance, my own invention, but so recently discovered that I have not yet named it: Szarházazine, perhaps, gentlemen—or would that be too whimsical? I can assure you that if we had had it some years ago the good cardinal would not have lasted twenty-four hours, much less than eighty-four. The combined effects of the three, after perhaps two doses of each, will be to reduce you to a state of absolute mental exhaustion and collapse. Then the truth will come, inevitably, and we will add what we will to your minds, and that, for you, will also be the truth."

"You tell us all this?" Jansci said slowly.

"Why not? Forewarned in this case is not forearmed; the process is irreversible." The quiet certainty in his voice left no room for any doubt. He waved away the white-coated attendants and pressed a button on his desk. "Come, gentlemen, it is time that you were shown your quarters."

Almost at once the guards were in the room again, releasing legs and arms one at a time from chair arms and legs, then reshackling wrists and ankles together, all with a swift and trained efficiency that precluded all idea of escape, much less escape itself. When Jansci and Reynolds were on their feet, the commandant led the way from the room; two guards walked on either side and a third, with pistol ready, behind each of the two men. The precautions were absolute.

The commandant led the way across the hard-packed snow of the courtyard, through the guarded entrance to a massively walled, window-barred block of buildings, and along a narrow, dim-lit corridor. Halfway along, at the head of a flight of stone steps leading own into the gloom below, he paused at a door, gestured to one of the guards, and turned to the two prisoners.

"A last thought, gentlemen, a last sight to take with you down into the dungeons below while you spend your last few hours on earth as the men you have always known yourselves to be." The key clicked in the lock, and the commandant pushed it open with his foot. "After you, gentlemen."

Hobbled by the shackles, Reynolds and Jansci stumbled into the room, saving themselves from falling by catching at the foot rail of an old-fashioned iron bedstead. A man was lying on the bed, dozing, and Reynolds saw, almost with no sensation of surprise—he had been expecting it from the moment the commandant had stopped outside the door—that it was Dr. Jennings. Haggard and wasted and years older than when Reynolds had seen him three days previously, he had been dozing on a dirty straw mattress; but he was almost instantly awake, and Reynolds could not resist a slow stirring of satisfaction when he saw that, whatever else the old man had lost, it certainly wasn't his intransigence: the fire was back in the faded eyes even as he struggled upright.

"Well, what the devil does this latest intrusion mean?" He spoke English, the only language he knew, but Reynolds could see that the commandant understood. "Haven't you damned ruffians pushed me about enough for a weekend without——" He broke off when he recognised Reynolds for the first time and stared at him. "So the fiends got you too?"

"Inevitably," the commandant said in precise English. He turned to Reynolds. "You came all the way from England to see the professor. You have seen him. Now you can say good-bye. He leaves this afternoon—in three hours' time to be precise, for Russia." He turned to Jennings. "Road conditions are extremely bad—we have arranged for a special coach to be attached to the Pécs train. You will find it comfortable enough."

"Pécs?" Jennings glared at him. "Where the devil is Pécs?"

"One hundred kilometres south of here, my dear Jennings. The Budapest airport is temporarily closed by snow and ice, but the latest word is that the Pécs airport is still open. A special plane for yourself and a—ah—few other special cases is being diverted there."

Jennings ignored him, turned, and stared at Reynolds.

"I understand that my son Brian has arrived in England?"

Reynolds nodded in silence.

"And I'm still here, eh? You've done splendidly, young man, just splendidly. What the devil is going to happen now, God only knows."

"I can't tell you how sorry I am, sir." Reynolds hesitated, then made up his mind. "There's one thing you should know. I have no authority for telling you this, but for this once only to hell with authority. Your wife—your wife's operation was one hundred per cent successful and her recovery is already almost complete."

"What! What's that you're saying?" Jennings had Reynolds by the lapels and, though forty pounds lighter than the younger man, was actually shaking him. "You're lying, I know you're lying! The surgeon said . . ."

"The surgeon said what we told him to say," Reynolds interrupted flatly. "I know it was unforgiveable, but it was essential to bring you home, and every possible lever was to be brought to bear. But it doesn't matter a damn any more, so you might as well know."

"My God, my God!" The reaction Reynolds had expected, especially from a man of the professor's reputation—that of an almost berserk anger over having been duped so long and so cruelly—completely failed to materialise. Instead, he collapsed on his bed as if the weight of his body had grown too much for his old legs to bear and blinked happily through his tears. "This is wonderful, I can't tell you how wonderful . . . And only a few hours ago I *knew* I could never be happy again!"

"Most interesting, all most interesting," the commandant murmured. "And to think that the West has the effrontery to accuse *us* of unhumanity."

"True, true," Jansci murmured. "But at least the West doesn't pump its victims full of actedron and mescaline."

"What? What's that?" Jennings looked up. "Who's been pumped full of——?"

"We have," Jansci interrupted mildly. "We're to be given a fair trial and then shot in the morning, but first comes the modern equivalent of being broken on the wheel."

Jennings stared at Jansci and Reynolds, the incredulity

on his face slowly changing to horror. He rose and looked at the commandant.

"Is this true? What this man says, I mean?"

The commandant shrugged. "He exaggerates, of course, but——"

"So it is true." Jennings' voice was quiet. "Mr. Reynolds, it is as well you told me of my wife: the use of that lever would now be quite superfluous. But it's too late now, I can see that, just as I begin to see many other things—and begin to know the things I shall never see again."

"Your wife." Jansci's words were statement, not question.

"My wife." Jennings nodded. "And my boy."

"You shall see them again," Jansci said quietly. Such was the quiet certainty, the unshakeable conviction in his tone, that the others stared at him, half convinced that he had some knowledge that was denied them, half convinced that he was mad. "I promise you, Dr. Jennings."

The old man stared at him, then the hope slowly faded from his eyes.

"You are kind, my friend. Religious faith is the prop ——"

"In this world," Jansci interrupted. "And soon."

"Take him away," the commandant ordered curtly. "The man goes mad already."

Michael Reynolds was going insane, slowly but inevitably insane, and the most terrible part of it was that he knew he was going insane. But, since the last forced injection shortly after they had been strapped in their chairs in that underground cellar, there had been nothing he could do about the relentless onset of this madness, and the more he fought against it, the more resolutely he struggled to ignore the symptoms, the pains, the agonising stresses that were being set up in mind and body; then the more acutely he became aware of the symptoms, the deeper into his mind dug these fiendish claws, chemical claws, claws that were tearing his mind apart.

He was secured to his high-backed chair hand and foot by a thigh belt and by a waist belt, and he would have given all he ever had or would ever have for the blessed release of throwing off these bonds, of flinging himself to the floor, or against a wall, or of contorting, convulsing his body in every fashion conceivable, of flexing and stretching, flexing and stretching every muscle he had, anything in a desperate attempt to ease that intolerable itch and frightening tension set up by ten thousand jumping, jangling nerve ends all over his body. It was the old Chinese torture of tickling the soles of the feet magnified a hundredfold, only here there were no feathers, only the countless insidious probing needles of actedron jabbing every screaming nerve end into a frantic frenzy, and the undreamed-of pitch of frenetic excitability.

Waves of nausea swept over him, his inside felt as if a wasps' nest had been broken there and a thousand buzzing wings were beating against the walls of his stomach, he was having difficulty with his breathing, and more and more frequently now his throat would constrict in a terrifying fashion; he could feel himself choke for want of air while waves of panic surged through him, then at the last instant release would come and the air surge gaspingly into his starving lungs. But his head, his mind—that was the worst of all. The inside of his head seemed dark and confused, the edges of his mind ragged and woolly and increasingly losing contact with reality, for all his conscious, desperate attempts to cling on to what shreds of reason the actedron and mescaline had left him. The back of his head felt as if it were being crushed between a vise, and his eyes ached abominably. He could hear voices now, voices calling from afar, and as the last vestiges of his reason slipped away from his powerless grasp and down into the darkness, he knew, even as his power of knowing left him, that the dark shroud of madness had completely enveloped him in its thick and choking folds.

But still the voices came—even down in the black depths, still the voices came. Not voices, something seemed to tell him, not voices but just a voice, and it wasn't speaking to him or whispering insanely in the dark corners of his mind as all the other voices had been; it was shouting at him, calling him with a strength that penetrated even through the folds of madness with a desperate, compelling urgency that no man with life at all left in him could possibly ignore. Again and again it came, endlessly insistent, seeming to grow louder and louder with every moment that passed, until at last something reached deep down into Reynolds' darkness, lifted a tiny corner of the shroud, and let him recognise the voice for a passing moment of time. It was a voice he knew well, but a voice he had never heard like this before: it was, he just dimly managed to realise, Jansci's voice, and Jansci was shouting at him, over and over again, "Keep your head up! For God's sake, keep your head up! Keep it up, keep it up!" Over and over again like some insane litany.

Slowly, ponderously, inch by agonising inch, as if he were lifting some tremendous weight, Reynolds lifted his head off his chest, his eyes still clamped shut, until he felt the back of his head press against the high chair back. For a long moment he stayed in that position, fighting for breath like a long-distance runner at the end of a gruelling race, then his head started to droop again.

"Keep it up! I told you to keep it up!" Jansci's voice was vibrant with command, and Reynolds was suddenly aware, clearly and unmistakably aware, that Jansci was projecting towards himself, making a part of himself some of that fantastic will power that had taken him from the Kolyma Mountains and brought him back alive across the uncharted, sub-zero wastes of the Siberian deserts. "Keep it up, I tell you! That's better, that's better! Now, your eyes—open your eyes and look at me!"

Reynolds opened his eyes and looked at him. It was as if someone had covered his eyes with thick sheaths of lead, the effort was so great, but open them he finally did and peered with unfocussed gaze across the gloom of the cellar. At first he could see nothing, he thought his eyes were gone; there was only a misty vapour swimming across his eyes, and then suddenly he knew it *was* a misty vapour, and he remembered that the stone floor was covered in six inches of water and the entire cellar festooned with steam pipes: the steaming, humid heat—worse by far than any Turkish bath he had ever known—was part of the treatment.

And now he could see Jansci: he could see him as if he were seeing through a misted, frosted glass, but he could see him, perhaps eight feet away, in a chair the duplicate of his own. He could see the head continually shaking from side to side, the jaws working constantly, the hands at the end of the pinioned arms opening and closing convulsively as Jansci sought to release some of the accumulated tension, the exquisitely agonising titillation of his overstimulated nervous system.

"Don't let your head go again, Michael," he said urgently. Even in his distress, the use of his Christian name struck Reynolds, the first time Jansci had ever used it, pronouncing it exactly as his daughter had done. "And for heaven's sake keep your eyes open. Don't let yourself go; whatever you do, don't let yourself go! There's a peak, a crisis of some kind, to the effects of these damned chemicals, and if you get over that—*don't let go!*" he shouted suddenly. Again Reynolds opened his eyes: this time the effort was fractionally less.

"That's it, that's it!" Jansci's voice came more clearly now. "I felt just the same a moment ago, but if you let go, yield to the effects, there's no recovery. Just hang on, boy, just hang on. I can feel it going already."

And Reynolds, also, could feel the grip of the chemicals easing. He had still the same mad urge to tear loose, to convulse every muscle in his body, but his head was clearing and the ache behind his eyes beginning to dwindle. Jansci was talking to him all the while, encouraging him, distracting him, and gradually all his limbs and body began to quieten; he grew cold even in the fierce tropical heat of that cellar, and bouts of uncontrollable shivering shook him from head to foot. Then the shivering faded and died away, and he began to sweat and grow faint as the humidity and the heat pouring from the steam pipes increased with every moment that passed. He was again on the threshold of collapse—a clear-headed, sane collapse this time—when the door opened and gum-booted warders came splashing through the water. Within seconds the warders had them free and were urging them through the open door into the clear, icy air, and Reynolds, for the first time in his life, knew exactly what the taste of water must seem like to a man who had been dying of thirst in the desert.

Ahead of him he could see Jansci shrugging off the supporting hands of the warders on either side of him, and Reynolds, though he felt like a man after a long and wasting bout of fever, did the same. He staggered, all but fell when the support of the arms was withdrawn, recovered, and steeled himself to follow Jansci out into the snow and bitter cold of the courtyard with his body erect and his head held high.

The commandant was waiting for them, and his eyes narrowed in swift disbelief as he saw them come out. For a few moments he was at a loss, and the words so ready on his lips remained unsaid. But he recovered quickly, and the professorial mask slipped effortlessly into place.

"Candidly, gentlemen, had one of my medical colleagues reported this to me, I should have called him a liar. I would not, I could not have believed it. As a matter of clinical interest, how do you feel?"

"Cold. And my feet are freezing—maybe you hadn't noticed it, but our feet are soaking wet—we've been sitting with them in water for the past two hours." Reynolds leaned negligently against a wall as he spoke, not because his attitude reflected his feelings, but because without the wall's support he would have collapsed on to the snow. But not even the wall lent him the support and encouragement that the approving gleam in Jansci's eyes did.

"All in good time. Periodic alternations of temperature is part of the—ah—treatment. I congratulate you, gentlemen. This promises to be a case of unusual interest." He turned to one of the guards. "A clock in their cellar, and where they can both see it. The next injection of actedron will be—let me see, it's now midday—will be at 2 P.M. precisely. We must not keep them in undue suspense."

Ten minutes later, gasping in the sudden, stifling heat of the cellar after the zero cold of the yard outside, Reynolds looked at the ticking clock, then at Jansci.

"He doesn't miss out even the smallest refinements of torture, does he?"

"He would be horrified, genuinely horrified, if he heard you mention the word 'torture,'" Jansci said thoughtfully. "To himself the commandant is just a scientist carrying out an experiment, and all he wants is to achieve the maximum efficiency from the point of view of results. He is, of course, quite mad, with the blind insanity of all zealots. He would be shocked to hear you say that too."

"Mad?" Reynolds swore. "He's an inhuman fiend. Tell me, Jansci, is that the sort of man you call your brother? You still believe in the oneness of humanity?"

"An inhuman fiend?" Jansci murmured. "Very well, let us admit it. But at the same time let us not forget that inhumanity knows no frontiers, no frontiers in either time or space. It's hardly the exclusive perquisite of the Russians, you know. God only knows how many thousands of Hungarians have been executed or tortured till death came as a welcome release—by their fellow Hungarians. The Czech SSB—their secret police—were on a par with the NKVD, and the Polish UB—composed almost entirely of Poles—were responsible for worse atrocities than the Russians had ever dreamed of."

"Worse than even Vinnitsa?"

Jansci looked at him in long, slow speculation, then raised the back of his hand to his forehead; he could have been wiping the sweat away.

"Vinnitsa?" He lowered his hand and stared sightlessly into the gloom of a far corner. "Why do you ask about Vinnitsa, my boy?"

"I don't know. Julia mentioned it—perhaps I shouldn't have asked. I'm sorry, Jansci, forget it."

"No need to be sorry— I can never forget it." He broke off for a long moment, then went on slowly. "I can never forget it. I was with the Germans in 1943 when we dug up a high-fenced orchard near the NKVD headquarters. We found ten thousand dead in a mass grave in that orchard. We found my mother, my sister, my daughter—Julia's elder sister—and my only son. My daughter and my son had been buried alive: it is not difficult to tell these things."

In the minutes that followed, that dark, furnace-hot dungeon deep under the frozen earth of Szarháza did not exist for Reynolds. He forgot their ghastly predicament, he forgot the haunting thought of the international scandal his trial would bring about, he forgot the man who was bent on destroying them, he could not even hear the ticking of the clock. He could think only of the man who sat quietly opposite him, of the dreadfully stark simplicity of his story, of the shattering traumatic shock that must have followed his discovery, of the miracle that he should not only have kept his sanity but grown into the kind and wise and gentle man he was, with hatred in his heart towards none that lived. To have lost so many that he loved, to have lost the most of what he lived for, and then to call their murderers his brothers . . . Reynolds looked at him and knew that he did not even begin to know this man, and knew that he would never know him. . . .

"It is not difficult to read your thoughts," Jansci said gently. "I lost so many I loved and, for a time, almost my reason. The Count—I will tell you his story someday—has lost even more. I, at least, still have Julia and, I believe in my heart, my wife also. He has lost everything in the world. But we both know this. We know that it was bloodshed and violence that took our loved ones away from us, but we also know that all the blood spilled between here and eternity will never bring them back again. Revenge is for the madmen of the world and for the creatures of the field. Revenge will never create a world in which bloodshed and violence can *never* take our loved ones away from us. There may be a better kind of world worth living for, worth striving for and devoting our lives to, but I am a simple man and I just cannot conceive of it." He paused, then smiled. "Well, we are talking of inhumanity in general. Let us forget this specific instance."

"No, no!" Reynolds shook his head violently. "Let us forget it, let's forget all about it."

"And that is what the world says—let us forget. Let us not think of it—the contemplation is too awful to bear. Let us not burden our hearts and our minds and our consciences, for then the good that is in us, the good that is in every man, might drive us to do something about it. And we can't do anything about it, the world will say, because we do not even know where to begin or how to begin. But, with all humility, I can suggest where we can begin—by not thinking that inhumanity is endemic to any particular part of this suffering world.

"I have mentioned the Hungarians, the Poles, and the Czechs. I might also mention Bulgaria and Rumania, where nameless atrocities have taken place of which the world has never yet heard—and may never hear. I could mention the seven million homeless refugees in Korea. And to all of that you might say: it is all one, it is all communism. And you would be right, my boy.

"But what would you say if I reminded you of the cruelties of Falangist Spain, of Buchenwald and Belsen, of the gas chambers of Auschwitz, of the Japanese prison camps, the death railways of not so long ago? Again you would have the ready answer. All these things flourish under a totalitarian regime. But I said also that inhumanity has no frontiers in time. Go back a century or two. Go back to the days when the two great upholders of democracy were not quite as mature as they are today. Go back to the days when the British were building up their empire, to some of the most ruthless colonisation the world has ever seen, go back to the days when they were shipping slaves, packed like sardines in a tin, across to

America—and the Americans themselves were driving the Indian off the face of their continent. And what then, my boy?"

"You gave the answer yourself: we were young then."

"And so are the Russians young today. But even today, even in this twentieth century, things happen which any respecting people in the world should be ashamed of. You remember Yalta, Michael, you remember the agreements between Stalin and Roosevelt, you remember the great repatriation of the people of the East who had fled to the West?"

"I remember."

"You remember. But what you do not remember is what you have never seen, but what both the Count and I have seen and will never forget: thousands upon countless thousands of Russians and Estonians and Latvians and Lithuanians being forcibly repatriated to their own home-lands where they knew that one thing and one thing only awaited them—death. You have not seen, as we have seen, thousands mad with fear, hanging themselves from every projection that offered, falling on their pocket knives, flinging themselves under the moving wheels of a railway wagon and cutting their throats with rusty razor blades, anything in the world, any form of painful, screaming self-ending, rather than go back to the concentration camps and torture and death. But we have seen, and we have seen how the thousands unlucky enough not to commit suicide were embarked: they were driven aboard their transports and their cattle cars—they were driven like cattle themselves—and they were driven by British and American bayonets. . . . Never forget that, Michael: by British and American bayonets. . . . Let him who is without sin . . ."

Jansci drew wet palms across an equally wet face to wipe off the sweat that was spilling out in the climbing humidity: both of them were beginning to gasp with the heat, to have to fight consciously for each breath they took, but Jansci was not yet finished.

"I could go on indefinitely, my boy, about your own country and the country that now regards itself as the true custodian of democracy—America. If your people and the Americans are not the world's greatest champions of democracy, you are certainly the loudest. I could speak of the intolerance and cruelties that accompany integration in

America, of the springing up of Ku Klux Klans in England, which once firmly, but erroneously, regarded itself as being vastly superior to America in the matters of racial intolerance. But it is pointless and your countries are big enough and secure enough to take care of their own intolerant minorities, and free enough to publicise them to the world. The point I make is simply that cruelty and hate and intolerance are the monopoly of no particular race or creed or time. They have been with us since the world began and are still with us in every country in the world. There are as many evil and wicked and sadistic men in London or New York as there are in Moscow, but the democracies of the West guard their liberties as an eagle does its young, and the scum of society can never rise to the top; but here, with a political system that, in the last analysis, can exist only by repression, it is essential to have a police force absolute in its power, legally constituted but innately lawless, arbitrary, and utterly despotic. Such a force is a lodestone for the dregs of our society, which first join it and then dominate it, and then dominate the country. The police force is not intended to be a monster, but inevitably, by virtue of the elements attracted to it, becomes a monster, and the Frankenstein that built it becomes its slave."

"One cannot destroy the monster?"

"It is hydra-headed and self-propagating. One cannot destroy it. Nor can one destroy the Frankenstein that created it in the first place. It is the system, the creed by which the Frankenstein lives, that we must destroy, and the surest way to its destruction is to remove the necessity for its existence. It cannot exist in a vacuum. And I have already told you why it exists." Jansci smiled ruefully. "Was it three nights or three years ago?"

"I'm afraid my remembering and my thinking are not at their best at the present moment," Reynolds apologised. He stared at the sweat dripping continuously from his forehead and splashing into the water that covered the floor. "Do you think our friend intends to melt us?"

"It would seem like it. As to what I was saying, I fear I talk too much and at the wrong time. . . . You don't feel even a little more kindly disposed towards our worthy commandant?"

"No!"

"Ah, well," Jansci sighed philosophically. "Understanding the reasons for an avalanche does not, I suppose, make one any the more grateful for being pinned beneath it." He broke off, hearing the heavy tramp of the footsteps in the corridor outside, and twisted to face the door. "I fear," he murmured, "that our privacy is about to be invaded yet again."

The guards entered, released them, pulled them to their feet, and hustled them out the door, upstairs, and across the yard in their usual efficient and uncommunicative fashion. The leader knocked on the commandant's door, waited for the command, then pushed the door wide, pushing the two men in in front of him. The commandant had company and Reynolds recognised him at once—Colonel Joseph Hidas, the deputy chief of the AVO. Hidas rose to his feet as they entered and walked over to where Reynolds stood trying to stop his teeth from chattering and his whole body from shaking: even without the drugs, the instantaneous hundred-degree alternations in temperature were beginning to have a strangely weakening and debilitating effect. Hidas smiled at him.

"Well, Captain Reynolds, so we meet again, to coin a phrase. The circumstances, I fear, are even more unfortunate this time than the last. Which reminds me: you will be pleased to hear that your friend Coco has recovered and returned to duty, although still limping somewhat badly."

"I'm distressed to hear it," Reynolds said briefly. "I didn't hit him hard enough."

Hidas raised an eyebrow and turned his head to have a look at the commandant. "They have had full treatment this morning?"

"They have, Colonel. A singularly high degree of resistance—but a clinical challenge after my own heart. They will talk before midnight."

"Quite. I'm sure they will." Hidas turned back to Reynolds. "Your trial will take place on Thursday in the People's Court. The announcement will be made tomorrow, and we are offering immediate visas and superb hotel accommodation to every Western journalist who cares to attend."

"There will be no room for anyone else," Reynolds murmured.

"Which will suit us admirably ... However, that is of little interest to me compared to another and somewhat less public trial that will take place even earlier in the week." Hidas walked across the room and stood before Jansci. "At this moment I achieve what I must frankly admit has become the consuming desire, the overriding ambition of my life—to meet, under the proper circumstances, the man who has caused me more trouble, more positive distress, and more sleepless nights than the combined efforts of all other—ah—enemies of the state I have ever known. Yes, I admit it. For seven years now you have crossed my path almost continually, shielded and spirited away hundreds of traitors and foes of communism, and interfered with and broken the laws of justice. In the past eighteen months your activities, aided by those of the luckless but brilliant Major Howarth, have become quite intolerable. But the end of the road has come, as it must come for everyone. I can hardly wait to hear you talk . . . Your name, my friend?"

"Jansci. That is the only name I have."

"Of course! I would have expected nothing——" Hidas broke off in midsentence; his eyes widened and color ebbed from his face. He took a step backwards, then another.

"What did you say your name was?" His voice this time was only a husky whisper. Reynolds looked at him in astonishment.

"Jansci. Just Jansci."

Perhaps ten seconds passed in utter silence while everyone stared at the AVO colonel. Then Hidas licked his lips and said hoarsely: "Turn round!"

Jansci turned and Hidas stared down at the manacled hands. They heard the quick indrawing of his breath, then Jansci turned round of his own accord.

"You're dead!" Hidas' voice was still the same hoarse whisper, his face lined with shock. "You died two years ago. When we took your wife away——"

"I didn't die, my dear Hidas," Jansci interrupted. "Another man did—there were scores of suicides when your brown lorries were so busy that week. We just took one the nearest to me in appearance and build. We took him to our flat, disguised him, and painted his hands well enough to pass any but a medical examination. Major Howarth, as you are probably aware by this time, is a genius with disguise." Jansci shrugged. "It was an unpleasant thing to do, but the man was already dead. My wife was alive—and we thought she might remain alive if I were thought to be dead."

"I see, I see indeed." Colonel Hidas had had time to recover his balance, and he could not keep the excitement out of his voice. "No wonder you defied us for so long! No wonder we could never break your organisation. Had I known, had I but known! I am privileged indeed to have had you for adversary."

"Colonel Hidas!" The commandant's voice was imploring. "Who *is* this man?"

"A man who, alas, will never stand trial in Budapest. Kiev, possibly Moscow, but never Budapest. Commandant, let me introduce you. Major General Alexis Illyurin, second only to General Vlassov in command of the Ukrainian National Army."

"Illyurin!" The commandant stared. "Illyurin! Here, in my room! It is impossible!"

"It is, I know it is, but there is only one man in the world with hands like that! He hasn't talked yet? No? But he will; we must have a complete confession ready when he goes to Russia." Hidas glanced at his watch. "So much to do, my commandant, so little time to do it in. My car, and at once. Guard my friend well against my return. I will be back in two hours, three at the most. Illyurin? By all the gods, Illyurin!"

Back once more in their stone-walled room, Jansci and Reynolds had little to say to one another. Even Jansci's usual optimism seemed to have failed him, but his face was as untroubled as ever. But Reynolds knew that everything was over, for Jansci even more than himself, and that the last card had been played. There was, he thought, something tragic beyond words about the man sitting quietly opposite him, a giant toppling into the dust, but quiet and unafraid.

And, looking at him, Reynolds was almost glad that he himself would die also, and he could not help being conscious of the bitter irony that his courage at the thought sprang not from courage but from cowardice: with Jansci dead, and because of him, he could not have faced Jansci's daughter again. Worse, even worse than that, was the thought of what must inevitably happen to her with the Count and Jansci and himself all gone, but the thought had no sooner come than he had thrust it violently, ruthlessly away from him: if ever there was a time that no weakness must touch his mind, that time was now, and dwelling on the laughter and the sadness of that mobile, delicate face that was all too easily evoked in his mind's eye was the highroad to despair. . . .

The steam hissed out of the pipes, the humidity spilled over the room, the temperature climbed steadily upwards— 120, 130, 140—and their bodies were drenched with sweat, their eyes blinded by it, and their breathing was the breathing of fire. Twice, three times, Reynolds lost consciousness and would have fallen and drowned in a few inches of water but for the restraining body belt.

It was as he was emerging from the last of these periods of unconsciousness that he felt hands fumbling at his fastenings, and before he properly realised what was happening the guards had him and Jansci once more out of the cell and into the bitter air of the courtyard for the third time that morning. Reynolds' mind was reeling as his body was reeling, and Jansci, too, he could see, was being half carried across, but even through the fog in his mind Reynolds remembered something and looked at his watch. It was exactly two o'clock. He saw Jansci looking at him, saw the grim nod of acquiescence. Two o'clock and the commandant would be waiting for them; he would be as punctual and precise about this as he was about every-thing else. Two o'clock and the commandant would be waiting for them: and so, too, would the syringes and the coffee, the mescaline and the actedron, waiting to drive them over the edge of madness.

The commandant was waiting for them, but he was not waiting alone. The first person Reynolds saw was an AVO guard, then two more, then the giant Coco leering at him with a wide, anticipatory grin on his seamed and bru-talised face. Then, last of all, he saw the back of a man leaning negligently against the window frame and smoking a black Russian cigarette in a tapered holder: and when the man turned round Reynolds saw that it was the Count.

9

REYNOLDS was certain that his eyes and his mind were deceiving him. He knew that the Count was safely out of the way and that his AVO superiors would not let him move an inch without guarding him like a hawk. He knew, too, that that last hour and a half in that steam oven of a dungeon had had an enormously debilitating effect and that his mind, dark and woolly and still confused, was playing curious tricks on him. Then the man at the window pushed himself leisurely off the wall and was sauntering easily across the room, cigarette holder in one hand, a pair of heavy leather gloves swinging in the other, and suddenly there could be doubt no more. It *was* the Count, alive, completely unharmed, the old mocking self that he had always been. Reynolds' lips parted in the first conclusive moment of shock, his eyes widened, then the beginning of a smile began to limn its lines on his pale and haggard face.

"Where on earth——" he began, then staggered back against the wall behind him as the Count slashed him across the face and mouth with his heavy gauntlets. He could feel the blood springing from one of the recently healed cuts on his upper lip and, with all he had already suffered, this latest pain and shock left him weak and dizzy, and he could see the Count only dimly, as through a haze.

"Lesson number one, little man," the Count said casually. He eyed a tiny spot of blood on his glove with evident distaste. "In future you will speak only when you have been spoken to." The look of distaste transferred itself from his gloves to the two prisoners. "Have these men fallen into a river, Commandant?"

"Not at all, not at all." The commandant was looking very upset. "Just undergoing a course of treatment in one of our steam rooms . . . This is most unfortunate, Captain Zsolt, really most unfortunate. It has destroyed the entire sequence."

"I wouldn't worry, Commandant," the Count said soothingly. "This is unofficial, and please don't quote me, but I understand that they are being brought back here either late tonight or early in the morning. I believe Comrade Furmint has the greatest of faith in you as a—shall we say—psychologist."

"You're sure of that, Captain?" The commandant was anxious. "You're quite sure?"

"Certain." The Count glanced at his watch. "We must not delay, Commandant. You know how essential haste is. Besides," he smiled, "the sooner they're away, the sooner they're back again."

"Let me not delay you then." The commandant was now affability itself. "I am quite reconciled to their departure. I am looking forward to completing my experiment, especially on so illustrious a personage as Major General Illyurin."

"It's not a chance which will come your way again," the Count agreed. He turned to the four AVO men. "Right, out into the truck with them, at once . . . Coco, my infant, I fear you are losing your grip. They are made of glass, you think?"

Coco grinned and took his cue. His shove, massive palm flat-handed against Reynolds' face, sent him staggering against the wall with wicked force, and two others grabbed Jansci and hustled him brutally out of the room. The commandant raised horrified hands.

"Captain Zsolt. Is it necessary——I mean, I want them back in good condition, so that——"

"Don't be afraid, Commandant," the Count grinned. "We, too, in our own crude way, are specialists. You will explain to Colonel Hidas when he returns and ask him to phone the chief? You will tell him, perhaps, how sorry I am to have missed him, but I cannot wait. Good. Thank you again, Commandant, and good-bye."

Shivering violently in their sodden clothes, Jansci and Reynolds were hustled across the courtyard into the back of a waiting AVO lorry. A guard accompanied the driver into the cab, and the Count, Coco, and another guard climbed into the back of the lorry, placed their guns on their knees, and kept a watchful eye on the two prisoners. A moment later the engine turned over, the truck got under way, and within seconds had passed by the saluting sentry at the gate.

Almost at once the Count pulled a map from his pocket, consulted it briefly, then replaced it. Five minutes later he passed by Jansci and Reynolds, slid back the inspection hatch, and spoke to the driver.

"Half a kilometre from here a side road branches off to the left. Take it, and drive until I order you to stop."

Within a minute the truck slowed, then turned off the road and went bouncing and jolting along a narrow rough track. So potholed was the road, so deep the frozen snow, that the truck constantly skidded from one side to the other, and the driver had the greatest difficulty in keeping it on the road at all, but the progress, if slow, was steady. After ten minutes the Count moved to the rear of the truck, stood up, and leant out the door as if looking for a familiar landmark, and after several minutes there he seemed to find it. He gave an order, the truck stopped, and he jumped out on to the snow, followed by Coco and the other guard. Obeying the implicit orders of the silently gesturing gun muzzles, Jansci and Reynolds jumped out after them.

The Count had stopped the truck in the middle of a thick wood, with a clearing to one side. He gave another order, and the driver used the space provided by the clearing for reversing the truck. It skidded and slipped on the snow-slicked grass, but heaving shoulders and a few broken branches under the back wheels soon had it back on the road again, facing the direction it had come. The driver stopped the engine and climbed out, but the Count made him restart it and leave it idling: he wasn't, he said, going to take the chance of the engine freezing up in that zero weather.

And it was indeed bitterly cold. Jansci and Reynolds, still in their same wet clothes, were shivering like men with the ague. The icy air turned chins and ears and nose tips red and blue and white, and the condensation of breath was heavy and almost like smoke, evaporating slowly like smoke in the still, frozen air.

"Speed, everyone!" the Count commanded. "You don't all want to freeze to death here, do you? Coco, you will guard these men. I can trust you?"

"To the death." Coco grinned evilly. "One slightest move, and I will kill."

"I don't doubt it." The Count looked at him thoughtfully. "How many men *have* you killed, Coco?"

"I lost count many years ago, comrade," Coco said simply. Reynolds, looking at him, knew with certainty that he was speaking the truth.

"Your reward will come one of these fine days," the Count said cryptically. "The rest of you—a shovel apiece. We have some work to do that will get your blood moving."

One of the guards blinked stupidly at him.

"Spades, comrade? For the prisoners?"

"You thought, perhaps, I was planning a garden allotment?" the Count asked coldly.

"No, no. It was just that you said to the Commandant ——I mean, I thought we were going to Budapest . . ." His voice trailed away into silence.

"Exactly, comrade," the Count said drily. "You have seen the error of your ways in time—in time and no more. Whatever else is required of you, comrade, heaven knows it is not thought. Come, or we all freeze. And do not be afraid. There will be no need to dig the ground, impossible, anyway, it's like iron. A little vale in the woods where the snow has drifted deep, a trench in the snow—and, well, at least Coco understands."

"I do indeed." The grinning Coco licked his lips. "Perhaps the comrade will permit me to——"

"Put an end to their suffering?" the Count suggested. He shrugged indifferently. "You may as well. What's only another two after you've lost count of all the ones that have gone before?"

He disappeared into the woods behind the clearing with the other three guards and, even in that crystal-clear, sound-carrying air, the men left behind could hear their voices growing fainter and fainter until they were only distant murmurs: the Count must have been leading them deep into the very heart of the wood. Coco, meanwhile, watched them with unblinking, venomous little eyes, and Jansci and Reynolds were both all too clearly aware that he was waiting only the slightest excuse to pull the trigger of the carbine that his great hands cradled as if it were a toy. But they gave him no such excuse: excepting only their uncontrollable shivering, they stood like statues.

Five minutes elapsed and the Count emerged from the woods, slapping a gauntlet against his polished high boots and the skirts of his long coat to free them of snow.

"The work proceeds apace," he announced. "Two more minutes and we will rejoin our comrades. They have behaved, Coco?"

"They have behaved." The disappointment in Coco's voice was all too clear.

"Never mind, comrade," the Count consoled him. He was marching up and down behind Coco, beating his arms to keep warm. "You haven't much longer to wait. Don't take your eyes off them for a moment. . . . How is—how is the pain today?" he enquired delicately.

"It still hurts." Coco glared at Reynolds and swore. "I am black and blue all over!"

"My poor Coco, you're having an uncommonly rough time of it these days," the Count said gently, and the sound of his viciously clubbing revolver was a pistol shot in the silence of the woods as the butt struck home accurately and with tremendous force just above Coco's ear. The carbine dropped from Coco's hands; he swayed, eyes turned up in his head, then crashed to the ground like a stricken tree as the Count stepped respectfully to one side to give a clear path to the giant's fall. Twenty seconds later the truck was on its way, and the clearing in the woods already lost to sight round a curve in the road.

For the first three or four minutes there was no sound, no word spoken in the cab of the truck, only the low, steady roar of the Diesel engine. A hundred questions, a hundred comments framed themselves on the lips of Jansci and Reynolds, but they didn't know where to start, and the shadow of the nightmare from which they had just escaped was still too vivid in their minds. And then the Count was slowing down and stopping, one of his rare smiles illuminating his thin, aristocratic face as he dipped into his capacious hip pocket and drew out his metal flask.

"Plum brandy, my friends." His voice wasn't quite steady. "Plum brandy, and God only knows that no one needs it more than we three do today. Me, for I have died a thousand deaths today—especially when our friend here nearly ended everything when he first saw me in the commandant's office—and you because you are soaking and freezing and prime candidates for pneumonia. And also, I suspect, because they did not treat you too well. I am right?"

"Right." Jansci had to answer, for Reynolds was coughing and choking as the grateful, life-giving warmth of the strong spirit burnt its way down his throat. "The usual breakdown chemicals, plus a special one he's just developed—and, as you know, the steam treatment."

"It was not difficult to guess." The Count nodded. "You did not look at all happy. In fact you had no right to be on your feet at all, but doubtless you were sustained by the sure knowledge that it was only a matter of time before I appeared on the scene."

"Doubtless," Jansci said drily. He drank deep of the brandy, his eyes flooded with tears, and he gasped for air. "Poison, sheer poison—but I have never tasted anything half as good!"

"There are times when one's critical judgments are better suspended," the Count admitted. He tilted the bottle to his mouth, swallowed as another man might swallow water, for all the apparent effect it had on him, and pushed the flask back in his pocket. "A most essential stop, but we must press on: time is not on our side."

He engaged the clutch and the truck moved forward. Reynolds had to shout his protest over the high-pitched roar of its first gear.

"But surely you are going to tell us———"

"Try to stop me," the Count said. "But as we drive along, if you don't mind. I will explain why later. However, to the happenings of today . . . First of all, I must tell you that I have resigned from the AVO. Reluctantly, of course."

"Of course," Jansci murmured. "Does anyone know yet?"

"Furmint does, I should think." The Count's eyes never left the road as he wrestled the skidding truck along between the narrow banks. "I didn't actually give notice in writing, but as I left him gagged and bound hand and foot in his own office, I don't think he could have been in much doubt about my intentions."

Neither Reynolds nor Jansci said anything—there seemed no remark to meet the occasion—and as the silence stretched out they could see the grin spreading over the Count's thin lips.

"Furmint!" It was Jansci who broke the silence, his voice sounding strained. "Furmint! You mean your chief ———"

"Ex-chief," the Count corrected. "None other. But let me begin from the morning. You will remember that I had sent a message out with the Cossack—incidentally, did he and his Opel arrive intact?"

"Both of them."

"A miracle. You should have seen his take-off. As I say, I told him that I was being sent out to Gödöllö—some security checkup, a big one. I should have expected Hidas to handle it himself, but he told me he had some important business elsewhere in Györ.

"Well, we went to Gödöllö—eight men, myself, and a Captain Kálmán Zsolt—an able man with a rubber truncheon, but singularly ungifted otherwise. And as we went I was worried—in a mirror I had caught the chief giving me a very curious look indeed just before I left the Andrassy Ut. Not, mind you, that there is anything remarkable about the chief giving anybody curious looks, he doesn't even trust his own wife, but it was curious coming from the man who had only last week complimented me on being the ablest AVO officer in Budapest."

"You are irreplaceable," Jansci murmured.

"Thank you . . . Then, just as we were arriving in Gödöllö, Zsolt dropped a bomb in my lap. He mentioned casually that he had been speaking to Hidas' chauffeur that morning and that he understood that the colonel was going to the Szarháza prison and wondered what the devil the colonel was going to that hellhole for. He kept on rambling about something or other, I don't know what, which was just as well, as I'm sure my face at that moment must have been a very interesting sight for anyone who cared to look at it.

"Everything fell together in my mind with such loud clicks that it's a wonder that Zsolt didn't hear it. Shoving me out of the way to Gödöllö, the chief's strange look, the lie Hidas had told me, the ease with which I had found out that the professor was in the Szarháza, the still greater ease with which I got the papers and stamps from Furmint's office. My God, I could have kicked myself when I remembered that Furmint had actually gone out of his way, quite unnecessarily, to tell me that he was going to hold a meeting with some officers, thereby letting me know that his office would be empty for some time to come—it was during the dinner hour when there was no one in his outer office . . . How they got on to me, I will never know. I'll swear that only forty-eight hours ago I was the most trusted officer in Budapest. However, that is by the way.

"I had to act, I had to act once for all, and I knew that my bridges were already burnt and that I had nothing to lose. I had to act on the assumption that only Furmint and Hidas knew about me. Obviously Zsolt knew nothing, but I wasn't banking on that—he's too stupid to be entrusted with anything—it's just that both Furmint and Hidas are naturally so distrustful that they wouldn't risk telling anyone." The Count smiled broadly. "After all, if their best man had defected, how were they to know how far the rot had spread?"

"How indeed?" Jansci said.

"Precisely. Immediately we arrived in Gödöllö we went to the mayor's office—not our local branch there, they were being investigated among others—threw the mayor out and took over. I left Zsolt there, went downstairs, collected the men, told them that their duty until five o'clock this evening was to consist of going round the cafés and bars, posing as disaffected AVO men, to see what they could turn up in the way of seditious talk. A job after their own hearts. I provided them with plenty of money for local colour: they'll be drinking away steadily for hours yet.

"Then I went dashing back to the mayor's place in a state of great excitement and told Zsolt that I had found something of utmost importance. He didn't even stop to ask what it was. He came tearing out of the office with me, dreams of promotion shining in his eyes." The Count coughed. "We will miss out the unpleasant part of it. Suffice to say that he is now incarcerated in an abandoned cellar not fifty yards from the mayor's office. Not bound or hurt in any way, but it will take an oxyacetylene torch to free him."

The Count stopped speaking, braked the truck, and got out to clear his windshield. It had been snowing quite heavily now for two or three minutes, but neither of the other two had noticed it.

"I took my unfortunate colleague's identity papers." The Count was on his way again both with truck and story. "Forty-five minutes later, stopping only en route to buy a clothes rope, I was at the door of our H.Q., and a minute later I was in Furmint's office—the very fact that I got as far as that showed that Furmint and Hidas had indeed been as close-mouthed about my defection as I had suspected they might be.

"The whole thing was ridiculously simple throughout. I had nothing to lose, I was still officially in the clear, and nothing succeeds like effrontery, especially on a massive scale. Furmint was so staggered to see me that I had the barrel of my pistol between his teeth before his jaw had time to close again: he is surrounded by fancy knobs and bell pushes all designed to save his life in an emergency, but they were not, you understand, designed to protect him against such as myself.

"I gagged him, then forced him to write a letter in his own hand to my dictation. Furmint is a brave man and he was most reluctant, but nothing overcomes high moral principles like the muzzle of a pistol grinding into your ear. The letter was to the commandant of the Szarháza prison, who knows Furmint's writing as well as he knows his own, authorising him to release you two to myself, one Captain Zsolt. Then hè signed it, covered it with practically every stamp we could find in his office, put it in an envelope, and sealed it with his own private seal, a seal not known to a score of people in all Hungary: I, fortunately, was one of them, although Furmint didn't know it.

"I had twenty metres of clothes ropes, and when I was finished Furmint was trussed like a fowl. All he could move were his eyes and his eyebrows, and he used these to great effect when I picked up the direct phone to the Szarháza and spoke to the commandant in what I pride myself was a perfect imitation of Furmint's voice. I think Furmint began to understand a great many things that had puzzled him over the last year or so. Anway, I told the commandant that I was sending Captain Zsolt to pick up these prisoners and that I was also sending a written authorisation, in my own personal writing with my own personal seal, with him. There were to be no slip-ups."

"What if Hidas had still been there?" Reynolds asked curiously. "He must have left only very shortly before you phoned."

"Nothing could have been better and easier." The Count gestured with an airy hand, then grabbed the wheel quickly as the truck slewed towards a ditch. "I'd just have ordered Hidas to bring you back immediately and waylaid him en route. ... When I was speaking to the commandant, I coughed and sneezed from time to time and let my voice seem a little husky. I told the commandant I had a devil of a cold coming on. I had my reasons for that. Then I spoke on the table microphone to his outer office and said that I wasn't to be disturbed, on any account whatsoever, for the next three hours, not even if a minister wanted to speak to me. I left them in no doubt as to what would happen if my orders were disobeyed. I thought

Furmint was going to have an apoplectic stroke. Then, still in Furmint's voice, I rang up the transport pool, ordered a truck to be brought round for Major Howarth at once, and ordered four men to be standing by in readiness to accompany him—I didn't want them, but I had to have them for local color. Then I bundled Furmint into a cupboard, locked it, left his office, locked that too, and took the key with me. Then we set off for Szarháza. . . . I wonder what Furmint's thoughts are at this very moment? Or Zsolt's? Or if any of the AVO men I left in Gödöllö are still sober? And can't you see Hidas' and the commandant's faces as the truth dawns on them?" The Count smiled dreamily. "I could spend all day just thinking of these things."

For the next few minutes they drove along in silence. The snow, although not yet blinding, was thickening steadily, and the Count had to give his exclusive attention to the road. Beside him Jansci and Reynolds, helped as much by the heat generated in the cab by the engine as by the second drink they had had from the Count's bottle, could feel the warmth gradually returning to their frozen bodies as the continuous shivering eased and gradually stopped and a thousand pins and needles jabbed their numbed legs and arms in the exquisite agony of returning circulation. They had listened to the Count's story in an almost complete silence and still sat in silence: Reynolds could think of no suitable comment on either this fantastic man or his story, and to know how even to begin to thank him was quite beyond his imagination. Besides, he had more than a shrewd suspicion that thanks would receive very short shrift indeed.

"Did either of you see the car Hidas arrived in?" the Count asked suddenly.

"I saw it," Reynolds answered. "A black Russian Zis—big as a house."

"I know it. Solid steel body and bulletproof windows." The Count was slowing down now, edging their truck close in to the shelter of some trees that crowded down on the roadside. "I think it unlikely that Hidas would fail to recognise one of his own trucks and pass by without comment. Let us see how the land lies."

He stopped, jumped out into the swirling snow, and the others followed him. Fifty yards took them to the junction of the main road, smooth and unbroken now under its fresh covering of snow.

"Obviously nothing's passed by here since the snow started falling," Jansci observed.

"Exactly," the Count agreed. He glanced at his watch. "Three hours almost to the minute since Hidas left Szarháza—and he said he would return within the three hours. He shouldn't be long."

"Couldn't we just run the truck across the road and stop him?" Reynolds suggested. "That would delay the alarm another couple of hours."

The Count shook his head regretfully. "Impossible. I've thought of it, but it's no good. In the first place, the men we left behind in the woods should make it back to the Szarháza in an hour—an hour and a half at the most. Then you'd require a crowbar or a stick of dynamite to break into a car armoured like the Zis, but even that's not the point: in this weather the driver almost certainly wouldn't see the truck until it was too late—and that Zis weighs almost three tons. It would wreck the truck—and if we are to survive at all, we want to keep that truck intact."

"He could have passed by in the first minutes after we left the road, before the snow started falling," Jansci put in.

"It's possible," the Count conceded. "But I think we should give him a few minutes——" He broke off suddenly, listened, and Reynolds heard it at the same time—the subdued hum of a powerful motor, closing rapidly.

They were off the road and into the shelter of a few trees just in time. The approaching car, Hidas' black Zis without a doubt, swept by in the swirling snow with a hissing crunch of wide snow tires and was lost to sight and sound almost immediately. Reynolds caught a glimpse of a chauffeur in the front and of Hidas in the back with what looked like another small figure huddled beside him, but it was impossible to be sure. They were racing back to the truck, and the Count was swinging it out on the main road: the hunt would be up in minutes now, and time was running out. The Count had barely changed up to top gear when he changed down again and brought the truck to a halt by the side of a small wood through which telephone poles and wires were strung to cut off the approaching corner. Almost at once two men, half frozen with the bitter cold and their clothes so matted with snow that they looked more like a couple of walking snowmen than human beings, came stumbling out of the wood and running towards the truck, each carrying a box under his arm. As they saw, through the windshield, Jansci and Reynolds sitting in the cab, they waved their arms in delight and grinned broadly, and there was no mistaking them now: Sandor and the Cossack, and their expressions were those of men welcoming friends back from the dead. They piled into the back of the truck with as much speed as their frozen limbs would allow, and the Count was on his way again within fifteen seconds of coming to rest.

The inspection door behind the cab pushed open and Sandor and the Cossack plied them with excited questions and congratulations. After a minute or two the Count passed back his brandy flask and Jansci took advantage of the sudden lull in talk to ask a question.

"What boxes were they carrying?"

"The small one was a telephone linesman's kit for tapping wires," the Count explained. "Every AVO truck carries one of those. On the way here I stopped at the inn in Koteli, gave it to Sandor, and told him to follow us to near the Szarháza, climb a telephone pole, and tap the private line from the prison to Budapest. If the commandant was still suspicious and wanted confirmation, Sandor would have answered: I told him to talk through a handkerchief, as if Furmint's cold, which I had already let the commandant know was developing, had become worse."

"Good lord!" Reynolds found it impossible to hide his admiration. "Is there anything you did not think of?"

"Very little," the Count admitted modestly. "Anyway, the precaution was not needed: the commandant, as you saw, had never a suspicion. The only thing I was really afraid of was that those dolts of AVO men I had with me might call me Major Howarth in front of the commandant, instead of Captain Zsolt I had coached them to call me, for reasons, I said, which Furmint would personally explain to them if any of them blundered. . . . The other box contains your ordinary clothes, which Sandor also brought on from Koteli in the Opel. I'll stop in a moment and you can nip into the back and change out of these uniforms. . . . Where did you leave the Opel, Sandor?"

"Back there, deep in the wood. No one can see it."

"No loss." The Count dismissed the matter with a wave

of his hand. "It wasn't ours in the first place. Well, gentlemen, the hunt is up, or will be any moment now, and it will be up with a vengeance. Every escape route to the West, from trunk roads down to bicycle tracks, will be blocked as they have never been blocked before: with all due respects to yourself, Mr. Reynolds, General Illyurin is the biggest fish that has ever threatened to escape their net. We will do very well indeed to escape with our lives: I do not rate our chances very highly. So what now, I wonder?"

No one had immediate suggestions to make. Jansci sat looking straight ahead, the lined face beneath the thick white hair calm and unworried, and Reynolds could almost have sworn that a slight smile was touching the corners of his mouth. He himself had never felt less like smiling, and as the truck roared steadily on from the whitely opaque world of snow behind to the whitely opaque world of snow ahead, he made a mental catalogue of his own successes and failures since he had entered Hungary only four days previously. The catalogue was not one that he could contemplate with either pleasure or pride. On the credit side, there could only be reckoned the contacts he had made, with Jansci and his men in the first place, and then with the professor—and he could derive no real satisfaction from these, without the Count and Jansci even these would have been impossible. On the debit side—he winced as he realised the length of the list on the debit side: being captured immediately after arriving in the country, making the AVO a gratis presentation of a tape recording that had ruined everything, walking into Hidas' trap and having to be rescued by Jansci and his men, having to be saved by Jansci from succumbing to the effects of the drugs in the Szarháza, almost betraying his friends and himself when his astonishment had overcome him at the sight of the Count in the commandant's room. He writhed in his seat as he thought of it. In short, he had lost the professor, split up the professor's family beyond recovery, been responsible for the Count losing the position that alone enabled Jansci's organisation to work smoothly—and, as bitter as anything, he had lost any hope he might ever have had that Jansci's daughter might look kindly on him again. It was the first time that Reynolds had admitted, even to himself, that he ever had any such hope, and he was lost for a long, long moment at the wonder of it. With a physical effort, almost, he shook off all thought of it, and when he spoke he knew there was only one thing he could say.

"There's something I want to do, and I want to do it alone," he said slowly. "I want to find a train. I want to find the train that's——"

"Don't we all!" the Count shouted. He smashed a gloved hand down on the steering wheel with a force that nearly broke it, and his thin face was alive with a grin of sheer delight. "Don't we all, my boy! Look at Jansci there—he's been thinking of nothing else for the past ten minutes."

Reynolds looked sharply at the Count, then more slowly at Jansci. It *had* been the beginnings of a smile that he had seen on Jansci's face, he realised now, and even as he watched the smile widened as Jansci turned towards him.

"I know this country like the back of my hand." The tone was almost apologetic. "It was about five kilometres back that I noticed that the Count was headed due south. I do not imagine," Jansci added drily, "that very much of a welcome awaits us across the border of Yugoslavia."

"It's no good." Reynolds shook his head stubbornly. "Just me, only me. Everything I've touched yet has gone wrong, just one more step towards the concentration camps. Next time there'll be no Count turning up with an AVO truck. What train is the professor on?"

"You will do this alone?" Jansci asked.

"Yes. I must."

"The man's mad," the Count announced.

"I can't." Jansci shook his white head. "I can't let you do it. Put yourself in my position and admit that you may be selfish. I have, unfortunately, a conscience to live with, and I would not care to face it every waking night for the rest of my life." He stared forward through the windshield. "Even worse, I would not care to face my daughter for the rest of my life."

"I don't understand——"

"Of course you don't." It was the Count interrupting, and he sounded almost jovial. "Your all-exclusive devotion to your job may be admirable—to be frank, I don't think it is—but it only tends to blind you to things that are dazzlingly clear to your elders. However, we argue, and uselessly. Colonel Hidas is even now having a fit in our worthy commandant's office. Jansci?" He was asking for a decision, and Reynolds knew it.

"You know all we need to know?" Jansci asked the Count.

"Naturally." The Count was hurt. "I had four minutes to wait while the—ah—prisoners were being produced. I did not waste those minutes."

"Very well, then. There it is, Meechail. The information in exchange for our help."

"I don't appear to have much option," Reynolds said bitterly.

"The sign of an intelligent man—he knows when he has lost an argument." The Count was almost purring. He jammed on the brakes, pulled a map from his pocket, made sure that Sandor and the Cossack could see it from the observation hatch behind, and jabbed at it with his finger. "Here is Cece—this is where the professor is being put aboard the train today—or, rather, has already been put aboard the train. Special wagon tacked on to the end."

"The commandant mentioned something like that," Jansci said. "A number of high-ranking scientists——"

"Pah! Scientists? High-ranking criminals bound for the Siberian taiga, and it's where they deserve to go. Nor is Dr. Jennings getting any special treatment—it's a convict coach, pure and simple, a front-loading cattle truck: the commandant made no bones about it." His finger traced the railway line down to the point where it intersected with the main road due south from Belgrade at the town of Szekszárd, sixty kilometres north of the Yugoslavian border. "The train will stop here. Then it follows the main road due south to Bálaszék—it goes straight through there—then turns west for Pécs, leaving the main road completely. It will have to be somewhere between Szekszárd and Pécs, gentlemen, and it presents quite a problem. There are plenty of trains I would derail, but not one carrying hundreds of my adopted countrymen. This is just a regular service train."

"May I see that map, please?" Reynolds asked. It was a very large-scale map, a road map but also a physical map showing rivers and hills, and as he studied it his excitement mounted, and his mind went back fourteen years to the days when he had been the youngest subaltern in the SOE. It was a crazy idea now, but it had been a crazy idea

180

then. . . . He pointed to a spot on the map, not far north of Pécs, where the road from Szekszárd, after cutting for almost forty kilometres across country, again paralleled the railway line, then looked across at the Count.

"Can you get the truck there before the train arrives?"

"With luck, with the roads not being blocked and, above all, with Sandor to lift me out of a ditch if I go into one—yes, I think I can."

"Very well. Here is what I propose." Quickly, succinctly, Reynolds outlined his plan, and at the end of it he looked at the others. "Well?"

Jansci shook his head slowly, but it was the Count who spoke.

"Impossible." He was very definite. "It cannot be done."

"It's been done before. In the Vosges mountains, 1944. An ammunition dump went up as a result. I know, because I was there. . . . What alternative do you propose?"

There was a short period of silence, then Reynolds spoke again.

"Exactly. As the Count said, it is an intelligent man who knows when he has lost an argument. We're wasting time."

"We are." Jansci had already made up his mind, and the Count nodded agreement. "We can but try."

"Into the back and change." The Count had made up his mind. "I'm on my way. The train is due in Szekszárd in twenty minutes. I'll be there in fifteen."

"Just so long as the AVO aren't there in ten," Reynolds said sombrely.

Involuntarily, almost, the Count glanced over his shoulder.

"Impossible. No sign of Hidas yet."

"There are such things as telephones."

"There were." It was Sandor speaking for the first time in minutes, and he showed Reynolds the pair of pliers in his huge hand. "Six cables—six snips. The Szarháza is completely cut off from the outside world."

"I," said the Count modestly, "think of everything."

10

THE ancient train rocked and swayed alarming-
ly along the ill-maintained track, shuddering and straining whenever a snow-laden gust of wind from the
southeast caught it broadside on along its entire length and
threatened for a heart-stopping moment, which was only
one of a never-ending series of such moments, to topple it
off the track. The carriage wheels, transmitting a teeth-
rattling vibration through a suspension that had long since
given up an unequal battle with the years, screeched and
grated in a shrilly metallic cacophony as they jarred and
leapt across the uneven intersection of the rails. The wind
and the snow whistled icily through a hundred cracks in
ill-made doors and windows, the wooden coachwork and
seats creaked and protested like a ship working in a heavy
seaway, but the ancient train battered on steadily through
the white blindness of that late afternoon in midwinter,
sometimes slowing down unexpectedly on a straight
stretch of track, at other times increasing speed unexpectedly round seemingly dangerous curves: the driver, one
hand almost constantly on the steam whistle that whispered and died to a muffled extinction only a hundred
yards away in the driving snow, was obviously a man with
complete confidence in himself, the capacities of his train,
and his knowledge of the track ahead.

Reynolds, lurching and staggering down the wildly
swaying length of a coach corridor, shared none of the
engine driver's obvious confidence, not in the safety of the
train, which was the least of Reynolds' worries, but in his
own capacity to carry out the task that lay ahead of him.
When he had broached the plan first of all to the others, it
had been with the memory in his mind of a soft starlit
summer's night and a train puffing gently along between
the wooded hills of the Vosges: now, just ten minutes after
he and Jansci had bought their tickets and boarded the
train at Szekszárd without let or hindrance, what he had
to do, what he must do, had assumed the proportions of a
nightmare impossibility.

What he had to do was simply enough stated. He had
to free the professor, and to free the professor he had to
separate the convict coach from the rest of the train, and

this could only be done by stopping the train and easing the tension on the coupling securing the convicts' coach to the guard's van. One way or another he had to reach the locomotive, which at the moment seemed impossibility enough, and then prevail upon the footplate crew to bring their engine to a halt when and where he told them. "Prevail" was right, Reynolds thought grimly. Perhaps he could persuade them if they were halfway friendly. Perhaps he could frighten them, but what was certain enough was that he couldn't force them. All they would have to do was to refuse to obey, and he would be helpless. The control cabin of a locomotive was a complete mystery to him, and not even for the professor could he shoot or knock out engineer and fireman and place hundreds of innocent passengers in danger of death or disfigurement. Even as he thought of these things, Reynolds could almost feel the physical sensation of cold, dull despair flooding into his mind, and he thrust these thoughts ruthlessly aside. One evil at a time. First of all, he had to get there.

He was rounding the corner of the coach, supported only by the one hand that clung to the window bar—his other was deep in his coat pocket supporting the weight of and concealing the suspicious bulge caused by the heavy hammer and torch there—when he bumped into Jansci. The older man muttered an apology, glanced at him briefly and without recognition, stepped forward till he could see the entire length of the corridor from which Reynolds had just emerged, stepped back, opened the door of the adjacent toilet to check that it was empty, then spoke softly.

"Well?"

"Not so well. They're on to me already."

"They?"

"Two men. Civilian clothes, belted trench coats, no hats. They followed me up front and back again. Discreetly. If I hadn't been looking for it, I wouldn't have noticed it."

"Stand out in the corridor. Let me know——"

"They're coming now," Reynolds murmured.

He glanced briefly at the two men lurching towards him as Jansci slid quietly inside the toilet, pulling the door till only a tiny crack was left. The man in the lead, a tall man with a dead-white face and black eyes, looked at Reynolds incuriously as he passed, but the other ignored him completely.

"They're on to you, all right." Jansci had waited till they were out of sight. "Worse still, they know you're on to them. We should have remembered that every train in and out of Budapest is being watched for the duration of this conference."

"Know them?"

"I'm afraid so. That man with the pale face is AVO—one of Hidas' hatchet men. As dangerous as a snake. I don't know the other."

"But it's an obvious assumption that he's AVO also. Surely the Szarháza——"

"They don't know about that yet. They can't. But your description has been out for a couple of days to every AVO man in Hungary."

"That's it." Reynolds nodded slowly. "Of course . . . How are things with you?"

"Three soldiers in the guard's van—there'll be no one in the wagon behind—they never travel in the same wagons as the prisoners. They're sitting with the guard round a red-hot wood stove, and there's a wine bottle circulating."

"Will you manage?"

"I think so. But how——"

"Get back!" Reynolds hissed.

He was leaning against the window, both hands in his pockets, and gazing down at the ground when the same two men returned. He glanced up indifferently, raised an eyebrow fractionally as he saw who it was, glanced down again and then sideways as he watched them stagger up the length of the corridor and then out of sight.

"Psychological warfare," Jansci murmured. "A problem."

"And not the only one. I can't get into the first three coaches."

Jansci glanced sharply at him but said nothing.

"The military," Reynolds explained. "The third carriage from the front is a mid-aisle coach, and full of troops. An officer turned me back. Anyway, it's no good: I tried an outside door handle when I turned my back to him, and it was locked."

"From the outside." Jansci nodded. "Conscripts, and the army is trying to discourage a premature return to civilian life. Any hope at all, Meechail? Communication cords?"

"Not one in the whole length of the train. I'll manage —I've damn well got to. You have a seat?"

"Second last carriage."

"I'll give you the tip-off ten minutes beforehand. I'd better go. They'll be back any second."

"Right. Bálaszék in five minutes. Remember, if the train stops there it means that Hidas has guessed and got through to them. Jump out on the blind side and run for it."

"They're coming," Reynolds murmured. He levered himself off the window and walked forward, passing the two men. This time both men looked at him with expressionless eyes and Reynolds wondered how much more time they would allow to elapse before making their pounce. He lurched forward the length of another two coaches, went into the toilet at the end of the fourth coach, hid his hammer and torch in the tiny triangular cupboard that supported the cracked tin washbasin, transferred his gun to his right pocket, and closed his hand round it before moving out to the corridor. It wasn't his own Belgian pistol, which had been taken from him, it was the Count's; it had no silencer on it and it was the last thing he wanted to use. But to live, he might be compelled to use it: it all depended on the two men who were shadowing his every movement.

They were running through the outskirts of Bálaszék now and Reynolds realised all at once that their speed had slackened perceptibly, and even as the realisation came he had to brace himself from sliding forwards as the air brakes went on. He could feel the curious tingling in the fingertips of the hand that held the gun. He left the toilet, moved into the middle of the passage between the two opposite doors—he had no idea on which side the station platform was going to be—made sure that the safety catch was off his gun, and waited tensely, his heart hammering heavily, slowly in his chest. They were still slowing down; he had to steady himself as the train battered violently across a set of points; then, so suddenly that the change of motion caught him off balance, the air brakes hissed off, the locomotive's whistle shrilled once, briefly, as the train started to accelerate again, and Bálaszék station was only a confused memory of a flickering row of palely blurred lights lost in the moment of seeing in the greyish-white curtain of driving snow.

Reynolds' grip on his gun eased. Despite the bitter cold of that coach corridor, he could feel the neckband of his collar wet with sweat. So, too, he realised, was his gun hand, and as he moved across to the left-hand door he withdrew it and wiped it up and down the outside of his coat.

He pulled the door window down a few inches, jammed it up a second later, and stepped back, gasping, to clear his eyes of the whistling blizzard that had lashed whiplike across his forehead and blinded him just in an instant of time. He leant back against the wood behind him, lit a cigarette, and his hands were unsteady.

It was hopeless, he told himself, worse than hopeless. With a steadily increasing wind gusting up to forty, perhaps even fifty miles per hour and the train doing the same speed diagonally into it, the combined total strength of that now howling wind outside was that of a whole gale, maybe a little more—and a whole gale that was no gale at all, just a screaming white wall of almost horizontally driving snow and ice. Even a split second of it on a tiny part of his body while standing in the relative warmth and security of the train had been too much; God only knew what it would be like outside, for minutes on end, with his whole life depending just——

Relentlessly he pushed the thought to one side. He moved swiftly through the concertina coupling leading to the next carriage, and glanced quickly down the corridor. No sign yet of the two men returning. He went back to where he had been, across to the door on the leeward side, opened it cautiously so as not to be dragged out of the train by the vacuum suction on that side, gauged the size of the bolt hole in the jamb that engaged the door catch, closed the door, checked that the window worked easily, then returned to the toilet. Here he used his knife to cut a small piece of wood off the small door below the basin and in a couple of minutes he had it trimmed to a shape and size just a fraction larger than that of the bolt hole. Then, as soon as he was finished, he moved out into the corridor again. It was essential that he be seen and keep on being seen by his two shadows: if they missed him, the hunt would be up the length of the train—and there were a hundred, maybe two hundred soldiers in the leading coaches who could be called upon to help them.

And this time he almost bumped into them as he closed the toilet door behind him. They had been hurrying, he could see, and the relief on the face of the shorter man showed clearly as he saw Reynolds emerging. The tall pale man's expressionless face did not change, but his reaction showed in so sudden a shortening of step that the other bumped into him. Both men slowed down, then stopped a couple of feet away from Reynolds. Reynolds himself made no move, he just leant into a corner to brace his body against the violent shaking of the train and leave both his hands free for use should the need arise. The pale man saw this and his dark, flat eyes narrowed fractionally before he brought a packet of cigarettes from his pocket and smiled with a smile that never got any further than the corners of his lips.

"Have you a match, comrade?"

"Certainly. Help yourself." Reynolds fished out a box of matches with his left hand and held them out at arm's length. At the same time his other hand moved slightly in its pocket, and the mouth of his gun sharply limned its circular outline through the thin gabardine of his trench coat. The pale man caught the slight movement and looked down, but Reynolds' eyes never left his face. After a moment the pale man looked up, regarded Reynolds unwinkingly over the flame of the cigarette, slowly handed back the matches, nodded his thanks, and continued on his way. Unfortunate, Reynolds thought, looking after them, but quite unavoidable: it had just been a silent challenge, a kite flown to see whether or not he had been armed; and if he hadn't convinced them, Reynolds felt sure, they would have nailed him there and then.

He looked at his watch for the tenth time. Three minutes to go, four at the most: he could feel the train's speed perceptibly easing as it started its gentle climb, and he could have sworn that he had just had his first glimpse of a road outside, almost paralleling the railway track. He wondered what the chances were of the Count and the others having made it there in time; he wondered what chances there were that they could make it at all. He could hear the wind now, clearly hear its high-pitched ululation above the rattle and the roar of the train, could see the almost solid wall of driving whiteness that limited visibility to only a few feet, and unconsciously shook his head. In this almost Arctic weather, a train on rails and a truck on tires were two vastly different propositions altogether, and it was all too easy to visualise the strained face of the Count peering through the ever-narrowing arcs before him as the wipers struggled vainly to clear the snow battering against the windshield.

But he *had* to depend on it, Reynolds knew that. He had to treat a remote possibility as a certainty. He took a last glance at his watch, let himself into the toilet once more, filled a big earthenware jug with water, put it in the cupboard, picked up the piece of shaped wood he had left there, took it outside, opened the leeward door again, and jammed the wood into the bolt hole, knocking it in firmly with the butt of his gun. He closed the door again, letting the latch gently into the wooden plug, and tested it carefully: the latch was clear of the bolt, but held firmly enough by the wood. Thirty pounds' pressure, maybe forty, would be required to tear the wood away.

He walked towards the rear of the train, quickly and softly. One carriage away, two men appeared from a dark corner and followed silently after him, but he ignored them. He knew they would try nothing while they were opposite the compartments with people in them, and when he came to the end of a coach Reynolds ran as quickly as possible through the concertina connection into the next. And then he was in the second last carriage, walking slowly, head straight on his shoulders so as to deceive the men behind, but his eyes to one side and searching the compartments.

Jansci was in the third compartment. Reynolds stopped abruptly, catching his shadows on the wrong foot, stood stiffly to one side to let them pass, waited till they were about ten feet away, nodded to Jansci, then ran back the way he had come, praying that he would not bump into anyone: a portly man blocking the corridors just then could have been the end of everything.

He could hear the footsteps pounding behind him, increased his speed, and that was almost his undoing: he slipped on a wet corner, struck his head against a window bar, fell, but forced himself to his feet, ignoring the sharp, almost stunning pain and the bright lights that flashed in front of his eyes, and ran on again. Two carriages, three carriages, four, and this was his; he rounded a corner sharply, dodged into the toilet, and banged the door shut behind him as loudly as possible—he didn't want his pursuers to be in a moment's doubt as to where he had gone—and locked it.

Once inside, he wasted no time. He picked up the big earthenware jar of water, stuffed a dirty towel into the top to retain as much of the water as possible, took a step backwards, and flung the jar with all his strength through the window. The crash was all that he had hoped for and more, the noise almost deafening in that confined space, and the sound of the shattering glass was still in his ears when he took the gun from his pocket, caught it by the barrel, switched off the light, softly eased the lock, and stepped into the corridor.

The shadows had the window down and were peering out, leaning as far as possible, crowding each other in their eagerness to see what had happened, where Reynolds had gone: they would have been less than human to have done anything else. Reynolds didn't even break step as he came through the door: one long stride, a leap propelled by all the strength of his legs, his feet stiffly in front of him smashing into the back of the nearest man, and the door burst open, one of the men catapulting out into the driving snow and the gloom before he had even time to cry out. The other, the pale-faced man, twisted impossibly in mid-air, caught the inside edge of the door with one hand, his face contorted with venom and fear as he fought like a wildcat to pull himself inside. But the whole struggle lasted perhaps only two seconds, and Reynolds was merciless, his downward clubbing pistol, aimed at the snarling face, changing direction in the last moment as the man's free hand came up in instinctive protection. The butt struck the fingers clinging to the doorway with a force that jarred Reynolds' arm to the elbow, and then there was no man in the doorway, only the gathering darkness of the night and a thin, high scream lost in the thunder of the wheels and the high threnody of the wind.

It took Reynolds seconds only to work the already loosened piece of wood free of the bolt hole and shut the door securely. Then he stuffed his gun into his pocket, retrieved the hammer and the torch from the toilet, and moved across to the opposite door of the coach, on the windward side.

It was here that he had his first setback, and one that

all but defeated him before he had even started. The train was now angling due southwest towards Pécs, the gale of wind and snow out of the southeast was blowing directly on the beam, and it seemed as if an even stronger man than himself were pushing against him on the other side. Twice, three times he heaved with all his strength, but the door gave no more than an inch.

Little enough time was left—seven minutes perhaps, eight at the most. He reached up, caught the metal grip at the top of the window, brought it right down in one convulsive jerk, and had he not dropped to the floor, the blast of wind and snow that shrieked in through the open window would have blown him clear across the other side of the coach. It was even worse than he had imagined it would be; he could understand now that the driver was slowing up not because of the incline but because he wanted to keep his train on the rails, and for one bad moment Reynolds was tempted to give up the whole suicidal project. Then he thought of the professor sitting alone in the last wagon among a pack of hardened criminals, of Jansci and all the others who were depending on him, of the girl who had turned her back on him when he had made to say good-bye, and the next moment he was on his feet, gasping as the bulleting snow lashed cruelly across his exposed face and sucked the breath from his lungs. He heaved with all his strength, once, twice, three times, unmindful of the fact that a sudden lull in the wind would have pitched him helplessly out into the snow, and on the fourth attempt managed to get the sole of his shoe stuck in the opening. He got his forearm into the crack, then his shoulder and finally half his body, pressed outwards with all the strength of his arms, reached down with a groping right foot until he found the snow-encrusted running board, and brought his left foot into the gap of the door. It was then that the hammer and torch in his pocket caught on the inside jamb of the door and he stood there for almost a minute, a minute that seemed an eternity, jammed between door and side of the coach, struggling frantically to free himself, fearing that at any moment someone might come along the corridor to investigate the source of the snow-laden gale that was whistling the length of the carriage. And then suddenly, with a ripping of buttons and tearing of cloth, he was free, freed with a jerk that caused his right foot to slip off the running

190

board, and he hung there for a moment supported only by his left hand and the left foot still jammed in the doorway. Then he hauled himself slowly, painfully upright—he could get no purchase anywhere for his right hand—regained his footing on the board, stood there for a moment until he had regained control of himself, got his left hand out, hooked it round the inside of the open window, and jerked his left sole free. The door shut with a crash, and he was now completely outside, supported only by the already numbing fingers of his left hand and the pressure of the wind pinning him against the carriage side.

It was dusk now, but though there was still enough light to see by, he could not see, for with the driving snow he was a blind man groping in a blind world. He was, he knew, at the very end of the coach, and the corner was only a foot from where he stood, but though he could reach his right arm almost two feet round the corner he' could find not the smallest projection to give him purchase of any kind. At the fullest stretch of his left arm he tried with his right foot and found the narrow lateral steel member that housed the bumpers, but it was at far too acute an angle to serve his purpose; he tried to find the bumper itself, but it eluded him.

His left forearm was beginning to ache with the strain of supporting his weight, and his fingers were now so numbed that he had no means of knowing whether they were slipping or not. He hauled himself upright outside the carriage-door window again, changed arms, cursed himself for his stupidity as he suddenly thought of his torch, changed hands again, and once more leant back and as far round the corner as he could, this time with the beam of the powerful torch probing through the gloom and the snow. It took him only two seconds to see all he wanted to see and to memorise the relative positions of the lateral steel member at the back of the coach, the concertina coupling, and the steel bumper that seemed to leap uncontrollably from side to side as every jolting sway of the train caused a violent change in position relative to the opposing bumper on the next carriage. He pulled himself quickly upright, thrust the torch back in his pocket, and didn't hesitate, because he was dimly aware, without admitting it to himself, that if he as much as paused to consider the near certainty of a miss, a slip, and being crushed to instant death under the wheels, he could never have brought himself to do what he now did at once without any thought for the consequences. He moved both feet along till they were at the very edge of the running board, released his grip with his left hand, stood there held against the outcurving side of the carriage by wind pressure alone, then lifted his right foot and stepped into blind space, his body curving far over to the left as he did so. For an instant of time he was poised there in mid-air, the toe of his left shoe the only contact he had left with the train, and then in the very moment of that toe slipping off the frozen running board the wind caught him and he flung himself forward into the darkness.

He landed with one knee on the lateral member, the shin of the other leg striking cruelly across the bumper even as his outstretched hands struck against the stiffly yielding side of the concertina coupling. Such was his momentum that his right leg slipped at once across the frozen metal of the bumper, but he tightened his leg muscles convulsively and hooked his instep round the narrowest part of the bumper as his knees pointed down to the track rushing by beneath. For a few seconds he hung there, supported only by the counteracting pressures of his arms and one shin, wondering vaguely whether his leg had been broken, then he felt his hands—for all the maximum pressure he was exerting against them—begin to slip helplessly down the smooth, snow-covered material of the coupling. Despairingly he flung out his left hand, struck it painfully against the back of the carriage he had just left, pushed it forward, and felt his stiffened, outstretched fingers slide in the narrow gap between the carriage and its coupling. He clutched the rough edge of the toughened, rubberised fabric as if seeking to drive his hooking fingers clear through it, and three seconds later he was standing upright on the lateral member, securely anchored by his left hand, and trembling uncontrollably from the reaction of his effort.

But the trembling was from the reaction only. Reynolds, afraid only moments ago as he had never been afraid before, had crossed that nebulous frontier between fear and that strange world of uncaring and selfless indifference that lies beyond. With his right hand he felt for his spring-knife, clicked open the blade, and thrust the dagger point into the material about waist height: there could have been a dozen people streaming through the inside of the concertina coupling at that instant for all he cared. A few seconds' vigorous sawing with the blade's razor edges and he had a hole cut in the material, large enough to accommodate the toe of one foot, and at head height he cut another for a handgrip. Then he thrust his right toe into the first hole, his left hand into the second, pushed and heaved upwards, and drove the blade into the hilt through the top of the coupling to give him a secure handhold. And then he was on top, clinging desperately to the handle of the knife as the full force of the wind caught him and sought to blow him over the other side of the wildly vibrating coupling.

The first carriage—the fourth from the front, that was—proved to be relatively easy. The narrow metal sheathing for the ventilation louvres ran the entire length of the carriage along the top, and it took him less than half a minute, lying on the leeward side of the roof with his face bowed against the knifing blizzard and overhanding himself along the sheathing, to reach the far end. All the way along his feet had hung out over the edge, but he could do nothing about this: he should have been able to get some purchase with his toes on the guttering, but it was blocked and smooth with frozen snow.

And now he was reaching out gingerly on top of the corrugations of the next carriage coupling and had no sooner let go of the security of the ventilation sheathing than he realised the mistake he had made. He should have launched himself across in a dive for the other side instead of exposing himself to that shrieking wind that was beginning to gust more dangerously now, one moment all but blowing him clear over the far side of the furiously vibrating coupling, the next easing so unexpectedly that he had to hang on grimly to prevent himself from toppling off into the wind, but by flattening himself as low as possible and working his handgrip from corrugation to corrugation he safely reached the end of the third carriage.

It was again a relatively easy matter to traverse this, and when he reached the front he sat up, swung his legs over on to the next coupling, bent low, and launched himself across the intervening space, barking one of his knees badly as it struck the sheeting on the second carriage, but getting a secure grip at the same time. Seconds later only, it seemed, he was at the front end of the second carriage, and it was then, as he swung his legs out on to the coupling, that he saw it: the wavering, dipping beams of headlights, vanishing and reappearing through swirling flurries of snow on a road that paralleled the railway track not twenty yards away. The elation that swept through Reynolds banished for the moment all thought of exhaustion and cold and numbed senseless hands that could not serve him very much longer: it could have been anyone, of course, driving that vehicle out there in the blinding snow, but Reynolds was oddly certain it wasn't. He stooped again, poised on his toes, and launched himself across on to the roof of the first carriage: it wasn't until he arrived there and was skidding along helplessly on his face that he realised that this carriage, unlike the others, had no ventilation sheathing running along the top.

For a moment panic returned again, and he scrabbled furiously on the ice-smooth, slippery surface of the roof, seeking for a handhold—any handhold. Then he forced himself to be calm, for that frantic threshing of legs and arms was exactly what was required to destroy what little friction coefficient there was between himself and the train and send him sliding helplessly over the side to his death. There must, he told himself desperately, be ventilators of some kind or other, and suddenly he knew what they must be—those little top-hatted chimneys spaced three or four to a coach—and it was just at that moment he realised something else: the train was curving round sharply into the wind, and the centrifugal force was sending him sliding slowly, remorselessly, towards the edge.

He was sliding feet first, face down, and his toes beat a furious tattoo on the carriage roof as he sought to crack the frozen snow that filled up the guttering and gain at least a toe hold. But the snow was frozen into ice; he smashed against it in vain, and the first he knew that he had failed was when his shins struck painfully against the edge of the carriage roof. And still the train kept curving round that interminable corner.

His knees now rested on the edge of the roof and his nails were breaking off as his fingers, hooked into rigid talons, furrowed through the smooth ice on the carriage top. He knew now nothing could save him, and he could never afterwards explain what strange, subconscious instinct—for in that moment of approaching death his mind had ceased to work altogether—had caused him to jerk out his knife, press the release catch, and bury the blade in the roof just before his hips reached the side and he passed the point of no return.

How long he lay there at the full stretch of his knife he did not know. It could have been only seconds. Gradually he became aware that the track beneath him had straightened out again, that the centrifugal force no longer had him in its murderous grip, and that he was free to move once more, although with infinite caution. Inch by inch he slowly pulled his legs back on to the roof again, freed the knife, stabbed it in further up, and gradually hauled himself on to the top. A moment later, still using his knife as his sole support, he found the first circular ventilator and clutched it as if he would never let it go. But he had to let it go, there could be only two or three minutes left. He had to reach the next ventilator. He reached out in its direction, raised the knife, and stabbed it down; but it struck some metal, probably a bolt head, with a jarring shock, and when he brought it up to his eyes he saw that the blade had been snapped off cleanly at the hilt. He flung the handle away, braced his feet against the ventilator, and pushed off along the roof, colliding heavily with the next ventilator, perhaps only six feet away. Seconds later, again using his feet to propel himself forward from one ventilator to the next, he had reached the third one and then the fourth; and then he realised he did not know how long the carriage was, whether there were any more ventilators, whether or not another push along the top of the carriage would send him skidding helplessly over the front of the carriage to fall to his death under the wheels of the train. He decided to risk it, placed his feet against the ventilator and was on the point of pushing off when the thought struck him that with any height at all he should be able to see from there into the cab of the locomotive and see limned against its brightness, perhaps, the edge of that coach, for the snow was beginning to ease at last.

He knelt upright, the ventilator clutched tightly between his thighs, and his heart turned slowly over as he saw the edge of the carriage, silhouetted clearly against the red glow from the locomotive's open firebox, a bare four feet away. In the cab itself through the flurries of snow, he caught a glimpse of the engineer and of his fireman turning and stooping as he shovelled coal from the tender into the firebox. And he could see something that had no right to be there but which he might have expected—a soldier armed with a carbine, crouched for protection from the cold close into the gaping red maw of the firebox.

Reynolds fumbled for his gun, but all the feeling had left his hands; he couldn't even get his frozen forefinger through the trigger guard. He thrust it back in his pocket and rose quickly to his feet, leaning far into the wind, the ventilator still locked between his legs. It was all or nothing now. He took one short step; the sole of his right shoe found the edge of the carriage with the second step. He was in mid-air; then he was sliding and slithering down the sloping, crumbling coal of the tender to land on his shoulder and side, temporarily winded, at the back of the footplate.

They turned to stare at him—all three, engineer, stoker, and soldier, turned to stare at him, their faces almost comical in bewilderment and disbelief. Perhaps five seconds elapsed—five precious seconds that enabled Reynolds partially to regain his breath—before the soldier abruptly recovered from his astonishment, unslung his rifle, swept the butt high in the air, and leapt towards the prostrate Reynolds. Reynolds grasped a lump of coal, the first thing that came to hand, and flung it despairingly at the advancing man, but his fingers were too numb, and as the soldier ducked low the coal flew high over his head, missing him completely. But the fireman didn't miss, and the soldier collapsed on to the footplate as the flat of the shovel caught him on the back of the head.

Reynolds scrambled to his feet. With the torn clothes and bleeding, frost-whitened hands, and face streaked with coal dust, he was an incredible spectacle, but at that moment quite oblivious of the fact. He stared at the fireman, a big, curly-haired youngster with his shirt sleeves rolled far up in defiance of the bitter cold, then transferred his gaze to the soldier at his feet.

"The heat." The youngster was grinning. "He was suddenly overcome."

"But why——"

"Look, friend, I don't know who you're for, but I know who I'm against." He leaned on his shovel. "Can we help you?"

"You certainly can!" Reynolds rapidly explained, and the two men looked at each other. The older man, the driver, hesitated.

"We have to think of ourselves——"

"Look!" Reynolds ripped his coat open. "A rope. Take it off, will you? My hands are about gone. You can tie each other's wrists. That should——"

"Of course!" The younger man grinned even as the driver reached for the air-brake lever. "We were held up. Five or six men at least. Safe home, my friend."

Reynolds hardly stopped to thank the men who helped him so casually with so little thought for themselves. The train was slowing down quickly on that incline, and he had to get to the back wagon before it stopped altogether and the tightening of the coupling chain, as the wagon tried to move back down the hill, made it impossible to free it. He jumped out from the lowest cab step, tumbled head over heels, regained his feet, and started running back. The train was almost stopped now as the guard's van crawled past him, and he had a momentary, heart-warming glimpse of Jansci standing in the open door at the rear of the van, a gun rock-steady in his hand.

Then the buffers were banging and rattling together as the locomotive up front came to a halt. Reynolds had his torch switched on and was lifting the towing links clear and knocking off the air-brake flange coupling with his hammer. He looked briefly for a steam coupling, but there was none—convicts didn't need heat—he had severed all connection between the last wagon and the train. All the carriages were now jolting backwards under the impetus of the releasing pressure of the compressed buffer springs; Jansci, a bunch of keys swinging in one hand and the leveled gun still in the other, was stepping across from the guard's van to the cattle truck, and Reynolds himself was just grabbing hold of the handrail when the guard's van bumped violently into the truck and gave it its initial impetus for the run down the long, gentle hill they had just climbed.

The big brake wheel was on the outside of the wagon and Reynolds was beginning to turn this, perhaps a mile after they had left the main train, when Jansci finally found the right key for the wagon, kicked the door open, and flashed his torch inside. Half a mile further on Reynolds was just giving the wheel its final lock and bringing the coach to a gentle standstill, watched by a smiling Jansci and a Dr. Jennings who had been at first dazed then unbelieving but now as wildly excited as any schoolboy.

And they had barely left the wagon and were striking out for the west where they knew the road lay when they heard a cry and saw a figure floundering towards them through the deep snow. It was the Count, all aristocratic reserve gone, yelling and shouting and waving his arms like a madman.

11

THEY arrived at Jansci's headquarters in the country, not ten miles from the Austrian frontier, at half-past six in the following morning. They arrived after fourteen consecutive hours' motoring over the frozen snowbound roads of Hungary at an average speed of well under twenty miles an hour, after fourteen of the coldest, most uncomfortable, most exhausting hours' travelling that Reynolds had ever done in his life. But they arrived, and for all their cold and hunger and weariness and sleeplessness, they arrived in tremendous spirits, their elation buoying them up above all their distress—all except the Count, who, after his first outburst of gladness at their safety and success, had relapsed, as the long hours of the night wheeled by, into his usual remote, detached mood of sombre cynicism.

They had covered exactly four hundred endless, gruelling kilometres in the course of that night, and the Count had driven every kilometre of the way, stopping twice only for petrol, rousing reluctant, sleeping pump attendants with the twin menaces of his voice and uniform. More than once, as the lines of strain had etched themselves more and more deeply into the Count's lean face, Reynolds had been on the point of suggesting that he take over, but each time his common sense had come to the rescue and he had refrained: as he had observed on that first drive in the black Mercedes, the Count, as a driver, was in a world all of his own and, on these snowbound treacherous roads, it was more important that they should arrive safely than that the Count's exhaustion should be relieved. And so for most of the night Reynolds had sat and dozed and watched him, as did the Cossack by his side, both of them being in the relatively warm cab for the same reason—to thaw out. The Cossack had been in far worse case than even Reynolds, and understandably so: for the last half of the distance between Szekszárd and Pécs—almost twenty miles—he had been perched outside the truck, jammed between fender and bonnet, keeping the windshield completely clear for the Count as he had driven through the blinding snow. And it had been on that fender that he had had his grandstand view of Reynolds' suicidal climb across the coach roofs, and there was no scowl now in his face as he looked at Reynolds, just a kind of awed wonder.

The direct route from Pécs to Jansci's house in the country would have been just under half of the actual distance they had covered, but both Jansci and the Count had been convinced that taking that route could only have had one end—a concentration camp. The fifty-mile stretch of Lake Balaton blocked off most of the escape routes to the Austrian border in the west, and both men had been sure that between its southern tip and the Yugoslavian border not even the most insignificant road would be left unwatched. The other routes to the West, between the northern tip of Balaton and Budapest, might or might not have been watched, but they had taken no chances. They had gone two hundred kilometres due north, circled round the northern outskirts of the capital itself, then taken the main highway to Austria, branching off to the southwest as they approached Györ.

And so it had taken them fourteen hours and four hundred kilometres, and brought them to their destination cold and hungry and exhausted. But once they were inside the safety and shelter of the house, these things fell from them like a cloak, and when Jansci and the Cossack produced a roaring fire in the wood stove, Sandor a cooking pot and a magnificent smell of cooking, and the Count a bottle of *barack* from a more than adequate stock he kept in the house, their relief at their safe arrival, their jubilation at having completely thwarted the AVO, expressed itself in talk and laughter and still more talk. And with warm food inside them and the Count's *barack* bringing life back to frozen bodies and limbs, all thought of weariness and sleep was forgotten. There would be time enough for sleep—they had all day for sleep—for Jansci wasn't going to make his attempt at the border till after midnight of that day.

Eight o'clock came, and with it the weather and news reports over the big, modern radio Jansci had recently installed in the house. Of their own activities and the rescue of the professor there was no mention, nor had they expected any: such a confession of failure was the last thing the Communists would make to their satellite subjects. The weather report, which predicted further heavy and continuous snowfall over almost the entire country, contained an item of extreme interest: all southwest Hungary, in an area stretching east from Lake Balaton to Szeged on the Yugoslavian border, was completely immobilised by the severest snowstorm since the war, every road, railway line, and airport being completely blocked. Jansci and the others listened in a silence more eloquent of their relief than any words could have been: had their attempt been made twelve hours later, both rescue and escape would have been impossible.

Nine o'clock came and with it the first grey tinges of dawn through the again thickly falling snow, the second bottle of *barack,* and the recounting of many stories. Jansci told of their sojourn in the Szarháza, the Count, already with half a bottle of brandy inside him, gave an ironic account of his interview with Furmint, and Reynolds himself had to tell, several times over, of his perilous journey across the top of the train. To all this, the most avid listener by far was the old professor, whose feelings towards his Russian hosts, as Jansci and Reynolds had observed when they had seen him in the Szarháza, had undergone a radical and violent change. The beginnings of the change and their change towards him had come, he said, when he had refused to speak at the conference until he knew what had happened to his son, and when he had heard that his son had escaped, he refused to speak anyway—the Russians' last hold over him was gone. Being thrown into the Szarháza had made him more furious than ever, and the final indignity of being imprisoned in the same freezing cattle truck as a band of hardened criminals had completed his conversion in no uncertain fashion. And when he had heard of the tortures inflicted on Jansci and Reynolds his fury knew no bounds. He swore in a most uncharacteristic fashion.

"Wait!" he said. "By heavens, just wait till I get home! The British Government, their precious projects, their missiles—damn their projects and their missiles! I've got more important things to do first."

"Such as?" Jansci asked mildly.

"Communism!" Jennings downed his glass of *barack* and his voice was almost a shout. "I'm not boasting, but I've got the ear of nearly all the big newspapers in the country. They'll listen to me—especially when they remember the damned poppycock I used to talk before. I'll expose the whole damned, rotten system of communism, and by the time I'm finished——"

"Too late." The interruption came from the Count, and the tone was ironic.

"What do you mean, 'Too late'?" Jennings demanded.

"The Count just means that communism has already been pretty thoroughly exposed," Jansci said soothingly, "and, without offence, Dr. Jennings, by people who have suffered for years under it, not just a weekend, as you have."

"You expect me to go back to London and sit on my hands——" Jennings broke off, and when he spoke again his tone was calmer. "Damn it, man, it's the duty of everyone—all right, all right, I'm late in seeing it, but I see it now—it's the duty of everyone to do what he can to stop the spread of this damnable creed——"

"Too late." Again the dry interruption came from the Count.

"He just means that communism outside its homeland is failing of its own accord," Jansci explained hastily. "You don't need to stop it, Dr. Jennings—it's already stopped. Oh, it works here and there, but only to a limited extent, and then only among primitive people like the Mongols, who fall for the fine phrases and the even finer promises, but not with us, not with the Hungarians, Czechs, Poles, or others, not in any country where the people are more politically advanced than the Russians themselves. Take this country itself—who were the most heavily indoctrinated people?"

"The youth, I should imagine." Jennings was holding his impatience in check only with difficulty. "They always are."

"The youth." Jansci nodded. "And the pampered darlings of communism—the writers, the intellectuals, the lionised workers of heavy industry. And who led the revolt here against the Russians? Exactly the same people— the young, the intellectuals, and the workers. The fact that I think that the whole rising was futile, crazily ill-timed, has nothing to do with it. The point is that communism failed most completely in those among whom it had the best chance of succeeding—if it were ever to succeed."

"And you should see the churches in my country," the Count murmured. "Crowded masses every Sunday—packed with kids. You wouldn't worry about communism so much then, Professor. In fact," he added drily, "the only thing to match the failure of communism in our countries is its remarkable success in countries like Italy and France, which have never seen one of these in their lives." He gestured with evident distaste at the uniform he was wearing and shook his head sadly. "Human nature is a wonderful thing."

"Then what the devil would you have me do?" Jennings demanded. "Forget the whole damned thing?"

"No." Jansci shook his head with just a trace of weariness. "That's the last thing I want you to do, that's the last thing I want anyone to do—there may be a greater crime, a greater sin than indifference, but I don't know of it. No, Dr. Jennings, what I should like you to do is to go home and tell your people that we in Central Europe have only our one little life apiece to lead, and time is running out. Tell them that we would like to smell the sweet air of freedom, just once, before we go. Tell them that we have been waiting for seventeen long years now, and hope cannot last forever. Tell them we don't want our children and our children's children to walk along the dark and endless road of slavery and never see a light at the end. Tell them we don't want much—we only want a little peace, green fields and church bells and carefree children playing in the sun, without fear, without want, without wondering what dark clouds tomorrow must surely bring."

Jansci leant forward in his chair, his glass forgotten, the tired lined face beneath the thick white hair ruddy in the flickering flames of the fire, earnest and intense as Reynolds had never seen him.

"Tell them, tell your people at home, that our lives and the lives of generations to come lie in their hands. Tell them that there is only one thing that ultimately matters on this earth, and that is peace on this earth. And tell them that this is a very small earth, and growing smaller with every year that passes, but that we all have to live on it together, that we all *must* live on it together."

"Coexistence?" Dr. Jennings raised an eyebrow.

"Coexistence. A terrible word, a big bogeyman word, but what else could any sane man ever offer in its place— all the nameless horrors of a thermonuclear war, the requiem for the lost hopes of mankind? No, coexistence must come, it must if mankind is to survive, but this world without spheres, the dream of that great American, Cordell Hull, will never come if you have impetuous fools, as you do have, Dr. Jennings, shouting for big results now, here, today. It will never come so long as people in the West think in terms of parachute diplomacy, of helping us to help ourselves—— My God! They've never seen even a single Mongol division in action or they wouldn't talk such arrant nonsense—it will never come while people talk dangerous drivel about the Russian people being their secret allies and say 'Get at the Russian people' or listen to the gratuitous advice of people who fled these unhappy countries of ours years ago and have lost all contact with what we are thinking and feeling today.

"Most of all, it will never come so long as our leaders and governments, our newspapers and our propagandists teach us incessantly, insistently, that we must hate and fear and despise all the other peoples who share this same tiny world with us. The nationalism of those who cry 'We are the people'—the jingoistic brand of patriotism—these are the great evils of our world today, the barriers to peace that no man can overcome. What hope is there for the world as long as we cling to the outmoded forms of national allegiance? We owe allegiance to no one, Dr. Jennings, at least not on this earth." Jansci smiled. "Christ came to save mankind, we are told—but maybe he has made a special exception in the case of the Russians."

"What Jansci is trying to tell you, Dr. Jennings," the Count murmured, "is that all you've got to do is to convert the Western world to Christianity and all will be well."

"Not quite." Jansci shook his head. "What I say applies to the Russians even more than the Western world, but I think the first move must come from the Western world— a maturer people, a more politically advanced people— and not nearly so afraid of the Russians as the Russians are of them."

"Talk." Jennings was no longer angry, not even ironic, just thoughtful. "Talk, talk, just talk. It'll require a great deal more than that, my friend, to bring about the millennium. It needs action. First move, you said. What moves?"

"Heaven only knows." Jansci shook his head. "I don't. If I did know, no name in all history would be so revered as that of Major General Illyurin. No man can do more, no man dare do more than make suggestions."

No one spoke, and after a time Jansci went on slowly.

"It is essential, I think, to hammer home the idea of peace, the idea of disarmament, to convince the Russians, above all things, of our peaceful intentions. Peaceful intentions!" Jansci laughed without mirth. "The British and the Americans filling the armouries of the nations of Western Europe with hydrogen bombs—what a way to demonstrate peaceful intentions, what a way rather to ensure that Russia will never relax its grip on the satellites it no longer wants, what a way to drive the men of the Kremlin—scared men, I tell you—inexorably nearer the last thing in the world they want to do—sending the first intercontinental missile on its way: the last thing they want to do, the last act of panic or desperation, because they know better than any that, though in their deep cellars in Moscow they may survive the retaliation that will surely come, they will never survive the vengeful fury of the crazed survivors of the holocaust that will just as surely engulf their own nation. To arm Europe is to provoke the Russians to the point of madness: whatever else we may not do, it is essential to avoid all provocation, to keep the door of negotiation and approach always open, no matter what the rebuffs may be."

"It is essential to watch 'em like hawks, I would say," Reynolds commented.

"Alas, I thought we had made him see the light," the Count mourned. "Perhaps we never will."

"Perhaps not," Jansci agreed. "But he's right, all the same. In the one hand the big gun, in the other the olive branch. But the safety catch must always be on, and the hand of peace always a little in advance, and you must be endlessly patient—rashness, impatience could bring the world to catastrophe. Patience, endless patience—what matter a blow to your pride when the peace of the world is at stake?

"You must try to meet them in as many fields as

possible—culture, sport, literature, holidays, all those things are important enough—anything that brings people into contact with one another and lets them see the idiocies of chauvinism is bound to be important—but the great opening lies in trade. Meet them in trade, and never care how many concessions you make—the losses would be negligible in exchange for the good will gained, the suspicions allayed. And get your churches to help, as they are helping now here and in Poland. Cardinal Wyszynski, who walks hand in hand with Gomulka of Poland, knows more about the way to achieve the peace of the world that must eventually come than I ever will. People all over Poland today walk in freedom, talk in freedom, worship in freedom, and who knows what another five years may bring?—and all because men of vastly different creeds, but of an equally great good will, determined that they were going to get together and get on well, no matter what sacrifices they had to make, no matter what blows to their pride they had received.

"And that, I think, is the real answer—not the proposing of courses of action, as Dr. Jennings suggested, but in creating the climate of good will in which those actions can flower and bear fruit. Ask the rulers of the great nations who should be leading our sick world to a better tomorrow what their greatest need of today is, and they will tell you scientists and still more scientists—those luckless, brilliant creatures who have long since traded in their birthright of independence, buried their consciences, and sold out to the governments of the world—so that they can strive harder and still harder until they have in their hands the ultimate weapon of destruction."

Jansci paused and wearily shook his head. "The governments of the world may not be mad, but they are blind, and their blindness is but one step removed from insanity. The desperate, most urgent need this world knows or will ever know is the need for an effort without parallel in history to get to know ourselves and the other people of the world even as well as we know ourselves, and then we will see that the other man is just as we are, that right and virtue and truth belong to him as much as they do to us. We must think of people not as a conglomerate mass, not conveniently, indiscriminately, as a faceless nation: we must always remember that a nation is made of millions of little human beings just like we are, and to talk about national sin and guilt and wickedness is to be wilfully blind, unjust, and unchristian, and while it is true that such a nation may go off the rails, it never goes off because it wants to, but because it can't help it, because there was something in its past or in its environment that inescapably has made it what it is today, just as some forgotten incidents, some influences that we can neither recall nor understand, has made each one of us what we are today.

"And with that understanding and knowledge there will come compassion, and no power on earth can compete against compassion—the compassion that makes the Jewish Society issue world-wide appeals for money for their sworn but starving enemies, the Arab refugees, the compassion that made a Russian soldier thrust his gun into Sandor's hands, the compassion—a compassion born of understanding—that made nearly all the Russians who were stationed in Budapest refuse to fight the Hungarians, whom they had come to know so well. And this compassion, this charity, will come, it must come, but men the world over must want to make it come.

"There is no certainty that it will come in our time. It's a gamble, it must be a gamble, but better surely a gamble from hope, however tenuous that hope, than a gamble from despair and pressing the button that sends the first intercontinental missile on its way. But for the gamble to succeed, understanding comes first; mountains, rivers, seas are no longer the barriers that separate mankind, just the minds of mankind itself. The intolerance of ignorance, not *wanting* to know—that is the last real frontier left on earth."

For a long time after Jansci had finished speaking only the crackling of pine logs in the fire and the gentle singing of a kettle broke the silence in the room. The fire seemed to fascinate, to hypnotise everyone sitting there, and they stared into it as if by staring long enough they could see the future of Jansci's dream. But it wasn't the fire that fascinated them, it had been the effect of Jansci's quiet, insistent, hypnotic voice, and what his voice had said and the memory lingered long. Even the professor had lost all his anger, and Reynolds reflected wryly that if Colonel Mackintosh could only know the thoughts that were running through his mind at that moment, he would be unemployed as soon as he arrived back in England. After a time the Count rose to his feet, walked round replenishing the empty glasses, then took his seat again, and all in silence. No one even looked at him as he was doing it; no one, it seemed, wanted to be the first to break the silence or even wanted the silence to break. They were all deeply sunk in their own private thoughts; Reynolds was thinking, almost inevitably, perhaps, of the long-dead English poet who had said centuries ago almost exactly what Jansci had been saying then, when the interruption came, the harsh strident ringing of a telephone bell, and it came so pat with Reynolds' thoughts that the one thing that leapt to his mind at that moment, a moment that he was never to forget, was to wonder for whom the bell tolled. The answer was not long to wait: it tolled for Jansci.

Jansci, startled out of a deep reverie, sat up, transferred his glass to his right hand, and picked up the telephone with his other. As the phone lifted off its receiver, the ringing stopped abruptly, and in its place, clearly audible to everyone in the room, came a high-pitched shriek, a long-drawn-out scream of agony which faded away into a thin, horrible whisper as Jansci pressed the phone to his ear. The whisper gave way to staccato words, then a lighter, higher, sobbing voice, but what the words were no one could distinguish, one ivory-knuckled hand was pressing the receiver so hard to Jansci's ear that only vague incoherent sounds could escape. The others in the room could do no more than watch Jansci's face, and as they watched, it hardened into a mask of stone and the ruddy color drained slowly from his cheeks until they were as pale, almost, as the snow-white hair above. Twenty seconds, perhaps thirty, passed without Jansci speaking a word, then there came a sudden crack and a splintering of glass, and the tumbler in Jansci's hand crushed and broke and shivered into a hundred fragments as it fell on to the stone floor, and the blood from the scarred, misshapen hand began to well and flow and drip steadily down among the shattered pieces of glass. Jansci didn't even know it had happened; his whole mind, his whole being was at that moment at the other end of that telephone wire. Then he said suddenly, "I'll call you back," listened for another few moments, whispered, "No, no," in a low strangled voice, and thrust the phone violently back on its rest, but not before the others had time to hear the same sound as they had heard when Jansci had picked up the phone, a hoarse scream of pain that ended as if sheared by a guillotine as the connection went.

"That was a silly thing to do, wasn't it?" Jansci, staring down at his hand, was the first to speak, and his voice was quiet and empty of all life. He drew out a handkerchief and dabbed at the streaming blood. "And such a waste of all that good *barack*. My apologies, Vladimir." It was the first time that anyone had ever heard him call the Count by his true name.

"What in the name of God was that?" Old Jennings' hands were shaking so that the brandy spilled over the lip of his glass, and his voice was a trembling whisper.

"That was the answer to many things." Jansci wrapped the handkerchief round his hand, clenched his fist to keep it in place, and stared into the dull red heart of the fire. "We know now why Imre went missing, we know now why the Count was betrayed. They caught Imre, and they took him down to Stalin Street, and he talked to them, just before he died."

"Imre!" the Count whispered. "Before he died. Heaven forgive me. I thought he had run out on us." He looked uncomprehendingly across at the telephone. "You mean that——"

"Imre died yesterday," Jansci murmured. "Poor, lost, lonely Imre. That was Julia. Imre had told them where she was and they went out to the country and took her, just as she was leaving to come here. And then they made her tell where this place was."

Reynolds' chair crashed over backwards as he rose to his feet, and his lower teeth were showing like a wolf's.

"That was Julia screaming." His voice was hoarse and unreal, totally unlike his normal voice. "They tortured her, they tortured her!"

"That was Julia; Hidas wanted to show that he meant business." Jansci's dull voice became muffled as he buried his face in his hands. "But they didn't torture Julia, they tortured Catherine in front of Julia, and Julia had to tell."

Reynolds stared at him uncomprehendingly. Jennings looked baffled and fearful, and the Count was swearing to himself, over and over, a meaningless, blasphemous litany of oaths, and Reynolds knew that the Count understood, and then Jansci was talking, mumbling to himself, and all of a sudden Reynolds understood also and he felt sick and fumbled his chair upright and sat down; his legs seemed to have become weak and nerveless.

"I knew she hadn't died," Jansci muttered. "I always knew she hadn't died, I never gave up hoping, did I, Vladimir? I knew she hadn't died . . . Oh God, why didn't you let her die, why didn't you *make* her die?"

Jansci's wife, Reynolds realised dully, his wife was still alive. Julia had said that she must have died, died within days of the AVO taking her away, but she hadn't died; the same faith and hope that had kept Jansci searching the breadth of Hungary in the sure knowledge that she lived must also have kept the spark of life burning in Catherine, firm in the faith that one day Jansci would find her. But now they had her, Hidas had left the Szarháza because he had known where to find her, these devils of the AVO had her . . . and they had Julia, and that was a thousand times worse. Unbid, shadowy pictures of her crossed his mind, the mischievous way she had smiled at him when she had kissed him good-bye near Margit Island, the deep concern in her face when she had seen what Coco had done to him, how she had been looking at him when he waked from sleep, the dead, dull look and the clouded eyes when foreknowledge of coming tragedy had touched her mind . . . Suddenly, without being aware that he had had any intention of doing so, Reynolds rose to his feet.

"Where did the call come from, Jansci?" His voice was back to normal again, no trace of the ice-cold rage showing through.

"The Andrassy Ut. What does it matter, Meechail?"

"We can get them back for you. We can go now and get them back. Just the Count and myself. We can do it."

"If any two men alive could do it, I can see these two before me now. But even you cannot do it." Jansci smiled, a slow, wan smile that hardly touched his lips, but nonetheless he smiled. "The job, only the job, nothing but your job. That is your creed, what you live by. Your job is done. What would Colonel Mackintosh think, Meechail?"

"I don't know, Jansci," Reynolds said slowly. "I don't know, and God knows I don't even care. I'm through, I'm finished. I've done my last job for Colonel Mackintosh, I've done my last job for our Intelligence Service, so with your permission, the Count and I . . ."

"One moment." Jansci held up his hand. "There's more

to it than that, it's even worse than you think. . . . What did you say, Dr. Jennings?"

"Catherine," the old man murmured. "What a strange coincidence, my wife's name is Catherine also."

"The coincidence affecting us is even deeper than that, I'm afraid, Professor." For a long time Jansci gazed sightlessly into the fire, then he stirred. "The British used your wife as a lever against you and now——"

"Of course, of course," Jennings murmured. He was no longer trembling, but quiet and unafraid. "It is obvious, is it not? Why else should they have rung up? I shall leave at once."

"Leave at once?" Reynolds stared. "What does he mean?"

"If you knew Hidas as well as I," the Count said, "you wouldn't have to ask. A straight trade, is it not, Jansci? Catherine and Julia returned alive in exchange for the professor here."

"That's what they say. They'll give them back to me if I return the professor." Jansci shook his head, slowly, finally. "It cannot be, of course, it cannot be. I cannot give you up, I cannot give you back. God only knows what they might do to you if they had hands on you again."

"But you must, you must." Jennings was on his feet and was staring down at Jansci. "They will not harm me, I am too useful to them. Your wife, Jansci, your family—what is my freedom compared to their lives? You have no choice in the matter. I am going."

"You would give my family back to me—and you would never see your own again. Do you realise what you are saying, Dr. Jennings?"

"Yes." Jennings spoke quietly, doggedly. "I do know what I'm saying. It's not the separation that's so important, it's just that if I go to them both our families will be alive—and who knows, freedom may come my way again. If I don't, your wife and daughter die. Surely you can see that?"

Jansci nodded, and Reynolds, even through his anxiety, through his almost overpowering anger, could still feel pity, could feel heart-sorry for any man presented with such a cruel, inhuman choice: and that the choice should be presented to a man like Jansci, a man who only moments ago had been preaching the creed of loving his enemies, of the need for understanding and helping and conciliating his Communist brother, made everything so bitterly intolerable. And then Jansci cleared his throat to speak, and Reynolds knew what he was going to say even before he said it.

"I am more glad then ever, Dr. Jennings, that I have helped, in what little way I could, to save you. You are a brave man, and a good man, but you shall not die for me or mine. I will tell Colonel Hidas——"

"No, *I* will tell Colonel Hidas," the Count interrupted. He crossed to the phone, cranked a handle, and gave a number. "The colonel is always so pleased to have reports from his junior officers. . . . No, Jansci, leave this to me. You have never questioned my judgment before: I beg of you don't start doing it now."

He broke off, stiffened slightly, then relaxed and smiled.

"Colonel Hidas? Ex-Major Howarth here . . . In excellent health, I'm glad to say . . . Yes, we have thought over your proposition, and have one to make in return. I know how grievously you must miss me—me, the most efficient officer in the AVO, a fact vouched for, you will remember, by no less a person than yourself—and propose to remedy this. If I can guarantee that Professor Jennings will not talk when he reaches the West, will you accept myself, a humble makeweight to be sure, in exchange for Major General Illyurin's wife and daughter? . . . Yes, yes, certainly I'll wait. But I haven't all day."

He cradled the phone in his hand and turned to face both the professor and Jansci, holding out a hand to stop their protestations and the professor's futile efforts to take the phone from him.

"Rest easy, gentlemen, and reassure yourselves. Noble self-sacrifice has little appeal for me: in fact, not to put too fine a point on it, it has none at all. . . . Ah, Colonel Hidas . . . Ah, so, I feared as much . . . A blow to my self-esteem, but then I am, I suppose, only a little fish . . . Then the professor it must be . . . Yes, he is more than willing . . . He will *not* go back to Budapest for the transfer, Colonel Hidas . . . do you think we are mad? If we go there, then you have all three, so if you insist on Budapest, then Dr. Jennings crosses the border tonight, and nothing you or any man in Hungary can do can prevent that. You know that better than—— Aha, I thought you would see reason—you always were so reasonable a man, were you not? Then listen carefully.

"About three kilometres north of this house—the general's daughter will show you the way here if you cannot find it easily—a side road branches off to the left. Follow this road—it ends about eight kilometres further on at a small ferry across a tributary of the Raba. Remain there. About three kilometres to the north there is a wooden bridge over the same stream. We are going to cross that, destroy it so that you will not be tempted to follow it, and make our way south to the ferryman's house opposite which you will arrive. There is a small, rope-operated boat there which we will use to effect the transfer of prisoners. All this is clear to you?"

There was a long pause; the faintly metallic, indistinguishable murmur of Hidas' voice was the only sound in the silence of the room, then the Count said, "Wait a moment," covered the mouthpiece with his hand, and turned to the others.

"He says he must have an hour's delay—they must have government permission. It's quite likely. It's also more than likely that, in normal circumstances, our dear friend would use that hour to call up the army to surround us or the air force to drop a few well-chosen bombs down the chimney."

"Impossible." Jansci shook his head. "The nearest army units are at Kaposvár, south of Balaton, and we know from the radio that they must be completely bogged down."

"And the nearest air force bases are up at the Czech border." The Count glanced through the window at the grey world of driving snow. "Even if they aren't unserviceable or closed in, no aircraft could ever find us in this weather. We take a chance?"

"We take a chance," Jansci echoed.

"You have your hour, Colonel Hidas." The Count had removed his hand from the mouthpiece. "Call us a minute later, and you'll find us gone. One other thing. You will come by way of the village of Vylok, and by no other way—we do not wish to have our escape route cut off, and you know the size of our organisation—we will have every other road north of Szombáthely covered, and if a car or truck as much as stirs along these roads, you will arrive here to find us gone. Until we meet then, my dear

Colonel . . . In about three hours, you would say? *Au revoir.*"

He replaced the phone and turned to the others.

"You see how it is, gentlemen— I get all the kudos and reputation for chivalry and self-sacrificing gallantry, without any of the distressing risks customarily associated with these things. Missiles mean more than revenge, and they want the professor. We have three hours."

Three hours, and now one of them was almost gone. It was an hour that should have been spent in sleep, they were all exhausted and desperately in need of sleep, but the thought of sleep occurred to none. It could not occur to Jansci, dazed though he was with joy at the thought of seeing Catherine again, because he was at the same time unhappy, consumed with anxiety and remorse, and still in his heart blindly determined that the professor should not go. It could not occur to the professor, for he had no wish to spend his last few hours of freedom in sleep, and it did not occur to the Cossack, because he was again at his interminable practice with his whip, readying himself for glorious battle against the accursed AVO. Sandor never thought of it; he had just walked up and down in the bitter cold outside by Jansci's shoulder, because he would not leave him at this hour. And the Count was drinking, heavily, steadily, as if he would never see a bottle of brandy again. Reynolds watched him in silent wonder as he opened a third bottle of brandy—and the Count had already consumed more than half of the others. He might have been drinking water for all the apparent effects.

"You think I drink too much, my friend?" He smiled at Reynolds. "You do not conceal your thoughts."

"Wrong. Why shouldn't you?"

"Why not indeed? I like the stuff."

Reynolds shrugged. "That's not why you drink."

"No?" The Count raised an eyebrow. "To drown my many sorrows, perhaps?"

"To drown Jansci's sorrows, I think," Reynolds said slowly. Then he had a moment of acute, unusual perception. "No, I think I know. You *know*—how you can be sure I do not know—but you *are* sure that Jansci will see his Catherine and Julia again. His sorrow is gone, but yours remains, and yours was the same as his, but now you have to bear yours alone, so you feel it with redoubled effect."

"Jansci has been talking to you?"

"He has said nothing to me."

"I believe you." The Count regarded him thoughtfully. "You know, you have aged ten years in a few days, my friend. You will never be the same again. You are, of course, leaving your Intelligence Service?"

"This is my last mission. No more."

"And going to marry the fair Julia?"

"Good God!" Reynolds stared at him. "Is it—is it as obvious as that?"

"You were the last to see it. It was obvious to everyone else."

"Well then, yes. Of course." He frowned in surprise. "I haven't asked her yet."

"No need. I know women." The Count waved a lackadaisical hand. "She probably has faint hopes of making something of you."

"I hope she has." Reynolds paused, hesitated, then looked directly at the Count. "You put me off beautifully there, didn't you?"

"Yes, I did. It was unfair— I was personal, and you had the grace not to rebuff me. Sometimes I think pride is a damnable thing." The Count poured a half tumbler full of brandy, drank from it, chain-lit another Russian cigarette, then went on abruptly, "Jansci was looking for his wife, I for my little boy. Little boy! He would be twenty next month—maybe he *is* twenty. I don't know, I don't know. I hope he lived."

"He was not your only child?"

"I have five children, and the children had a mother and grandfather and uncles, but I do not worry about them, they are all safe."

Reynolds said nothing; there was no need to say anything. He knew from what Jansci had said that the Count had lost everything and everybody in the world—except his little boy.

"They took me away when he was only three years old," the Count went on softly. "I can still see him standing there in the snow, wondering, not understanding. I have thought of him since, every night, every day of my life. Did he survive? Who looked after him? Had he clothes to keep the cold out? Has he still clothes to keep the cold out? Does he get enough to eat, or is he thin and wasted? Perhaps no one wanted him, but surely to God— He was such a little boy, Mr. Reynolds. I wonder what he looks like; I always wondered what he looked like. I wondered how he smiled and laughed and played and ran. I wanted all the time to be by his side, to see him every day of my life, to see all the wonderful things you see when your child is growing up, but I have missed it all, all the wonderful years are gone, and it is too late now. Yesterday, all our yesterdays, can never come again. He was all that I have lived for, but to every man there comes a moment of truth, and mine came this morning. I shall never see him again. May God look after my little boy."

"I'm sorry I asked," murmured Reynolds. "I'm terribly sorry." He paused, then he said: "That's not true, I don't know why I said that. I'm glad I asked."

"It's strange, but I'm glad I told you." The Count drained his glass, refilled it, glanced at his watch, and when he spoke again he was the old Count, his voice brisk and assertive and ironic. "*Barrack* brings self-pity, but it also dispels it. Time we were moving, my friend. The hour is almost up. We cannot stay here—only a madman would trust Hidas."

"So Jennings must go?"

"Jennings must go. If they don't get him, then Catherine and Julia . . ."

"Finish. Is that it?"

"I'm sorry."

"Hidas must want him badly."

"He wants him desperately. The Communists are mortally afraid that if he escapes to the West and talks—and that would be a blow from which they would not recover for a long time—the damage would be irreparable. That is why I phoned and offered myself. I knew how badly they wanted me; I wanted to find out how badly they wanted Jennings. As I said, they want him desperately."

"Why?" Reynolds' voice was strained.

"He will never work for them again," the Count answered obliquely. "They know that."

"What you mean is——"

"What I mean is that they only want his everlasting silence," the Count said harshly. "There is only one way you can ensure that."

"God above!" Reynolds cried. "We can't let him go, we can't let him walk to his death and not do——"

"You forget about Julia," the Count said softly.

Reynolds buried his face in his hands, too confused, too dazed to think any more. Half a minute passed, perhaps a minute, then he jerked upright as the harsh, strident ring of the telephone bell cut through the silence of the room. The Count had the receiver off its rest within two seconds.

"Howarth here. Colonel Hidas?"

Again the listeners—Jansci and Sandor had just hurried in through the doorway, heads and shoulders matted with snow—could hear the metallic murmur of the voice in the earpiece, but were unable to distinguish anything. All they could do was watch the Count as he leaned negligently against the wall, his eyes moving idly, unseeingly around the room. Suddenly he straightened off the wall, the contracting muscles of his eyebrows etching a deep, vertical line on his forehead.

"Impossible! I said an hour, Colonel Hidas. We cannot wait any longer. Do you think we are madmen to sit here till you can take us at your leisure?"

He paused as the voice at the other end interrupted him, listened for a few moments to the urgent, staccato chatter, stiffened as he heard the click of a receiver being replaced, looked for a moment at the lifeless phone, then slowly returned it to its hook. His right thumb, as he turned to face the others, was rubbing slowly, gratingly against the side of his forefinger, and his lower lip was caught between his teeth.

"Something's wrong." The voice reflected the anxiety in his face. "Something's very wrong. Hidas says the minister responsible is at his country retreat, the telephone lines are down, they've had to send a car to fetch him and it might be another half hour, or possibly—— You damned idiot!"

"What do you mean?" Jansci demanded. "Who——"

"Me." The uncertainty had vanished from the Count's face, and the low controlled voice was alive with a desperate urgency that Reynolds had never heard before. "Sandor, start the truck—now. Grenades, ammonium nitrate to take care of that little bridge at the foot of the road, and the field telephone. Hurry, all of you. For God's sake, hurry!"

No one stopped to question the Count. Ten seconds later they were all outside in the heavily falling snow, piling equipment into the truck, and within a minute the truck was jolting down the bumpy path towards the road. Jansci turned to the Count, one eyebrow raised in mute interrogation.

"That last call came from a call box," the Count said quietly. "Criminal negligence on my part not to catch on to it right away. Why is Colonel Hidas of the AVO telephoning from a call box? Because he's no longer in his Budapest office. It's a hundred to one that the previous call wasn't from Budapest either, but from our divisional H.Q. in Györ. Hidas has been on his way here all the time, desperately trying to delay us, to keep us here with these bogus phone calls. The minister, government permission, broken phone lines—lies, all lies. My God, to think that we fell for that sort of thing! Budapest— Hidas left Budapest hours ago! I'll wager he's no more than five miles from here at this very moment. Another fifteen minutes and he would have nailed us all, six good little flies waiting patiently in the spider's parlour."

12

THEY waited at the foot of the telephone pole by the side of the wood, peering through the momentarily thinning snow and shivering almost continuously. Too little sleep, too much exhaustion, and the treacherous, quickly evaporating warmth of the brandy were no fit preparation for even so brief a vigil in the bitter cold.

And it had been a brief vigil, so far. A scant fifteen minutes had elapsed since they had left the house, driven down the dirt track across the little humpbacked bridge, then turned west along the main road till they had come to this wood, perhaps two hundred yards from the turn-off, with its hiding place for the truck. The Count and Sandor had been dropped at the bridge, to place the charges of ammonium nitrate, while Reynolds and the professor had run into the wood, improvised rough and ready switches from dead branches, hurried back to the bridge, and helped the Count and Sandor to conceal their tire tracks and the wiring which led from the nitrate to the wood where Sandor was now in hiding with the plunger in his hand. By the time the others had returned to the truck Jansci and the Cossack, the latter agile as a monkey on any pole or tree, had already connected up their field set to the overhead telephone wires leading to the house.

Another ten mintes passed, twenty, then half an hour. The snow still fell thinly, the cold reached more deeply for the marrow of their bones, and both Jansci and the Count, with the AVO now long overdue, had become suspicious and anxious. It was not like the AVO to be late, especially when such a prize was at stake; it was most unlike Colonel Hidas, the Count declared, to be late at any time. Perhaps they were being held up by bad roads or impassable roads. Perhaps Hidas had disregarded instructions, perhaps his men were at that very moment sealing off every road to the frontier and encircling them from the rear, but the Count thought it highly unlikely: he knew that Hidas was under the impression that Jansci had a large and far-reaching organisation and that Jansci should neglect the obvious precaution of posting lookouts on the roads for miles around would probably never even cross his mind. But that Hidas had some stratagem in mind, the Count was now convinced. Hidas was a formidable adversary at any time, and the concentration camps held all too many people who had underrated the astuteness and persistence of that thin and embittered Jew. Hidas was up to something.

And it became immediately plain when Hidas did finally turn up, he had indeed been up to something. He came from the east, and he came in a big, green, closed-in truck which, the Count said, was his mobile H.Q.-cum-caravan accompanied by another, smaller brown truck, almost certainly with some of his AVO killers inside. So much Jansci and the Count had expected. But what they had not expected, and what amply accounted for the AVO's delay in arriving, was the presence of the third vehicle in the convoy, a big lumbering, heavily armoured half-track, equipped with a vicious-looking high-velocity anti-tank rifle, almost half the length of the vehicle itself. The watchers by the telephone pole at the woodside stared at each other in perplexity, at a loss to discover any possible reason for this display of armed might. They were not left to wonder long.

Hidas knew exactly what he was doing—he must have learned from Julia that Jansci's house had two blind-gable end walls—for he didn't hesitate, not even for a moment: he had his men well briefed and trained, and the manoeuvre was executed with smooth and effortless efficiency. A few hundred yards distant from the track leading off the road to the house the two trucks accelerated, leaving the half-track behind, then changed down almost in perfect unison, braked, swerved off the road, and across the little humpbacked bridge, raced up to the house and fanned out, one on either side of it, coming to rest opposite and several yards distant from either of the blind-gable walls. Immediately the trucks had stopped, armed men leapt out and took up crouching positions behind the trucks and behind the little outbuildings and some of the trees that bordered the back of the house.

Even before the last man had taken up position, the big half-track had swung off the road, scraped between the low walls of the hump bridge, with the snout of its long gun pointing grotesquely skywards, plunged down the other side and ground to a halt about fifty yards away from the front of the house. A second elapsed, then another, then there came a flat, whiplash crack as the big gun fired and a roar and eruption of smoke and flying debris as the shell exploded in the wall of the house just below the ground-floor windows. A few more seconds passed, the dust from the first explosion hadn't even had time to settle, when the next shell smashed into the house, perhaps a yard away from the first, then another and another and another, and already a hole almost ten feet in length had been torn in the masonry of the front wall.

"The treacherous, murderous swine," the Count whispered. His face was quite expressionless. "I knew I couldn't trust him, but I didn't know till now just how much I couldn't trust him." He broke off as the big gun fired again, and waited until the rolling echoes had died away. "I've seen this a hundred times—this is the technique that the Germans first perfected in Warsaw. If you want to bring a house down without blocking the streets, you just knock the bottom out and the house falls in upon itself. They also discovered, just by way of an extra dividend, that everyone hiding in such a house would be crushed to death at the same time."

"And that's what they are trying— I mean, they think we're in there?" There was a tremor in Dr. Jennings' voice, and his horror showed in his pale face.

"They're not just amusing themselves by having target practice," the Count said roughly. "Of course they think we're there. And Hidas has his terriers stationed all around the house in case the rats should try to bolt from their hole."

"I see." Jennings' voice was steadier now. "It would appear that I have overestimated the value of my services to the Russians."

"No," the Count lied. "No, you haven't. They want you all right—but I suspect they want Major General Illyurin—and myself—even more. Jansci is Communist Hungary's enemy number one, and they know this chance would never come their way again. They couldn't pass it up—and they were prepared to sacrifice even you to make the most of this chance."

Reynolds felt a slow stirring within him—a stirring of anger and admiration—anger for the way the Count was hiding the truth from Jennings, for letting him think that they could still trade him without any danger to himself, admiration for the ready skill with which he had invented so plausible an explanation.

"They're fiends—they're inhuman fiends," Jennings was saying in wonder.

"It is certainly difficult to think of them as anything else at times," Jansci said heavily. "Did—did anyone see them?" There was no need to ask whom he meant by "them," the mute headshakings showed that all had understood. "No? Then perhaps we had better call our friend up there. The phone connection is under the gable. It shouldn't have been damaged yet."

And it hadn't. There was a lull in the firing, and in the still, frosty air it was quite easy for them to hear the ringing of the bell inside the house as Jansci cranked the handle of the field telephone; easy, too, to hear a shouted order and see the man who ran round the corner of the house, waving a signal to the gunners in the half-track: almost at once the big rifle dipped to one side. Another order, and the crouching soldiers round the house broke quickly from their hiding places, some running towards the front of the house, some towards the back. At the front, the watchers could see the AVO men stooping low along the gaping ruin that was all that remained of the wall, then jumping up and poking their carbines through the shattered windows while a couple of men kicked the front door back off its broken hinges and passed inside. Even at that distance there was no mistaking the first of the two men who had gone inside; there was no mistaking the giant, gorilla-like figure of Coco anywhere.

"You begin to understand, perhaps, why the worthy Colonel Hidas has survived so long?" the Count murmured. "One could hardly accuse him of taking unnecessary chances."

Coco and the other AVO men reappeared at the front door, and at a word from the giant the other men watching at the windows relaxed while one of them disappeared round the corner of the house. He reappeared almost at once, followed by another, who went straight inside the house, and that this other could only have been Colonel Hidas was obvious when they heard his voice coming tinnily through the field phone's headset seconds later: Jansci had only one of the receivers to his ear, and the voice came clearly enough through the second for all the others to hear.

"Major General Illyurin, I presume?" Hidas' voice was calm, composed, and only the Count knew it well enough to detect the faint edge of anger underneath.

"Yes. Is this the way the gentlemen of the AVO keep their bargains, Colonel Hidas?"

"There is no room for childish recrimination between the two of us," Hidas replied. "Where are you speaking from, may I enquire?"

"That, too, is irrelevant. You have brought my wife and daughter?"

There was a long pause, while the receiver went dead, then Hidas' voice came again. "Naturally. I said I would."

"May I see them, please?"

"You do not trust me?"

"A superfluous question, Colonel Hidas. Let me see them."

"I must think." Again the phone went dead, and the Count said urgently:

"He's not thinking—that fox never requires to think. He's stalling for time. He knows we must be somewhere we can see him—so he knows he can see us. That was what his first pause was for—he was telling his men to——"

A shout from the house brought confirmation of the

Count's guess, even before he had made it in words, and a moment later a man came rushing out the front door and ran down pell-mell towards the half-track.

"He's seen us," said the Count softly. "Us or the truck behind us. And now guess what?"

"No need to guess." Jansci dropped the field set. "The half-track. Take cover! Will it blast us from there—or will it come to seek us out? That's the only question."

"It'll come for us," Reynolds was certain. "Shells are useless in a wood."

He was right. Even as he was speaking, the big Diesel of the half-track had growled into life, and now it was lumbering up to the clear space in front of the house, stopping and going reverse.

"He's coming all right." Jansci nodded. "They didn't have to move to fire from there—that rifle turret can traverse through 360 degrees." He moved out from the cover of his tree, jumped over the snow-filled ditch on to the road, and held both arms, just touching, high above his head—the agreed signal to the hidden, waiting Sandor that he was to press the plunger.

No one was prepared for what happened, not even the Count, who had underestimated how desperate Hidas had become. Faintly, through the field telephone lying on the ground, he heard Hidas shouting "Fire!" and before the Count had time even to call out a warning several automatic carbines had opened up from the house and they leapt back behind tree trucks to escape the whistling hail of rifle fire that smashed into the wood around them, some shells striking into the boles with solid hammer blows, other ricocheting off and whining away evilly to bury their misshapen metal in tree trunks still deeper in the wood, and yet others just breaking off branches and twigs to bring tiny flurries of frozen snow sifting down gently to the ground. But Jansci had had no time, no chance and no warning, and he toppled and swayed and crashed heavily to the road as might one of the trees behind him when the feller's axe had struck the last blow at its base. Reynolds straightened from his shelter and had just taken his first plunging step towards the road when he was grabbed from behind and hauled roughly behind the tree he had just left.

"Do you want to get yourself killed too?" The Count's voice was savage, but the savagery was not directed at

Reynolds. "I don't think he's dead—you can see his foot moving."

"They'll fire again," Reynolds protested. The crackling of the carbines had ended as abruptly as it had begun. "They can riddle him lying there."

"All the more reason why you shouldn't commit suicide."

"But Sandor's waiting! He hadn't time to see the signal ——"

"Sandor's nobody's fool. He doesn't require any signal." The Count edged an eye round a corner of his sheltering tree, saw the half-track rumbling down the dirt road towards the bridge. "If that bridge goes up now, that damn tank can stop and pulverise us from where it stands: worse, it can reverse and cross the ditch, tracks first, on to the main road. Sandor knows it. Watch!"

Reynolds watched. The half-track was almost on the bridge now. Ten yards, five yards, it was climbing up the far hump of the bridge. Sandor had left it too late—Reynolds knew he had left it too late—then there came a sudden flash of light, a low dull roar nothing like so loud as Reynolds had expected, followed first by the rumbling of falling masonry, then a grinding, metallic screeching and a crash which shook the ground almost as much as the explosion had done as the half-track plunged nose first into the bed of the stream and the far abutment of the bridge, its long rifle smashing against what was left of the wall of the bridge, fracturing and bending sharply upwards at a crazy angle, as if it had been made of cardboard.

"Our friend has a superb sense of timing," the Count murmured. The dry, ironic tone accorded ill with the set, bitter mouth, the fury barely in check. He picked up the field phone, cranked the handle viciously, and waited.

"Hidas? . . . Howarth here." The Count bit each word out separately. "You mad, crazy fool! Do you know who you've shot?"

"How should I know? Why should I care?" The easy suavity had gone from Hidas' voice, the loss of his half-track had shaken him badly.

"I'll tell you why you should care." The Count had his control back again, and his voice was silky with menace. "That was Jansci you shot, and if he's dead you will be well advised to accompany us when we cross the border into Austria tonight."

"Fool! Have you taken leave of your senses?"

"Listen, and judge who is sane. If Jansci is dead, we have no further interest in either his wife or daughter. You may do what you like with them. If he is dead, we will be across the border by midnight and within twenty-four hours Professor Jennings' story will be splashed in banner headlines across the front page of every newspaper in Western Europe and America, every paper in the free world. The fury of your masters in Budapest and Moscow will know no bounds—and I shall take great care that every paper will publish a full account of our escape and the part *you* played in it, Colonel Hidas. For you, the Black Sea Canal if you're lucky, perhaps Siberia, but almost certainly just a disappearance, shall we say? If Jansci dies, you die also—and no one knows it better than you do, Colonel Hidas."

There was a long silence, and when Hidas finally spoke, his voice was no more than a husky whisper.

"Perhaps he is not dead, Major Howarth."

"You can but pray. We shall see— I'm going to see now. If you value your life, call off these murderous hounds of yours!"

"I shall give the orders immediately."

The Count replaced the phone, to find Reynolds staring at him.

"Did you mean that? Would you have turned Julia and her mother over——?"

"My God, what do you think I am? . . . Sorry, boy, didn't mean to bite. I must have sounded convincing, eh? I'm bluffing, but Hidas doesn't know I am, and even if he wasn't more scared right now than he has ever been in his life before and realised that perhaps I was bluffing, he wouldn't even dare to try to call the bluff. We have him by the hip. Come, he should have called his dogs off by this time."

Together they ran out on the road and stooped to examine Jansci. He was lying on his back, his limbs outflung and relaxed, but he was breathing steadily and evenly. There was no need to search for the injury—the welling red blood from the long wound that stretched from the temple back past the ear was in shocking contrast to the snow-white hair. The Count stooped low, examined him briefly, then straightened.

"No one could expect Jansci to die as easily as that." The wide grin on the Count's face was eloquent of his relief. "He's been creased and concussed, but I don't even think that the bone has been chipped. He'll be all right, perhaps in a couple of hours. Come, give me a hand to lift him."

"I will take him." It was Sandor speaking, he had just emerged from the wood behind and he brushed them gently aside. He stooped, caught Jansci under the body and legs and lifted him with the ease with which one would have lifted a little child. "He is badly hurt?"

"Thank you, Sandor. No, just a glancing blow ... That was a splendid job down by the bridge. Take him into the back of the truck and make him comfortable, will you? Cossack, a pair of pliers, up that telephone pole, and wait till I give you the word. Mr. Reynolds, you might start the engine, if you please. She may be cold."

The Count picked up the phone and smiled thinly. He could hear the anxious breathing of Hidas at the other end.

"Your time has not yet come, Colonel Hidas. Jansci is badly hurt, shot through the head, but he will live. Now listen carefully. It is painfully obvious that you are not to be trusted—although that, I may say, is no recent discovery on my part. We cannot and will not carry out the exchange here—there is no guarantee that you will keep your word, every possibility that you won't. Drive along the field for about half a kilometre—it will be difficult in the snow, but you have the men and it will give us time to be on our way—and you will come to a plank bridge that will take you on to the road again. Then drive straight to the ferry. This is clear?"

"It is clear." Some of the confidence was back in Hidas' voice. "We will be there as soon as possible."

"You will be there an hour from now. No more. We do not wish to make you a present of the time to send for reinforcements and cut off escape routes to the West. Incidentally, do not waste precious time in attempting to summon help by this telephone. I am about to cut all the wires now and shall cut them again about five kilometres north of here."

"But in an hour!" Dismay was back in Hidas' voice.

"To clear these fields so deep in snow—and who knows what this side road to the river you speak of is like. If we are not there in an hour——"

"Then you will find us gone." The Count hung up the receiver, gestured to the Cossack to cut the wires, looked in to the back of the truck to see if Jansci was comfortable, then hurried round to the cab. Reynolds had the engine running, moved over to make room for the Count behind the wheel, and within seconds they were bumping out of the wood, on to the main road, and off into the northeast, where the first dusky fingers of twilight were beginning to touch the snow-capped hills under a dark and leaden sky.

Darkness was almost upon them, and the snow was beginning to fall more heavily again, with the chill promise of still more to come, when the Count swung the truck off the river road, drove a couple of hundred jolting yards up a narrow dirt track, and stopped at the bottom of a small, abandoned stone quarry. Reynolds started out of his deep reverie and looked at him in surprise.

"The ferryman's house—you've left the river?"

"Yes. Just about another three hundred metres from here—the ferry, I mean. Leaving the truck in plain view of Hidas when he arrives on the other side would be too much of a temptation altogether."

Reynolds nodded and said nothing—he had spoken barely a dozen words since they had left Jansci's house, had sat in silence beside the Count all the way, had hardly exchanged a word with Sandor as he had helped him to destroy the bridge they had so lately crossed. His mind was confused; he was torn by conflicting emotions, consumed by a torturing anxiety that made all previous anxieties fade into insignificance. The most damnable part of it all was that old Jennings was now become talkative and positively cheerful as he had never been since Reynolds had first known him, and was trying all he could to raise the flagging spirits of the others—and Reynolds suspected, without in any way having reason for his suspicion, that the old professor knew, in spite of what the Count had said, that he was going to his death. It was intolerable, it was unthinkable, that such a gallant old man should be allowed to die like that. But if he didn't, nothing was more certain than that Julia would die. Reynolds sat there in the gathering darkness, his fists clenched till forearms ached, but far at the back of his mind he knew, without in any way consciously admitting his decision to himself, that there could be only one answer.

"How is Jansci, Sandor?" The Count had slid open the inspection hatch at the back of the cab.

"He stirs." Sandor's voice was deep and gentle. "And he is muttering to himself."

"Excellent. It takes more than a bullet in the head to account for Jansci." The Count paused a moment, then continued. "We cannot leave him here—it is altogether too cold, and I don't want him to wake up not knowing where he is, not knowing where we are. I think——"

"I will carry him to the house."

Five minutes later they reached the ferryman's house, a small white stone building between the road and the heavily shingled, sloping bank of the river. The river here was perhaps forty feet wide, and very sluggish, and even in the near darkness it looked as if it might be very deep at that particular spot. Leaving the others at the door of the ferryman's house—the door faced on to the river—the Count and Reynolds jumped from the steep bank on to the shingle and went down to the water's edge.

The boat was doubled-ended, perhaps twelve feet long, without either engine or oars, the sole means of propulsion being provided by a rope stretched tight between concrete-embedded iron posts on either side of the river. This rope passed through screwed pulleys, one at either end of the boat and one on a raised amidships block, and passengers simply crossed from one bank to the other by overhanding themselves along the rope. It was a type of ferry Reynolds had never seen before, but he had to admit that, for a couple of women who probably knew nothing whatsoever about boats, it was a foolproof system. The Count echoed his thoughts.

"Satisfactory, Mr. Reynolds, very satisfactory. And so is the lay of the land on the other side of the river." He gestured at the far bank, at the curving half moon of trees that swept back from either bank, enclosing a smooth treeless expanse of snow unbroken but for the bisecting road that reached down to the water's edge. "A terrain which might have been specifically designed to discourage our good friend Colonel Hidas, who is no doubt at this very moment entertaining pleasant visions of his men lurking at the water's edge with their hands full of machine guns. It would have been difficult—I say it with modesty—for anyone to have chosen a better spot for effecting the transfer. . . . Come, let us call upon the ferryman, who is about to enjoy some unexpected and, no doubt, unwonted exercise."

The ferryman was just opening the door as the Count raised his hand to knock. He stared first at the Count's high-peaked hat, then at the wallet in the Count's hand, then licked suddenly dry lips. In Hungary it was not necessary to have a bad conscience to tremble at the sight of the AVO.

"You are alone in this house?" the Count demanded.

"Yes, yes, I am alone. What—what is it, comrade?" He made an attempt to pull himself together. "I have done nothing, comrade, nothing!"

"That's what they all say," the Count said coldly. "Get your hat and coat and return immediately."

The man was back in a matter of moments, pulling a fur cap on to his head. He made to speak, but the Count raised his hand.

"We wish to use your house for a short time, for a purpose that is no concern of yours. We are not interested in you." The Count pointed to the road leading south. "A brisk walk, comrade, and let an hour elapse before you return. You will find us gone."

The man looked at him unbelievingly, looked wildly around to see what the trap was, saw none, and scuttled round the corner of the house and up on to the road without a word. Within half a minute, his legs going like pistons, he was lost to sight round a corner of the road.

"Putting the fear of death in one's fellow man becomes, as a pastime, increasingly distasteful with the passing of the days," the Count murmured. "I must put an end to it. Bring Jansci inside, will you, Sandor?" The Count led the way through the little lobby and into the ferryman's living room, paused at the door, expelled his breath gustily, and turned round.

"On second thoughts, leave him in the lobby. It's like a damn furnace in this room—it'll only send him off again." He looked closely at Jansci as Sandor propped him in a corner with coats and some cushions taken from the living room. "See, his eyes open already, but he is still dazed. Stay with him, Sandor, and let him come out of it by

228

himself. . . . Yes, my boy?" He raised an eyebrow as the Cossack came rushing into the lobby. "You are perturbed about something?"

"Colonel Hidas and his men," the Cossack gasped. "They have arrived. Their two trucks have just pulled up at the water's edge."

"Even so." The Count screwed one of his Russian cigarettes into his holder, lit it, and sent the match spinning out through the dark oblong of the open doorway. "They are punctual to a degree. Come, let us go and pass the time of day with them."

13

THE Count walked the length of the lobby, stopped abruptly, and barred the doorway with his arm. "Remain inside, Professor Jennings, if you please."

"I?" Jennings looked at him in surprise. "Remain inside? My dear fellow, I'm the only person who is *not* remaining here."

"Quite. Nevertheless, remain here for the present. Sandor, see that he does." The Count wheeled and walked quickly away, without giving the professor opportunity for reply. Reynolds was at his heels, and when he spoke his voice was low and bitter.

"What you mean is that it requires only one single, well-directed bullet into the professor's heart and Colonel Hidas can retire, complete with prisoners, well satisfied with his night's work."

"Something of the kind had occurred to me," the Count admitted. His feet ground on the shifting shingle, then he halted by the boat and looked about the dark, cold waters of the sluggish river. The truck and each individual figure, each man, were easily seen against the white background of snow, but it had already grown so dark that it was nearly impossible to distinguish features or uniforms, just black, empty silhouettes. Only Coco was recognisable, and that by virtue of his great height; but one man stood in advance of the others, his toes by the water's edge, and it was to this man that the Count addressed himself.

"Colonel Hidas?"

"I am here, Major Howarth."

"Good, let us not waste time. I propose to effect this

exchange as quickly as possible. Night, Colonel Hidas, is almost upon us, and while you're treacherous enough in the daylight, God only knows what you're like when darkness falls. I don't propose to stay long enough to find out."

"I shall honour my promise."

"You shouldn't use words you don't understand. . . . Tell your drivers to reverse till they come to the wood. You and your men are also to fall back as far as that. At the distance—two hundred metres—it should be quite impossible for you to distinguish any of us in any way. From time to time guns are accidentally discharged, but not tonight."

"It shall be exactly as you say." Hidas turned, gave some orders, waited till the two trucks and his men had started to move back from the riverbank, then turned to face the Count. "And now what, Major Howarth?"

"This. When I call you, you will release the general's wife and daughter, and they will start walking towards the ferry. At the same moment, Dr. Jennings will get into the boat here and cross over to the other side. Once there, he will climb up to the bank, wait there till the women are close, pass by them as they approach the river, then walk slowly towards you. By the time he's there, the women should be safely across and it should, by then, be too dark for anyone, on either side, to achieve anything by indiscriminate shooting. The plan, I think, is foolproof."

"It shall be exactly as you say," Hidas repeated. He wheeled, scrambled up the shelving bank, and started to walk back towards the dark line of trees in the distance, leaving the Count gazing after him and thoughtfully rubbing his chin.

"Just that little bit too compliant, just that little bit too eager to please," he murmured. "Just a little . . . Tchah! My endlessly suspicious nature. What can he do? The time has come." He raised his voice. "Sandor! Cossack!"

He waited till the two men had come out from the cottage, then spoke to Sandor. "How is Jansci?"

"Sitting up, still swaying a bit. His head hurts very badly."

"Inevitably." The Count turned to Reynolds. "I want to say a few words to Jennings, alone—Jansci and I. Perhaps you understand. I won't keep him a minute, I promise you."

"Be as long as you like," Reynolds said dully. "There's no hurry for me."

"I know, I know." The Count hesitated, made to say something, then changed his mind. "You might launch the boat, will you?"

Reynolds nodded, watched the Count disappear into the house, and turned to give the others a hand to pull the boat down the shingled beach into the water. The boat was heavier than it looked; they had to pull it gratingly across the pebbles, but with Sandor's help it was in the water in a matter of a few seconds, tugging gently on its rope as the sluggish current caught it. Sandor and the Cossack walked back up to the top of the bank, but Reynolds remained at the water's edge. He stood there for a few moments, pulled out his gun, checked that the safety catch was on, and thrust it in his coat pocket, his hand still round it.

It seemed that only moments had elapsed, but already Dr. Jennings was at the door. He said something that Reynolds couldn't distinguish, then came Jansci's deep voice, and then the Count's.

"You—you will forgive me if I remain here, Dr. Jennings." The Count was hesitant and unsure for the first time that Reynolds had ever known. "It's just—I would rather——"

"I quite understand." Jennings' voice was steady and composed. "Do not distress yourself, my friend—and thank you for all you have done for me."

Jennings turned away abruptly, took Sandor's arm to help him down from the highbank, then stumbled awkwardly down the shingle, a stooped figure—until this moment Reynolds had never quite realised how stooped the old man really was—with his collar turned high against the bitter chill of the evening and the skirts of his thin raglan coat flapping out pathetically about his legs. Reynolds felt his heart go out to the defenceless, gallant old man.

"The end of the road, my boy." Jennings was still calm, but just a little husky. "I am sorry, I'm terribly sorry to have given you so much trouble, and all for nothing. You came a long way, a long way—and now this. This must be a bitter blow for you."

Reynolds said nothing, he couldn't trust himself to say anything: but the gun was coming clear of his pocket.

"One thing I forgot to say to Jansci," Jennings murmured. "*Dowidzenia*, tell him I said that. Just '*dowidzenia!*' He will understand."

"I don't understand, and it doesn't matter." Jennings, moving towards the boat, gasped as he walked into the barrel of the gun held rigidly in Reynolds' hand. "You're not going anywhere, Professor Jennings. You can deliver your own messages."

"What do you mean, my boy? I don't understand you."

"There's nothing to understand. You're just not going anywhere."

"But then—but then Julia——"

"I know."

"But—but the Count said you were going to marry her!"

Reynolds nodded silently in the darkness.

"And you're willing—I mean, you will give her up ——"

"There are some things even more important than that." Reynolds' voice was so low that Jennings had to stoop forward to catch the words.

"Your final word?"

"My final word."

"I am well content," Jennings murmured. "I need now hear nothing more." He turned to retrace his steps up the shingle, and, as Reynolds made to thrust his gun back in his pocket, pushed him with all his strength. Reynolds lost his footing on the treacherous pebbles, fell heavily backwards, and struck his head against a stone with force enough to leave him momentarily dazed. By the time he had shaken his head clear and risen dizzily to his feet, Jennings had shouted something at the top of his voice—it wasn't until much later that Reynolds realised that it had been the signal for Hidas to send Julia and her mother on their way—scrambled into the boat, and was already halfway across the river.

"Come back, come back, you crazy fool!" Reynolds' voice was hoarse and savage, and quite without realising the futility of what he was doing he was tugging frantically at the rope which stretched across the river, and then he dimly remembered that the rope was fixed and the boat completely independent of it. Jennings paid no attention to his call, did not even so much as look over his shoulder: the bow was grinding on the pebbles of the far side when Reynolds heard Jansci calling him hoarsely from the door of the ferryman's cottage.

"What is it? What is happening?"

"Nothing," Reynolds said wearily. "Everything is going just according to plan." He climbed up the bank as if his legs were made of lead and looked at Jansci, looked at the white hair and face and the blood that caked one side from temple to chin. "You had better get cleaned up. Your wife and daughter will be here at any moment— I can see them crossing the field now."

"I don't understand." Jansci pressed his hand to his head.

"It doesn't matter." Reynolds fumbled a cigarette into his hand and lit it. "We've kept our side of the bargain, and Jennings is gone." He stared down at the cigarette end glowing in his cupped palm, then looked up. "I forgot. He said I was to say '*dowidzenia*' to you."

"*Dowidzenia?*" Jansci had taken his hand from his head and was staring in perplexity at the blood on his fingers, but now he looked strangely at Reynolds. "He said that?"

"Yes. He said you'd understand. What does it mean?"

"Farewell—the Polish *Auf Wiedersehen*. Till we meet again."

"Oh, my God, my God!" Reynolds said softly. He spun his cigarette into the darkness, turned, and walked quite slowly along the lobby into the living room. The sofa was over in the far corner, by the fire, and old Jennings, hatless, coatless, and shaking his head from side to side, was trying to prop himself into a sitting position. Reynolds crossed the room, with Jansci now just behind him, and steadied the old man with an arm round his shoulders.

"What happened?" Reynolds asked gently. "The Count?"

"He was here." Jennings rubbed an obviously aching jaw. "He came in and took two grenades out of a bag and put them on the table, and I asked him what they were for and he said, 'If they're going back to Budapest with these trucks, they're going to have a damned long shove.' Then

233

he came across the shook hands with me—and that's all I remember."

"That's all there is, Professor," Reynolds said quietly. "Wait here. We'll be back soon—and you'll be with your wife and son within forty-eight hours."

Reynolds and Jansci went out into the lobby, and Jansci was speaking softly.

"The Count." There was warmth in his voice, something that touched on reverence. "He dies as he has lived, thinking never of himself. The grenades end the last chance of our being cut off before the border."

"Grenades!" A slow, dull anger was beginning to kindle deep down inside Reynolds, a strange anger he had never felt before. "You talk of grenades—at this hour! I thought he was your friend."

"You will never know a friend like him." Jansci was filled with a simple conviction. "He is the best friend that I or any man could ever have, and because he is that to me I would not stop him now if I could. The Count has wanted to die, he has wanted to die ever since I have known him; it was just a point of honour with him to postpone it as long as possible, to give as many suffering people what they wanted of life and freedom and happiness before he himself took what he wanted of death. That is why risks did not exist for the Count; he courted death every day of his life, but not openly and I have always known that when the chance came to seize it with honour, he would grasp it with both hands." Jansci shook his bloodstained head, and Reynolds could see from the light streaming out of the living room that the faded grey eyes were misted with tears. "You are young, Meechail, you cannot possibly conceive of the dreariness, the purposelessness, the dreadful emptiness of living day after interminable day when the wish to live has long since died in you. I am as selfish as any other man, but not so selfish as to buy my happiness at the expense of his. I loved the Count. May the snow lie softly on him tonight."

"I am sincerely sorry, Jansci." Reynolds spoke with genuine regret, and in his heart he knew he *was* deeply sorry, but for what or for whom he could not at that moment have said: all he clearly knew was that the fire of anger within him was slowly increasing, burning more brightly than ever. They were at the front door now, and he strained his eyes to pick out what he could on that white expanse of snow on the other side of the river. Julia and her mother he could clearly see, making their way slowly towards the riverbank, but at first he could see no signs of the Count. But the pupils of his eyes were now widening steadily since he had left the brightness of the room behind him, and he finally picked out his moving figure, no more than a half-seen blur against the dark line of the trees beyond him—and, Reynolds suddenly realised, far too near the trees. Julia and her mother were as yet hardly more than halfway across the field.

"Look!" Reynolds grabbed the elder man's arms. "The Count's almost there—and Julia and your wife are hardly moving. In the name of heaven, what's the matter with them? They'll be caught, they'll be shot——What the devil was that?"

A loud splash, a thunderclap of a splash in the silence of the night, had startled him with its unexpected suddenness. He ran to the bank and saw the cold dark waters of the river churning to a foam as unseen arms threshed through them: Sandor had seen the danger even before he had, had flung off his overcoat and jacket, and now his great arms and shoulders were carrying him across to the far bank like a torpedo.

"They are in trouble, Meechail." Jansci, too, was on the bank now, and his voice was tense with anxiety. "One of them, it must be Catherine, can hardly walk—you see how she drags her steps. It is too much for Julia . . ."

Sandor was at the other side now, out of the water, up the shingled shore and over the three-foot bank beyond as if it didn't even exist. And then, just as he cleared the bank, they heard it—a sharp, flat explosion, the unmistakable crack of a grenade, from the woods beyond the field, then another through the trees even while the echoes of the first explosion were still rolling away, and then immediately afterwards the harsh, staccato rattle of an automatic carbine—and then silence.

Reynolds winced and looked at Jansci, but it was too dark to see the expression on his face; he could only hear him murmuring something over and over again to himself, but Reynolds could not distinguish the words, they must have been Ukrainian. And there was not time to wonder; even at that very moment Colonel Hidas might be stooping over the man whom he had thought to be Professor Jennings. . . .

Sandor had reached the two women now, an arm round each of them, and was plunging back through the frozen-crusted snow towards the riverbank as if he had been leading two fleet-footed runners by the hand instead of virtually carrying them, which he was. Reynolds wheeled round to find the Cossack standing just behind him.

"There's going to be trouble," Reynolds said quickly. "Get up to the house, stick the submachine gun through the window, and when Sandor drops below the level of the riverbank——" But the Cossack was already on his way, his feet churning up the gravel as he raced for the house.

Reynolds turned round again, the fists by his side clenching and unclenching in his anxiety, his frustration at their helplessness. Thirty yards to go now, twenty-five, twenty, still a strange absence of all sound and activity from the woods in the background, and Reynolds was just beginning to hope against hope when he heard the excited shouts from the trees, a barked command, and at once an automatic carbine opened up with its harsh staccato cough, the very first shells whistling by only inches from Reynolds' head. He dropped to the ground like a stone, dragging Jansci with him, and lay there with his open hand beating at the pebbles in his impotence while the bullets whined harmlessly overhead, but even at that moment he found time to wonder why only the one man was firing—one would have expected Hidas to bring his entire arsenal to bear.

Then, muffled though the sound was by the thick snow, there suddenly came to his ears the thud-thud of pounding feet and a moment later, in a waist-high flurry of flying snow, Sandor came over the top of the far bank like a charging bull, literally lifting Julia and her mother clear off their feet, and landed with a grating, sliding crunch on the pebbles at least ten feet beyond and below, and even while he was still stumbling, still recovering his balance on that treacherous footing, a machine gun with a different cyclic rate had opened up—the Cossack had timed it without the loss of a second. It was doubtful whether he could see anybody against the dark background of trees, but the AVO machine gun was pointing directly at him and must have betrayed its position, flash cover or not, by the red fire streaking from the mouth of the barrel. In any event, the firing from the wood stopped almost immediately.

Sandor had reached the boat now and was lifting somebody into it. A moment later he helped the second person inside, dragged the heavily laden boat off the gravel with one mighty heave, and was overarming himself so powerfully across the river that the gurgling water at the forefoot piled high into a bow wave that gleamed whitely even in the darkness of the night.

Jansci and Reynolds, on their feet again, were at the water's edge, waiting, hands reaching out ready to grab the boat and drag it ashore, when all at once there came a hiss, a soft crack, and a blinding white light burst into life not a hundred feet above their heads, and almost on the instant a machine gun and several rifles opened up again, still from the trees but much further to the south, where the wood curved in to meet the river.

"Shoot the flare down!" Reynolds shouted to the Cossack. "Never mind the AVO. Shoot that damned flare down!" Blinded by the glare, he plunged into the river just as he heard Jansci doing the same thing, swore softly as the side of the boat struck painfully against his kneecap, grabbed the gunwale, jerked the boat up on the shelving pebbled beach, staggered as someone who had incautiously stood up in the boat pitched forward against him, recovered and caught her up in his arms just as the flare above the river died as suddenly as it had come to life. The Cossack was proving himself that night. But the guns from the wood across the river still coughed and chattered, the men behind them were firing from memory, and bullets were still whistling and ricocheting all around them.

There was no doubt whom Reynolds had in his arms. It must have been Jansci's wife; she was too frail, too light altogether for Julia. Guided now only by the slope of the pebbled shore—the darkness, after the blinding whiteness of the flare, was now quite impenetrable—Reynolds took a step forward and all but collapsed to the ground as the pain in his momentarily paralysed knee struck at him. He freed one hand, grabbed at the tautened rope to steady himself, heard a thud as if someone had fallen heavily, felt someone else brush by him and heard steps running up towards the bank, clenched his teeth against the pain and limped up the shingles as quickly as he could. He felt a bullet pluck at the sleeve of his coat. The three-foot bank that he had to scale with his aching leg and the woman in his arms loomed as an unsurmountable obstacle in his mind, then a great pair of hands caught him from behind and he was standing on top of the bank, still clutching the woman, before he had more than dimly realised what was happening.

The oblong of pale light that was the door of the ferryman's cottage was before him now, not ten feet away, and, even as he saw it, even as he heard bullets smashing against the stonework of the cottage and whining away into the darkness, Jansci, who had been the first to reach the house, reappeared in the doorway, suicidally silhouetted against the light behind him. Reynolds made to shout a warning, changed his mind—it was too late now if any marksman had drawn a bead, and it was only two seconds away—moved forwards, heard the woman in his arms say something, knew instinctively, without understanding the words, what she wanted and set her gently on her feet. She took two or three faltering steps forward, then flung herself into the outstretched arms of the waiting man, murmuring, "Alex! Alex! Alex!" then she seemed to shudder, leaned heavily against him as if she had been struck from behind, but that was all Reynolds saw: Sandor had bundled them all into the lobby and crashed the door shut behind him.

Julia was half sitting, half lying at the far end of the corridor, supported by an anxious-looking Dr. Jennings. Reynolds reached her in two strides and fell on his knees beside her. Her eyes were shut, her face very pale; there was the beginning of a bruise upon her forehead, but she was breathing, shallowly but evenly.

"What's happened to her?" Reynolds asked huskily. "Has she been—has she been——"

"She'll be all right." Sandor's voice behind him was deep and reassuring. He stooped and lifted her in his arms and turned towards the living room. "She fell getting out of the boat and she must have struck her head on the stones. I'll take her in to the couch here."

Reynolds watched the giant, the water dripping steadily from his soaking clothes, carry her through the door as if she were a child, rose slowly to his feet, and almost bumped into the Cossack. The youngster's face was alive with exultation.

"You should be at your window," Reynolds said quietly.

"No need." The Cossack's grin stretched from ear to ear. "They've stopped firing and gone now back to the trucks— I can hear their voices in the woods. I got two of them, Mr. Reynolds, two of them! I saw them fall in the light of the flare, just before you shouted at me to shoot the flare out."

"And you did that too," Reynolds acknowledged. That accounted, he realised, for the lack of any more of the pistol flares: a double-edged weapon, it had turned disastrously in Hidas' hand. "You've saved us all tonight." He clapped the proud boy on his shoulder, turned to look at Jansci, and then stood very still.

Jansci was kneeling on the rough wooden floor, and his wife was in his arms. Her back was to Reynolds, and the first thing he saw was the round, red-ringed hole in her coat, high up below her left shoulder. It was a very small hole and only a little blood, and the stain wasn't spreading at all. Slowly Reynolds walked the length of the corridor and sank on his knee beside Jansci. Jansci lifted his white, bloodstained head and looked at him with sightless eyes.

"Dead?" Reynolds whispered.

Jansci nodded without speaking.

"My God!" Reynolds' shock showed in every line of his face. "Now, now—to die now!"

"A merciful God, Meechail, and understanding far beyond my deserts. Only this morning I asked Him why He hadn't let Catherine die, why He hadn't *made* her die. . . . He has forgiven my presumption, He knew far better than I. Catherine was gone, Meechail, gone before the bullet ever touched her." Jansci shook his head, a man marvelling at the splendour of it all. "Could there be anything more wonderful, Meechail, than to pass from this earth without pain at the moment of your greatest happiness? Look! Look at her face—see how she smiles!"

Reynolds shook his head without speaking. There was nothing to say, he could think of nothing to say, his mind was numbed.

"We are both blessed." Jansci was talking, almost rambling to himself; he eased his arm, so that he could look down on his wife's face, and his voice was soft with memory. "The years have been kind to her, Meechail;

239

time loved her almost as much as I. Twenty years ago, five and twenty years ago, drifting down the Dnieper on a summer's night— I see her now as I saw her then. She has not been touched." He said something in a tone so low that Reynolds couldn't catch it, then his voice came more clearly again. "You remember her photograph, Meechail, the one you thought did Julia more than justice? Now you can see: it could never have been anyone else."

"It could never have been anyone else, Jansci," Reynolds echoed. He thought of the photograph of the beautiful, laughing girl and stared down at the dead face in Jansci's arms, at the thin white hair, the grey face haggard and emaciated as he had never seen a face before, a pitifully wasted face sculpted and graven into the deep lines of premature old age by unimaginable privations and hardships, and he felt his eyes go blind. "It could never have been anyone else," Reynolds repeated. "The portrait did her less than justice."

"That's what I said to Catherine, that's what I always said to her," Jansci murmured. He turned away and bent low and Reynolds knew that he wanted to be alone. Reynolds stumbled blindly to his feet—he had to feel for the wall to support and guide him—and walked slowly away, the numbness in his mind slowly giving way first of all to a confusing maelstrom of conflicting thoughts and emotions, then slowly clearing and settling till there was only one thought, one fixed immovable purpose left in his mind. The slow anger that had been smouldering within him all evening now burst into an intense white flame that consumed his mind, his every thought, to the exclusion of all else, but there was no trace of this blazing fury within him when he spoke quietly to Sandor.

"Could I ask you to bring the truck here, please?"

"In a moment," Sandor promised. He gestured at the girl lying on the couch. "She is just coming to. We must hurry."

"Thank you. We will." Reynolds turned away and looked at the Cossack. "Keep a good watch, Cossack. I will not be long." He walked along the corridor, went past Jansci and Catherine without looking at either of them, picked up the automatic carbine that leaned against the wall, and passed out through the door, closing it softly behind him.

14

THE dark, sluggish waters were ice-cold as a tomb, but Reynolds didn't even feel their freezing touch, and though his whole body shuddered involuntarily as he had slid silently into the river, his mind had not even registered the shock. There was no room in his mind for any physical sensation, for any emotion or thought of any kind, except for that one starkly simple, primeval desire, the desire that had sloughed off the tissue veneer of civilisation as if it had never been—that of revenge. Revenge or murder—there was no distinction in Reynolds' mind at that moment, the absolute fixity of his purpose permitted of none. That frightened boy in Budapest, Jansci's wife, the incomparable Count—they were all dead. They were dead primarily because he, Reynolds, had set foot in Hungary, but he had not been their executioner: only the evil genius of Hidas could be held accountable for that. Hidas had lived too long.

Automatic carbine held high above his head, Reynolds breasted his way through the thin film of crackling ice that stretched out from the far bank, felt his feet touch bottom, and scrambled ashore. Stooping, he filled a spread handkerchief with handfuls of tiny pebbles and sand, tied the corners, and was on his way, without even pausing to wring or shake any of the icy water out of his clothes.

He had run two hundred yards downriver before making his crossing, and now he found himself in the perimeter of the wood that curved east and south to the bisecting road where the two trucks were parked. Here in the shadow of the trees he could not be seen, and the frozen snow on the ground beneath their laden branches was so thin that his stealthy progress could have been heard barely ten feet away. He had slung his automatic carbine now, and the weighted handkerchief in his hand swung gently to and fro as he picked his wary way from tree to tree.

But for all his soft-footed caution, he had covered the ground swiftly and was alongside the parked trucks within three minutes, peering out from the shelter of a tree. There was no sign of life from either truck, their rear doors were closed, there were no signs of life at all. Reynolds straightened, preparing to glide across the snow to Hidas' truck, then froze into immobility, rigid against the bole of his tree. A man had moved out from behind the shelter of Hidas' truck and was coming directly towards him.

For a moment Reynolds was certain that the man had seen him, then almost at once relaxed. AVO soldiers didn't go hunting for armed enemies in a dark wood with their gun carried under the crook of one arm and a lighted cigarette in the other hand. The sentry obviously had no suspicions, was just walking around to keep his blood moving in that bitter cold. He passed by within six feet of Reynolds and as he began to move away, Reynolds waited no longer. He took one long step out from the concealing shelter of the tree, his right arm swinging, and just as the man started to whirl round, his mouth open to cry out, the weighted cloth caught him with vicious force at the nape of the neck. Reynolds had time and to spare to catch both the man and his gun and lower them silently to the ground.

He had the carbine in his hand now, and half a dozen steps took him to the front of the brown truck—a truck, Reynolds could see, with its engine hood blown off and motor damaged by the explosion of the Count's grenade—then he was moving silently across to Hidas' caravan, his eyes so intently watching the back door that he all but tripped over the crumpled shape lying at his feet on the ground. Reynolds stooped low, and although he knew even as he stooped who it was that was lying there, nevertheless the shock of confirmation made him grasp the barrel of his carbine as if he would crush it in his bare hands.

The Count was lying face upwards in the snow, his AVO cap still framing the lean aristocratic face, the chiselled acquiline features even more aloof and remote in death than they had been in life. It was not hard to see how he had died—that burst of machine-gun fire must have torn half his chest away. Like a dog they had shot him down, like a dog they had left him lying there in the darkness of that bitter night, and the gently falling snow was beginning to lie on the cold, dead face. Moved by some strange impulse, Reynolds removed the hated AVO cap, sent it spinning away into the darkness, pulled a handkerchief—a handkerchief stained with the Count's own blood—from the dead man's breast pocket, and spread it gently across his face. Then he rose and walked to the door of Hidas' caravan.

Four wooden steps led to the door, and Reynolds walked up these as softly as a cat, kneeling at the top to peer through the keyhole. In the space of a second he could see what he wanted to see—a chair on the left-hand side, a made-up bunk on the right-hand, and, at the far end, a table with what looked like a wireless transmitter bolted to the top of it. Hidas, back to the door, was just seating himself in front of the table, and as he cranked a handle with his right hand and picked up a telephone with his left, Reynolds realised that it was no transmitter but a radiotelephone. They should have thought of it. Hidas was not a man to move about the country without means of instant communication available to him, and now, with the skies clearing, he would almost certainly be calling in the air force in a last, desperate gamble to stop them, but it didn't matter any more. It was too late, it made no difference now, none to those whom Hidas was pursuing and certainly none to Hidas himself.

Reynolds' groping hand found the knob, and he passed through the well-oiled door like a shadow, not quite closing it behind him: Hidas, his ear filled with the sound of the ratchety whirr of the call-up handle, heard nothing. Reynolds took three steps forward, the barrel of his carbine gripped in both hands and the stock raised high above his shoulders, and, as Hidas began to speak, brought it swinging down over Hidas' shoulder and smashed the delicate mechanism to pieces.

Hidas sat for a moment in petrified astonishment, then whirled round in his chair, but he had lost the only moment he would ever need. Reynolds was already two paces away, the carbine again reversed in his hands, the muzzle trained on Hidas' heart. Hidas' face was a stone mask carved in shock, only his lips moved, but no sound came from them as Reynolds slowly retreated, picked up the key he had seen lying on the bunk, felt for the keyhole, and locked the door, his eyes never once leaving Hidas. Then he moved forward and halted, with the mouth of the carbine, rocklike in its steadiness, just thirty inches short of the man in the chair.

"You look surprised to see me, Colonel Hidas," Reynolds murmured. "You should not be surprised, you of all men. Those who live by the sword as you have lived by the sword must know better than any man that this moment comes to all of us. It comes to you tonight."

"You have come to murder me." It was statement and not a question. Hidas had looked on death too often from the sidelines not to recognise it when its face turned towards himself. The shock was slowly draining out of his face, but no fear had yet come to replace it.

"Murder you? No. I have come to execute you. Murder is what you did to Major Howarth. Is there any reason why I shouldn't shoot you down in cold blood as you shot him? He hadn't even a gun on him."

"He was an enemy of the state, an enemy of the people."

"My God! You try to justify your actions?"

"They need no justification, Captain Reynolds. Duty never does."

Reynolds stared at him. "Are you trying to excuse yourself—or just begging for your life?"

"I never beg." There was no pride, no arrogance in the Jew's voice, just a simple dignity.

"Imre—the boy in Budapest. He died—slowly."

"He withheld important information. It was essential that we got it quickly."

"Major General Illyurin's wife." Reynolds spoke quickly to fight off a growing feeling of unreality. "Why did you murder her?"

For the first time a flicker of emotion showed in the thin, intelligent face, then vanished as quickly as it had come.

"I did not know that." He inclined his head. "It is no part of my duty to wage war on women. I genuinely regret her death—even though she was dying as it was."

"You are responsible for the actions of your AVO thugs?"

"My men?" He nodded. "They take their orders from me."

"They killed her—but you are responsible for their actions. Therefore you are responsible for her death."

"If you put it that way, I am."

"If it were not for you, these three people would be alive now."

"I cannot speak for the general's wife. The other two—yes."

"Is there then—I ask you for the last time—any reason why I shouldn't kill you—now?"

Colonel Hidas looked at him for a long moment in silence, then he smiled faintly, and Reynolds could have sworn that the smile was tinged with sadness.

"Numerous reasons, Captain Reynolds, but none that would convince an enemy agent from the West."

It was the word "West" that did it—but Reynolds was not to realise that until long afterwards. All he knew was that something had triggered open a floodgate, released a spate of pictures and memories in his mind, pictures of Jansci talking to him in his house in Budapest, in the dark agony of that torture cell in the Szarháza prison, with the firelight on his face in the cottage in the country, memories of what Jansci had said, what he had said over and over again with a repetitive persistence, with a passionate conviction that had hammered his ideas deeper home into his mind than Reynolds had ever suspected. Everything he had said about—— Deliberately, desperately, Reynolds forced the thoughts and pictures from his mind. His carbine jabbed forward another six inches.

"On your feet, Colonel Hidas."

Hidas rose and stood facing him, his hands hanging by his sides, and stared down at the gun.

"Clean and quick, Colonel Hidas, eh?"

"As you wish." His eyes lifted from Reynolds' whitening trigger finger and found his face. "I would not beg for myself what has been denied so many of my victims."

For a fraction of a second longer Reynolds continued to increase the pressure on the trigger, then, almost as if something had snapped inside him, he relaxed and took one pace back. The white flame of anger still burnt within him, burnt as brightly as ever, but with these last words, the words of a man quite unafraid to die, he had felt the bitterness of defeat welling in him so powerfully that he could taste it in his mouth. When he spoke his voice was strained and hoarse, he scarcely recognised it as his own.

"Turn round!"

"Thank you, but no. I prefer to die this way."

"Turn round," Reynolds said savagely, "or I'll smash both your kneecaps and turn you round myself."

Hidas looked at his face, saw the implacability, shrugged to the inevitable, turned away, and collapsed without a sound across his desk as the butt of the rifle caught him behind the ear. For a long moment Reynolds stared down at the fallen man, swore in a bitter fury that was directed not against the man at his feet but at himself, turned, and left the caravan.

There was a feeling of emptiness, almost of despair, in Reynolds' mind as he descended the steps. He was no longer particularly careful to conceal his presence, that fury within him had still not found its outlet, he would have welcomed the chance to turn his automatic carbine on the armed AVO men within that other truck, cut them down without compunction as they came pouring out the door silhouetted against the light behind, just as they had cut down Jansci's wife silhouetted in the light of the door of the ferryman's cottage. And then suddenly he broke step and stood still, stood very still indeed: he had just realised something that he should have realised minutes ago had he not been so bent on his reckoning with Colonel Hidas. The brown lorry was not only quiet: it was far too quiet to be true.

In three steps he had reached the side of the truck and pressed his ear against the side. There was nothing to be heard, just nothing at all. He ran round to the back, flung open a door, and peered inside. He could see nothing, it was pitch-dark inside, but he did not need to see anything: the truck was empty, and no one moved or even breathed inside.

The truth struck with such suddenness, such savage force, that he was for the moment numbed, incapable of all action, capable of nothing but the realisation of the enormity of his blunder, the thoroughness, the appalling ease with which he had been deceived. He might have known, he might have guessed—the Count had been suspicious of it even at the beginning—that Colonel Hidas would never have accepted defeat, never have given up, far less given up with such submissive ease. The Count would never have fallen for it, never. Hidas' men must have been on their way to make the crossing of the river to the south when the flare had been fired, and both he and the Cossack had blindly accepted as genuine the noisily faked withdrawal through the woods. They would be there by now, they were bound to be there by now, and he, Reynolds, was missing at the very moment his friends needed him as they had never done before—and to crown the folly of his night's work, he had sent Sandor, the one man who might have saved them, to collect the truck. Jansci had only the boy and the old man to help him—and Julia was there. When he thought of Julia, when he thought of her and the leering, gargoyle face of the giant Coco, something snapped inside Reynolds' mind and released him from his motionless thrall.

Two hundred metres lay between him and the bank of the river, two hundred metres covered in deep, frozen snow. He was exhausted from sleeplessness and privations and weighed down by heavy boots and saturated clothes, but he covered the distance in less time than he had ever done before. It was not anger now—although it was still there—that lent wings to his heels and kicked the flying gouts of snow head-high as he pounded along; it was not anger, it was fear, fear such as he had never known before.

But it was not numbing, paralysing fear, but a fear, instead, that seemed to sharpen all his senses and lend him an abnormal clarity of mind. He braked suddenly, arms windmilling violently as he approached the bank of the river, slid noiselessly over the edge on to the shingle, cat-footed down to the water's edge, and pushed himself out into the icy current without even the tiniest splash. He was almost halfway across, swimming smoothly and powerfully, one arm holding the carbine far above his head, when he heard the first shot from the ferryman's cottage, followed immediately afterwards by another and another.

The time for caution was gone—if ever there had been such a time. Churning the water madly, Reynolds reached the far side in a few seconds, touched bottom, scrambled up the far shore with his driving feet slipping desperately on the sliding shingle, swarmed over the bank, clicked over the carbine switch from automatic to single-shot firing—a machine gun was less than useless, it was positively dangerous, if friend and enemy were fighting in the same confined space—and ran, crouching through the pale oblong of light that was the ferryman's front door. Ten minutes at the most had elapsed since he had walked out through that door.

Jansci's wife was no longer in the corridor, but the corridor was not empty. An AVO man, carbine in hand, had just come out of the living room and was shutting the door behind him, and even at the moment Reynolds realised that that could mean only one thing—the fight inside, if there had been a fight and not just a massacre, was over. The AVO man saw him, tried to bring his gun up, realised he could not make it in time, and the warning shout died in his throat as the stock of Reynolds' carbine caught him terribly across the head and side of the face.

Carbine again reversed in his hands, Reynolds gently toed open the door. One swift, all-encompassing glance at the tableau before him and he knew that the fight was indeed over. Six AVO men Reynolds could see inside the room, four of them still alive: one lay almost at his feet in that strangely crumpled relaxation that only the dead can achieve, another by the wall on the right-hand side, not far from where Jennings was sitting with his head almost on his knees as he shook it slowly from side to side. In one far corner a man held a carbine on a bleeding Jansci while another bound his hands to the chair on which he was sitting; while in the other corner the Cossack, lying on his back, was struggling desperately with the man who, lying on top of him, was bludgeoning him with short arm blows to the head; but the Cossack fought on, and Reynolds could see how he was fighting: he was pulling with all his strength on the stock of his whip, whose sixteen-foot length was wrapped round and round the throat of the man above, inexorably turning his face a strange bluish color and slowly strangling him. Near the centre of the room stood the giant Coco, contemptuously ignoring the girl who struggled so futilely in the crook of one great arm, grinning with wolfish expectation as the AVO man fighting with the Cossack stopped belabouring him, reached back with his right hand, fumbled with his belt, and came clear with a sheath knife.

Reynolds had been trained, and ruthlessly trained, by wartime professionals who had survived similar situations a score of times and survived by neither demanding surrender nor wasting the tiniest fraction of a second in unnecessary announcement of their presence. Those who kicked open a door and said "Good evening, gentlemen," never lived to talk about it. The door was still swinging gently on its hinges when he fired the first of three deliberate, spaced, carefully aimed shots. The first pitched the Cossack's assailant into the corner of the room, the knife falling from his upraised hand and clattering to the floor;

248

the second took the man who held the gun on Jansci; the third, the man who had been tying Jansci's hands. Reynolds was just lining up for the fourth shot, sighting for Coco's head with an almost inhuman lack of haste—the giant AVO had swung the girl round in front of his body for protection—when a rifle barrel smashed across his carbine and left forearm, sending his gun clattering heavily on the floor. Yet another AVO man had been behind the door as it had opened and been completely hidden: he must have thought it had been the man who had just left returning, until Reynolds had fired his first shot.

"Don't shoot him, don't shoot him!" The quick hoarse order had come from Coco. With a careless shove he sent the girl across the room to land heavily on the couch and stood there with his hands on his hips, while his fury at what had just happened and his elation at seeing Reynolds powerless before him fought for supremacy in the darkly evil face. The struggle didn't last long. Lives, even the lives of his comrades, mattered little to Coco, and a grin of unholy anticipation spread across the brutalised face.

"See if our friend is armed," he commanded.

The other man searched Reynolds briefly, hands running up and down the outside of the clothes, then shook his head.

"Excellent. Catch this." Coco threw his carbine across to the other and drew his open palms slowly up and down across the front of his tunic. "I have an account to settle with you, Captain Reynolds. Or perhaps you have forgotten."

Coco meant to kill him, Reynolds knew, meant to have the joy of killing him with his bare hands. His own left arm was useless—it felt as if it had been broken—and useless it would remain for some time to come. Deep inside him he knew that he had no chance in the world, that he couldn't hold Coco off for more than a few seconds, but he told himself that if ever he was to have a chance it was now, before the fight had started, while the element of surprise still existed as a possibility, and even with the thought he was hurling himself across the room, his legs jackknifing open as his feet reached for the giant's chest. Coco was almost taken by surprise—almost, but not quite. He was moving away even as the feet struck him, making him grunt with the pain, and one of his flailing arms caught Reynolds behind the head so that he all but somersaulted, his back striking painfully against the wall by the couch with a force that drove all the breath from his body with an explosive gasp. For a moment he lay quite still, then, badly winded and aching though he was, he forced himself to struggle to his feet again—if Coco's feet reached him while he was still on the floor, Reynolds knew that he would never rise again—moved to meet the advancing giant, and struck out at the sneering face before him with all that remained of his strength, felt his fist strike home jarringly against solid bone and flesh, then coughed in agony as Coco contemptuously ignored the blow and struck him with tremendous force in the middle of the body.

Reynolds had never been hit so hard, he had never imagined any peron could have been capable of hitting so hard. The man had the strength of an ox. In spite of the sea of pain below his chest, in spite of his rubbery legs and the waves of nausea that threatened to choke him, he was still on his feet, but only because his splayed hands were supporting him from the wall against which he had been hurled. He thought he could hear the girl calling his name, but he couldn't be sure, he seemed to have become suddenly deaf. His vision, too, was blurred and dimmed; he could just vaguely distinguish Jansci struggling frantically with the ropes that secured him, when he saw Coco coming at him again. Hopelessly, despairingly, Reynolds flung himself forward in a last futile attempt to lash out at his tormentor, but Coco just side-stepped, laughed, placed the flat of his hand against Reynolds' back, and sent him reeling crazily across the room to crash into the jamb of the open door and slide slowly down to the floor.

For a few brief moments consciousness left him, then slowly returned, and he shook his head dazedly. Coco was still in the middle of the room, arms akimbo, triumph in every line of the seamed and evil face, the lips drawn back in wolfish anticipation of pleasure yet to come. Coco meant him to die, Reynolds realised dimly, but he meant him to die slowly. Well, at this rate, it would not be much longer. He had no strength left; he had to fight for every gasping breath he took, and his legs were almost gone.

Weakly, dizzily, he pushed himself somehow to his feet and stood there swaying, conscious of nothing but the reeling room, the fire in his body, the salt taste of blood on his lips, and his indestructible enemy standing there laughing in the middle of the floor. Once more, Reynolds told himself dully, once more—he can only kill me once—and he was reaching his hands behind him to launch himself on his last tottering run when he saw the expression on Coco's face change and an iron arm reached across his chest and pinned him to the corner as Sandor walked slowly into the room.

Reynolds would never afterwards forget how Sandor looked at that moment, like something that belonged not to this world but to the ice halls of Scandinavian mythology. Fifteen minutes, perhaps twenty, had elapsed since Sandor had plunged into that freezing river, and most of the time since then he had spent out in the sub-zero cold. He was coated now with ice, coated almost from head to foot, and the falling snow had clung to him and turned to ice also. In the light from the ferryman's oil lamp he glistened and glittered in that rigid, crackling suit of ice like some eerie visitor from another and alien world.

The AVO man by the door stood open-mouthed in shock, recovered with a visible effort, dropped one of the two carbines—his own and Coco's—that were encumbering him, and tried to line the other up on Sandor, but he was too late. Sandor caught the rifle with one hand, tore it from the man's grasp as one would take a stick from a little child, and pushed the man back against the wall with his free hand. The man swore, took two running steps, and leapt snarling at him, but Sandor just plucked him out of the air, whirled round in a complete circle, then flung him across the room with dreadful force to smash high up against a wall, where he hung grotesquely for a moment as if held there by invisible hands, then fell to the floor like a broken, crumpled doll.

Even as the AVO man had leapt at Sandor, Julia had slid off the couch and thrown herself at Coco's back, flinging her arms round him, trying to delay him if only for a second. But her hands could not even meet round his chest; he had broken her grip as if it were cotton and pushed her to one side without as much as looking at her, and had already fallen upon an off-balance Sandor, bludgeoning him with great swinging sledgehammer blows, so that Sandor fell heavily to the floor with Coco on top of him, his great hands already round Sandor's throat. There was no grin on Coco's face now, no gleam of anticipation in the small black eyes: he was fighting for his life, and he knew it.

For a moment Sandor lay motionless, while Coco's iron fingers tightened inexorably round his throat, the massive shoulders hunching as he put all his great strength into the effort. Then Sandor stirred, reached up his hands, and caught Coco round the wrists.

Reynolds, still weak and barely able to stand upright, Julia beside him now and clutching his arm, stared in fascination. Reynolds' entire body seemed a sea of pain, but even through that pain he seemed to feel again something of the agony he had felt when Sandor had once caught him by the forearms and squeezed and squeezed with the flat of his fingers and not as he was now doing, with his hooked fingertips digging deep into the tendons on the inside of Coco's wrists.

Shock it was that showed first in Coco's face, the shock of unbelief, then pain, then fear as his wrists were crushed in the vise of Sandor's grip and his fingers round Sandor's throat slowly forced to open. Still holding Coco's wrists, Sandor pushed him to one side, rose to his feet, pulled Coco after him so that the AVO giant towered high above him, swiftly released the wrists, and had his arms locked round Coco's chest before Coco had had time to appreciate what was happening. Reynolds thought at first that Sandor meant to throw the other, and from the momentary relief on Coco's face it seemed that he had thought so also; but if he had so thought, the disillusion and the pain and the fear came soon and all in an instant as Sandor buried his head deep into Coco's chest, lifted his shoulders high, and began to crush the giant in a murderous bear hug which Coco must have known in a sudden flash of certainty he would never live to feel relaxing, for the fear in his expression gave way to contorted terror as his face turned bluish-red from the lack of oxygen, as he moaned deep in his throat while his starving lungs fought for air and his fists hammered in frantic madness against Sandor's back and shoulders with as much effect as if he were beating them against a rock of granite. But the memory of the moment that Reynolds took with him was not of Coco's threshing panic and darkening, pain-contorted features, not even of Sandor's expressionless face with the still gentle eyes, but of the steady crackling of ice as Sandor crushed ever more tightly, more remorselessly, and

of the horror on Julia's face as he caught her to him and
tired to shut out from her ears as best he could the hoarse,
horrible scream that filled the room, then slowly faded and
died.

15

IT was just after four o'clock in the morning
when Jansci halted them in the centre of a thick clump of
head-high reeds, turned, and waited until the others had
caught up with him. They came in single file, Julia, Reynolds, the Cossack, and Dr. Jennings with Sandor beside
him, half helping, half carrying him across the frozen
marshes, all with their heads bent low, all except Sandor
with the trudging, stumbling gait of those very close to
exhaustion.

They had reason, and more than reason, for their exhaustion. Two hours and three miles lay between them
and where they had left the truck, two hours of winding in
and out between the frozen reeds that snapped and
crackled at the lightest touch, two hours of interminable
stumbling and crunching through the thin ice of freezing
marshes, ice just not strong enough to bear their weight,
but more than strong enough to impede their progress,
compelling them to lift each foot high to clear it before
moving on to the next step, where they would sink down
again through ice and frozen mud, often beyond their
knees. But that same ice was their salvation that night; the
dogs of the border guards would have found the conditions hopeless for operation and could only have floun-
dered along, helplessly out of their depth. Not that they
had seen or heard either dogs or guards once in these
three miles: on a night such as this even the fanatical
guards of the AVO huddled high in their stilted border
towers round the warmth of a stove and let who would
pass by.

It was a night such as the night on which Reynolds had
crossed the border into Hungary, with the cold stars riding
high in a cold and empty sky and a wind sighing gently
through the marshes, a bitter wind that touched their
cheeks with icy talons and carried their frozen breath
drifting away through the softly rustling reeds. For a
moment Reynolds himself was lost in the memory of that

first night, when he had lain in the snow, as cold and even colder than he was now, and had felt the icy wind in his face and seen the stars high above, and then, with an almost physical effort, he wrenched his mind away from that night, for his thoughts had moved on to the police hut and the appearance of the Count and he felt sick to his heart when he remembered for the hundredth time that the Count would never come again.

"No time for dreaming now, Meechail," Jansci said gently. He nodded with his roughly bandaged head, leaned forward, and parted high reeds for Reynolds to have a glimpse of what lay beyond—a sheet of ice, perhaps ten feet wide, that stretched in both directions as far as he could see. He straightened again and looked at Jansci.

"A canal?"

"A ditch, that's all. Just a little drainage ditch, but the most important in all Europe. On the other side lies Austria." Jansci smiled. "Five metres from freedom, Meechail, freedom and the success of a mission. Nothing can stop you now."

"Nothing can stop me now," Reynolds echoed. His voice was flat, empty of all life. The longed-for freedom interested him hardly at all, the complete success of his mission even less: the success was ashes in his mouth, the cost had been too cruelly high. Worst of all, perhaps, was what was to come, and he knew with a sombre certainty what that was. He shivered in the bitter cold. "It grows even colder, Jansci. The crossing is safe—no guards are near?"

"The crossing is safe."

"Come then—let's not wait any longer."

"Not me." Jansci shook his head. "Just you and the professor and Julia. I remain here."

Reynolds nodded heavily and said nothing. He had known what Jansci was about to say, and he knew with equal certainty that dissuasion was useless. He turned away, not knowing what to say, and even as he turned Julia broke loose from his arms and caught her father by the lapels of his coat.

"What did you say, Jansci? What was that you said?"

"Please, Julia. There is no other way, you know there is no other way. I have to stay."

"Oh, Jansci! Jansci!" She was pulling at his lapels, shaking them in her anxiety. "You can't stay, you mustn't, not now, not after all that's happened!"

"More than ever after all that's happened." He put his arms around her and pulled her close and said: "I have work to do, I have much work to do, and as yet I have hardly begun. If I stop now, the Count will never forgive me." He smoothed the blond hair with his scarred and twisted hand. "Julia, Julia, how could I ever accept freedom for myself while I know there are hundreds of poor people who will never know freedom unless it comes through me? No one can help them as well as I, you know that. How can I buy for myself at the expense of others a happiness that would be no happiness at all? Can you expect me to sit at my ease somewhere in the West while the young men here are still being dragged off to the Black Sea Canal or dying old women being driven out to work in the beet fields, and the snow still on the ground? Do you indeed think so little of me, Julia?"

"Jansci." Her face was buried in his coat and her voice was muffled. "I can't leave you, Jansci."

"You can and must. You were not known before, but you are known now and there is no place for you in Hungary. No harm will come to me, my dear—not while Sandor lives. And the Cossack, too, will look after me." In the starlit gloom the Cossack seemed to straighten and grow tall.

"And you can leave me? You can let me go?"

"You no longer need me, my child—you have stayed with me all these years because you thought I needed you—and now Meechail here will look after you. You know that."

"Yes." Her voice was more muffled than ever. "He is very kind."

Jansci caught her by the shoulders, held her at arm's length, and looked at her.

"For the daughter of Major General Illyurin, you're a very silly girl. Do you not know, my dear, that if it were not for you, Meechail would not be returning to the West?"

She turned and stared at Reynolds, and he could see that her eyes were shining in the starlight with unshed tears. "Is—is this true?"

"It's true." Reynolds smiled faintly. "A long argument, but I lost it. He won't have me at any price."

"I'm sorry. I did not know." The life had gone out of her voice, "This is the end of it then."

"No, my dear, only the beginning." Jansci caught her

close and held her as her body shook with dry soundless sobs, looked over her shoulder, and nodded at Reynolds and Sandor. Reynolds nodded in return, shook the scarred, misshapen hand in silence, murmured his good-bye to the Cossack, parted the tall reeds, and went down to the ditch, followed by Sandor, who held one end of the Cossack's whip while Reynolds held the other and moved out gingerly on the ice. On the second step it broke under his weight and he was standing on the muddy bottom, covered to the thighs in freezing water, but he ignored the numbing cold of it, broke the ice in front of him, and pulled himself up on to the far bank. Austria, he said to himself, this is Austria, but the word meant nothing to him.

Something splashed into the water behind him and he turned to see Sandor forging his way through the water and broken ice, carrying Dr. Jennings high in his arms, and as soon as Reynolds had him safely on top of the bank, Sandor waded back to the Hungarian side, gently took the girl away from Jansci, and carried her in turn across the ditch. For a moment she clung to him almost desperately, as if she was terrified of breaking the last contact with the life she was leaving behind her, then Reynolds stooped down and raised her on to the bank beside him.

"Do not forget what I told you, Dr. Jennings," Jansci called softly. He and the Cossack had come through the reeds and were standing on the far bank. "We are walking a long dark road, but we do not want to walk it forever-more."

"I will not forget." Jennings was shaking with cold. "I will never forget."

"It is good." Jansci bowed his white bandaged head in a barely perceptible token of farewell. "God be with you. *Dowidzenia.*"

"*Dowidzenia,*" Reynolds echoed. *Dowidzenia*—till we meet again. He turned, caught Julia and Dr. Jennings by the arms, and led them, the shivering old man and the silently crying girl, up the gentle slope to the field and the freedom that lay beyond. At the top he turned, just for a moment, and he could see the three men walking slowly away across the Hungarian marshes, never once looking back, and by and by they were lost to sight behind the tall reeds and he knew that he would never see them again.